# THE SPIDER ROOM

4/18 ?!
419 !
420

4/01
403
404
410

# THE SPIDER ROOM

by

## TIM KELLY

Published by
Lil's Closet Publications
130 Harris Ave
Bethel, Ohio 45106
thespiderroom@fuse.net

This novel is a work of fiction. Any references to real people, places, events or entities are intended to add a sense of authenticity and reality to the fiction and, as such, are the product of the author's imagination or are used fictionally.

# TABLE OF CONTENTS

# DEDICATION

The utmost thanks and appreciation to my wife, Doreen, for tolerating the many years I spent with my head up my past trying to get this right. I can't recall the number of times I completed a revision and declared with absolute certainty, "It's done", only to realize upon re-inspection that it was still half-baked. After a while, with each successive declaration, she would just congratulate me and smile knowingly. To be honest, I thought I would never finish this book and it probably spent more time on the closet floor than it did upon my desk. In a way, I don't think it will ever truly be done because certain matters raised on its pages are resolution proof and I simply lack the skill and the artistry to bring them to a final resting place.

So, thank you, Doreen, for your patience and for giving me the freedom to get this as finished as it will ever be. I love you five.

# PERSPECTIVES

*There is no present or future - only the past, happening over and over again - now.*
- Eugene O'Neill


*All human beings should try to learn before they die*
*What they are running from, and to, and why*
- James Thurber


*When I meditate on the gulf towards which I traveled and reflect on my youthful disobedience, for these things I weep, mine eye runneth down with water.*
- John Woolman


*You'll find true north somewhere, somehow*
*When the road ends and spits you out*
*You'll call your friends and wipe your nose*
*You'll find true north and stumble home*
- Jillette Johnson, from "True North"

# PROLOGUE

*The boy sat alone in a dark room.*
*A disembodied voice whispered softly, "What's wrong?"*
*"I'm afraid", the boy responded.*
*The voice whispered again, "What are you afraid of?"*
*"I don't know."*

# PREFACE

*He woke up in a drooly stupor, drenched in sweat and coated with an oily layer of grime. His joints all ached and, after a disoriented time-and-space readjustment, he remembered that he had been sleeping on the filthy wooden floor of a sweltering boxcar, thousands of miles from home. The radio in his brain was playing, "In the desert you can remember your name cause there ain't no one for to give you no pain". He winced, shook his head and tried to switch stations and conjure up a different tune, but failed.*

*He sat erect, balled up his fists, and ground them into his itchy swollen eyes. Through blurred vision he squinted at the graffiti on the boxcar wall, which began, "Everyone is a no one".*

*"Yup", he nodded in agreement, carefully inserting a pinky finger into his left ear and swiveling it around like a Q-tip.*

*As he yawned awake and evaluated his predicament, he threw his head back, made a megaphone of his hands, and shouted in resignation at the top of his lungs, "What the fuck am I doing here? How the fuck did I even get here?", and then laughed like a lunatic at the dingy ceiling. He thought he sensed an ominous presence just behind his left shoulder and spun his head around to be certain he was alone. A slight sulfurous stench crept up his nostrils and a shiver of panic rippled through his heart. He propped his bent elbows up on his hunkered knees, hung his head in his hands, closed his eyes, and took a series of deep breaths.*

*"Quick! Snap back!", he thought. "No! Not here! Not now! Don't worry! Everything is going to be okay!"*

*He had been dreaming of his dead father. "Matthew. Come here, son", the old man had summoned. "I've got something important I have to tell you." And just as he reached for the knob to the secret door that led to the chamber where his father was playing pool, at the first creak of the rusty hinge, the dreamscape transmogrified and a powerful vacuumous force sucked him through a frigid tunnel and tossed him tumbling into a dark bunker filled with hundreds of daddy-long-legs and matted-up clumps of spider webs, tying and tangling him up from head to toe in a straitjacketed mess of thick black cords, like a crab in a fisherman's net.*

*He tried to scream but was paralyzed by fear and unable to utter a sound. His heart was racing madly and he knew he was going to have a heart attack. He was terrified. He knew where he was. He was in the spider room.*

# PART ONE

"A spider is a predatory invertebrate animal that injects venom to kill prey. It symbolizes patience for its hunting with web traps, and mischief and malice for its poison and the slow death it causes."
—Wikipedia

# CHAPTER I

Matt Mahoney stood with arms outstretched like a shaman conductor, gripping the sides of the Wurlitzer as the jukebox needle hissed and popped in its vinyl groove like a snake slithering through pulverized shards of glass. He pulled his hair back into a ponytail and measured its length with his fists. Then, he ran his thumbnail across the reeded edge of a silver 1959 Washington quarter and peered with serious gaze through the glass of the multicolored altar, divining guidance as he scrutinized the musical selections with a superstitious intensity. With an intuitive sense of precision, he poised his offering at the lip of the chute, attained a calm sense of certainty, and let it drop sacrificially into the dark slit. And then, the metallic swallow and click. Feeding the monster. No. The Goddess.

With eyes closed in meditation and feet propped in the corner booth, he drummed upon the tabletop with the fingers of his right hand, ran the fingertips of his left hand across the table's underside, brushing across the upside down mountains of petrified bubble gum that coated it like a strange indecipherable Braille, and sang along to an old song he had loved since he was a kid:

*I'm a travelin' man and I've made a lot of stops all over the world and in every port I've owned the heart of at least one lovely girl.*

He dissolved into a romantic Ricky Nelson universe of cute little Eskimos, sweet Frauleins, and pretty Polynesian babes and imagined each one in his arms, so soft, so generous of flesh, the smooth of their skin, their ruby lips warm and moist upon his, their honey tongues mingling. But then he flinched when the reproachful voice trickled in.

"No. Too pure. Too perfect. Maybe should not touch." Then, as if on command, his self-pitiful thoughts drifted back to stewing over several recent disappointments.

Behind the counter stood Matt's friend, Vinny, known to all as the V-Man, his confectioner's apron a stained display of favorite flavors. Blenders whirred and phosphates fizzed in the carbonated air. On the huge saloon-style mirror, in festive crayon lettering, a hand-drawn sign boasted the annual return of Raphaelo's "Famous Fresh Peach Sundae." Vinny caught Matt's eye in his and gestured to him over a blast of whipped cream and a sprinkling of nuts.

After his customers had been served, the V-Man snuck a quick break, hung up his apron, and sat down opposite Matt, stirring him from his reverie with their customary greeting.

"Hey Matt. How they hangin', my man?"

"Low and loose and full of juice." They both gave their customary chuckle.

"I didn't see you come in," Vinny said. "A whole bunch of kids were here. I was taking care of them and trying to keep my eyes on the magazines at the same time. But when I heard this song, I knew it had to be you."

"Really?" Matt was flattered.

"Yeah. Nobody plays that one anymore. At least not since my brother died. He loved that song. That's why we've kept it so long. My old man refused to get rid of it. Now I only keep it here for you."

Matt nodded. Sad thoughts. Change subject? "Thanks. I appreciate that." His gaze roamed across the map of Vinny's face. The plump cheeks, the heavy jowls, the secret scars, the already world-weary eyes. Matt avoided the subject of Vinny's older brother, Frankie, who was born with a cerebral palsy kind of disease and had died a couple years earlier. He walked with herky-jerky marionette motions and spoke garbled words, which only his family understood. It was a familiar sight around that part of town to see Frankie struggling home from high school by himself, each step a balancing act of supreme effort, negotiating curbs and steps as he endured the ridicule of kids who laughed at him out loud as though he were a comedy matinee spectacle.

"Nobody else realized it because they never took the time to get to know him," Vinny went on, "but he was smart as a whip. Inside that body was a regular kid who was no different than you or me. He knew his classmates laughed at him when he walked down the street. They treated him as if he were stupid. And, you know—he was my big brother. I looked up to him. He was my hero, my profile in courage. He never gave up. And there was nothing I could do to help him." Vinny stopped short. "I guess we saw the best and the worst of people."

Matt couldn't get that twisted image or the misery thoughts out of his head. Then came a cringe of guilt because he remembered laughing the first time he saw Frankie bouncing across the street on his way to the family store. But now Matt revered him as if he were an unrecognized martyr or a saint whose life and death had, in some intangible way, made him want to be a better person.

"Are you working anywhere?" asked Vinny.

"I was. At Coleman's. I quit on Friday while I still had all my fingers."

"Quit? What happened?"

"Well, it's quarter to seven and I'm walking to work with my brown lunch bag, my egg salad sandwiches, a couple cream-filled cupcakes, and I'm on Creek Street by the old broom factory and there were about a million birds zooming around and the squirrels and chipmunks are already leaping through the trees, chirping and having a very important conversation in a language I didn't understand, and then, out of the blue, I got hit on the head with an acorn and I started to think about what a beautiful day it already was and, well, I just couldn't do it. I could not waste another gorgeous day inside that grimy sweatshop with my ass glued to my forklift. So, basically, I got fed up and turned myself around, ate my lunch for breakfast, hitched to Vandenburg's, and spent the day at the beach catching some rays. And now it's official. I am once again a gentleman of leisure."

"Gotta watch out for those acorns. They can pack a wallop. But, hey, a man's gotta do what a man's gotta do. You are to be commended, my son." Vinny cracked a smile. "I miss high school. Everything was more predictable. We didn't have to worry about our futures. Our biggest decisions were whether to go to the basketball game or to the movies on a Friday night."

"That's true. In high school, I couldn't wait to get out of there. I thought all my dreams would come true once I graduated. Part of me wishes I could go back."

"Be careful what you wish for." Vinny extended an index finger and wagged it at Matt.

"But there was one other thing," Matt added. "The night before that, I was working overtime, driving my forklift and loading the rickety freight elevator up with pools and pool tables and storing them up on the top floor, and I was getting into it. It was mindless, but I could see that I was accomplishing something. Most everybody was gone, and everything was fine until one of the owner's sons from Chicago or New York comes over and ruins everything. Some spoiled rich kid. Not much older than me. He starts yelling at me. Said I damaged one of the skids. I knew I didn't, but he didn't believe me. And besides, half of 'em are already busted when we get 'em. I should have told him 'fuck you' and clocked out, then and there. But I kept my mouth shut. Then all night I thought about everything I should have said and done. So in the morning I woke up and 'Maggie's Farm' is playing over and over in my head like a broken record. And the more I thought about it the more pissed off I got. So I had no choice. I had to quit that job."

Vinny, ever receptive, nodded his head behind a smirk, clapped his hands, and said, "Once again I applaud your philosophy. I wish I could have been there to witness your epiphany. I'm lucky here. I'm my own boss. I can run the place pretty much how I want to. I don't need any rich brats from Chicago to tell me how to do my job."

Matt smiled, pretending to know what an epiphany was. He was pleased that he had not yet said anything blatantly regrettable. *Oh good*, he thought, *maybe can sleep tonight*. He envied people who didn't care about anything, who could say or do whatever they wanted without self-consciousness or remorse and always slept well and looked forward to the future without a hint of concern for the screw-ups of their past. Some people congratulate themselves for all their deeds, overlooking all their flaws and imperfections. Matt, on the other hand, carried his embarrassments around like debts, debts with interest rates so high they could never be paid off, and always criticized himself for whatever he couldn't do and felt defined and crippled by his failures, secretly preoccupied with his own mediocrity, plagued by self-blame and nailed to a cross of permanent regrets.

"Can I get you something? A sundae? Ice cream soda?"

"No thanks. I just came by to say hi and play my song." He hesitated, starting to worry that he had monopolized the conversation and that further talk might ruin things. Change focus.

"So now that you're out of school, you got any plans? Are you gonna be running the store full-time or what?"

The V-Man shrugged, lips compressed. "I guess so. At least for now. I've got to keep up the family tradition. My folks rely on me. But what I plan to do, if I can break away from the store, is to use my degree and start my own newspaper. An upstate Village Voice. Get into movie and book reviews, concerts, the arts, do interviews, cover controversial issues. An alternative to the Register. Disturb the status quo. Piss off a few people. Instead of scooping ice cream I should be scooping the news. I'm gonna call it 'The Inside Scoop.'" He grinned. "What about you? Have you got any plans for your future?"

"Ah yes. The future." Matt scratched at his stubbly promise of an eventual beard in a Shakespearean pose of mock contemplation, attempting to find humor in the subject, attempting to disarm his fear. How could he know what he wanted to do in the future if he didn't even know what he wanted to do now? He was stuck in that in-between place, no longer a child but not yet a man. From the vantage point of his teetering present, all future prospects looked so bleak, like a crystal ball filled with a swirling glob of black clouds.

"Yeah, actually I do," Matt said. "I'm gonna go to Canada and hitch around for a while. I read this National Geographic article about the Maritimes. Especially Nova Scotia. Looks incredible. That's where I was thinking of going."

"Canada? You're not getting drafted are you?"

"Hell no. I had a high number. I'm not eligible anymore. I just want to see Canada."

"When are you leaving on your trip?

Matt thought, *It's a journey, not a trip*, but knew it would sound silly if he tried to make a point of that distinction. "Tomorrow. Soon as I can get my shit together, I'm outta here."

"But you just got back, didn't you? I guess the nest is getting a bit too small. Gotta spread those wings and fly." Vinny fluttered his fleshy hands like dainty little bird wings.

"Hey, before I go, you got any new Junior Editor Quiz questions?" Matt asked. This was a tradition of theirs, posing brainteasers and riddles to each other.

"I thought you'd never ask. This one came to me a while ago, as I was watching an album spinning around on my turntable. I got sucked into it and started thinking about the grand scheme of things and how we're all just tiny microscopic particles, insignificant specks in the vastness of the universe, and that none of it matters. We think our lives are important, but they're not. Just look up at the stars on a clear night and you'll realize that we mean nothing. And I must confess, my perceptions were somewhat herbally enhanced at the time. But, to the point, I want you to think about this when you're stranded on the side of the road in East Bumfuck, Nova Scotia. Ready?" Matt nodded. "Okay. What spins around faster? The beginning of the first song on an album or the end of the last one?"

Matt had a befuddled expression. "What do you mean, faster? It's all going the same speed. You know, 33 $\frac{1}{3}$. And anyway—"

Vinny cut him off. "Just hold on for now and think about it. Ruminate deeply, amigo. Put on your thinking cap. We'll discuss it when you get back."

Vinny was drawn back behind the counter by a couple of teenage boys who, with an unconvincing air of nonchalance, were sheepishly purchasing a corncob pipe, just as Matt and his friends had done when they were that age. Matt began to leave. From the half-opened screen door, he caught Vinny's eye and gave a goodbye nod.

"Who are you going with?" Vinny shouted.

"Just the three of us—me, myself and I. The unholy trinity."

Matt knew he had to do this one on his own, as a total stranger in unfamiliar territory. That was the only way to shake free of his ragged old self. This was between him and It.

"Have a good time. Send me a postcard from Halifax." The V-Man assumed a solemn-faced priestly stature, dipped the scooper in the cloudy rinse water and sprinkled it toward Matt, a confectioner's blessing, and, tracing it through the sign of the cross, intoned, "Adios to those dominoes and Nabiscos. Now go and sin some more."

As Matt slipped out of the store with a self-satisfied wave, a jukebox voice queried: "Did you write the book of love? And do you have faith in God above?" And then the slam of the crooked screen door.

Matt felt himself easing into one of those elastic moments. He stood there staring at the surprising tininess of the quaint old-fashioned candy store, at the blatant glare of the neon sign casting an alluring glow in the waning-light doldrums of this early summer's night, and at the unkempt teenagers with fashionably scraggly long hair and frayed bell-bottom jeans as they loitered near the entrance, squatting languidly on the concrete steps, rehearsing hipness as they smoked self-rolled cigarettes and mumbled disaffected coolisms among themselves.

Tobacco fumes blended with the choking blue exhaust of an old oil-burning clunker that idled driverless at the curb. Matt dragged his sad and empty heart down Jefferson Ave. beyond the mothy halo of the neon sign, his somber shape vanishing into the humid and ever-so-still summer darkness with his head down and his hands planted deep in his pockets, worrying that it had been rude of him to not purchase anything, and, most of all, dredging through his dusty old vault of misery thoughts about Helen.

# CHAPTER II

"Matthew Anthony, I don't know what I'm going to do with you. You're just like your father. If you could only have more confidence in yourself, you could do anything you set your mind to. You've got to think of your future. You have so much potential. Don't waste it." Mrs. Mahoney shook her head and gave her son the Mom Look as she sat across from him at the table in her ever-tidy kitchen.

There it was again. The future. The vacant black screen he preferred not to think about. Instead, he preferred navigating forward with his eyes glued to the rear view mirror, preoccupied more with where he had been than where he was heading.

*What could I possibly ever be?* he wondered. *A teacher like my father?* Definitely not. The mere thought of standing in front of a classroom full of students was panic-inducing and, in its own twisted way, felt literally life threatening. Even the prospect of going to college, though he had been accepted at a couple, filled him with fear and insecurity. Was he smart enough for college? Would he be able to pay attention in class? What if he didn't get along with his dormmates?

"Don't worry, Ma. I'll be okay. I can take care of myself."

"But you just got back." She averted her eyes to conceal her wounded frown. "And you never know who is going to be picking you up. They could be anybody. You're putting your life into the hands of perfect strangers. It's so dangerous."

He loved that expression: perfect strangers. "Don't worry, Ma. I promise. I won't take any chances." He kept it short, knowing that nothing he said could defeat the art and science of her worrying. At a loss for words, he feigned interest in an address book from The New

Holland Company, which, on its cover in gold embossed lettering, stated, "God Gives Every Bird Its Food—but He Does Not Throw It Into the Nest."

Mrs. Mahoney sat in the kitchen, her glasses balanced at the tip of her nose, perusing the latest TV Guide. Merv Griffin smiled at Matt from the cover. Sitcom reruns and "Crazy Eddie" commercials from the New York City stations flickered on the portable black and white TV. An Ellery Queen mystery magazine was spread down, mid-read, beside a bouquet of fresh-cut garden flowers that erupted into a riot of color from a white porcelain vase. At her feet lay her crocheting handbag with its skeins of colorful yarn. Long plastic needles spiked out haphazardly from their rainbow nest. Snorting and drooling in the corner lay Eustace, an English bulldog known variously as "The Big, the Fat and the Ugly," "The King of Farts," and "Gaseous Clay." Though fierce in appearance, with Eustace it was definitely "The Call of the Mild." At the sight of his face—with the droopy, goopy eyes, the hammered-in snout, and the warthog fangs that stuck upward—people were universally inspired to remark, "He's so ugly, he's cute," as if the observation were original. Viewed from behind, his balls bulged out in a tight and proud little package of studly doghood.

"Are you hungry? Can I fix you something to eat?" A son is always presumed to be hungry.

"That's okay, Ma. I'll make myself something."

When Matt was a boy, his mother was the most beautiful mother in the world. Then, when he reached that certain age and beauty became a thing of glamour, a gallery of glossy and idealized images of Hollywood starlets or magazine hussies, he no longer considered her beautiful. He grew critical. All his life she had been the woman who lived in the shoe, so busy with so many children that he often felt lost in the shuffle, overlooked and forgotten, and not certain that she loved him. Maybe he blamed her for that. As Matt got older, that mother of many became beautiful again, and he was ashamed of himself for his lapse of love. He should have known better than to listen to those deceptive voices. These days her nest was nearly empty, the shoe roomier, and, on most evenings, he could slip easily into the comfort and luxury of her undivided presence without having to compete for her attentions.

Beneath the habituated hum of the refrigerator, a silence came over the kitchen as Mrs. Mahoney absorbed herself in her yarn and Matt studied the week's newspapers that were piled on the table. "Hmm," he muttered, "let's see."

A partial solar eclipse to begin precisely at 3:22.45.3 p.m. and end at 5:45.11.0 p.m. Only one second of carelessness on Earth in watching the Sun could produce permanent blindness. Must use a filter. Happening tomorrow. Better be careful!

A letter to the editor praising the blind man named Derby who runs the newsstand at the Post Office. Another letter complaining about the unfinished windmill that had been long in construction beside the thruway exit and urging that it either be completed or demolished. "I believe the windmill is a shame and disgrace to the New Holland area," the letter read. "It is half-finished, neglected and almost forgotten" and, as such, the writer supposed, "it is possibly the most fitting monument to the city."

And yet another letter, bemoaning the fact that the city's captains of industry, as symbolized by the numerous factories that had made New Holland their home for the past century or more, fueling the livelihoods of tempest-tossed generations, were all shutting down operations and moving south where labor was cheaper. "What are we to do?" the author asked. "What will happen to the thousands of people who are losing their jobs? Who will pay their mortgages? Their rent? How will they all survive? And what will become of the city when the industry has all left and there is nothing to take its place? I have lived in New Holland my whole life and worry for its future. It will always be my home, even if I have to abandon it to find work." It was signed, "A concerned former factory employee."

An editorial about the proposed downtown mall: "The Mall— Now. The New Holland people are overwhelmingly in favor of a mall." The Junior Editors Quiz: "Where Did the Dachshund Originate?" Two dogs long and a half a dog high. Then to the funnies and his favorite character, Henry, the infantile bald-headed mute boy. Lucky stiff. A world without words. Just pure thought. And then to "Sketches" by Ben Burroughs, the syndicated newspaper poet who harped out simple rhymes about commonplace subjects:

*Don't waste your time on ugly things*
*Beauty is all around*
*Look for only happy things*
*Hear well a joyful sound*
*For every ugly thing in life*
*There are ten beautiful things*
*Look at the flowers and the trees*
*And birds with magic wings*
*Watch little children as they play*
*What better thing than this*
*To fill the world with wonder*
*And mountains of sweet bliss*
*There will be darkness to be sure*
*And yet who can deny*
*The beauty of a glowing sun*
*Or a starlit sky*
*So spend your borrowed time on Earth*
*Looking for the good*
*Cast aside the hate and fear*
*Seek only brotherhood*
*Then when the Master calls you*
*To a peace sublime*
*You'll spend eternity with Him*
*Because you did not waste time*

*What a bunch of happy horseshit*, thought Matt. *Talk about looking at life through a filter. Are you blind? Hey buddy, you been out of your house lately?*

Mrs. Mahoney reached into her blouse and adjusted the padded insert that replaced the cancer-eaten breast that had been removed when Matt was in the seventh grade. She was a no-nonsense mother who always knew her mind immediately but revealed only as much as was necessary. Born in New Holland into an old-world immigrant household and raised by a shrewd but loving Polish mother with a knack for languages and a self-assured, fastidiously coiffed Italian father who whistled operas as he strolled home from the factory, Mrs. Mahoney shunned the old country superstitions, rejected both foreign worlds, and professed only to being an American. There were times, however, while she was troweling dirt with rolled-up pants legs and a bandana knotted around her forehead, planting flowers or harvesting dandelion greens, or when climbing the stairs at night in slow studied steps, that her immigrant heritage insinuated itself in the crow's feet of her watchful eyes, in the heavy corners of her mouth, and in the worry that had carved its thick wrinkled signature into her forehead. At those moments, she seemed inhabited by the wandering spirit of her deceased mother and looked no more than a few steps removed from the ship that had transported her mother to this country eight decades earlier as a three-year-old child.

Matt scooped a spoonful of peppermint tea into a stainless steel tea ball, screwed it shut, dangled it by its chain like a censer and slowly submerged it into a cup of boiling water to let it steep. The minty steam wafted upon his face as he oozed a gooey spoonful of Yucatan honey into the cup and watched it dissolve. *Oh, it's a miracle. Transforming water into tea.*

He then cracked two eggs into a soup bowl and stabbed and blended them with a fork. He put a tab of butter in a Teflon frying pan and, when it melted, poured in a small portion of the egg batter and waited for it to start sizzling. The batter collected on one side of the pan and, as the heat set in, it assumed the shape of California. He spilled in the rest of the batter, beat it up for a while, and made a scrambled egg sandwich, dipping it with each bite into a puddle of Karo syrup.

They watched TV until a public service announcement came on and a cautionary voice spoke through a grainy screen: "It's 10:30. Do you know where your children are?" Mrs. Mahoney exhaled through her nostrils, glanced at the clock, and turned off the TV. When she put her cup in the sink, Matt rose, gave her a big Jackie Gleason hug and a kiss on the forehead, and said "Baby, you're the greatest." It was his way of saying "I love you" without having to say the actual words. She smiled, hugged him back, and then climbed the stairs to her bedroom.

# CHAPTER III

## A. The Narrow Escape

Matt made a couple calls to see if he could find his younger brother, Rory. From all reports, it appeared that he had been making the rounds, but his present whereabouts was unknown.

So far, Matt's evening had been smooth sailing. If he went to bed right away and was the early bird in the morning, he could start his journey first thing, fresh from a peaceful night's sleep. But he never knew what to expect. On the best of nights, he drifted to sleep like a normal person, entertained until dawn by pleasantly bizarre dreams which, time permitting, he collected in his journal. On those other nights, however, the curse of obsessive introspection took over his mind and his memory vault sprang open and all the stupid forgotten things he had said during the day leapt out and bombarded him with the ferocity of those flying monkeys in the Wizard of Oz. He prayed for God to strike him dumb. His life would be so much simpler and happier if he were mute.

The refrigerator suddenly stopped its incessant hum, the hum that goes unnoticed until it ceases, filling the kitchen with an ominous silence. The depression started to soak into his pores. He tried to stave it off. He moved to the living room, turned all the lights off, sat on the couch, got more and more depressed, tried to relax, and tried to gather his senses. He traced the path of a narrow shaft of light backward from a triangular golden patch on the carpet beside his foot and then up and across the pitch-black room to where it sparkled in the antique gold-leaf mirror and then back across the room where it escaped through a gap in the curtains and then continued outside and upward for a quarter million miles until it landed on the moon.

His foot began tapping as if keeping beat to a mad rampant tune in his head. The room quivered. He felt a tremor. Shadows crept across the walls in a slow crawl. Then, in the space of a single split second, his mind ruptured and all hell broke loose as he felt It, that unspoken of It, enter the room and fill it with Its suffocating predatory presence. It was The Watcher. There It stood, infallible, poised on the knick-knack shelf among his mother's Hummels, like a dark lord harping and spewing out its unholy scripture as it unlatched the lid of his Pandora's box of personal miseries, leaning so near to Matt's shoulder that he could smell the sulfur of Its foul breath.

It spoke.

"You fucking asshole." Each word jack-hammered into his brain. His heart raced. God, how he hated this.

*I am dying. I know I am dying*, then *Relax. Relax. It's not real. It's only in my head. Ignore It and It will go away.*

Once The Watcher arrived, though, emerging Christ-like in the lethal gloom of the den, Matt could not stop It. Nor could he stop the poison from coursing through the blood stream of his tainted, taunted self as the disintegration process began and his own version of the Jekyll-and-Hyde curse transformed him from the fairly normal-but-not-quite-cool Matt into the Weird Matt. So remote. So utterly riddled with self-pitying regrets. Then, as The Watcher closed in on Matt and his panic flowered, It began speaking to the man inside his head and they spoke in a common tongue about the demeaning of life as he listened mutely and only half-understandingly to their disturbing chatter, afraid to interrupt or do anything that might draw too much attention to himself.

The more he tried to cope with his invisible onslaught, the more he panicked, overcome with that pinned-down feeling. His weakling heart still racing and threatening to explode. He felt trapped and paralyzed and empty of breath. His throat went tight as though he was being choked. The walls closed in upon him and squeezed all the oxygen from the room. He wanted to scream. He stood his ground for as long as he could. It was like holding his breath underwater or being smothered by a heavy pillow. As his panic continued to escalate, he darted out the back door, overwrought, desperate for air, away from The Watcher and from his own boxed-in craziness.

Outside, in the backyard, awash in moonlight, Matt collapsed. He took in the night air with a deep breath like a drowning man cast suddenly ashore, inhaled the fresh scent of dewy grass, and looked around for a clue to something reassuring, anything that might matter enough to ward off this ambush. Finding nothing, he faced the garage as if it were a holy shrine and knelt on the driveway in an erect and reverential schoolboy position of prayer, scratched his fingertips against the gouges in the rough-textured blacktop until it hurt, and hurriedly recited The Our Father and The Hail Mary, hoping both that the neighbors would and would not see him. He tried to talk to a distorted version of the God he was not even sure he believed in, the anonymous God, whoever he or she or it may be. But he didn't know what to say, what favors to ask for, what sins to confess or what weaknesses to betray. Everything sounded so selfish, as if God was nothing more than Santa Claus with a halo. And he, all pathetic and undeserving, was a sorry sight for any self-respecting lord on high. Besides, prayers were always his last resort. He was an emergency-only supplicant, leaving a message just in case. But he didn't figure he'd be a high priority on any heavenly callback list, given his less-than-stellar record as a Catholic and his rocky relationship with his maker. It nonetheless occurred to him that kneeling was the most proper and prayerful of all positions. It was submissive and vulnerable and created, even for the unhumble, the appearance of humility before the Lord or at least the idea of the Lord. It might work in a pinch. But it was too much like begging. Matt, disgusted with himself, vowed never again to beg for anything from the Lord. It's all just inane superstitions anyway, like the Greek myths, but not as creative or insightful. He stood up, embarrassed by his display of false devotion, scrubbed away the driveway pebbles

17

embedded in his kneecaps, and tried to regain his composure and maintain his cool.

## B. Sewer Tomatoes

Matt's head was a noisy battlefield of screamin' demons chattering and slashing about like a rowdy drunken mob looking for a helpless victim. The tranquil night, with its safe, deserted streets, so silent and uncomplicated, soothed and massaged his maimed and throbbing brain and encouraged him to go for a walk. The only way he could sanitize his head was to walk himself into a state of exhausted mindlessness. It was his well-practiced late-night antidote to whatever had contaminated his mind. Lowering his eyes, he advanced down his driveway and took a left onto Peak Street. He proceeded eastward like a pilgrim into a sacred darkness and dragged his anvil of troubled memories along the sidewalk until he reached the long steep descent of Incline Avenue, where he turned right.

He raised his head against the undertow that sucked him downward and inward and he looked forward across the basin of the valley to the rise of hills, invisible in darkness on the far side of the Iroquois River. As a child, he thought that was where the Indians lived. But no, he eventually learned, that was where the Italians lived. The South Side. His mother had been raised there. In the daytime, the view from the top of Incline Avenue was immaculate all the way over to the panoramic layering of the green and rolling hills of the far, far country south of town, above and beyond the firefly fields and the lazy cow pastures and the winding country roads where he and his friends cruised at night, riveted to music as they got stoned in their smoky cars. At night, however, it was all just an inky black screen, its beauty a total mystery. He strained his eyes into the dim distance as though from the crow's nest of a wayward ship and sailed forward.

He peered through the storefront window of Bud's Confectionery. Like Raphaelo's, Bud's was a struggling vestige of the swiftly disappearing mom and pop corner candy store with its old-fashioned soda fountain and its cushioned booths pocked with burn holes and reinforced with duct tape, where kids congregated after school to act cool, sneak cigarettes, and whisper exaggerated tidbits of urgent gossip. The store was in disrepair and was a much-shrunken version of the building that loomed so large in Matt's memory. The clatter and drone of the air conditioner jutting from the side window was amplified by the nighttime silence and Matt knew that Shirley would be royally pissed off when she opened up in the morning and discovered that whoever closed up the night before had neglected to shut it off.

Throughout his teen years, Bud's had been the hangout and headquarters for his group of friends known somewhat facetiously as The Hill Hoods. The diminutive owners, Bud and Shirley Domiano, had suffered through those turbulent times as surrogate parents to the gang as a whole, tolerating and forgiving their many screw-ups and oftentimes shaking and scratching their heads in bewildered disbelief. He could still see Bud, a tiny man with serious features and eyebrows thick and dark like an owl's, reprimanding him with one of the many sermons which had earned him the nickname "The Reverend Mr. Bud."

New groups of adolescents had long since taken their place on Incline Avenue and The Hill Hoods were now the retired and supposedly wiser elder statesmen of teenaged street delinquency. Truth be told, there wasn't a real hood among them. They had always been a tame gang, middle-class kids who didn't like fighting or breaking any significant laws. By now the tight bonds of friendship between them all had loosened, college and girlfriends had driven them hither and yon, and Matt, having been so dependent upon the security of those bonds for such a long time, saw his old order dissolving and all his friends drifting in different directions, creating new alliances, and moving forward without him.

He was haunted by what his mother said about wasting his potential. It worried him because he didn't think he had any. His friend Buzz had once put it best during one of their marathon late-night walk-

and-talks along the dark residential tree-lined streets of New Holland just after he had graduated from college.

"My first job," Buzz had said, "was as a junior engineer for the EPA. I had to visit a wastewater treatment plant in the New York metro area. They have these sludge drying beds. Right there, in the midst of all the sewage, you'd see these huge juicy tomato plants. The seeds had passed through the body and were flushed down into the sewer. These beds provided the perfect conditions for them to become what they were designed to become—tomato plants. Big and red. Looked delicious, but you couldn't eat them. Anyway, my point is that potential is like a seed. If it's not nurtured properly, it will always remain just a seed. All it needs is a chance, and then its true nature takes over, whether it's in a sea of shit or your mom's backyard garden. Some kids our age still think it's important that they got high scores on those IQ tests we took in fifth or sixth grade. But those old tests, they don't mean anything anymore. You need to act on your potential or it will be wasted. Someone who is half as smart will go twice as far if he works at it rather than just waiting around for someone else to admire his potential and turn it into something. After a certain point, if you don't take matters into your own hands, the potential is wasted, and you're nothing more than a high test score or a dried-up seed."

"I don't know, Buzz. I don't know what my potential is. In all seriousness, the only ambition I have right now is hitchhiking and traveling. Nothing else comes to mind at the moment."

"Just stick with it. There's no rush. You're a smart guy. Right now, you're more interested in enjoying life. You'll find something eventually."

Matt guessed it might have appeared that way, that he was enjoying life, but inside, Matt was thinking that he might be one of those flushed seeds with the potential to become nothing more than an inedible sewer tomato, thriving in the subterranean mire of his own shit.

Matt stood in front of the little store, illuminated by a streetlight. He wondered what kind of a seed he was and laughed because he was still proud of his high scores on those old tests. He still enjoyed sitting at Bud's counter, joking around with Shirley or shooting the shit with Sally, Marie, Liz, or Gail as they mixed strawberry ice cream sodas or blended him a specially concocted chocolate-malted milkshake with an extra heap of Horlich's powdered malt. Although he still indulged in its simple comforts on occasion, he now saw Bud's as an institution from which he had graduated, a shrine at which he no longer knelt and prayed. He gazed through his distorted image in Bud's front window and made a face, curling his lip Elvis style. Mimicking the King, he drawled, "Thank you very much" to Bud and Shirley, whose invisible presence permanently inhabited the space in which he was standing. He hummed and whistled and continued down Incline Avenue, singing in his thoughts:

*Oh to live on Sugar Mountain*
*With the barkers and the colored balloons*
*You can't be twenty on Sugar Mountain*
*Though you're thinking that you're leaving there too soon.*

## C. Infinite Regress

When he reached Ash Avenue, he took a right and then a quick left down Sullivan Street, a verdant dead-end lane, until he came upon the house where Helen lived. She was his first girlfriend. He had fallen head-over-heels in love with her and, during their time together, his heart was glad and full. Those happy days with Helen all existed in a bygone Eden, a forsaken space to which he could never return. Before the unraveling. Whenever he tried to make sense of what had happened way back then, his mind began to swirl and his guilty conscience filled with a diseased blend of self-hatred and bitter remorse. Then, the familiar scalpel and the tired old postmortem, slicing and carving away, studying the symptoms, looking for the disease.

As far as he could tell, there was a self-destructive glitch in his thought process, a malfunction, as if his needle had gotten jammed inside some pocked groove on a warped album. He would close his eyes and follow his mind like a bloodhound on a scent, tracking down a body. He would follow and follow the train of thought to see if he could keep it on a safe track, trying to prevent it from taking that unexpected turn that led to all those death-wish dead ends. But after a certain point he would get distracted, lose his concentration, and before he knew it, his mind had already gone all haywire with a will of its own. He tried to pinpoint the fault line where the dysfunction would take control, but he could detect no seam, no crack, no split, like a deep imperceptible paper cut. He didn't know if it was an irreparable factory defect or if a quick tune-up at the garage would set him straight.

*Elevator to the brain hotel,* he thought. *Broken down, but just as well.* He looked wistfully at the dangling sashes in the darkened windows of Helen's house, thought of the note he had sent her, and imagined how much she and everyone else there must despise him now and how he would never be able to explain himself to them even if he got the chance. He couldn't even explain it to himself. Somewhere along the line, he had turned into a different person, a damaged Bizarro version of the one he used to be, someone even he himself did not like. It was as if he did things he didn't want to do for reasons he didn't understand. All that crazy, sad stuff was beyond his reach and grasp, all disfigured and distorted in its own hall of mirrors, and he could never quite make it out except he knew that it haunted him with a kind of insurmountable misery.

## D. Swoons and Cheers

Misery thoughts. Quick. Snap back. *Don't wanna go completely nuts just yet.* So he trudged through the overgrown lot at the end of Sullivan Street and crept through brittle backyard silences back onto Ash Avenue, pulling himself away from his memories like an insect trying to escape being swallowed by the whirling current of a gulping drain. He turned right on Margaret Avenue and continued to its end at Plane Street, braced and strengthened by thoughts of all his friends who lived there.

He turned left and walked past the laundromat that he and a few friends had vandalized when he was fifteen—it was a dumb prank gone awry but had taught him a valuable lesson about how not to behave— then past the old-fashioned brick fire station where, on sweltering summer days, the firemen used to let all the kids come in for sips of ice-cold spring water from their special bubbling cooler and, if they were lucky, a slide down the pole. He continued to Kaiser Street.

"Lucky" Luke Piersall lived on the corner of Kaiser Street and Plane Street. He had just graduated from college and was going to start teaching in September. Mrs. P. was probably by herself, sitting at the kitchen table, drinking a cold glass of Utica Club, puffing on her Kents and scribbling through the daily crossword puzzle in the Register. If it wasn't so late and he wasn't in such a vile mood, he would have popped in to say hello and tell her about his upcoming journey and let her know that her son had agreed to drive him into Canada. Luke, always the mature one, had what could only be described as a sparkling personality. Matt, an unemployed dropout with no career ambitions and no skills, was a child by comparison, and he wished he could polish himself up so he would shine like Luke.

He turned right on Kaiser Street, a short stump that dead-ended at Mitchell Street. Matt attended sixth grade in Miss Arnold's class at the Mitchell Street School, which stood at that corner. It was an imposing brick edifice, which, with its paved fenced-in playground, had the look of a high-security prison. It was there where he used to play kickball during recess and the lunch hour, attempting with all his might to impress the schoolgirls by booting the ball onto the roof of the building as they cheered on the sidelines, like so many pretty maids all in a row.

Little sixth-grade Matt envisioned his long stride, the smooth stroke and powerful release of muscular tension and the explosion when his foot connected with its target and then the upper atmospheric arc of the ball as it disappeared from view. Then, of course, the chorus of girls swooning with admiration as he rounded third and jogged across the chalk-drawn home plate with a broad and triumphant Mickey

Mantle grin. In reality, the best he ever mustered was a mediocre drive against the side of the brick fortress, just shy of the second row of wire-meshed windows, just shy of swoons and cheers.

He attended his first dances at that school. Friday night record hops in the gym. The giggly sixth-grade girls in their fluffy petticoated dresses and exuberant fairy tale aspirations. Awkward boys with bad manners, ill-fitting dress clothes, scuffed shoes, and shiny hair thick and dripping with more than just little dabs of Wildroot and Brylcream. And the dance contests in which wiry kid bodies, twisted, jitterbugged and mash-potatoed, limbs all a-flailing in wild contortions to the rollicking beats of the latest, greatest top ten 45 RPM smash hit singles as spun by dowdy middle-aged teachers who worried that they might be complicit in promoting the devil's agenda.

What ever happened to that hot-stepping eleven-year-old kid who danced unselfconsciously with each week's girl of his dreams, arms and legs swinging and kicking with serious competitive energy during the two-and-a-half-minute whirlwind of each dance contest? Although he never won, he always fantasized that it was he who was the best dancer in the gym and that, one of these nights, he would receive the recognition he deserved and all the girls would want him for their partner. That was the fuse that drove those furious feet so long ago before he quit dancing and retreated into a bashful rigidity that feared motion.

## E. The Queen of Vegetables

Matt continued dragging his memories of those things that did and did not happen and slid still deeper down the long thigh of Cliff Street and into the guts of the sleeping city. From this height the view was clear to the South Side. A refreshing breeze blew over the river from the hills beyond the opposite rim of the valley to cool his damp forehead, carrying with it a slight whiff of curdled waters. Lights from South Side houses twinkled like stars from a nearby galaxy, and he was surprised by how otherworldly it all looked against the silky, nighttime backdrop. Gravity increased with each downward step, and he had to flex his calves and brace his weight against his knees to prevent himself from being sucked down into a free-falling tumble. Partway down he turned onto Cypress Avenue and walked to the two-family house where Carla lived. In the backyard was a small but thriving vegetable garden, which was tended by a blue-robed plaster statue of the Virgin Mary with chipped and pitted heavenward eyes that were both blissful and agonized.

"Hail Mary," he saluted. "Full of grapes."

Carla was an authentic Sicilian-born Italian with nut-brown Mediterranean skin, Sophia Loren eyes, and an ethereal beauty that captivated Matt from the first time he beheld her, like a vision, strolling up Incline Avenue with her friends on a Friday night in summertime. She had been his Holy Grail object of desire since the end of his second junior year in high school. The way she floated along the sidewalk, her frayed bell-bottom jeans brushing against the pavement, seemed to foretell that he had found "the one." He grew so immersed in his obsession for her that he lost all perspective and continued to pursue her even though she did nothing to encourage him or give him hope. Had he been wiser—and less afflicted by her spell—he'd have realized that she was merely tolerating his attentions out of politeness.

But still, nothing would deter him from his belief that he and Carla were a matched pair, predestined to be as one. He knew that he was more of an acquired taste than a delicacy, but he kept thinking that if he tried long enough and hard enough, she would get to know the real Matt and fall in love with him just as Helen had. Somehow, though, no matter how hard he tried to act normal when he was with her, it was always Weird Matt who showed up and foiled his plans with all his insecurities and inhibitions. No matter how much passive rejection she fed him, he continued to stand first in line, Johnny-on-the-spot, eager for his next full serving of indifference, as if he were wedded to his infatuation. Always pushing boulders uphill. Always getting flattened.

Now, here he stood on this new night in the midst of a farewell ramble, grinding his teeth and looking with vain eyes at Carla's house, still uncertain whether he should be worshiping at her shrine or destroying it. He threw a kiss at the lonely and lovely Madonna, she so full of grace, that glorious queen of the vegetables, and cringed at the memory of what a spectacle he had made of himself.

## F. Cannibals

He completed the Cliff Street descent, crossed Park Avenue, and passed by the Calvin Coolidge Junior High, which he attended in seventh and eighth grades. He moved on to Johnson Street and the "New" New Holland Apartments, a recently constructed low-rent apartment complex. Adjacent to it, towering above, was the senior citizens' high-rise apartment building, a monolithic structure that landed unexpectedly from outer space one night when nobody was looking, reducing everything around it to rubble. These were, in good part, the refuge for those who had been displaced by the cyclonic effects of urban modernization.

New Holland was in the process of being "revitalized" with, in addition to the new housing, the proposed construction of a downtown mall. Amid optimistic guarantees of a robust economy, the wrecking balls flew, the glass shattered, the bricks exploded, and the city's old buildings crumbled into dusty heaps. Apparently, in order for the city to be renewed, it first needed to be destroyed; now the downtown looked like a World War II bombsite, more like a death than a renewal.

As with Matt himself, New Holland's old identity had become possessed by a new, weird imposter. It was already impossible to recall how everything had looked just a few months earlier, which shop was where, or how all the bulldozed streets and alleys had run, though he had been down them all hundreds of times and would've sworn he had them all committed to memory. Its history was being erased, structure by structure, and would soon be lost to a time gone by forever. All the old gray ghosts that had once been perched upon the ravaged rooftops of the century-old buildings were being shooed away to some other-dimensional homeless shelter to reminisce about the great city that was no more and to rock themselves away into oblivion, for there was no place left to haunt. He stood in the midst of these pulverized ruins. His city had become a museum of collapse. He was a stranger upon its new streets and hated his helplessness and the inevitability of everything disintegrating around him. It was pitiful—the sight of a city gasping and dying like a proud old man being cannibalized by his grandchildren—all for the sake of building a mall. Surveying the destruction around him and visualizing the destruction still to come, Matt didn't know what to think except that it had better be a pretty good goddamn mall.

## G. Esmerelda, Queen of the Moon

He turned left on Guy Street, walked past the medieval-looking St. Teresa's Episcopal Church and the YMCA, then hanging a left onto Merchant Street and a quick right onto Orchard Street through an eerie darkness over the polluted waters of the Skanatoga Creek, a convenient toilet for the slimy sewage spewed from all the upstream factories huddled around it. The Skanatoga was like a perverted industrial rainbow that always took on the color of whatever dye was being used and flushed out of the factories on that particular day. Matt pitied any fish so unfortunate as to inhabit that befouled creek as it plunged down to the brown-trout sludge waters of the Iroquois River.

As he approached the Andrew Carnegie Free Public Library at the corner of Orchard and Chapel Streets, he heard a muffled voice seemingly engaged in one half of a spirited conversation. It was coming from the dim-lit alcove of the library's side entrance. His sudden presence intruded upon the moment, and he expected to see a romantic couple disentangling themselves from a heavy session of necking and petting and hurriedly buttoning, tucking, and zipping. Instead, he saw a dwarfish figure, flashlight in hand, dressed in little girl clothes and tiny pink ballerina slippers, sitting crunched in the corner as she studied the colorful illustrations of an oversized children's book. Around her neck hung a large bronze medallion studded with glass jewels that projected constellations of kaleidoscopic shards of light against the chambered walls. She held up the medallion, with all its would-be rubies and sapphires and emeralds, and spoke toward it as if it were a walkie-talkie. In the direct yellow beam of her flashlight, her face appeared painted and theatrical as it coalesced into a grotesque but somehow sweet elvin mask with a carnival grin. The childlike image was confounded by bad teeth and the crow's feet that articulated her eyes.

"I've been waiting for you," she said behind an attentive countenance, not the least bit startled by his unannounced arrival. "Do you have the keys, kind sir?"

There was a formal curtsy in her voice. He loved the rusted growl of the ill-meshed gears of her vocal chords, yet her enunciation was precise and rang Shakespearean in the shadows of this cloistered midnight stage.

Her name was Esmerelda. She was a miniature woman possessed with the look of a munchkin and the innocent mind of a child. Matt had known her since junior high school when he and his friends discovered her on their lunchtime break as she was wandering the streets of downtown New Holland as if it were her own personal wonderland.

"What keys?"

"The keys to the library. My books were due today. If they're late, the lady won't let me have any more books. And that will never do. No. That'd be a dill pickle now, wouldn't it?"

"Why don't you put them in the overnight return in front of the library? You can put books there anytime."

"Oh no. I can't do that. That's too willy-nilly. I talked to Roger and he told me that you would be here with the keys. He said the keys to the kingdom would be delivered by a brave young man on a white stallion." Her eyes darted sideways, as though in search of his tethered beast. She whispered, with an index finger to her lips, "Shhh. The walls have ears and the ears have walls."

Matt had never met Roger but knew him by reputation. He was the King of Mars. Esmerelda was the Queen of the Moon. Together they ruled the universe. They carried on long interplanetary conversations through Esmerelda's glimmering medallion. As a matter of fact, she was in the process of reading Roger one of the children's stories when Matt interrupted her.

Though most kids, sensing her supernatural nature, treated her with kindness, there were some who picked on Esmerelda and ridiculed her for her eccentric appearance and her fantasy-world beliefs. They told her that she belonged in the nuthouse in Utica, but she always just smiled at them, confident as a queen in her convictions and her exalted cosmic status. Matt was captured by the gravity of her happy and peaceful universe. He wouldn't mind living in a world like that, a loyal subject to his Queen Esmerelda.

She opened one of her books, a Disney book adorned with colorful pictures of animals, and spoke as if to an old friend: "Oh, I love animals," she said. "They're so beautiful. I love them all and they all love me. I am their favorite flower." She spoke like a frog princess as she swooned and turned the pages. "Oh I love Walt Disney. He is such a wonderful man and he makes such wonderful movies. So fair and square and hunky-dory." Her voice, rich with wonder, crackled and her eyes twinkled.

Matt didn't know where Esmerelda lived or how she got out so late at night. She must have snuck out of her house to return her books, and for that he applauded her gumption. Uncertain what to do and not wanting to leave her there by herself, he suggested that he walk her to the police station just around the corner on Skanatoga Street. She agreed, commenting on how wonderful policemen were and how they had always been so kind to her. Her eyes and ears perked up.

"Maybe I'll get to ride in the police car."

This unique woman, who had always seemed to be such a freak of nature, now seemed a rare exotic flower with wondrous, perhaps magical, qualities, a strange Dorothy forever at large in her own perpetual Oz—too unspoiled, too innocent, too delicate for this coarse and cruel world. As he walked her toward the station, he was tempted to take hold of her hand and realized that, if he had done so, it would have been for his own comfort.

As they approached the station, she looked up at Matt and whispered, "Don't tell them about the overdue books." He assured her he would not.

Entering the squat, outdated, inadequate, and soon-to-be-obliterated structure, Matt groaned as he recognized the cartoonish clone behind the counter. It was Officer Dumas, known to every kid in the city as Officer Dumb Ass. In his ill-fitting uniform, he appeared weirdly skinny and lanky except for the emerging middle-aged Humpty-Dumpty paunch that tested the cinch of a military-style belt left over from his trimmer years. He enjoyed grasping his holstered pistol when he talked to you.

Matt straightened his long hair and attempted to explain to the Officer what had happened.

Dumas gave him a shrewd once-over and, paying no attention to anything that had been said, responded, "I remember you. Yer Prof. Mahoney's kid. The one was in the car, that old junk, middle of the night on River Street. Parked there by yourself waiting on somebody."

"Yeah. That was me. But I was just parked there. I wasn't waiting for anybody. I wasn't doing anything."

"Yeah, right. I remember you said that then, too. We shoulda hauled you in that night. If it was up to me—"

The officer had no insight into the true nature of either the mixed-up, well-intentioned kid or of the charmingly deluded mini-woman standing before him like a colorful pair of mismatched socks, nor did he appreciate the spell of serendipity that commingled his fate with theirs on this midsummer's night.

Officer D. looked at Esmerelda, his eyebrows raised and questioning. "Ma'am, has this man been bothering you? Has he hurt you or taken anything from you?"

"Oh no officer. He's a wonderful man. He loves animals. He's such a nice man. So fair, and square and hunky-dory." For a moment Matt felt like Walt Disney.

"Yeah, okay. Right." He shook his head and redirected his attention to Matt. "What are you doing with her so late at night? Something is wrong here. Your eyes are all red and puffy. Something is definitely wrong here."

Matt's eyes had always been red and itchy since he was a kid. "Chronic blepharitis," he was told, but now, in this psychedelic age, the redness always led people to believe he was stoned or tripping. They were only sometimes correct. Lately, with his insomnia taking on new and unprecedented dimensions, his already irritated eyes were more swollen and crusty and bloodshot than ever and had ugly bags beneath them.

"I told you. I found her by the library. She was all alone. I don't know—she was confused or something. I was just trying to help. If I was trying to do anything wrong I wouldn't be bringing her here." He raised his voice in defense as invisible hands strangled at his Adam's apple, giving it that queasy feeling that was just shy of fury. He stifled the anger and frustration quaking inside him and silently called the officer a four-syllable name that involved his mother.

"You." The officer aimed a cocked-and-loaded index finger. "Lower your voice and sit down over there. We'll deal with you later."

Esmerelda looked at Matt and whispered, "Do you think they'll let me ride in the police car?"

Duty bound, though he knew it would rub the officer the wrong way, and partly for that reason, Matt said, "She wants you to take her home in the police car."

He saw Esmerelda's eyes light up in appreciation and anticipation.

The officer was not amused. "I told you to keep your mouth shut and sit down. Don't worry. We'll take care of her—and you."

Officer D. and a second officer conferred in hushed conspiratorial tones. Phone calls had already been made. Matt wanted to leave but dared not. Esmerelda sat like a well-behaved schoolgirl outside the principal's office, a doll baby in a grownup chair, studying her books and swinging her stumpy legs as she chanted a nursery rhyme:

*Namby-pamby*
*Dilly-dally*
*Hunky-dory do,*
*Huggy-kissy*
*Lovey-dovey*
*All the whole night through.*

The second officer sauntered in lackadaisically as though he was not professionally committed to Officer Dumb Ass's antics and told a delighted Esmerelda he would drive her home.

"Oh that would be wonderful," she said to the officer. "You are such a nice man."

"Can I leave now?" asked Matt.

The officer shook his head. "No. You better wait around."

As Esmerelda passed Matt on her way out the door, she looked him in the eye and said, "Thank you for helping me, kind sir."

Matt smiled and said, "No problem, kind lady," and, pointing to her medallion, said, "Say hello to Roger for me."

She caressed the medallion and smiled back through crinkled and squinty eyes and, speaking in a prophetic voice with unintentional astuteness, intoned, "Isn't it like they say? No good deed goes unpunished."

A few minutes later, Officer D. came back out and spewed the venom of some misplaced old grudge into Matt's face. Matt was nervous even though he had nothing to hide and had done nothing wrong. He was accused of being high and trying to take advantage of Esmerelda. He was patted down and made to empty his pockets. He was taunted with vague physical threats and knew that the officer was goading him to react in a way that would invite a moderate drubbing. Matt took the abuse stoically until the officer got tired of being a bully and said, "I'm letting you go this time. But I'm watching you. And I'm watching that brother of yours, too."

Knowing that it would be a waste of time to argue with someone whose mind was already made up, Matt said nothing and left before the officer had a change of heart, if that is the correct word. When he was outside on the sidewalk, beyond reach, he protested with a middle finger, muttering, "Perch and rotate, you asshole," and continued on with his nighttime walk, which was now solemn and malicious.

## H. Conquered in a Car Seat

Skanatoga Street led to River Street, which was silent and vacant, as usual for this hour, but well-illuminated with streetlights, giving it an expansive and glittery aura. The roar of eighteen-wheelers bellowed down the valley from the thruway and the rumblings of a centipedal freight train rattled and echoed in the crumbling alleys and side streets like dinosaurs in a canyon. The hands of the old clock on the Farmers' National Bank building were at 12:51. He took a left onto River Street and followed its current across Chapel Street, walking past the remaining downtown stores of what always seemed, in the universe of his boyhood, to have been such a bustling metropolitan business district. With all of them slated for demolition, the city's future now rested upon the uncertain success of the ever-impending New Holland mall.

The intersection of River and Chapel Streets was where he had been parked on the night of his previous run-in with Officer Dumas. It was a few months earlier on another one of his insomniac nights that he got behind the wheel of his short-lived fluid drive 1948 Dodge and prowled the night to escape a fresh barrage of predator thoughts.

*He drove a highly conspicuous big black tank of a car with a fat splotch of pink Bondo by the front wheel well. Its monstrous trunk was spacious enough to sneak four of his friends into the drive-in theater. After cruising aimlessly around the deserted streets for a while, he parked on River Street to relax, forget about time and futures, and seek the sanctuary of good thoughts with the engine running, the heat blasting and the radio squirting out tunes in the lonesome cave of his car. The streets were all newly plowed following an 18-inch dumping of wet snow—"good packing," as they used to say, referring to the ease with which an arsenal of heavy-duty snowballs could be crammed into shape for their wintry war games. Parking meters protruded like periscopes through the snowbanks that obscured the curbs and sidewalks in front of Holzheimer and Shaul's, where unclothed no-nipple mannequins studied him from their window displays, oblivious to their nakedness. He blew a kiss to the prettiest, gave the customary tube to her dickless companion, and slouched back in his seat, eyes closed, hands clasped behind his head. He turned up the volume on the FM college station and sang along, perhaps a little too loud:*

> *Maybe the lateness of the hour*
> *Makes me seem bluer than I am*
> *But in my heart there is a shower*
> *Hope she'll be happier with him*

*It was around 3 a.m. on a frigid mid-January night. The downtown, his downtown, felt so holy and meditative at that late hour. So cozy and safe.*

*Then, out of nowhere, two police cars came screeching to a halt, blocking him fore and aft, their glaring lights pulsating in the frozen air. Four cops in heavy winter SS officer trench coats lunged from their cruisers and surrounded him. One of them was carrying a shotgun. With no explanation, Dumas ordered him onto the half-shoveled sidewalk where he stood, without a coat, in a fit of shivers, for half an hour while they conducted their Keystone Kops interrogation and search. They ransacked the car, pillaging through his glove compartment and trunk, removing and searching beneath his back seat cushions and inspecting the ashtray and dashboard with comical precision. He was questioned, accused, searched, re-searched, and, at every turn, disbelieved. They mocked his long hair, making the typical unimaginative comments he had come to expect from narrow-minded half-wits. As it turned out, they had hatched the brilliant theory that he was waiting for a drug connection with a presumed but unidentified dealer from New York City, a notion so absurd that even in those circumstances, Matt had to suppress his laughter.*

*"Yeah right," he thought, "with all of New York State at my disposal, I'm going to make a big-time drug deal beneath the streetlights at 3 a.m. in plain sight on River Street around the corner from the police station." He wished he had the nerve to say that out loud.*

*One of the officers, Tony M., taunted him with questions about how his mother was doing, feigning concern, trying to lull him into a false sense of camaraderie, and then followed up with accusatory questions about drugs, hoping that his smooth technique would persuade Matt to spill the beans on himself. They told Matt his eyes were red and they knew he was stoned, but he wasn't. After they were done tearing his car apart and making wild accusations, the officers chuckled among themselves and told him he would be arrested for loitering and littering if he didn't clean up and move along. They left everything, including his back seat, littered in the snow. His only witnesses were a family of mannequins who just stood there in sympathy, mourning his misfortune with mute compassion.*

Good thing I'm white*, he thought, pondering what the outcome might have been if he were black or Puerto Rican and thankful that they hadn't discovered the roach and the pile of residue in the back seat ashtray.*

Now, here he was again, suspicious for doing nothing other than walking the streets and acting the Good Samaritan for the enchanted Queen Esmerelda. He had no defenses against such an ambitious and random menace. His only refuge was in the safety of the fond memories engendered by each familiar store front, each dirty alley, each echoing movie theater, school, and church. But even fond memories could no longer be trusted. They somehow always led to self-reproach that escalated into despondency, his thoughts swirling around like a needle on a scratchy old album, stuck in one ever-dizzying groove, convincing him that he's doomed and that life is hopeless and that there is no worthwhile future to attain.

## I. Superman and the Hulk

He continued dragging his anvil like an old man, navigating east on River Street, trudging the ground where the much-anticipated mall would soon be constructed, past the still-standing-for-now Tryon ("Now Playing—The Godfather") and Iroquois ("Closed") Theaters, where he had seen hundreds of movies since he was old enough to walk downtown by himself. He walked on beyond Pink & Rock's bar and the piss-drenched steep and narrow stairway that led up to Worm's third floor penny-a-minute pool hall. Onward still to St. Brigid's Catholic Church where, as a devout and obedient young congregant all decked out in his Sunday best, he attended high mass on Sunday mornings, fidgeting in his pew during Father Krouse's interminable sermon, and struggling with guilt for the bewildering but pleasurable longings occasioned by the teasing sight of the sensuous women in their stylish dresses, their black veils thin like lingerie as they genuflected at their pews, bathed in opulent streams of morning sunlight.

Their fingertips and foreheads still moist with holy water dipped from the marble font. And the choir girls, so pure and virginal, so full of grace, gliding like a procession of angels up the center aisle and kneeling at the communion rail with shut eyes and heads tilted back, their wetted tongues revealed to absorb the body of their savior through their barely-parted lips. And where, no matter where he sat or in which direction he looked, the stern judgment-day eyes of the unforgiving stained-glass-window saints penetrated to the dark and dreggy recesses of his sin-hidden soul, straight to the core of his impure thoughts.

Behind the church, on Mercy Street, was St. Brigid's School. Matt had gone there from kindergarten until the beginning of the second grade, when his teacher, Sister Jeronima Clare, punished him in a way he could no longer remember but which had frightened him so badly that he refused to return to her classroom. Mrs. Mahoney, unable to persuade, coerce, or bribe him back, transferred him to Ash Avenue School, which was just three blocks walking distance from their home. Thus he became what the nuns derisively referred to as a "public schooler," which was almost as bad as being a Protestant.

Second-grade Catholic-school Matt couldn't understand why anyone would ever be a Protestant. The nuns had taught him that all Protestants were going straight to hell no matter how they lived their lives. No "Get Out of Hell Free" card. No questions asked. And God, the biggest Catholic of all, hated Protestants with a vengeance. God's greatest love was a good Catholic and, of course, heaven was for Catholics only. According to those women of the veil, however, even most Catholics would end up in hell anyway because all it took was one bad act to smite the heavenly home you were building, brick by brick, by being a good Catholic. The soul was just a lifelong construction site, teetering on destruction at all times. At best, he might get to spend most of eternity in the mind-numbing doldrums of purgatory, but anything was better than that pit of flames or the nothingness of the dreaded limbo. In purgatory you were at least on heaven's waiting list, though it could take millions of lifetimes to get called up from the torment of God's minor leagues to the joy of his celestial majors.

*God must be peculiar*, he thought, *to create us in his image and profess to love us so much, and then send most of us to the hell he had created for those who did not live up to his standards. The Creator condemning his creations and torturing them for their flaws. It was not fair. He should have built us better.*

All those "Jesus versus God" images confused both Little Matt and, to some extent, the current version of Matt, who felt he should by now have grown beyond worrying about such frivolous things. It was the good cop/bad cop relationship where the merciless, unforgiving God would beat you and bloody you up into a state of terrified submission, and then Jesus bops in like a leading man, so handsome and understanding and loving and forgiving, healing all your wounds, and you would do anything to please him, anything to avoid getting beaten up again. They were the superheroes. Jesus was the invulnerable "I can do anything" Superman who would always save the day and wouldn't harm a fly. But God was different. He was the Hulk or an evil nemesis with violent outbursts and a bad temper, making unreasonable demands and never satisfied, an angry and jealous in-your-face superhero who left bodies strewn about in the wake of his vengeful acts. You definitely did not want to piss him off.

Oddly, the fear-mongering elementary school nuns, in their full-bodied black armor that revealed nothing other than a frightening stony-faced countenance, were always more interested in Satan and his sly ways than in the Savior Son or any Almighty God. They couldn't stop bragging about Satan and his awesome dark powers. They were more enraptured by the mysteries of his wickedness and the art of spiritual torture and the thrill of eternal damnation than in the rewards of a blissful afterlife. They did not love God. They feared him like a slave fears a sadistic master. Any obedience they extracted from the children in their classrooms would not have been inspired by any holy impulse in the child but rather by the fear of being dragged to hell, impaled upon the tines of the devil's pitchfork to burn forever in their beloved inferno. It was all just a conspiracy of fear, and they, the gullible lambs of God, were constantly warned that they had better always be good. "For he who loves the danger will perish in it," they were told, not quite comprehending what variety of danger was being referred to. It was clear to Matt by the fourth grade that the only way he would ever deserve heaven was to be murdered as he was leaving church, immediately after having made a full confession and saying his penance, thus being restored to a perfect state of grace, and dying quickly before he'd had any impure thoughts or muttered any profanity. One could only hope.

There was more, but he didn't want to think about it, so he continued his trek and walked past the Columbian Hall where, several centuries earlier at a Friday night dance, he had first set his eyes upon Helen, and she upon him, as The Galaxies amped out their too-loud renditions of the latest British Invasion hits. That first glimpse, through a tunnel of indifferent faces and the distracting buzz of a hundred conversations across the sparkling mirror-ball twilight of the dance floor, was a genuine love-at-first-sight experience that sent Matt's heart cartwheeling with the absolute certainty that he had to meet her and, for some reason, run his fingertips across her cheek. To hope for more would be greedy and impure.

## J. Conquistadors

He crossed Phillips Street and strolled past the East River Street School into the East End. Continuing past Carmel's—a popular late-night greasy-spoon diner where the rabble of last-call drunks congregated each weekend at 2 a.m. when the bars shut down—he felt the discomfort of being so conspicuous, so upper-middle-class and pale skinned. Anyone could tell by the sight of him, and the slight reserve in his gait, that this was not his turf. The East End was a flavorful and intriguing foreign colony embedded within the bland perimeter of his own conventional white world. On most warm summer nights, the street was alive with the bouncy rhythms of Spanish music from opened windows and car radios, with bold, narrow-eyed men and the sensuous señoritas—exotic and alluring in tight denim short-shorts— and a cast of colorful charismatic actors and sidekick characters who hung around outside the bars, slumping against the hoods and trunks of the curbside cars, cursing one another in black jive or rapid-fire Spanish which was incomprehensible to most Anglos. He enjoyed the ring and rhythm of the language and the cocky bravado that set it afire even though he didn't understand it, and he imagined how cool it would be if he could speak it and join them in the secrecy of their foreign lingo.

In seventh grade, when Matt first became aware that these Spanish-speakers were moving into town, he was curious because the mere sight of them inspired images of courageous Pizarro and

Cortez conquistadors in crested helmets and golden breastplates as well as the ravishing raven-haired women with fiery ebony eyes, twirling seductively in scarlet skirts and loose low-cut white blouses, a dazzling display of cleavage and thighs. His shyness, however, couldn't overcome the language barrier when dark-skinned Yammo and Armando, fresh from Puerto Rico, joined his eighth-grade class and knew only one sentence in English: "Yammo smokey ceegar." He liked the way they looked in their tight, pegged pants and their spit-shined tap-heeled Beatle boots, which were cool when the Beatles wore them but were disparaged as PFCs, Puerto Rican fence climbers, when worn by the likes of Yammo and Armando. It had surprised Matt to learn that there was a bitter prejudice and even hatred against these new arrivals that manifested themselves in crude jokes and racist epithets. No one had told him in advance that he wasn't supposed to like them.

After he graduated from A. L. Henderson High School, he worked on and off for a couple years at several of the local sweatshops: Coleman's, Regent Enterprises, and Cove Industries. There he indulged himself in fantasy love affairs with the Hispanic factory girls sweating alongside him on the assembly lines. He was infatuated by their walnut skin, their laughing eyes, and their sexy Puerto Rican accents. Most of them had Spanish boyfriends who sat with them during their breaks or walked them home when the factory whistle put an end to another day of robotic labor. Matt knew he wasn't man enough for any of them anyway and that his fantasies were ludicrous. They'd probably laugh at him and his asinine Anglo ways if he tried to get close to them—or he'd get beat up by one of their boyfriends.

## K. The Bad Lads

Matt wished he were more like his brother, Rory, who was all confidence and charm and didn't worry about all those things that nagged Matt. His was a colorful spectrum as compared to Matt's featureless beige. Rory was at ease in the East End and spent a lot of time there, carousing its streets and bars with his notorious gang of friends, the Bad Lads. The Lads were brash and boisterous and were known as troublemakers, the way they attracted attention bunched together and strutting in a noisy pack in front of the shops on River Street, dominating the sidewalk as they wrestled with each other, wolf-whistling at every girl who caught their wandering eyes. The Evening Register sensationalized their reputation and increased their sex appeal by describing them as "a roving gang of wild youth," which evoked images of anti-social Marlon Brando wild ones and disrespectful, brooding James Dean rebels. Thus, the Bad Lads were feared by the elderly, who believed what they read in the newspaper as if it were their bible, and were decried citywide by parents seeking to protect their own children from such a bad influence. They were prized, though, by romantic teenaged girls looking for misunderstood hoodlum boyfriends to rehabilitate.

In truth, though they did have their scrapes, the Lads were not as dangerous as many townspeople were so inclined to believe or as they themselves imagined. Nonetheless, they became the easy scapegoats for unsolved crimes and anonymous complaints and were never given the benefit of any doubt nor a fair chance to prove themselves as anything other than miscreant juvenile delinquents.

Matt walked by the bodega and saw two of the Lads leaning against a corner mailbox. They greeted each other with power handshakes and the obligatory round of "Hey brother, what's happenin'?" Willie and Charlie were two of Rory's best friends. Willie was a soft-spoken Black kid from the East End. He was looking dapper in his cheap shades and cool duds. Charlie, wearing his faded Bioyah hat, was a gregarious pasty-skinned Italian kid from the West End. He was good-natured but, when crossed, had a short fuse and a feisty temper. He was known to a select few as the Day-Glo Dago because his bedroom was painted black and was illuminated with black lights. The walls and ceilings were decorated with cosmic Day-Glo posters and his own hand-painted psychedelic Day-Glo murals that sucked you into them when you lay riveted to the floor in the phosphorescence of the black-lit darkness amid the musky aroma of a bubbling bong and the hypnotic spell of whatever album was spinning you through the private universe of his bedroom. Twirling a beat-up silver flute like a cheerleader's baton, Charlie brought it to his lips and pretended to play for a few seconds, all the while jumping up and down on one leg and making exaggerated facial expressions. Then, with his husky atonal voice, he began singing:

*He hears the silence howling*
*Catches angels as they fall*
*And the all-time winner*
*Has got him by the balls*

Charlie added unneeded accentuation by grabbing his crotch with his free hand and shouting, "My God! What have you done?"

Willie peeked over his shades, rolled his eyes and shook his head. "Motherfucker's crazy, man."

Charlie nodded. "I'm not a motherfucker. I'm a family fucker. And I'm coming to your house next."

Both Willie and Matt had heard that one before. Matt exhaled a laugh. "Are you guys stoned or what?"

Charlie stopped mid-pose, suspended in air like a cartoon character, and said, "To the bone, man. To the fuckin' bone."

Willie mumbled behind half-mast eyes, "Hey, you got any grass on you?"

"No," Matt said. "Good thing, too. I just got searched down at the police station by that asshole, Officer Dumb Ass." He told them the entire story, exaggerating the degree of his own defiance and customizing it with several self-aggrandizing details.

Charlie and Willie snorted with laughter. Charlie said, "Fuck that shit, man. That is one fucked-up story. Fucking pigs. They hassle you even when you're being good and shit. Police brutality, man."

"Dumb Ass, man," said Willie. "Last time I saw him, he told me I was insolent. I had to look it up. Motherfucker was right."

"Too bad you didn't have any grass on you," Charlie added. "You could have gotten high with Esmerelda. Man. Now that woulda been a trip."

"Absafugginlutely," emphasized Willie. They all laughed at the thought of a stoned Esmerelda.

For several minutes they kept reality at bay with ridiculous banter to keep the tide of stony hilarity flowing and to stem the ever-rising tide of boredom. When things quieted down, Matt spit out the question that had been on the tip of his tongue all along. "Hey, have you guys seen Rory?"

"Yeah. For about two minutes. Then he went off with Carmelita. The dude's getting whipped, man." Willie shook his head, lifted his pinky finger, and wriggled it in circles.

Carmelita was a beautiful, petite Puerto Rican girl with a pinky worthy of being wrapped around. Like Mrs. Mahoney, she was a smart, no-nonsense girl who, even at such a young age, knew her own mind and spoke it with her heels dug into the ground. She was a positive influence on Rory and was able to keep him away from the trouble that arose when he and the Bad Lads were patrolling their turf.

## L. King of the Mountain (The Uphill Struggle)

With spirits sufficiently lifted, Matt bid adieu to the wasted Lads and continued along East River Street past the series of cozy residential side streets that all dead-ended at the railroad tracks that ran parallel to the rat-happy river. He preferred dead ends to parallels. B-sides to hits. He walked past Ray's Place, Pal's Market, and the Our Lady of Vilnius Lithuanian Church and the side street where, half a century earlier, a certain child had lived before he had grown up and changed his name to Doug Kirkland, the famous movie star.

When he reached Moorman Avenue, where he could hear "I'll Follow The Sun" blasting from an open-windowed bedroom, he took a left and began pushing his boulder up the mountainous climb to the part of town known as Polack Hill. Dragging anvils and pushing boulders—that was all he ever did.

The climb challenged the shredded muscles of Matt's empty legs. Each step was a pessimistic struggle against gravity. With its unrelenting grade, it might as well have been Mt. Everest. Leaning into the hill, straining at his knees and calves, lungs gasping, leg muscles burning, his forehead breaking into a drippy perspiration and his heartbeat pulsing in his eardrums, Matt was "The Little Engine That Couldn't." *I know I can't, I know I can't.*

But he could and he did. Soon enough the punishing grade softened. The high houses with steep, impossible-to-mow lawns fell behind him, and he stood on flat ground and planted his flag in the land of the Poles, new sweat soaking through his t-shirt and trickling from his brow into his eyes.

Polack Hill had first been known as Cork Hill after the influx of Irish immigrants in the mid-nineteenth century. Matt's Irish great-grandparents had lived there, but by that century's end, the Poles and the Italians began surging into town to fill the menial labor jobs at the carpet mills and the dozens of other sweatshops that fueled the industrial engine that groaned and belched from the gritty underbelly of New Holland's version of the American dream.

The Italians laid claim to the west end of town and the entire south side of the river; founded their own Little Italy; opened up their own grocery stores, pizzerias, bars, shoe repair, and tailor shops; and didn't bother much with Merchant Hill or Cork Hill. As the story went, the Poles of the East End set their sights on Cork Hill and made strategic advances to run the Irish out and claim it for themselves. Their conquest was complete when they successfully established their own Polish-speaking St. Adalbert's Church and elementary school. But that was before Matt's day. To him it had always been Polack Hill.

Such was the pattern of the social climb in New Holland. It was a warped version of the children's game King of the Mountain but drawn out over decades and played for real-life stakes. Many of the newest immigrants started out in the East End, establishing proud neighborhoods amid the industry of the noisy mills, the odious river, and the clattering of the tracks. When the East End began bursting at the seams and could no longer accommodate the steady flow of "huddledmasses yearning to breathe free," new lands were sought. They soldiered up the mountain against the resistance of the reigning hill-dwellers, clawing ever upward in search of status, security, and acceptance, claiming new streets and neighborhoods, always trying to preserve the old-world ways from new-world erosion even as they adopted new American habits. Despite their own struggles, or perhaps because of them, each new clan staking out their own domain at the top of the mountain then turned around and fought to defend their hard-earned turf against the struggles and advances of any new breeds that may be following in their path. Prejudice and contempt regenerated itself over and over again through a series of new underdogs and top dogs.

Matt's own Polish grandmother, an immigrant resident of Polack Hill in its conquering years, was disowned and shunned by her old-world parents when she broke their tribal pact and married Matt's grandfather, a South Side Italian immigrant. As a result, Matt had many Polish great-aunts, great-uncles, and cousins of varying degrees of kinship whom he had never met and knew nothing about, even though, unbeknownst to him, some cousins had been his classmates in school. Nevertheless, the prejudices dissipated over the decades as the children and children's children of the immigrant Poles, Italians, and Irish all started sampling new flavors and raising all-American generations of half-and-halfs. As the wizen-eyed immigrant grandparents began dying off and their old country traditions and superstitions were threatened by extinction, the old ways became less and less relevant, and the distinctions between Polack Hill and the Italian South Side, though still evident, became distinctions without much of a difference. Now it was the Puerto Ricans who were the strange new kids on the block, looking up at the mountain that stood tall and steep before them, planning their ascent, appraising their struggle.

*At least their struggle is real*, thought Matt. *Mine is just a whiny fabrication.*

## M. A Scent of Death

He continued, turning left, walking past the lumber yard and the string of tidy homes with American flags mounted on their porches, the daffodil gardens and the yard ornaments and the meticulous vegetable patches. He saw a birdbath on a neatly manicured postage-stamp front yard and, mysteriously drawn to it, winced at the sight of a dead bird floating in the murky slime. He prodded it gently, as if not wanting to disturb its slumber, and, as it bobbed in response, he recoiled as a repugnant scent of death rose to his nostrils, and he saw that its twig legs were broken and its eye sockets had already been eaten empty.

As Matt approached the antiquated three-story tenement building where his friend David lived, the fragile serenity of the night was pulverized as a huge thick-necked Marmaduke of a guard dog pounced at him and let loose a feral blood-curdling howl that scared the heart from Matt's chest and sent him to the sidewalk in a frightened defensive collapse. The dog stopped mid-air and mid-leap at the top of the flimsy fence as he reached the end of his tether, froze in place for a moment, as though time had stopped, chomping ravenously in Matt's direction, and then dropped back to Earth in a slobbering plop, its hackles on full alert and its hot snout dripping snot.

"Jesus Christ!" Matt was trembling from the shock. He rose and spoke in a whisper, "Hey there, Cerberus. I am sure glad you're on a chain. You scared the bejeebers out of me. I just about crapped my pants thanks to you."

There was a good three feet between the still-growling beast and the back porch that led up to David's apartment. He considered crashing there for the night, he was so exhausted, but he didn't want to wake up his friend or perhaps interrupt something intimate. Maybe the dog had woken him up. He monitored the apartment for a minute or two, hoping to see an alerted head poking out the window, but there was no sign of life or light, and he lacked the confidence to risk the harsh startle of a late night knock. Besides, he worried that time had driven a wedge between them and that, as David and all Matt's other friends were rapidly evolving into adulthood, he was being left behind in his detested state of arrested adolescence.

*It was David who, less than a week earlier, had taken Matt aside and said, eye-to-eye, directly, and matter-of-factly, "Maybe it's none of my business, but I saw Carla last night. She was with Socket. I'm only mentioning this because I know you said you were supposed to be with her and she told you she had something she had to do with her family. I thought you would want to know." Lenny "Socket" Toomey was Matt's age and a casual acquaintance.*

*Matt pretended it was no big deal and hoped that nothing in his reaction revealed otherwise, but inside he felt like a public spectacle. His stupidity was maddening. "It's more than the human mind can bear," he recited in an attempt at a British accent, conjuring images from a Velvet Underground song, images of Carla swooning to "the smooth soothings of some Neanderthal." My name really suits me, Matt thought, forgiving only his redundant "t."*

*That same night he went to a party at a friend's apartment. He was inundated by the throb of music, the waves of intoxicating smoke, the periodic drifts of patchouli, and the jumbled-up mesh of conversations in the dim-lit room. His friend Benjamin used exquisite care to control the pulse of the party and fine-tune the hip ambiance by expertly selecting choice cuts from album after album. Matt sat in his bubble, aloof and brooding, observing couples tumbling into playful interactions and sharing telltale glances in dark corners where certain intimacies are permitted. They all seemed part of a secret clique, and he couldn't figure out how they knew the things they knew about each other. The clever conversation and the private details that broke through barriers and made connections possible. It was as if there were classes about growing up that he had missed, classes he didn't even know were offered and lessons he had never learned. And now here he was, stuck in grade school while everyone else advanced through the ranks and got their degrees. So he avoided contact, retreated into muteness, and memorized theoretically clever somethings to say in case someone tried to start a conversation with him.*

*Seeking refuge in music, he fingered through dozens of Benjamin's albums and made one request: "Blue," by Joni Mitchell, the side with "The Last Time I Saw Richard." Benjamin took the request without comment. Over an hour later, despite a few reminders, Ben still hadn't played it, and Matt still hadn't spoken with anyone. When he could take it no longer, he blurted out, "Jesus Christ, Ben. Can't you play the goddamn album?" His voice was an intrusive blast, shattering the protective musical shell of the living room. Conversations ceased and all eyes were trained on Matt, anticipating his next move.*

*Benjamin took him aside—lately everyone was taking him aside for one reason or another—and delicately said, "Matt, I can't play that. This is supposed to be a party. That album's too down. It'll kill the room. It's..."—he wanted the correct word—"depression." He searched Matt's eyes, but there was no traction. Matt was long gone. He had thought the album would be a hit for the crowd. He was broken and lost in the embarrassment of his outburst and in the unbridgeable distance between himself and everyone else in the room. Most of all he was lost in wondering how he had gotten so screwed up and in wishing he were mute so he would no longer have to suffer the humiliation and regret of every foolish sentence he uttered. He felt erased, just an ugly black smudge, a stain on the carpet. He wanted to say he was sorry but didn't know how. He didn't know why he wanted to infect the party with his sulking soundtrack. Maybe he should just stop all his self-pitiful whining and get it over with once and for all. Maybe it was his cowardice that held him back. He hated the person he had become. He was so sick of it—that same old tired program running on and on in his Crazy Eddie brain—and he didn't know how to turn it off.*

*Benjamin returned to his duties at the turntable. The music remained upbeat and cool. The party continued uninfected. A voice crooned, "You can send me dead flowers every morning" as Matt snuck out the back door, knowing no one would miss such a killjoy, but nonetheless hoping that some sympathetic girl from the party, someone, anyone, would notice, take interest or even pity—at that point he didn't care which—and follow him down the back stairs and ask him what was wrong and let him collapse into her arms, to rescue him before he exploded. But that only happens in the movies, and besides, there was something pretty pathetic about that whole scenario. Instead, he took a long walk around town to scrub his mind free of all thought before returning home, putting on his headphones, and listening over and over to "Repent Walpurgis," which was the musical mirror to his fugue mood. But it was an ineffective antidote. He was nothing more than a hamster stuck in a cage, racing on an ever-spinning wheel, getting nowhere fast. The entire city had become his cage, but it was too small for the walk he now needed to take, and his spinning was out of control. He was afraid that, without that longer walk, he might do something desperate and unforgivable, something irreversible that would convert his emptiness into nothingness. He knew he had to escape his cage.*

*Shit*, he thought, *there I go again, wasting my time on ugly things*. He took a last look up at the frowning gape of David's apartment windows. *Quick. Snap back.* He continued past Cork Hill Liquors, the last bastion of Irish home rule remaining on Polack Hill, crossed Upper Chapel Street, which was the main artery, and then over the Upper Skanatoga Creek on the Thaddeus Kosciusko Bridge. But first, he slipped into the bushes to take a long-overdue whiz. He marveled at how loud his piss sounded as it crashed and cascaded against the leaves and weeds and dug a frothy little pond into the loose dirt.

"Pissing my life away," he said, making a whooshing sound and spraying the noxious amber fluid around as if he were a fireman putting out a fire with a big, long hose.

The residential neighborhood on the other side of the bridge was now deserted, but in the dimming hours of a warm summer night, the front porches of the rows of homes along these streets were populated with Polish and Ukrainian grandmothers keeping a watchful eye on the pedestrian traffic like sentinels guarding a cherished homeland. Matt recalled the dozens of times he and Helen walked these streets, joking about the wrinkled old ponnies in their babushkas, rocking in the secrecy of their dark porches, peering out and studying their every move as they strolled hand in hand on the stage that was the sidewalk.

Matt half-hoped, half-dreamed, but never quite dared to expect that on one of his late-night meanderings, while the rest of the world lay dormant, he would discover her, Helen, wandering aimlessly like himself. In the comfort of the uncomplicated night, his bundle of fears would all dissolve and he and Helen would once again join hands and walk together, just as they used to, and in the majesty of the moment he would have the time and courage to apologize for everything and explain his thoughtless behavior and purge himself of his all-consuming guilt and his ever-growing weirdness. She would understand and absolve him once and for all and then everything would be okay again, the same as it was, like in a movie when it has all been a bad dream or a temporary spell. The demons and The Watcher would vanish as though they never existed, and the newly liberated Matthew A. Mahoney would become the Matthew A. Mahoney he knew he could become in the freedom of an unfettered self—triumphant and victorious, achieving his fully realized potential for the promising future, all that kind of stuff. No sewer tomato     he! He shook his head at the absurdity of his thoughts, pinning all his hopes on such a chance encounter, even though the teasing night was rich with such far-fetched impossibilities. It was not a good strategy, but Matt knew that it was too late for everything to ever be the same again, for everything can only be as it is, not as it was.

## N. Dead and Dying Sons

The mountainous Moorman Avenue ascent had taken the spunk from Matt's legs. Exhaustion dumbed him down. His body and mind and emotions were running on empty as he plodded past St. Benedict's

Church and along the tedious length of Rensselaer Street, knee deep in his own sludge. He wondered why he never saw any other wanderlusting insomniacs roaming the streets during his nocturnal promenades. Wasn't anyone else curious about the nighttime? Wasn't anyone else kept awake and driven from their bed by their antagonistic thoughts?

His throat was parched as if he were crossing a desert, and the thought of curling up on someone's lawn for a nap, just a quick one—he was so tired—seemed a reasonable idea. As a diversion, he began to count his steps, but he had to quit counting when the addictive robotic monotony of the mathematics of walking began to control his thoughts like an evil hypnotist and brainwash him with the mystery of numbers. All those loose digits created a racket inside his head, like seeds in a shaken gourd, and soon that imaginary racket became as real as the nerve-wracking thoughts he had been attempting to drown out.

Matt's mind spun back to Vinny's brainteaser and wondered what he could have meant. Wasn't it obvious that all tracks of an album revolve at the same speed? He bent his neck backward and gazed at the stars and the moon and the heavens above him, all spinning around in different grooves on the celestial turntable that was this vast vinyl universe. His stymied mind started racing as if it were an out-of-control album going 16 RPM then accelerating through 33, 45, 78 and still ever-increasing speeds, all just more numbers messing with his mind, driving him crazier.

He shook the numbers out of his head as best he could and, as he mushed past Biscanno's Pizzeria, he substituted the linear numerical menace with the free-form anarchy of his melancholy reminiscences of himself and Helen enjoying greasy pizza in a joint packed with other classmates from Bishop Brannan High School who recognized them as a couple, "the perfect couple," someone had said, and with the usual brood of destructive memories that swarmed with it.

*Ah, shit. It's just one disturbing slide show after another. Why can't I turn it off?* He tried reprimanding the projectionist inside his head but couldn't get his attention, so the show continued, despite his protests. But that ever-present master of disguises, that Jack of all trades, that cunning keeper and unleasher of the screamin' demons and the harbinger of It, was not pestered by Matt's efforts to restrict him, to oust him from his inner perch where he commanded an easy control over all of Matt's thoughts. Matt had even written him a poem. It started out like this:

> *There's a man who lives inside my head*
> *Who says he wishes I were dead*
> *Who speaks in such a cocksure voice*
> *That he seems to leave me little choice*
>
> *He makes no bones of his intention*
> *He wants my death to be his invention*
> *And so every chance he gets, he takes,*
> *To confound me with my life's mistakes*

Onward he marched up the tiny but nonetheless dispiriting hump at the end of Rensselaer Street and onto Crocus Ave, to the Seventh Ward Honor Roll, a modest and neglected memorial to the local veterans of World War II. He skimmed down the inscribed columns of names of forgotten soldiers, knowing that behind each name was a story.

There were no markings to distinguish the survivors from the war-fallen. There should have been gold stars beside the names of the dead ones so their downtrodden souls could rest easier in the knowledge that their ultimate sacrifice had received at least some recognition, even if with just a measly star, as if they'd been given an A+ on whatever final test they had faced on whatever foreign battlefield they had last stood upon split seconds before that bullet shattered their skull or that bayonet sliced through their guts or whatever implement of destruction had by some other manner delivered them their earthly ruin. A token recognition. Maybe just a dab of fatherly acknowledgment. A simple, "I'm proud of you, son. I'll miss you."

*Every dead or dying son deserves at least that much,* Matt thought.

## O. A Plague of Locusts

This street, lower Crocus Avenue, was yet another land of too many memories, a plague of locusts, each step laden with the stab of flashbacks of those happier times. He dwelt on the sharp contrasts between his then and his now and wondered how his world had become such a loveless shambles in which every thought reminded him of something depressing. Accentuate the negative. Eliminate the positive. The world was all bass-ackward.

*My glass is neither half-full nor half-empty. My glass is cracked.* He longed to run away from everyone who reminded him of anyone and from everything that reminded him of anything, to unmesh the grinding gears of his self-destructive dysfunction. He needed to get fixed.

"My Life as a Hole," he sighed, imagining a title for his autobiography, pondering, *Why is it that I'm not happy unless I'm not happy?*

The deep wooded yards on the west side of Crocus Avenue were dense and foreboding. The protective trees lining the street were thick with rugged corrugated bark. A pungent fragrance seeped from the bushes and dripped from the leafy branches that reached out and sheltered the sidewalk. The ornate homes were hidden behind a row of spear-tipped wrought-iron fences, their turrets and gables and balconies and wraparound porches buried beneath ancient towering pines in a shroud of shadows. He had never known anyone who lived in those homes and wondered who they were and what they did and if they were rich. *House of Usher? Or Seven Gables?*

Preoccupied by haphazard thoughts, he tripped against the uneven frost-heaved W.P.A. sidewalks, their wide cracks packed with cushiony moss, struggling patches of grass, and trampled-down dandelions, and nearly fell to the ground. *Stumbling blocks. So many stumbling blocks.* He righted himself and noticed the gooey coat of pit juice caking under his arms and dripping onto the sides of his chest like a syrupy extract, or maybe a new skin. It turned cool as it dried onto his real skin.

He heard a voice singing. He looked and beyond the shadows saw a woozy figure staggering toward him, unaware that he had an audience.

> *I got a baby's brain and an old man's heart*
> *Took eighteen years to get this far*
> *Don't always know what I'm talking about*
> *Feels like I'm living in the middle of doubt*
> *'Cause I'm eighteen*
> *And I don't know what I want...*

When they were ten yards apart, the figure looked up and gasped at the shock of seeing Matt standing there with a big grin on his face.

"Damn, bro, you trying to scare the shit out of me or what?" It was Yoyo. He was barefooted and shirtless and had three cans of Genny Screamers dangling in a plastic six-pack ring from one hand and a loose grip on an open can in the other. Beer dribbled through his lips and onto his chest. He was shit-faced drunk.

"Hey, Yoyo. What are you doing out here? You're plastered, man. You better be careful, singing so loud. It's late. Somebody'll call the cops on you."

"Hell, I don't care. It won't be the first time. Besides, my girlfriend just broke up with me 'cause she wants to go out with Denny. That fuckin' prick. Supposed to be my friend and everything. That's uncool, man. So I kinda went ballistic on her and decided to get drunk."

He started sobbing like a wounded hyena. His eyes were swollen red slits. "I'm such a fog, man. I think she's been screwing him all this time, and I never even suspected. Fuckin' ball buster. Hell, she never even screwed me! We came real close a couple times, you know what I mean, and I got kinda scared and, well, it didn't work out. This shit, damn, it's got me all con—, con—, confuzzled, man. What should I do, man? You're older. You must know all about this kinda stuff."

Matt was equally confuzzled because he didn't know Yoyo well enough to be having this conversation with him. The beer had magnified their degree of friendship for the poor kid. And Matt didn't know as much about all that kind of stuff as Yoyo gave him credit for.

"Tell you what. Go over to the fields, find a quiet spot and try to get some sleep. It's a nice night and nobody will bother you there. Everything will work out. You'll find another girlfriend. You'll get yourself good and laid and you'll forget all about how bad you're feeling right now. Everything's gonna be fine. I promise."

Yoyo took Matt's advice, and, singing inordinately grateful praises, he stumbled off the curb and zigzagged across the street, beer spilling from the open can like piss onto his smudged toes. "Thanks, man. I owe you big time, man. I owe you fuckin' big time and I will pay you back, I swear to you. I will not forget this."

Matt watched until the still-mumbling drunk had landed on the other side of the street beyond the glow of the streetlight and into the safe green comfort of the ball field and was certain that Yoyo's eternal gratitude would be forever forgotten in ten minutes max.


## P. Butterfly Angels


At Wallace Street, across from Soldier Field and the no-longer "New" New Holland Municipal Pool, he cut across to Creek Street and to the entrance into Vedder's Woods. From where Matt stood, camouflaged by darkness on the sidewalk in front of the Vedder residence, the driveway weaved down through thick woods and across Bunn Creek and up the hill to its end at Merchant Street.

These woods had been the wonderland of his youth, his own private Sherwood Forest. He had practiced the heroics of his childhood navigating the pale waters of its creek and conquering its hills and exploring its paths, climbing its trees, catching crayfish and frogs, collecting its fossils and precious stones, digging for buried treasure, swinging like Tarzan from its jungle vines, rolling and tumbling and daydreaming among the wildflowers and lush summertime fragrances and, in wintertime, riding sleighs and saucers down its snowy alpine trails and trudging its frozen tundra to the North Pole of its arctic winter wilderness.

As a teenager his adventures were more of the nighttime variety and consisted of getting drunk—and usually sick—on Boone's Farm Apple Wine or Martini & Rossi sweet vermouth chugged straight from the bottle or getting stoned with his friends within the safety of the spooky woods. Now, he no longer bore any similarity to that Tom Sawyer pathfinder who had mapped each inch of these woods or even to the Holden Caulfield dropout who had puked and passed out in its bushes. He wasn't sure who he was now or who he wanted to be, but for the moment he assumed the identity of the Neil Young loner, mysterious and unknowable, concealed by shadows. Even though he knew that he was not cool enough to pull that off and that it contradicted his true nature, whatever that was, he still enjoyed picturing himself behind that façade.

*Step aside. Open wide. It's the loner.* He walked up the driveway beneath tall evergreens and penetrated through the spotlit entrance as if he had a license to trespass and was swallowed down the throat of the woods that lay ahead. When he was in grade school, it was considered an act of bravery to go into the woods at night, for all the big kids, axe murderers, and other terrors lurking in its secret spaces. Even though Matt was now a big kid himself and he knew that all those fears were illusory, his skin still crawled and his heart beat louder and faster when the black specter of the woods closed its arms around him.

Beyond the light, the woods were an impenetrable wall of darkness. He pictured himself wandering off the paved way and falling into the prickers. He took each step with caution, as if entering an unlit cave, until his pupils made a dark adaptation and cured his blindness. The driveway angled down and around an ancient stone retaining wall and through tangled thickets and trees with gnarled and intertwined branches and into an open meadow and then over the old stone bridge where he and his friends used to have pissing contests.

He was never any serious competition for the Mileski brothers who could lean against the wall on one side of the bridge and project their piss in a high and powerful arc across the entire width of the one-lane driveway and over the opposite wall where it went splashing down into the creek below like a liquid homer. Though that was years before, the competitive spirit lived on, and Matt now regretted taking that piss on Polack Hill because his overfull bladder had erupted with a force and pressure that might have challenged the old records set by the Mileskis and, if he had only held it, might have blasted over that far wall like a mighty Mickey Mantle swat.

He looked around and realized that these woods were no longer the Sherwood Forest of his childhood. They had shrunken back to the woods they had always been before his imagination had transformed it so many years ago. Now, only his memories remained large. The low roar of the churning creek babbled a lazy hypnotic rhythm, which was echoed and amplified beneath the bridge, and then rippled down and over the placid waterfall that fed into a quaint little storybook pool. He stood there, closed his eyes, and meditated on the mossy scent wafting upward and on the whoosh of running water, tinkling like bells, dripping and plinking from ledges and over rocks, swirling through sculpted-out basins, ringing and mingling together in a watery chorus of musical whispers.

Just beyond the bridge was a path that shot off the driveway and climbed the hill to the backyard of Matt's old house. This was where little Matt had dashed carefree through bushes and hid behind trees while playing heart-pounding games of hide and seek, freeze tag, chase, and sardines on hot summer nights in a long-gone world. When he lived there, that path had always been well worn in summer, and in winter it was a high-speed Olympic sled run for him and all his friends. Now, those days were trampled beneath new dirt, and the path was now overgrown with weeds and shrubs.

He continued up the driveway to the top of the hill where there was a clearing with a robust chestnut tree spreading its thick limbs up against the stars. During all the summers of his childhood, that tree had provided him with a rich vault of chestnuts, which he collected as though they were golden nuggets. They were so shiny and beautiful and all the more so because they served him no purpose other than to be admired.

The tree still stood sturdy though not yet ready to yield its annual treasury of strange fruit. On certain summer evenings, when the sun was just right, there was a brief spell when the final streams of sunlight filtered through the canopy of the overhanging limbs of the woods and set the clearing ablaze in a fiery red and orange sunset glow as though it were the light of a different world.

On one evening at that bewitched hour, when he was still innocent enough to be enchanted, Matt looked down into the woods from his backyard and saw hundreds of monarch butterflies flapping and floating in gracefully interwoven orbits about the shining tree. He ran down and joined them, and they all danced together until night descended through the trees and the butterflies flitted away like angels to whatever world they had come from. Only Matt remained, alone in twilight and wishing he could follow the butterflies to their mystic lair where all things were possible and all wishes came true. But that was a long-ago lifetime in a long-ago world. And the butterflies never returned.

## Q. The Spider Room

He stood near the end of the driveway, still confined within the pale of the mumbling leaves and the trembling of the haunted woods, and felt comforted within its eerie presence. His passage to Merchant Street was blocked by the wrought iron gate that had been latched shut and locked. He would have to go through the bushes.

Flanked beyond this last clutch of undergrowth was his old home, summoning him with its undeniable heartbreaking presence. A beacon of light pierced through the darkness and caught Matt's eye. A quick shiver skimmed across his flesh. The light came from a lamp in the room where his father died and delivered with it the heavy duffel bag of recollections he had been dragging around since that day of death.

As he looked upon the house, that monolith of memories, his mind was beset by a crossfire of emotions. The resurrected remnants of long-buried tensions lured him toward his father's death room. He tiptoed up the side yard and pressed his face against the window and surveyed the room but saw nothing. He dropped to his knees and peeked through a lit-up basement window. The pool table was still there, and beyond that in the farther room, he could see the half-opened door to what was called the spider room. It was a scary little storage space with a low ceiling and neither windows nor lights. It was filled with spindly legged spiders and dusty cobwebs and the threat of other undefined terrors that, to a boy's mind, were both fascinating and frightening, imaginary and real—a private cell where all his deepest fears could come true.

As children, he, Rory, Elaine, and their older sister, Julia, played a game in which they took turns locking each other in the spider room for a few minutes at a time as an initiation into a nonexistent club. They called it a bravery test. One time, Matt was abandoned in the room after being locked in. He waited an eternity for someone to let him out, growing more and more panicky with each second that ticked by. He refused to shout or bang on the door until he felt the feathery tickle of a daddy long legs on his hair and then on his face, and he envisioned an army of predatory spiders moving in on him, smothering him as they weaved his final death web. He started screaming and banging on the door, but it wouldn't open. No one was there. His heart started to pound as loudly as his fists against the door, and he was afraid to breathe because he thought the spiders would crawl into his lungs and swarm him from inside. He couldn't stop himself from hyperventilating, sucking in those malicious spiders, and expecting his heart to explode from the escalating fear, until the door opened and his mother grabbed him away from the infested spider room and into the safety of her arms. Now, as he knelt and spied from outside his old house, he heard the whispers of that terrifying day stirring from his inner well of banished voices that had never quite left him, and they were resonating with the still-lingering spectral presence emanating from the spider room, and he wished he could climb through the basement window and, for God's sake, shut that fucking door!

He wiped the cobwebs from his thoughts and dragged himself to the summit of Merchant Street and away from the house that still contained the skeletons and the odd hidden bits of his old self that he hoped no one would ever find. Then, defeated and depleted, he turned left on Peak Street.

*Full circle, or full something or other, at least,* he concluded. He crossed Incline Avenue, and with his last ounce of energy proceeded down the final stretch, the home stretch, with a single unanswered question chanting itself in his head like a foreboding mantra: *Am I a good person?*

## R. Sunrise and Flowers

Eustace snorted and danced and squirted out excited piss squiggles on the linoleum as Matt crept through the back door and into the kitchen. He looked like a stodgy Winston Churchill dog with his saggy jowls and his chew bone sticking out of his mouth like an oversized cigar. It was 3:30. Matt's face was flushed and perspiring, his ears were burning at the edges, and his feet were flat and throbbing as if his bones had been crushed down. He looked around. It was safe. The Watcher and all the screamin' demons were gone, and the man inside his head was silent.

He went to his bedroom, took off his clothes, and slipped between the sheets. Eustace followed him up the stairs, past the thunder of Mrs. Mahoney's rumble-house snoring, and swaggered into Matt's room, leapt like a cow onto the bed, and slathered Matt's face with a goodnight lick or three. A buzzing from the windowsill converted his indifferent lips into a momentary smile. Matt knew that his insomnia was now no match for the exhaustion he had worked so hard to cultivate, but even sleep was no longer a sure sanctuary. On several recent occasions, he had woken up in a cold sweat, quaking from nightmares about rats nibbling at his face as he lay frozen in place, horrified to his core but unable to fight them off or run away as his flesh was being slowly gnawed. One night he awoke from such a dream and, while still in a half-hallucinatory state, began shouting that there were rats under his bed. When his mother came running into his room, she found him standing on his bed, naked, screaming at her to run before the rats got her.

Now, as he lay in bed, he unfolded a sheet of paper from his wallet and sank into the comfort of his poetry before collapsing into what he hoped would be a safe sleep. He began to read, "When I was young and the girls were blouse-blooming and bursting like sunrise and flowers..."

# PART TWO

I see a vision of a great rucksack revolution thousands or even
millions of young Americans wandering around with rucksacks,
going up to mountains to pray, making children laugh and old men
glad, making young girls happy and old girls happier, all of 'em
Zen Lunatics who go about writing poems that happen to appear in
their heads for no reason and also by being kind and also by strange
unexpected acts keep giving visions of eternal freedom to everybody
and to all living creatures.
—Jack Kerouac, *The Dharma Bums*

# CHAPTER IV

For Matt, rising each day was like being reborn into the bad dream his life had become. Daylight yanked at his crusted eyelids like a burning yellow forceps. A sour wad of depression sickened his stomach. He couldn't remember ever wanting to get out of bed in the morning. He flexed and stretched and discovered that in the course of the night he had been pushed to one side and was clinging to the leftover space. Eustace had claimed the middle of the bed, was sprawled out like a sea otter, and even had his drooly head on the pillow. It was not unexpected. Matt had even written a limerick in honor of Eustace's bed-hogging habits:

*If my dog sleeps with me in my bed*
*And my pillow is under my head,*
*When I wake the next day*
*From a sound sleep, I say,*
*"How did you get my pillow instead?"*

After three or four false starts, one in which he fell back asleep and dreamed that he had already risen and gotten dressed, and then the spark of a cold wet nose from Eustace, Matt extracted himself from his bed. A fat fly buzzed around his head and came to rest against the warm window, seeking rejuvenation from a soak of morning sunlight.

"Morning, Harold," Matt said. Harold had been living against Matt's window for a week or so now and he fancied it as an exotic pet.

He checked the back bedroom and was relieved to see Rory sound asleep beneath a mountain of blankets, his long black hair spread across the pillow like a silky scarf. The air conditioner was on full blast, and the room was cold as an icebox. Matt shivered as he entered Rory's fortress of solitude. Against the wall was a half-filled gallon jug, which at one time had contained some Gallo wine but was now used as a convenience in the middle of the night.

The click of the door must have awakened Rory. He looked at Matt through heavy-slitted eyes. "Jesus Christ, Rory, you're gonna freeze your balls off in here."

Rory reached down under the covers, groped a bit, and said, "Nope. Balls are fine. Nice and warm."

Pointing at the jug, Matt asked, "When're you gonna dump that out?"

"Shit. It's not even full yet."

"Does Mom know you've been pissin' in that bottle?"

Rory grinned. "I highly doubt it."

"She was worried about you last night. You should call her if you're going to be out all night."

"I wasn't out *all* night. And if I called to ask, she wouldn't let me. Look who's talking. I got home before you did."

"You know what I mean. She saw that commercial again and got all bummed out." Not wanting to appear his brother's keeper, Matt changed the subject.

"I saw Charlie and Willie last night. They said you were with Carmelita."

"Yeah. We hung out at her house for a while." Affecting a Puerto Rican accent, he then said, "Had some rice and beans, man."

The way Rory avoided talking about Carmelita proved his affections. She was a genuine catch. But so was Rory. Girls flocked around him in a way Matt could not comprehend, drawn to his leading-man smile, his charismatic ways, and his good looks. Over the past couple of years, he was a devoted body builder at the YMCA and had an honest-to-God muscle man physique. Unfortunately, Matt moped, he hadn't inherited any of Rory's lucky charms, and his physique was nothing but skinny and scrawny. He was nothing like Rory. He was the mediocre and immediately forgettable Matt

Mahoney, a klutz around girls, vacillating between a crippling shyness and an irrational fear. For him it was hard work and miserable results, and he worried that he had become too weird and too ugly and too undesirable to be a contender for anyone's affections.

"I wanted to say goodbye. I'm heading to Canada. I'm gonna hitch around for a while."

"What do you mean, 'Goodbye'? You just got back. Mom gets worried when you take these trips."

"Yeah, I know. She worries about both of us."

When Matt went downstairs there were two familiar figures watching the morning quiz shows at the kitchen table. His niece, Samantha (Sam for short) screamed at the top of her lungs, "Grandma! Uncle Matt's awake! Can we make noise now?"

She sprinted over and jumped into his arms. "Give me a piggy-back ride."

Nieces and nephews were Matt's saving grace. Being an uncle was the only thing he took pride in. He loved to laugh at all the funny things they did and said, and he marveled at their innocence. It pleased him that they craved his attention and laughed at his corny jokes and funny faces. There was nothing he enjoyed more than playing the role of the longhaired hippie uncle, pretending to be hip and cool, because no matter how depressed or discouraged he became, he always felt like a big shot around them, and they knew no better than to look up to him and like him. He never wanted to do anything to ruin that.

His nephew, Todd, glanced up from his sketchpad where he was scratching out pencil portrayals of Sonny and Cher in various TV costumes and, with a bemused grin, said to Matt, "Aren't you glad you got up?"

"Hey, Sambo. Skin me, man." Matt extended an upturned palm.

She knew the drill. She brushed her palm against his, struck a pose, snapped her fingers and said, "Cool man."

Todd tolerated his younger sister's antics but couldn't resist rolling his eyes and saying, "Oh Sam, you're so far out and groovy."

Sam was breathless. "Hey Uncle Matt. Grandma says you're going on another trip. Will you get me another present? I still have the other presents you gave me."

Matt had given her a lustrous seashell the size of a quarter that he'd found that spring on the beach in Sitges, Spain. He had placed it and a scoopful of sand in a matchbox he'd gotten in London and told Sam that leprechauns used the seashell to fill the matchbox with scooped-up gold dust.

"Sure thing, Sambo. I'll put you on my gift list. And could you do me a favor?"

"What?"

"Could you call Tates and tell him I went to Canada and I'll see him in a couple months?"

Her eyes lit up because, of all Matt's friends, Tates, a brawny and fearsome-looking lumberjack-sized kid with wild hair, was her favorite.

"Yeah!," she beamed.

It was a good day to begin a journey: clear skies, and not too hot. From his bedroom window he could see his mother in the backyard garden weeding around the tomatoes and fixing the wobbly wire fence that was meant to keep Eustace from the vegetables and flowers. Eustace sniffed and snorted, patrolling the yard as Mrs. Mahoney's diligent protector-in-chief, dancing and romping around her feet like a pet pig and gazing up at her with sad, goopy eyes. She took the pooper-scooper and deposited Eustace's business into the waste receptacle that was dug into the yard and then put the lid back in place. These were his do-dos. The occasional indoor droppings were, according to Mrs. Mahoney, his "don't-don'ts."

Matt loaded up his rumpled old Boy Scout pack stained with toothpaste and grease, which some former scout had given him a few years earlier. Just for the hell of it, he threw in a lucky rock he found in Boulogne-Sur-Mer and a few wishbones he had been saving. He held his camera for a moment, just a cheap Instamatic, but didn't pack it. Picture taking was not the hippie thing to do. He was a traveler on a journey, not a tourist on a vacation. From the top of his nightstand, he grabbed a book he'd been reading about Genghis Khan, the Jack Kerouac paperback *The Dharma Bums*, and his yellow spiral notebook which, on the cover, had written in bold capital letters, "**IF FOUND, RETURN TO MATT MAHONEY, 33 PEAK STREET, NEW HOLLAND, NEW YORK.**"

The first two pages of the notebook had lists of curious words: timorous, prelapsarian, chiaroscuro, nondescript, lugubrious, pentagram, perlustration, rapture, cacoepy, sidewinder, stumbling block or stepping stone?, vainglorious, commodious environs, Occam's Razor. Elsewhere were snippets of conversations he had heard, such as "I was taught that the meek shall inherit the earth," to which someone had responded, "Yeah, right. Six feet of it." Then there were examples of word play he had made up: "A roamin' Catholic," "Depression is the better part of squalor," "The monarch had no charm," "attics and cellars—addicts and sellers," "incremental/excremental," "penance/pennants," "The presidents had ten spiders," "The teacher was a cheater," "Plastered on punch at a pre-prom party," "She spurned the burn of his yearn," "inert « inept," and "adoption « abortion." Next he has some sayings such as "Is it an eye for an eye or turn the other cheek?" "A word once uttered can never be unsaid," and "Straight from the heart of a bird," which had come to him in a dream. Then there were two recent words: "dromomania—an abnormal obsession for roaming and traveling" and "drapetomania—an insane or uncontrollable impulse to wander away from home." In the margins he squeezed in Vinny's gift: "epiphany—a comprehension or perception of reality by means of a sudden intuitive realization."

From his nightstand he picked up his poem "When I Was Young" and folded it back into his wallet where he always kept it. As he walked out of his bedroom, all packed up and raring to go, he took a last look at the poster on his wall. Sue, a girl he met at Brant

Community College, had drawn it for him using colored pencils on poster board. In a bright rainbow spectrum of stylized lettering was written, "Today Is the First Day of the Rest of Your Life," illustrated with cheerful drawings of butterflies and birds and flowers.

"Hey Ma!" he shouted from the kitchen. "Let's get this show on the road."

He had $120 in his wallet and no idea how long that would last. He tucked his denim jacket between the folds of his rolled-up sleeping bag and slung it over his shoulder with an elastic rubber strap.

"Can't go anywhere without my denim jacket." It was his protective cloak. When he put it on, he was at ease and, if not cool, at least invisible and safe.

As he headed for the door, Sam shouted, "Hey, Uncle Matt. Don't forget this." She handed him his Wham-O Frisbee.

"Thanks Sam. You're the greatest. Now it's time to skedaddle."

He was now equipped and ready for the road. The hamster was escaping his cage.

Mrs. Mahoney drove Matt down Merchant Hill, across the river and up through the South Side to the Thruway. Todd and Sam were in the back seat. On the radio, Boom Boom Brannigan announced, "It's 1540. WPTR. Where the sounds abound and the hits won't quit. Bringing you the latest and greatest from all the bands in the land."

A hay truck passed them in the other direction. Honoring a childhood superstition, Matt closed his eyes, made a wish, and did not look back until the hay truck was gone.

"Now Matthew, are you sure you've got enough clothes? It's cold in Canada."

It was as if there was an immediate climatic shift at the Canadian border and then—presto!—before you know it you're tripping over the Arctic Circle and consorting with Eskimos in igloos and polar bears on glacial fields.

"Mom," he said, "why do little boys wear sweaters?"

"I know, I know. I can't help it. I worry about you. Please be careful. It's a scorcher out there today." They'd been through this before and she knew the answer: little boys wear sweaters to keep their mothers warm.

It was Monday, about noontime. He shook hands with Todd and gave Sam a kiss on the cheek. "Don't forget my present," she reminded her uncle. He gave her the thumbs up.

He kissed his mother goodbye, told her not to worry, and promised to be careful and call her collect. She drove off and as soon as she disappeared, he already missed her. He was concerned that maybe he loved her and depended on her too much. He sought to be more independent and yet love her no less.

He waved farewell to the picturesque city across the river and registered a lasting gaze in case he never returned. "So long, Hamsterland."

He placed his gear on the roadside and, with the wind in his face, assumed the comfort and confidence of his hitchhiker's stance by the entrance to the Thruway and even waved to the tollbooth operator. He was already relaxed and free, feeling a thousand pounds lighter. He was a travelin' man now, a rolling stone, a freewheeling hitchhiking hippie. The person known as Matt had slipped away and was nowhere to be seen nor would he be missed by this new guy who was standing there is his stead, wearing Matt's clothes and brandishing Matt's thumb. He had retreated into the safety of anonymity. His world ripped wide open, and now anything was possible. When he extended his arm and flicked his thumb into the streaming sunlight and saw the far westward shadow it cast, he was overcome by a surge of independence and an optimistic resolve to rise from the ashes of his past and be born anew. And then, as that first car passed him by without a second glance, he rejoiced inside and thought, "One car closer to my redemption," but wasn't sure what he meant by that.

He thought about it for a moment and lapsed into a daydream. When he snapped back, he scribbled an urgent note on a torn-out scrap of notebook paper and tucked it into an empty pickle jar littered in the weeds and grasses. He crossed the roadway and buried the jar in a shallow grave beneath bushes and leaves and the shade of roadside trees.

Hitchhiking was against the law but was usually tolerated at the Thruway exits as long as you didn't go beyond the tollbooth. Matt expected a long wait because most traffic entering the Thruway at this exchange headed east toward Albany and New York City, but after waving his thumb for only fifteen minutes, a VW bus with Pennsylvania plates pulled over and gave him a ride all the way west to Syracuse.

New Holland vanished from the rear view mirror and ceased to exist. Matt, with all his quirks and imperfections, also ceased to exist. In his place was an embryonic blob of yearnings and a wandering destiny that was impossible to predict. He was a nobody now, just the way he liked it. He yearned to evolve himself over and over again with each new ride and each new highway Samaritan to whom he would be a blank slate with an erased past—no longer just one of many, no longer the spoiled professor's kid or somebody's baby brother. Neither was he the spoiled son wasting his potential and throwing away his future. The guy who couldn't even find a girlfriend because he so feared the electric shock of the female touch, the mere anticipation of which caused his mind to roll up into a ball and become unresponsive like one of those little bugs.

His future was now just a series of rides with an endless chain of strangers. Perfect strangers. Each one an unsuspecting accomplice along the obstacle course of Matt's journey to learn whatever it was he must learn to become whoever it was he must become to fulfill whatever it was that he needed to fulfill in order to achieve his life's purpose. Maybe, one day, without warning, a hundred, a thousand, or maybe a million miles down the road, the nondescript entity known to some as Matt would wake up and realize, just like Pinocchio, that he had become a real person like he imagined he used to be before whatever happened *happened* and everything somehow unraveled and got so crazy and convoluted and sad and oh so lost.

The driver was the superintendent of an apartment building in Scranton. The chilly air between him and his female companion gave Matt the impression that they picked him up to create a diversion in an argument they were having, but Matt didn't care why they picked him up. He was just relieved to be on the road again, disentangled and disengaged, safe in the care of a perfect stranger who was unaware that the soft-spoken, apparently well-adjusted, and intelligent young man in his midst was on a mad-dash escape from the invisible forces that threatened his existence. No one, neither family nor friends, had any inkling of the secret cancer that ate away at his insides while, on the surface, he joked and laughed with the crowd. It was when he was alone that he crumbled and even wept for incomprehensible reasons, but he never told anybody because he was ashamed of being so weak and immature. It all sounded so absurd when he tried to put his ordeal into words. He supposed that maybe everyone lived the same kind of repressed double life, harboring undetectable quiet desperations beneath a calm facade. For his own selfish sake, he hoped so.

The radio filled the long lulls between forced tidbits that never quite grew into a full-blown conversation, other than the driver bemoaning that the Phillies were having "a shit year" and if they knew what was good for them they'd get rid of "that shit manager." Matt, though he had lost most of his interest in baseball over the years, was still a Yankees fan. He couldn't brag much about their mediocre season, but at least they were doing better than the Phillies.

He gazed heavenward for any hints of the scheduled eclipse, but the skies had turned dark and cloudy, rendering the phenomenon unobservable and, he hoped, eliminating all risks of blindness. As with his own self, his own life, it seemed that the true nature of the bedlam unfolding within him went unnoticed, even by himself, obscured by clouds, and he was always none the wiser.

He heard the quaint strains of a bouncy little tune that had followed him around England that spring and had stowed away stateside in his backpack to invade the American airwaves:

71

*In a little while from now*
*If I'm not feeling any less sour*
*I promised myself I'd treat myself*
*And visit a nearby tower...*
*I may as well go home*
*I decided on my own*
*Alone, again, naturally*

He identified with the casual despair of the suicidal lyrics and found himself repeating it over and over in his head long after it had been played and long after he had grown tired of its incongruously merry melody. But today Matt was feeling alert and energetic and identified more with the melody than the sentiment. Pleasant daydreams and fanciful notions bred like rabbits in the grassy leisure of his atypically positive Ben Burroughs outlook. Yes. "Look for only happy things. Hear well a joyful sound." It was already working. Something about getting away from home always unwedged him and freed him up to new possibilities and new degrees of personal freedom. It was his therapy. If salvation were the product of religious devotions, then hitchhiking was his religion and the roads of the world were his spiritual path.

He thanked the driver, parachuted out of the van at Exit 36, and landed onto the pavement of his newly-spun universe, all zipped up into a new skin suit, sewn and stitched and tailor-made just for him on the special occasion of his journey. The new and improved Matt Mahoney was ready and willing to enjoy the freedom to not be himself and was eager for a divine sign that his transformation, or at least its promise, was real and that his tired old self, his saggy worn-out bag of skin, had been left behind on the floor of that van along with the hometown dirt from the bottom of his shoes.

Suddenly, without adequate warning, a flotilla of angry thunderclouds erupted into cannon blasts and a barrage of military-grade raindrops pummeled the earth. He closed his eyes, opened his mouth, and tilted back his head to let the downpour baptize his face and anoint his throat like holy water trickling from the fingertips of an anonymous God. Again, at the flip of some celestial switch, the cloudburst ended and a river of gold streamed through a rupture in the mass of clouds in the same manner that had awed him when he was a child and had thought that such a showering of sunlight through clouds emanated directly from heaven. Steam lifted from the pavement as if from an overheated skillet. His flesh tingled from the invigorating tropical fragrance of the fresh rainy vapors and his mind was wonderfully empty.

He attempted to hitch the last few miles but soon gave up the ghost and opted to call Luke. It was bad form and a bit of a defeat to holster his thumb before reaching his destination, especially on his first day, but with his friend at such close range and a pay phone in sight, his lapse was forgivable.

Luke arrived in a matter of minutes, driving his maroon 1966 Ford Mustang with its immaculate black leather seats. He was beeping his horn and making wild gestures, braying, "Get out of the road, you dirty hippie!"

He was mimicking the state patrolman who had given them each a ticket for hitchhiking at that same exit the previous summer. The two boys had bicycled from New Holland to Kingston, Ontario, a three-day trip, but the fun and freedom of cycling, as well as the novelty, had by that time given way to the discomfort of sore legs and asses. So they sold their bikes in Kingston and then hitched back home. At the Syracuse exit on the way back, an overly aggressive Patrolman Bortig, a New York State Police Officer, pulled over and screamed at them like a drill sergeant, his jutting jaw operating mechanically beneath cool reflective shades. Rather than haul them down to the station, he read them the citation and explained in loud militaristic commands that they could either plead guilty and pay the fine by mail or they could appear in person before the Honorable Herman Harding at the Liverpool Town Hall on August 4th at 7:30 p.m. to enter a plea of not guilty or, perhaps, insanity. When the officer finished the blunt end of his spiel, he told the boys that they could continue to hitch, "but I better not see you when I come back here."

Luke thought the incident was funny and, whenever he told the story, called Officer Bortig "The Evil Giant." Matt never paid the ticket, choosing instead to keep it as a souvenir of the officer's absurd Barney Fife conduct."

Luke got out of his Mustang flashing his confident million-dollar movie-star smile.

"Hey, Lucky Luke," Matt called out.

"Hey, Mighty Matt. Did you bring all that rain?"

Luke advanced a handshake and a one-armed hug. He was a year older than Matt, which still seemed to make a difference. They had been good friends since working together at the River Street Pharmacy when Matt was a sophomore, squeezing fresh-made orange juice and serving phosphates and flavored cokes and homemade ice cream from the soda fountain counter to the after-school students and the downtown regulars.

Luke would joke and say, "Yeah, we used to be soda jerks. Now we're just jerks."

Matt always enjoyed Luke's company, but their get-togethers had become less and less frequent during Luke's college years, and, as he slid his wet ass onto the shiny leather of the Mustang, it was like an overdue reunion with a long-lost friend.

"Hey, it's good to see you. How was England?" Luke asked.

"It was great, but I didn't get to see as much as I wanted to. Me and Boone hitched through France and made it to Spain for a week or so. I'm gonna save up and go back and do it right. Go to Ireland. Maybe do that Magic Bus trip to India. Have you heard about that? That would be wild."

"Did you meet any girls? Or should I say 'birds'?"

"Naw—unfortunately. You know me."

At Luke's apartment, Matt quizzed his friend on his upcoming career as an elementary school teacher.

"Aren't you nervous about it?" The prospect of having such a responsible job was frightening to Matt, parents trusting him with their children and depending on him to make important decisions. He couldn't even imagine being able to stand in front of a class without dying of nervousness and fear.

"Nah. I got over that during my student teaching."

"Do I have to start calling you Mr. Piersall now? Mr. Piersall, can I please go to the lavatory? I gotta take a number two real bad." Matt was straining and raising his hand like an insistent schoolboy who was holding it in with all his might. "When I was a kid at St. Brigid's, the nuns used to make us raise our hand if we had to go the bathroom. We had to put up either one or two fingers, depending on what we had to do. It was so embarrassing. I didn't want anyone to know what I was doing so if I had to do a one I put up two fingers and vice versa. It was less embarrassing that way for some reason. Man, those battleaxe nuns were experts when it came to humiliating us little kids. Damn penguins."

Later that night, they went to a diner and talked over coffee and homemade rhubarb pie. Luke said, "I think I'm ready to settle down, get married, have kids, find a nice little house in a nice little neighborhood. When I find the right girl, then everything else will fall into place. I'll know immediately that she's 'the one.' Maybe I'm naïve, but I still believe in that old love-at-first-sight thing. Of course it's got to be mutual."

"Yeah. You're screwed if it's not mutual."

"It feels strange. On one hand I think I've turned into an adult— graduating from college, getting a real job. On the other hand I still feel like a goofy kid inside, and I wonder how they could ever hire me to teach these kids. I'm barely more than a kid myself, and I'm afraid that the other teachers and the parents will see through me and realize they made a mistake, that I'm just pretending to be a real adult."

"Luke, you're not pretending. You've always been an adult, even when you were a kid. You're just now growing into it."

That evening, Matt and Luke stood at the crux of their diverging lives, each venturing into a world the other did not understand. Matt was trapped in that in-between place and was in the midst of fleeing the demons of his troubled past while pursuing the hoped-for angels of the future that awaited him. His only refuge was his thumb and the prospect of something unexpected and unpredictable that would intervene and rescue him from the mess he had made of his life—fleeing and pursuing and searching the world for that someone to accompany him on his life's quest.

Luke, rather, was rooted on the brink of adulthood. He would soon be a teacher of children, a giver of tests, and a grader of homework. Hundreds of students and parents would soon be calling him Mr. Piersall, asking his opinions and relying on his judgment. He would have a checkbook and grownup bills like rent, utilities, car loans, and insurance and would even have his name in the phone book.

Luke had always been the mature one, the responsible one. Even as a teenager he had a special license with adults. He called them by their first names and knew their gossip and conversed with them about adult matters. Even Mrs. Mahoney, who didn't trust Matt to drive her new Oldsmobile 98, allowed Luke to use it to run errands for her in a pinch. Luke had *always* been an adult with already-developed adult sensibilities. It seemed that, somehow, he had bypassed all the pitfalls of adolescence that still snared Matt. When Matt looked at Luke, he saw a confident young man with a promising future that was beckoning him forward. When he looked at himself in the mirror, all Matt saw was an overgrown and immature child stuck in a broken-down past that was holding him back.

Matt knew that he and Luke were fundamentally different and that it was their differences that were now becoming more prominent. With the world spinning around him in a maelstrom of confusing relationships and circumstances and having no safe center, Matt clung to his friends like buoys as he bobbed about in the discomfort of his own social ineptness. But the friends were drifting away and apart and there was less and less to cling to. And Matt felt himself sinking.

That night he lay awake in his sleeping bag, overwrought by fears that it was a mistake to be traveling alone. He worried that homesickness would get the best of him and send him scurrying back with his tail between his legs, that he would miss his mother, or that he would have a heart attack and die on the side of some godforsaken back road in the wilds of Canada. He felt a shiver from within, like he had swallowed an ice cube. He was so alone. Outside, the gossiping buzz of crickets and other insects lulled his mind into submission and transported him back in time to another sleepless night when he was five years old.

*From his old bedroom, he could hear the lonesome moan of the whistle from a downtown train. The glow of a streetlamp radiated like a miniature sun. Shadows leapt across the drawn shades like a stampede of ghostly horsemen galloping outside his window. Restless and afraid, he rolled out of his bed, dressed in his Davy Crockett pajamas, and marched through the dimly lit house to his mother's bedroom. He tapped her shoulder and woke her up with a startle.*

*"Mommy. I can't sleep." He knew she would be able to help him.*

*"Go back to bed, honey. It's late. You'll fall asleep if you just lay in bed and keep your eyes closed."*

*"But I can't sleep, Mommy." He was wide-awake and wanted her to comfort him in the warmth and security of her bed where he would fall asleep all cuddled up beside her.*

*"Did you say your prayers?"*

*"Yes. Three times. Once on my knees and twiced in bed. But it didn't help."*

*"Go to bed, Matthew. It's late. You'll fall asleep."*

*"But Mommy."*

*"What?"*

*"I'm ascared."*

*"Why honey? What are you afraid of?"*

*"There's a monster in my room. It keeps talking to me. Make it go away."*

*She reached her arm around his sagging head and whispered in his ear, "Oh, Matthew. Don't worry. There's nothing to be afraid of."*

*As he trudged back to his bedroom through the mesh of shadowy crisscrossing patterns cast around the hallway by streetlights and headlights and moonlight streaming through window panes and stairway railings, the night's eerie aura absorbed straight into his skin and illuminated some newly discovered chamber deep within himself that opened up into an immense reservoir of emptiness as he realized that there was nothing anyone could do—not even his mother—that would help him fall asleep and that he was standing there, helpless and all alone in this vast, vast world, and that he would always be all alone.*

# CHAPTER V

It was early afternoon when Luke returned from class, saddled up the Mustang, and galloped north on Route 81. Luke, breezy and free, cranked up the volume when his favorite new song came on the radio:

*You just call on me brother*
*When you need a hand*
*We all need somebody to lean on*
*I just might have a problem*
*That you'll understand*
*We all need somebody to lean on*

At Watertown they turned west on route 12E and stopped at Ma & Pa's Bakery in Chaumont. On the wall was a hand-drawn sign that said, "If you want what you smell, just ask Ma," and beneath it there was a large color photo of an elderly woman delivering a flavorful variety of donuts to an expectant group of hungry customers, beaming with smiles. The boys had stopped there on their bike trip the previous year and had talked for quite a while with the pint-sized high-spirited dynamo running the place, presumably Ma. She had praised their bicycling efforts and gave them extra doughnuts for the road. Matt and Luke were betting on whether Ma would remember them a full year later.

Sure enough, she remembered them as "those nice young boys on the bicycles." Matt knew it was really Luke she remembered. Ever the ambassador of good will, he chatted her up in his affable good-natured way, generously portraying Matt as the world traveler embarking on a new adventure. In her white sneakers and short gray wig, Ma smiled and said, "My goodness. I think it's… well… it's amazing" and gave them each a hug.

Luke was outgoing and free with kind remarks and thoughtful actions. Matt thought kind thoughts and envisioned himself performing good deeds as though he was a saint at heart, but more often than not he fell shy of acting upon his good intentions. He wondered if kind thoughts and good intentions without the good deeds that brought them to fruition were enough to add the necessary quota of bricks to build his mansion in heaven. There were contradictory sayings about that sort of thing. How can the road to hell be paved with good intentions if it is the thought that counts? If good thoughts alone could earn you a luxurious home in paradise, was it also true that bad thoughts would damn your soul even though you never acted on them? Matt had both good and bad thoughts. Kind and unkind.

There were also the unavoidable impure thoughts the nuns had always warned him about even before he knew what that meant, like previews of coming attractions. Those thoughts had a life of their own. Would they, by their very nature, without even acting on them, be enough to tip the scales on his wavering soul? If so, and if his damnation is assured either way, then what incentive is there to lead a moral life or follow a Christian ideal? Besides, when he was a student, the nuns and priests did not teach him to be loving and kind, nor did they demonstrate those qualities. Instead, they taught him to obey and do what he was told or else suffer dire consequences. They ruled through fear, not love. It had nothing to do with Jesus or any supposed God or Lord on high. It was all about discipline and maintaining control of the classroom, and in the manner of their teaching, it seemed that heaven and hell had nothing to do with good or evil.

That's why Matt had long ago ceased believing in either of those mythological places and instead focused on just doing his best while still here on Earth, where he could be his own judge according to his own ethical code, without promise of heavenly reward or fear of hellfire. Based on his own informal research, those self-appointed moral standard bearers of the world did not even come close to living by the standards they imposed on others. They certainly did not lead a life that came near to resembling the life of the Jesus whose love they were so keen on crowing about.

Cape Vincent was a fifteen-minute drive from Chaumont. It gazed westward into Canada from the empty eye socket at the ridge of New York State's brow. From there, the ferry carried Luke's Mustang across a narrow strait to a port on the east side of Wolfe Island, which was Canadian territory. Then it was a quick drive to the other side of the island where they would catch another ferry to Kingston, Ontario. The plan was for Luke to tell the border guard that they were going to Kingston for a few hours and would be returning on the last ferry. He withheld the fact that Matt, however, would not be returning. Matt was being dropped off in Kingston so he could hitchhike around Canada as a grateful beneficiary of the coast-to-coast network of inexpensive youth hostels. It was unbelievable to Matt that the government would show concern rather than disdain for the long-haired hippies infesting their roads and cities throughout this or any summer. That would never happen in America, where the official view was that the rootless youth generation was an existential threat to the traditional American way of life, whatever that was.

Matt had run into border problems the year before when he attempted to hitchhike back to Canada to meet up with a friend he and Luke had made in Kingston. He was refused entrance at both of the Niagara Falls crossing points because he was a longhaired hitchhiking hippie with a dirty backpack and only sixty dollars in his pocket and had no reputable reason for entering Canada. They might have thought he was a draft dodger. But that was last year. He had been by himself. He wasn't going to allow his ineptitude to stop him this year. So, with Luke as his smiling envoy, Matt was confident of an open-armed Canadian welcome, and he was not disappointed.

Luke performed commendably, cool as a cucumber, smiling and joking with the border guard. They sailed victoriously into Kingston and drove to the hostel. Matt paid his fifty cents for the night and became an official foreign "transient," which was the word used to describe the hostelers on the list of rules posted upon the bulletin board:

> *"NOTICE TO ALL TRANSIENTS: There shall be no drugs. No alcohol. No weapons. No smoking. No fighting. You must clean up after yourself and assist in kitchen cleanup after meals. Lights out and doors locked at 11 PM. The hostel is locked from 10 AM and reopened at 5 PM, and no transients may remain upon the premises during those hours. There is a three-day maximum stay for all transients. Transients shall be held responsible for damages caused to property. Any violation of these rules shall be cause for expulsion from the premises."*

It appeared that the person who devised these rules had a fondness for the word "transients."

Matt tried to talk Luke, who objected to being referred to as a "transient," into spending the night, but he had classes, responsibilities, and obligations and was less than half-regretful. "Just one night, Luke. For old times' sake." But Luke's arm resisted all twisting.

"So," Luke asked, subverting Matt's efforts to convince him to stay, "where are you headed?"

"I don't know. I'll go to Ottawa for a few days, then Montreal and Quebec, and then hitch through the Maritimes and come back through Maine. I read this great article in National Geographic about Nova Scotia—lots of fantastic scenery. Man, it was beautiful."

"That sounds good. I wish I could go with you, but I've got to get ready for school. Send me a card, and feel free to give my number to some of those French girls. Tell them to call Lucky Luke."

"Or you could come with me and meet them in person," said Matt, certain that Luke's company would improve his odds.

As they shook hands and said goodbye, Luke looked right into Matt's eyes with that Hollywood smile and Matt felt like a little kid being farewelled by his father.

Matt thought of his own grade-school days and of his fall from grace at the tender age of seven. He wished he'd had a kind and smiling teacher like Luke to greet him upon his arrival to his new second grade class at Ash Avenue School. Though it was a life-saving relief to have escaped that reign of terror, he still worried that he had displeased God by choosing to banish himself from the sanctity of his Catholic education at St. Brigid's School and to willingly consort with so many Protestants. His sturdy brick home in God's backyard had been swapped for a mud hut on some desolate trail in purgatory— or perhaps a custom built kiln in hell. If he had learned anything in Catholic school, it was that you were never too young to receive the promise of eternal damnation.

Even after becoming a dreaded public schooler, and no longer within ruler's reach of his cloaked tormentor, Matt continued to pray for salvation and remained fearful of angering The Lord or The Sweet Baby Jesus or his own personal Guardian Angel, with whom he shared his chair, or the Blessed Virgin Mary, who observed his every act and who knew his every desire from within his very heart, or the holy host of haloed angels on high and the martyred saints too numerous to name and too vicious to ignore. He knew that this traitorous switching of schools had delayed his First Confession and his First Holy Communion and that he would have to stew in the sludge and slime and stench of his original sin for an additional full year and allow the clever devil that much extra time to gain a foothold in the fertile turf of his impure soul.

To atone for the lapse of becoming a public schooler, Matt was required to make the long walk from Ash Avenue School to St. Brigid's every Wednesday afternoon to attend religious instruction classes and resume his lessons in the Baltimore Catechism. It was the medicine he was prescribed to ward of the ill effects of spending so much time around so many Protestants. He shuddered to learn that Sister Jeronima was to be his instructor. It surprised him to find that, instead of the cruel knuckle-rapping taskmaster from whom he had fled at the risk of God's wrath, Sister Jeronima went overboard with kindness and gave him a special welcome on his first day, as though he had been her favorite student. He was not so easily fooled, however, and he realized that she could not be trusted, that her smile was a ruse and that her seeming kindness had a darker purpose. He had been liberated, and she wanted to lure him back into her clutches not to save his soul but to continue to condemn it.

Americans outnumbered Canadians at the hostel. Matt laid out his sleeping bag on a cot next to Brian, a conscientious objector who was a taxi-driver in Toronto.

"Hostel? Man, they shouldn't call 'em hostels. They should call 'em friendlies."

He and Matt talked for a while, joking around back and forth, sensing each other out. Then, hushed and serious, he asked, "So, uh, Matt, you got a student deferment or a 4-F or something like that?"

"No, I was lucky. I had a high number. I wasn't in school, and even if I were, I wouldn't have applied for a 2-S."

"Why the hell not? I would have taken a 2-S, no doubt. You can bet your fuckin' bippy on that."

"I don't know. Why should students be treated any different? I didn't think it would be fair for somebody to be sent halfway around the world to get killed in a senseless war just because they're poor or don't want to go to college."

"Yeah. Or just because they're dumbasses." Brian accentuated the last word self-referentially. "I flunked out and lost my deferment, and about a day later got my letter. I thought, 'Fuck my luck, man. I certainly ain't no fortunate son.' So, hey, here I am, a fugitive draft dodger. Guilty as charged, your honor."

"Well, if my number were a little lower, I'd be right here with you, driving my own cab. Either that or I'd be living in Sweden."

"Sweden. Yeah. I considered it. I hear those Swedish girls have a thing for conscientious objectors. If I spoke Swiss I'd go over there. I shit you not."

"You mean Swedish."

"Swedish, Swiss, Swish, who cares. All I know is they are gorgeous."

"I *did* burn my draft card," added Matt.

"You did? Were you at a protest or something? Did you get arrested?"

"No. Nothing as daring as that. I did it by myself in the backyard. I thought it was a big deal at the time, as if an alarm was gonna alert the cops to come and get me. But nothing happened. No one knew, and nothing changed. I thought I was making a huge statement, but after I did it, I realized that it made no difference at all. It was totally symbolic. Maybe I should have done it downtown, in front of the police station. Or the selective service office. Then I stopped registering myself at the draft board. I thought they'd come down on me about that, but nobody said anything. I guess they didn't miss me."

"Yeah. I'm not sure if they're missing me either, but I'm afraid that serious shit shall ensue if I try to cross the border. My mom's pretty cool about it. She visits me every couple of months and brings me a care package with lots of goodies. Chocolate chip cookies, stuff like that. Gives me some money. Sweaters.

"But my father, that's another story. He fought the Germans. Battle of the Bulge—you know, serious wartime shit. He told me I was a traitor and that I was anti-American. I told him that I am pro-American but anti-war and anti-Nixon, and that just pissed him off even more, so I didn't try to talk about it with him anymore. He won't visit. He pretty much disowned me. He thinks I'm a candy ass. Told my mom that I ain't good for shit. She said not to let it get my dandruff up, that he'll come around after a while. But that's okay. I'm over it now. In the big picture, what's the diff? And who gives a flying fuck what anybody thinks? Would I even be here if I gave a shit what anybody thinks?" His whole face drooped.

At dinner, Brian and Matt sat with two girls, Ann and Diane, who came from Moose Jaw, Saskatchewan. He loved the way they talked. It was the same but different. After dinner, they all went to the park and threw Matt's Wham-O around until it was too dark. The boys showed off, sprinting and lunging and trying to outdo one another with spectacular catches as if part of a mating ritual—which, in fact, it was.

Ann had an understated beauty and preferred the relative anonymity of Diane's shadow. She wore tight cut-off jeans that accentuated the athletic thighs that sprang into steel bands when she ran. As Matt ran his eyes over the bulge of her calf, he imagined her to be a ballerina or a gymnast. When she laughed, she threw her head back and gazed upward as if inhaling sunlight.

Diane was barefooted and wearing a sleeveless chartreuse peasant dress with a billowy top that suggested ample features beneath. She seemed to glide across the grass. Her slender body was illuminated by the x-ray effect of the sunlight, and Matt could identify the unmistakable anatomy of her silhouette and that she wasn't wearing anything beneath her flimsy frock. He could see the sumptuous curvature of her embraceable womanly hips and the burnt sienna tint of her nipples penetrating through the gauzy garment, jiggling as she laughed and danced around. He tried not to stare but couldn't help drinking in every last drop of such an enticing vision and being swept into the vacuum of her naked loveliness as his mind flourished and consummated the act that had been eluding his body. Brian was even worse, drooling through his eyes at every heave and swell of Diane's unencumbered image.

He whispered to Matt, "Whew. Hubba hubba! Did you see what I saw? She's giving me whiplash, man. I am definitely the owner of a boner."

*Ah yes*, Matt thought, *my slaved senses perched and buzzing beside their dripping petals.*

They sat on the grass within the penumbral twilight of a lamppost, trying to be both deep and funny in alternate turns, talking about this and that and nothing in particular and everything in general, while sharing a six-pack of Labrador, compliments of Brian. Matt pretended to enjoy the beer but could barely manage to choke one down, never having developed a taste for it and at a loss as to how anyone could savor such a bitter brew.

The girls were nursing students in Moose Jaw and confessed to having boyfriends back home. They both declined when Brian laid back and offered himself up for a complete physical exam.

Diane adjusted her hemline above her folded knees and made Matt's day by saying, "What about you, Matt? You must have a girlfriend, such a sweet guy like you." She held his eyes in hers and, leaning forward, grabbed the toe of his sneaker and shook it playfully.

Matt lied. "There's a couple of girls I kind of see, but nothing serious."

Brian jumped in. "Hey, what about me? I'm a nice guy, too."

The girls declared Brian incorrigible and challenged him to convince them that he was, despite all appearances, a nice guy. They wanted proof. He had a good sense of humor—a fact he listed as reason number one—and so he played along as they ravaged his character. Matt didn't say much. His Adam's apple froze, and his mind fixated on Diane's image and the luxurious swells and curves of her body illuminated in sunlight and the imploring look in her eyes when she grabbed his foot.

They hung around and finished the six-pack. Matt, unable to choke down a second can, surreptitiously spilled much of the remainder out on the grass behind him. As the joke went, when he was caught doing this with his drinking buddies down in Vedder's Woods, the squirrels would lap up the spilled puddles, get drunk, and fall out of the trees. It earned him the embarrassing but short-lived nickname "Squirrel."

They walked back four abreast, holding and swinging their hands in a chain, singing "Hey Jude" in semi-unison, taking long synchronized strides, then harmonizing at the top of their lungs through the extended refrain, with Brian shouting, "Shake it Jude" and "JU-JU-JU-JUDY, JUDY, JUDY, JUD–OW!" as he slid up into a sloppy discordant falsetto. Matt was holding Diane's hand, trying to calculate the perfect degree of squeeze required to attract her and could not help but admit that at that moment, way down deep inside, he felt like a million bucks.

When they reached the hostel, Matt said, "I'm not tired yet. I need to walk around a bit more." He hoped that Diane would volunteer to join him, that maybe she would want to walk with him with joined hands, and maybe more. But he was afraid to ask. He was dismayed that everyone else, Diane included, wanted to go to bed. Keeping up the façade, he let them retire to their dorms as he walked the abandoned streets and then sat down in the park near the brittle lake, all quiet and dark and alone, and felt waging within himself that all-too-customary tug of war between rapture and despair.

His joyousness had worn off and was replaced with disappointment. That's when the spoiling began. When the dark chamber opened wide and each minor transgression emerged ferocious. He cursed himself over and over again for lying about having girlfriends, for pretending to like beer, for being so uptight and self-critical, for not keeping his goddamn mouth shut and his thoughts to himself, for needing others. And especially for leering with hungry eyes at Diane's body and, fool that he was, expecting that she might have welcomed the opportunity to share his company. Most of all, he damned himself for wanting her in a forbidden way, a way in which he did not want to want her.

He thought with two minds that argued back and forth with contrary purposes but was unable to reconcile his vivid desires with his idealized platonic notions of true storybook love and his veneration of woman as a virtuous and chaste creature, transcendent of all lustful longings. Caught and paralyzed by the headlights of such a moral conflict, which despised the very act it craved, he sometimes felt qualified for the priesthood.

"I'm nothing but a stupid Waldo," he rasped in disgust. These were the thoughts, the misery thoughts, that sent his mind into that dizzy downward spiral into the tangle of depressive ideations and to that place where life was futile and where the conquering voice of that man inside Matt's head would take charge like the captain of its own pirated vessel.

A song visited his head:

*Everybody has been burned before*
*Everybody knows the pain*
*Anyone in this place*
*Can tell you to your face*
*Why you shouldn't try to love someone*
*Everybody knows it never works*
*Everybody knows, and me*
*I know that door*
*That shuts just before*
*You get to the dream you see.*

Though it was past midnight, the door was unlocked when he returned. After a couple pieces of bread with some butter and strawberry jelly, he slipped into the men's dorm where the lights were out and everyone was sound asleep.

Brian stirred and moaned, "I think I'm in love. Hmmm. Gotta get me some of that sweet stuff."

"Which one?" Matt hoped it would be Ann.

"Both." His face beamed a silly grin and his lips puckered into a make-believe kiss as he added, "Boner city, man."

"Absafugginlutely," sighed Matt, then tumbled into an uncertain alien sleep and dreamed that he started screaming in the middle of the night, waking up everyone in the room. When he rose in the morning and had a chance to think about it, he wasn't sure that it was just a dream.

# CHAPTER VI

Diane and Ann boarded an early morning bus to Montreal. Matt and Brian walked them to the station where they exchanged hugs and addresses and optimistic vows to stay in touch. Ann, more composed and less expressive than her friend, surprised Matt by clinging longer and closer with her hug. He detected a slight scent of perfume. It both embarrassed and pleased him, her tight embrace, the way he could feel her softness pressed against his chest.

"Be sure to look us up if you go through Moose Jaw," she said to Matt, and even made a little joke: "Don't worry. We don't bite. Well, at least I don't."

*Geez, maybe I was barking up the wrong tree.* He wanted to kiss her or whisper something poignant in her ear but did neither. Poignancy was not his strong suit. And kissing, well, that was too presumptuous, too risky.

Brian gathered his gear and hitched back to Toronto. "My chariot awaits," he announced like a squire. Then he stiffened to let one rip and said, "Ah. Farting is such sweet sorrow," and walked off toward the highway. Matt's heart—despite the fart, which was a good laugh—was sad and empty after he waved goodbye to the first new friends of his journey, knowing he would never see them again.

He spent the next couple of days in Kingston, marching its streets and soaking up the sights and sounds through the eyes and ears of an émigré in training. He yearned for that foreign feeling, but he didn't feel like a foreigner. Kingston, on its surface, though larger, was no different than New Holland, and the girls seemed no different, overall, than American girls. That would change, he hoped, when he made it to French-speaking Quebec. Maybe then he would be a foreigner.

The first afternoon was spent at the library where he finished reading his book about Genghis Khan, jotted out letters and postcards to friends and family back home, and then strained to write some poetry. All he got was this:

> *I have viewed many worlds*
> *with a mixture of delight and despair*
> *but I have never managed*
> *to make myself feel like more than just an alien*
> *taking a never-ending outside look*
> *at a forever-impenetrable society.*

Perusing library shelves, he sought out two of his father's favorite authors, James Thurber and Eugene O'Neill. He recalled how the old man would laugh out loud at a Thurber story and how O'Neill would bring unashamed tears to his eyes and, according to Matt's mother, drive him into depths of depression for weeks at a time.

Matt wondered if the comedy or the tragedy of life was more in the eye of the beholder than the nature of the actual circumstances. He thought that if you took Thurber and O'Neill, had them spend a year together, and then write about it, you'd still end up with a comedy and a tragedy. Thurber would laugh at a funeral because the corpse had a big nose and a funny looking tie. O'Neill would cry at a birth because of the inherent futility of life. Perhaps everything is whatever you want it to be.

He used to ask his father, a professor of literature, to recommend books, but he would always refuse.

"You should choose your own reading. I don't want to influence you."

His father's refusal enraged him, but he said nothing and thought, *I am your son and your spitting image. I want to be influenced by you. You tell your students what to read. Why not me?* His spitting image. That's what everyone said. When he was a child and still admired the man, it was a source of pride. It distinguished him. His sense of personal worth was founded on his unshakable trust in his father's love for him and his belief in there being an inherited twinship with a man so great. But if his father shared any of that pride, he never demonstrated it. Now, this current version of Matt just wanted to be his own self with his own image, free of spit, detached and loosed of any bogus fatherly comparisons.

After much persistence, Professor Mahoney relented and gave Matt two books: O'Neill's *A Long Day's Journey Into Night*, and Thurber's *Fables Of Our Time*. Now, sitting there in the Kingston library, Matt warded off his typical dejected attitude as it started seeping in. He damned his O'Neill tendencies and wished he had more Thurber in him. He suddenly had a miniature epiphany, his first since learning the word. He quickly scribbled it on a piece of notebook paper before he forgot it: "Humor transcends drama."

He thumbed through a collection of Dylan Thomas poems, which contained "Fern Hill," his favorite, and then stumbled onto someone he'd never read, Francois Villon, the 15th-century rogue poet who had been mortally infatuated by an unattainable femme fatale named Katherine de Vausselles. In Matt's hands the book opened itself to a predestined page:

> *If she whom once I used to serve,*
> *Freely and faithfully—who brought*
> *Me so much torment, broke my nerve*
> *And tortured me—had only thought*
> *To say she merely wanted sport*
> *When first we met (no mention, none),*
> *I might have ducked the net she caught*
> *Me with and had a little fun*

Those words pierced the bulls-eye of Matt's heart so deeply that he wrote it down and put it in his wallet, next to his own poem, along with a rejection slip from *The New Yorker*, which read, "We regret that we are unable to use the enclosed material. Thank you for giving us an opportunity to consider it. The Editors." Not even the courtesy of a name, his or theirs. *And fuck you very much, too*, he thought.

Matt fancied himself a reincarnated Villon, curse intact, and that the transfixing spirit of his beloved Katherine had somehow found new life in the bosom of his very own precious and unattainable Carla. Now, here they were again, Katherine and Francois, reunited in new physical form after half a millennium of cold death.

Like Villon, Matt had once confessed his infatuation in a poem:

*The fire's warmth draws you nigh when you are cold*
*But venture none too near*
*For the flames will burn you*

*The cool waters of a mountain lake will refresh you*
*When the day becomes too hot*
*But venture none too far from the shore*
*For the lake may drown you*

*She is both a flame that beckons me closer*
*And a lake that challenges me with its depths*
*And I am just a fool*
*Unheeding of the lessons that nature demonstrates*

His first poems had all been written for Helen. It just started to happen, spontaneously, born of the captivating spell of first love. In retrospect, he realized that she had been his real-life muse, empowering him with her praise and encouragement. Once, in the intimate darkness behind the City Hall, he gave her his latest composition in which he referred to her as "the Queen of my nights." She read it, told him he was a poet, and rewarded him with a tender kiss. "You're *my* poet," she said. "A prince and a poet." They both laughed because they knew it sounded corny.

"Nah," he said. "I'm just a toad. But you can keep trying to turn me into a prince if you want. Don't let me stop you." He asked with his eyes for another kiss and, when she obliged him, he felt strong and proud imagining her, his own very princess, safe within his princely arms. She was the only person he had ever dared to share his poetry with. He tried once, a few years later, with Carla, giving her a poem he had written for her. She took it without comment, stuffed it in a pocket without reading it, and never mentioned it. He hoped that she had not shared it, mockingly, with all of her friends.

He had written his most recent poem while he was tramping in England. It was his best yet, but he refused to submit it to any magazine for fear that even his best work would be inferior, so he carried it around in his wallet in the event of a rare poetic emergency.

Before leaving the library, he looked through an encyclopedia and found that it took Pluto 248 Earth years to revolve around the sun and that it took Mercury only about 87 days. He scratched it down on a piece of scrap paper and put it in his bulging wallet.

That evening after dinner he went back to the park and played Frisbee with a rag-tag batch of hitchers and drifters from the hostel: skinny transients who could barely keep their pants up. A scrappy little polio kid with acorn knees who ran around like a marionette, sucking on an inhaler and laughing with his one-leg-shorter-than-the-other limp saying, "Mr. Dillon, Mr. Dillon. I'm coming, Mr. Dillon." Beautiful Earth-mamas with frizzed-out Janis Joplin non-hairdos or flaxen Joni Mitchell bangs and an unadorned mane draping their shoulders. Matt had no preference. The girls were all splendid and beautiful as they ran across the grass with their hair springing and flowing behind them in a miniature whirlwind.

Wanting to impress the girls, Matt attempted to catch the Frisbee in his mouth, as a dog might do, as it sliced through the air. He waited for the right toss and, when it sailed in his direction at just the right height and speed and angle, he positioned himself in a crouch and opened his mouth as wide as it would go. He flinched and closed his eyes at the last moment, and the swiftly spinning disc smacked against his teeth and gouged his lips. He should have known better. He had tried it once before at Vandenburg's Beach with the same result. Now, as then, he fell backward. Everyone, himself included, laughed out loud. He was half-embarrassed, half-proud as one of the girls bounced over to him and asked if he was okay. She smiled and said, "That was cute. But you should leave that to the dogs." He was going for cool, but cute would do.

Their eyes caught together for a moment. She had hair like Grace Slick on the cover of *Surrealistic Pillow* and was dressed in a tunic clinched at the waist with a rainbow sash, and her smile reminded him of Helen's smile. And though he thought he still knew Helen's face by heart, every freckle and crinkle and the happy squint of her eyes, the remembered likeness was now just a dream image re-summoned by these occasional reminders. It was a pleasant reminder.

One of the advantages of hostel life was that it offered the easy company of so many girls from so many different places, all looking for someone to hang out with for the evening, but without the anxiety of a phone call, the parental introductions, or the specter of rejection. It was just adventurous kids, away from home, hanging out on their own and having a good time. Kids. They all still referred to each other as kids. But Matt was at that age when it began to feel awkward calling himself a kid, though he could not yet, with a straight face, call himself a man.

Everybody got together and threw in quarters and a few bills to buy six joints from a local hippie. They squatted in the park getting high and bubbling over with their wild stoned-out ramblings. A scruffy Canadian kid with a superciliary scar was hitching around with his dog, a Collie mix he called Laz. Between tokes somebody asked him how the dog got his name. The kid explained that Laz was short for Lazarus. He was the runt of the litter who had nearly suffocated when his mother accidentally laid on him while she was nursing the other puppies.

"I thought he was dead. So I got down on all fours and tried to take its pulse and all that other. But I didn't know what I was supposed to do. So I put my ear against its chest but I didn't hear nothing in that aspect. So I opened his mouth and it was all drooly and had bad breath but I put my mouth over his and started to huff and puff and the whole nine balls of wax but he's got, like, this long snout and I thought all the air was getting out of the sides so I tried to shove as much of it as I could into my mouth without gagging and whatnot. I started saying to myself, 'Just pretend you're blowing up a balloon.' It wasn't really anything like blowing up a balloon, but that was what I told myself anyway. By this time I didn't notice the drool or anything 'cause it was all just blending in with mine anyway, and I kept trying to figure out what I was supposed to do and I had this flash that I could save him if I kept trying so I just kept blowing air into that dog and I was getting ready to give up and all of a sudden I started—I know this sounds stupid—I started crying and praying on my knees, holding him and this and that and I said, 'Please God, don't let this poor little puppy dog die just 'cause he's such a runt. It's not his fault he's a runt,' and I thought that I've always been kind of a runt myself and so in that aspect I said 'I promise, I swear, that if you let him live I'll always take care of him for as long as he lives' and 'Please God, just this one time' and, well, to make a long story short, all of a sudden, the dog started making whimpery sounds and all that kind of stuff, and the first thing I thought was that this dog was dead just a few seconds ago and that God gave him a second chance because I had promised to take care of him. I've always been unsure about God and all this Jesus stuff, so I went to see my parents' minister and told him about it and he told me, quotely, that if you are pure of heart and aren't doing something for selfish reasons, that God will always answer your prayers, and he told me I should name the dog Lazarus because it was a miracle that he was still alive and all that other."

No one said anything for a while except for a half-under-the-breath, "Wow, that was deep, man," and "That was heavy."

The kid, whose eyes loomed large and veiny from the smoke, and also from the adrenaline rush of reliving the miracle of a canine resurrection, took a deep hit off the joint he'd been holding while he told the story, released the smoke dreamily, and said, "Man, this is pretty good shit."

The next morning Matt went to a job bank with four other hostelers, all of them Canadian. The man turned Matt away with a scowl because he was a foreigner, but he referred three of the others to day jobs.

"Here you go. Go to this address and tell them I sent you." The man handed them a card and sent them off. The fourth guy was a dark, street-smart French Canadian named Tim who spoke broken English with a French accent and described himself as Quebecois. He told Matt, "He refused you because you are American. He refused me because I am Quebecois. But there will be no jobs for the other boys, either. They are wasting their time."

Tim had just hitched back from Vancouver. He said that the Rockies in British Columbia were "magnificent" and "very, very wild" and had to be seen to be believed. He gestured to fill in some of his lapses in the English language and, wagging a stiff index finger, mentioned a place called Wawa and said, "It is not a good place. Do not go there. You will get stuck." He also warned Matt to always be careful or he would get ripped off, "especially Vancouver," where a boy had his wallet stolen from his rucksack by his bed while he was in the shower for only ten minutes, and no one saw anything. Matt, knowing how devastating it would be to lose his wallet, was already cautious and always slept with it and his passport under his pillow. Besides, Matt was going east, not west, and would not have to worry about Wawa or Vancouver. Nonetheless, he vowed to be extra careful in the future.

Together, under Tim's tutelage, the two boys scoured local churches until they found a receptive minister who wished them a safe journey and gave them meal tickets for a free lunch at the well-named Robin Hood Cafeteria.

They walked several blocks to the cafeteria and slid into a booth. Upon seeing the meal tickets, the waitress took a maternal interest in the boys.

"So, where are you boys from?" When Matt said he was from New Holland, the waitress chatted enthusiastically about a religious retreat she had taken at Ossernenon Shrine, which was located not far from his hometown. She let them choose from the regular menu rather than give them what she called the "charity plate" and treated them as family rather than beggars. Matt played peek-a-boo with a pig-tailed girl in the next booth but stopped when her mother cast an arched brow his way. The girl talked nonstop, asking questions and making interesting observations of first impressions.

"Mommy, what's that stuff?" she asked, pointing to a bowl of cottage cheese. And then, "Mommy, can babies eat applesauce?" And then, after her mother sniffed the coffee creamer, crinkled her nose and asked the waitress how old it was, the girl sniffed at her own glass of ice water, crinkled her nose and asked, "Mommy! How old is water?" When they were piling their dirty dishes in a neat stack, the girl asked, "Am I being a good helper, Mommy?"

Matt glommed down the Salisbury steak, mashed potatoes, peas, Jell-O and Coke as well as the extra helpings and extra smiles the waitress heaped upon them. He noticed that Tim ate the English way, as Matt had learned to do during his recent trip, keeping his fork in his left hand and stacking food on the back of it with his right-handed knife for each bite, which could be a balancing act, depending on what you were eating.

"Here. Let me get you boys another pop," she insisted. Matt wasn't used to having a soda referred to as a pop but he knew what she meant. He just about licked the plate clean like a drooling dog even though he'd only been on the road a few days and hadn't yet gone hungry. Though they tried, the waitress wouldn't let them leave a tip. "You boys need it more than I do. You need to put some meat on those bones." Matt figured that she must have had a son about their age.

Tim was world-wise beyond his years. Matt was awed by his uncocky confidence and his deftness with adults. He had handled all the interactions with the ministers and the one priest, a humorless old curmudgeon who looked down on them with executioner's eyes but said nothing before turning his back and retreating into his rectory, shaking his head in judgment, disgusted by their nerve.

Matt was reminded of a long-buried memory from the early days, before he became a public schooler. He was still a Catholic schoolboy at St. Brigid's, toiling away at the task of building his heavenly home of bricks. He had even wanted to be a priest, but that all ended the day Father Mahan, looming unannounced from behind, ridiculed him in the crowded cafeteria in front of all his friends, including the girl he had a secret crush on. He called Matt a mysterious name—a glutton—and forbade him from continuing to indulge in the sloppy pleasure of eating his spaghetti in a sandwich, between two thick and fluffy buttered slices of Italian bread.

"Haven't you any manners? Do you eat like a pig at home too?"

"No, Father. I'm sorry, Father."

"Well you should be. God frowns upon gluttons."

Matt squirmed in the heat of Father Mahan's admonishment, not knowing what a glutton was but knowing that he was a sinner for being one, feeling frightened for having caused God to frown upon his sad, sunken soul. He knew the bricks had once again all crumbled into ruins, but he regretted his apology because it had been used to condemn him, not to forgive him. He devised a self-protective rule: never apologize to a priest.

Thus he learned humiliation before even knowing the word as all the children around him laughed and oinked for the eternal duration of the lunch period. He knew then that he could never be a priest. No. Not a glutton such as he. Not anymore. Not now that he has made God frown.

He quivered at the memory and at the absurd notion of going to hell for eating a spaghetti sandwich and wished that the fucking priest had told him quietly instead of turning him into a public spectacle and that there should be people hired to protect little kids from the nuns and priests of the world.

As it turned out, Tim was right about the other boys. Not one of them found work. They wasted half the day waiting around on a greasy bench in a smelly room until the would-be employer laughed and told them to get lost.

It rained that night, and everyone stayed in. Matt and Tim divvied up the time playing board games. The long evening petered out after a final game of Scrabble, during which they did not keep score or quibble over words because they were more interested in finishing the game than playing it. As usual, Matt stayed up later than anyone else. He sat in the kitchen and began to read *The Dharma Bums*. As he was taking his final leak before bed, he noticed this graffiti in one of the bathroom stalls:

*She offered her honor*
*He honored her offer*
*And for the rest of the night*
*He was on her and off her*

# CHAPTER VII

Having exhausted his three-day limit, Matt hitched to Ottawa and made it in two easy rides despite having been warned by that hostel warden that there had been a prison break just west of Kingston and that rides might be "as scarce as hen's teeth." He was unsure of the Canadian hitchhiking laws but assumed he would find out soon enough. His first lift was with a round and rosy-faced, burly man who had just returned home from a cruise in a friend's sailboat. They had navigated the St. Lawrence Seaway through Quebec into the Atlantic and around the Maritimes and then down the eastern seaboard to Florida. He was still vibrating from the experience and insisted on taking the longer scenic route along the St. Lawrence River so he could impress Matt with all the sights.

As a younger man, he explained, he promised himself he would sail to Florida before he turned fifty. "I had my own business, and, I tell you what, I didn't own that business. That business owned me. Then fifty came and went. I was inactive and lazy and depressed and I started having health problems.

"I got scared and thought, 'Hey, I wanna live before I die.' To make a long story short, I lost my shirt and decided to go on sabbatical. I got off my duff, sold the business, and did it, sailed the whole way, and it's the best thing I've ever done. It gave me the time and leisure I needed to readjust my perspective and clean out a lot of the crap that had built up inside my head. I gave myself a long overdue mental enema and now my thoughts are flowing free and easy for the first time in years." He scrunched up his cheeks and lips to make a loud expulsive sound to accentuate his point. "Think of this," he pointed his index finger. "At every moment of your life, you are older than you've ever been before and younger than you'll ever be again. You've got the right idea. See the world while you're still a spring chicken and healthy enough to enjoy it. Believe me, fifty will be here before you know it, and then you'll be an old fart like me.

"Here's what I learned. It's all an inside job. It's about reading the wind and working the rudder. You gotta have faith in the process. You've got to learn the ropes and live in the moment. Not tomorrow. Not yesterday. Just—" he snapped his fingers, "right now. You know what I mean? You gotta grab it." He mimicked catching a mosquito and said, "There. Got it." He did that several more times and said, "See what I mean? That's all that exists. Right—" and he snapped his fingers one more time, "now!"

Then he recited a short poem he had written. "I am not a poet. But here goes." He cleared his throat in a theatrical manner, stroked the unkempt shock of his mariner's beard, adjusted his Adam's apple, and raised his chin:

*Thirty didn't faze me*
*When forty hit I didn't give a lick*
*But fifty hit me from behind*
*And dropped me like a ton of fucking bricks.*

Matt was uncomfortable talking about the man's age and mortality and wasn't sure whether to laugh or try to think of something serious to say about the poem or the enema. He was spared the decision when the man, who was on a roll, stated, "My next trip will be through the Panama Canal and over to the Galapagos Islands and then up to Vancouver. Then I can die. But for now, I'm not yet ready to lower the sails and gather in the lines." He started singing "Swing Low, Sweet Chariot" and then said, "That's how I want to go. BAM!" Another finger snap. "Dead before I even know I'm dying. No time for self-pity or repenting. No pathetic last confession. Just take my soul, God. Take it as it is. No spit and polish. No last minute tidying up. I want an honest death."

There are all kinds of reasons for picking up a hitchhiker, in addition to the general truth that people enjoy being kind. Some see their own son or daughter out there and are being parental in guiding a stranger safely onward. For some, they are honoring the memory of their former hitchhiking selves before life tied them down. Some others may be looking for conversation to pass the time away and restore alertness. For the army of wanderers bumming around in their patched-together VW vans, picking up hitchhikers was simply the hippie thing to do. It was an expression of their shared generational bond and a celebration of that bond with the ritualistic inhalation of the smoke of the burning herb. For this man, in his current state of existential flux, over-bubbling with a revitalized zest for life, he wanted an audience to help make his transformation real and to bolster up his resolve to shed his old skin and be newly born. To practice being his new self to someone who didn't know his old self. Any old hitchhiker would do.

No sooner had Matt stretched out his legs on the roadside than a VW van with Nova Scotia plates beeped, pulled up ahead, and a hand emerged from the driver's window and waved him forward. The driver was a kid from Truro who was trying to cram as much adventure and freedom as possible into his two-week vacation before offering himself back up to the God of whatever his weekday grind happened to be. Matt dubbed him "The Traveling Truroan." Behind the wheel of his van, he was the commander of his own vessel, the master of his own destiny.

The interior was rigged for makeshift living and was cultivating its own traveling-bachelor atmosphere and its own funky, lived-in smell of musty clothes and old food. There was a twin mattress, a rumpled sleeping bag, camping gear, candy bar wrappers, crunched-up soda cans, and other garbage plus the inevitable dirty socks, t-shirts, and underwear scattered about. The kid said, "I've never been west before," indicating that, from his Nova Scotian vantage point, eastern Ontario was west. He didn't have any maps because he wanted to wing it and "listen to the road."

"In about four or five days," he said, "the road better shut up because I've got to be back to work. I'm low man on the totem pole and wouldn't be missed all that much if they let me go. Till then, I'm still the travelin' man. But when that time arrives, I'll be the homebound man. An entirely different creature," he said, looking at his left wrist, which was not sporting its customary watch.

Matt thought, *Half past a freckle and quarter to a hair*.

When a Led Zeppelin song came on the radio, the kid turned up the volume and sang his version of the opening lyrics: "With a pebble up her ass and a fifty cent ham."

The hostel was in a large athletic facility on the grounds of the University of Ottawa. The building was brimming with vagabond kids with tousled hair, all impressed by the palatial spaciousness of their temporary digs—their "commodious environs"—roaming the halls and taking stock of every bit of leisure this facility afforded them. As in Kingston, it cost fifty cents for the night, meals and showers included. He planned to spend a couple of days exploring the city and the canal and the parks before pointing his thumb east into French-speaking territory.

He borrowed a map and plotted a simple route to Halifax. From there he would ferry to Bar Harbor or Portland and then swing down to see one of his sisters in Massachusetts, another in Connecticut, and yet another in New Jersey before his victory lap home. Matt loved how the mapped world was so well ordered and logical and somehow even happy within its four corners, a world where even perilously steep and swervy roads and precipitous drops all appeared straight and safe, where every road delivered you safely to your destination, and no one ever got lost.

The locker rooms were a godsend, with steamy hot showers to wash off the sweat and grime of the day's ramble and an abundant supply of cottony "Property of University of Ottawa" towels to buff his glossy skin. In the common room, braless and freshly showered girls flung their heads forward to tease out the tangles and tendrils from their waterfalling hair with their rat-tailed brushes, their t-shirts wet and transparent against their slippery flesh, all awash in the fragrance of their fruity shampoos and soaps. There were bobby pins and curlers, lotions and sprays. Some practiced the art of applying lipstick while gazing into their compact pop-up mirrors. Long-haired hippie boys with intense faces made combs of their open-fingered hands, stroked back their hair, closed their hand into a fist at the ponytail end, and wrung out little rivulets of water.

Matt wished he had hair like Jimmy Page on the back cover of the first Led Zeppelin album or Stevie Winwood on the front of the second *Traffic* album. He always tried to brush it into that style, but it tended to frizz the wrong way or curl off in a haphazard direction. It was simpler to just tie it back and forget about it.

He returned to the expansive dorm room where the rogues' gallery of restless transients tended to their own select turf, each with their own peculiarized sense of decorum. Sleeping bags were laid out perpendicular to the walls with girls at one end of the room and boys at the other with nothing but an imaginary curtain separating them, reminiscent of Clark Gable and Claudette Colbert in *It Happened One Night.*

Matt lay on his sleeping bag, closed his eyes, breathed deeply and contentedly, and listened to the swarm of voices. He rose and wandered from his own little acre and ended up outside, sitting like a monk beneath a shade tree reading *The Dharma Bums.* The pages turned themselves until it was time to eat.

The cafeteria monitor was a broad-shouldered and full-bellied Viking of a man known as Erik the Head. He was a graduate student in classical studies at the university. Beneath his rainbow-colored pith helmet was a rebellious and poorly contained bush of auburn hair. His gruff voice boomed instructions like cannon blasts. With his contagious smile and brawny sense of humor, he was an easy favorite among the free-spirited maidens over whom he ruled with an extra measure of lordly beneficence.

Dinner was a clamorous banquet of fresh-faced ambassadors from all over North America, with a handful of Brits, Aussies, Germans, and

Scandinavians thrown in for flavor. Everyone was clean, shimmering, and radiant as they feasted over hot meals, chatting, telling jokes, and exchanging tales of the road. Matt listened to conversations in three different languages in addition to a Scotsman who rambled on about wee bairns and braes and bonny lasses and about how he longed to return home for a proper feed of haggis.

"What's haggis?" chirped a skeptical admirer.

"Aye," he said. "It's a sheep's guts and the organs and all the nasty bits that get swept up off the floor after it's been butchered. A meal fit for a Scottish king." He added some additional descriptives, but nobody could understand what he was saying. Some of the girls chuckled and rolled their eyes as the more smitten of them shrieked a bit in horror.

After dinner, wayward travelers lounged and meandered the wide halls, wrote letters and postcards back to wherever home was, mingled with strangers, or pretended to meditate in a conspicuous corner. There were nameless drifters who buried their heads in books and shy kid philosophers who thought they knew more than they did about Zen and metaphysics and existentialism. It didn't matter, though, because no one else knew very much, either, but everyone went along with it anyway, attempting to give the impression of quiet comprehension. Guitars appeared and would-be troubadours drew a hodgepodge of fans with their best renditions of "Catch the Wind," "Fire and Rain," "Blackbird," and "For What It's Worth." One brave girl attempted "White Rabbit" but failed spectacularly to her own good-natured delight.

There were two squinty, malnourished-looking, pauper kids from Halifax counting out their five hundred pennies, all they had to get to Vancouver. Somebody threw them a dollar. They threw it back, saying, "Just pennies, man. We're gonna get there on pennies." So everybody scrounged and scraped the bottoms of their pockets and packs for whatever chump change they could dig out and showered them with copper. "Pennies from heaven," one of them said, his arms raised, exultant and carefree, while the other one pocketed the coins.

When an Afro-haired girl with round blue-tinted granny glasses asked how they were going to get back from Vancouver, the boys, who possessed more verve than vision, looked at her and each other with question marks in their eyes.

In the gym, a bunch of kids pulled a mat from an equipment room and were competing to see who could do the longest headstand. One kid with an erect military posture, squared shoulders, and bulging Popeye biceps remained poised on his crew-cut head with his legs aligned and his toes pointed perfectly skyward, outlasting challengers as they rose and fell in defeat, one by one.

In the cafeteria, a huddle of curious travelers played cards, learning new games from different parts of the world, telling jokes and stories ,and perpetuating the myths and legends that inhabited the heads of hitchhikers. Matt showed off his card shuffling skills, meager though they were, while some watched and others spun more tales.

An English kid with a Scouse accent instructed a tableful of eager onlookers on a card game, All Fours, which Matt recognized as being identical to Pitch, the game that he and all his friends had played at Bromski's, a bar in New Holland.

Another spoke up: "Whatever you do, don't get stuck in Wawa. If you're hitching west out of the Soo, you gotta get a ride going all the way to Thunder Bay."

"Why? What's so bad about Wawa?"

"First of all, Wawa is more than 100 miles from anywhere. The hostel's a dump. A row of leaky old army tents that smell bad when they get wet, and there's no real toilets or showers, just a couple outside crappers. And if you get dropped off there, you can never get out. People will *not* pick you up. You'll be left in the lurch, man. You have to beg rides from people who have cars. One hitchhiker was there for, like, two or three weeks—couldn't get out—so the townspeople felt sorry for him, and they all pitched in and got him a bus ticket. Another was stuck there and ran out of money. The hostel kicked him out after three days, so, in order to save up a few bucks, he got a job washing dishes at a diner where he met a waitress. They fell in love, got married, and now he lives there. Now he's stuck for life."

"How long were you stuck there?" someone asked him.

"Well, I haven't actually been there," he blushed, "but that's what I've heard. That it's the worst spot in all the provinces."

"How many providences are there?" one American kid asked.

"You mean other than the one in Rhode Island?" the Canadian said with a disapproving snarl.

At some point during the evening, Matt revamped his itinerary, scrapped the eastern Maritimes, and decided to head west the next day. He wanted to step into Kerouac's shoes and toss his rucksack into a few freight cars and hop the legendary Zipper, the express freighter that ran along the California coast. He wanted to be a Zen lunatic. His mind argued against it, for fear that heading west would break him out of his safe orbital path, beyond the security of his hometown gravitational field and would, perhaps, propel him into a careless and dangerous drift far away from home. His heart, though, was all in, so for once in his life, his courage trumped his fears, and he told his mind to shut the fuck up so he could properly answer his calling like a man, or a reasonable facsimile thereof.

Matt was bristling. He spent some of his excess energy by calling his mother. He pondered whether Kerouac would have done that and figured that even the greatest of the travelin' men must have loved their mothers.

"Mom, I'm heading west. Yes, I'm fine. Yes, I've got enough clothes. Yes, I've got enough money. Yes, the hostels are clean and safe. Yes, I am enjoying myself. No, it doesn't get too cold at night. I'll be in touch in a few days. Postcards are on the way. Yes, I'll call collect."

When the conversation ended, Matt wanted to tell her he loved her but didn't dare. It was not the kind of thing they ever said. But he felt it more than ever and wished he could say it, a simple "I love you,

Mom," in a way both casual and heartfelt at the same time. And then, maybe, she might say it back.

He hung up, let the distance set back in, and went into the gym with his Frisbee. Moments later, a short, athletic girl with curly brunette ringlets bounded through the opposite doorway, all zest and vigor, and before he knew it they were both sprinting and leaping in their bare feet, chasing after the Frisbee as it hummed across the length of the gym. It was love at first toss. Her name was Maureen.

Matt still remembered how he felt in kindergarten the first time he'd seen Linda with her glimmering eyes, russet-haired Sylvia in fourth grade, dark-eyed Kathy in seventh, and, of course, Helen at the end of his freshman year. One time, on a weekend visit with friends at Fordham University, while riding the D-Train from the Bronx to Greenwich Village, he made eye contact with an extraordinary-looking Puerto Rican girl who was waiting at the 125th Street station as passengers all around her entered and exited the train. The crowd between them seemed to part as she smiled at him from the platform and through the filthy subway window to where her sat, and—he imagined—she almost waved at him as his train eased along the tracks and then sped him away into the lonely oblivion of its subterranean passageway. All night long he was obsessed with the memory of her transfixing image and the magnetic allure of her dreamy gaze, and he ached at the knowledge that he would have to live the rest of his life without ever seeing her again, without ever touching her walnut skin.

Carla had also had that effect upon him and given, the fiasco of that fascination, Matt swore that he would never let it happen again. He would not let himself become so hopelessly captivated by anyone, no matter how tempting she may be, and he would never again surrender himself or his heart to such self-deceptive and self-destructive devotions. She had been the unwitting decoy for his affections, and he had been the stupid smitten duck who couldn't tell the difference between love and infatuation no matter how many times he'd been shot down and incinerated by the failure of his foolish expectations. He vowed to keep a sensible head and a level eye. But Maureen was reaching him in that same vulnerable place and in that same immediate and irrational way, and he feared that his paper defenses would be no match for the fire he felt within. It scared him. So, please, no, none of that ridiculous love-at-first-sight nonsense ever again. No more Holy Grail quest to find "the one."

Nevertheless, he loved watching Maureen's nubile frame stretch with a well-honed athletic agility and, strong and graceful, grab that thing in flight and whip it back to him like a discus. A visual poem. He swooned in silence. *If there is a heaven,* Matt thought, *it is a broad meadow filled with beautiful girls in gauzy dresses all playing Frisbee in sunlight forever. Ah yes. All in a timeless forest at the world's angel-ancient edge.*

Afterward, worn out and sweaty, they talked for a while. She was hitching alone and heading home to Michigan. She had a rabbit's foot swinging from a belt loop and a knife strapped to her side in a leather sheath. She said, "If anybody messes with me, they'll be sorry."

"Have you ever had any problems hitching? I mean, as far as having guys come on too strong?"

"Not yet," she said with a smirk, patting her weapon. "Everybody's been good. Just the typical. A couple of guys came on kinda strong, giving me their dumb macho rap, but they backed off when they saw I wasn't buying it. And I'm not going to let the fact that I'm a girl stop me from hitching by myself. I've tried traveling with friends and it just does not work for me."

"Yeah, but it *is* a gamble, isn't it?" Matt sounded like his mother.

Maureen looked at him with riveting tough-as-nails eyes and said, "She who never gambles always loses."

The night drifted on. Maureen drifted to bed. Matt stayed up listening to a lanky James Taylor kid sing folky ballads in an echoey stairwell, to an Irish kid named Finbar singing a lament about the hanging death of the rebel Roddy McCorley "on the bridge of Toome today," and then to a wheat-haired Joni Mitchell girl in a threadbare pair of hip-hugger bell-bottoms sing "The Circle Game," a repertoire of originals and then a soulful rendition of "Sad-Eyed Lady of the Lowlands." She sang well but stumbled when she forgot the beginning of the third verse. Matt wanted to impress her by knowing it, which he did, but in the pressure of the moment, he couldn't quite grab it. Later, in his sleeping bag on the dark dormitory floor, amid the already familiar whiffs of skunky socks and sneakers and moldy clothes, as dreamy hallucinations kidnapped his mind, it came to him all at once and with clarity:

> *The Kings of Tyrus with their convict list*
> *Are waiting in line for their geranium kiss*
> *And you wouldn't know it would happen like this*
> *But who among them really wants just to kiss you*

# CHAPTER VIII

CLANG! CLANG! CLANG! CLANG! CLANG! "Get up. Get out of bed. Drag a comb across your heads." It was Erik the Head sounding an early morning alarm and banging a big aluminum pan with a stainless steel ladle.

"Shut the fuck up," someone retaliated.

"Rise and shine, my little pretties. The rosy fingers of dawn and the heroic Grecian sky are upon us, and the long and winding road beckons. I am here to deliver you forth upon the road and to your destiny. Now string your knees and get your asses out of bed. Breakfast awaits you." He laughed with glee and continued clanging.

The booming metallic din was too penetrating and persistent to ignore. Drowsy-eyed heads emerged from sleeping bags and from beneath pillows like baby birds squinting against an assault of morning light. Resistance fizzled. Everyone knew the Viking would win the day.

Matt shuffled into the men's room, groggy and still half-asleep, and was startled to attention as two mischievous girls walked out and announced in triumph, "The bathrooms have been liberated." Sure enough, to his delight there was a gaggle of girls brushing their teeth and socializing nonchalantly at the men's sinks. A pretty pair of feet with toenails displaying a chipped rainbow of colors was peeking out from one of the stalls.

"Oh my God," said one girl. "Look at my hair. It looks like the wreck of the Hersperus."

"What's that mean?" said another.

"Oh, I don't know. That's just something my mother says."

Matt marveled at the immodesty of some of the guys who used this as an opportunity to challenge the girls by proudly swinging their dicks around like chubby breakfast sausages, and he marveled even more at the girls who were not fazed by it.

At breakfast the girls complained about wet toilet seats and everyone chimed in.

One guy said, "Who cares if the seat's wet? It's just your ass, for God's sake."

Another said, "Don't worry about it. You girls just hover over public toilets anyway."

A girl said, "You guys are so gross. What you need on those things is a nozzle. It might improve your aim."

"You're just jealous. You wish you could be packing one of these pistols."

"Oh, please. You must be kidding. I'd rather die than have one of those things jangling around between my legs. All wrinkled and ugly. Yuck!" She scrunched up her face as if she had taken a big bite from a lemon while all the other girls laughed and nodded their heads in agreement.

One guy said, "They're not always wrinkled. Sometimes they straighten out and all the wrinkles vanish. It's magic. Wanna see?"

Another said, "Hey, why is it that only the men's bathrooms were liberated? That's not fair. That's sexist."

"It's a woman's prerogative," said one girl.

"Squatters rights," said another.

"But, come on. Admit it. You dug it. It gave you a chance to show off your little weenies and act real macho in front of us poor, defenseless girls." She mocked up a saccharine Shirley Temple smile, her mouth gleaming with braces, and fluttered her eyelashes. "Besides, we don't want you stinking up our bathrooms or messing up our toilet seats with your tinkle juice."

There were multiple responses: "Did you say 'little' weenies? I guess you didn't see mine," and, "Yeah—like your shit doesn't stink."

"That's right," the girls spoke in a chorus of confidence.

Matt tried to think of something clever to say but was afraid it would backfire, so he kept his mouth shut.

When the conversation got more graphic, a sparsely-whiskered loner dude with his head bobbing over a breakfast bowl, having been disturbed from sleepy morning ruminations, said, "Please! I'm trying to eat my oatmeal," and everyone laughed.

"You sit on your tongue there, breakfast boy," the bravest girl responded.

"I'd rather have *you* sit on *my* tongue, sweetie." He made a V with his index and middle fingers, pressed them against his lips, and lapped his tongue through the opening in a lewd manner. "Mmmm. Yummy."

Undaunted, the brave girl looked at the breakfast boy, cocked her head, and said, "Suck my dick."

Matt had an outdated 1965 Esso Touring Map of Ontario bearing the stamp of Gay's Esso Service, Henderson, New York. He would be hitching the Trans-Canada Highway and hoped that by nightfall he would make it to Sudbury, 315 miles west of Ottawa. He started his westward trek with Ted, a blue-eyed kid from Queens, "the best of the Boroughs." Matt originally thought Ted was Canadian because he had a red and white maple-leaf patch sewn into his backpack.

"A lot of Canadians don't care for us Americans. You know, Viet Nam, Nixon, the ugly American, and all that. I figured I'd have better luck if people think I'm Canadian. I don't want to deal with all that anti-American bullshit."

After three rides, which brought them a mere fifteen miles out of Ottawa, they had a long discouraging wait in gray weather. Matt grew impatient, knowing that each of them alone had a better chance of a ride than both of them together. They agreed to split up and meet that night in Sudbury. Matt forfeited the chance of the first ride by letting Ted keep the hitching spot while he walked westward down the road, the Queensway, the Trans-Canadian highway. From a distance, Matt called back to Ted, "A buck says I beat you" and gave him a good-natured farewell salute, and that was the last they ever saw of each other.

This road was nothing like an American interstate. It was your basic two-laner with regular intersections. There were no on-ramps, off-ramps, special service areas, or tollbooths. Unfortunately, on this day, there was also no traffic.

He walked for miles, lost in his customary tangle of thoughts, fighting against the urge to investigate the lure of every side road, wondering where they would all take him, imagining all the intrigues and love affairs awaiting him and plotting a lifetime of aimless meandering throughout the humdrum of the great nowhere and into the heart of the serendipitous great everywhere with its spider's-web network of intermeshed roads and highways that would deliver him to all places and satisfy all of his wanderlusting runaway restlessness. He was being carried away by a swell of intoxicating thoughts, but just as he was starting to levitate, he was interrupted by a flash of lightning, a blast of thunderclaps, and a few million bucket-loads of rain. He was already soaked when a trucker, who had furry caterpillar eyebrows, took pity on him and gave him a lift to Renfrew.

As he was walking out of Renfrew, a carload of hippie travelers heading the opposite direction stopped and gave him half a joint. The driver said, "It's for the head, man. It'll keep you nice." Matt toked it up as he walked, relishing an image of himself as a stoned hobo at large upon life's never-ending ribbon of highway.

He next caught a short ride with a traveling salesman in an old station wagon that was loaded with a jumble of boxes containing a multitude of household items. On the dashboard was a thick catalog titled "The Queen City of the Lakes Mercantile" which boasted "Serving Your Needs Since 1883." He was from Buffalo, had just received a promotion and was motivated to prove himself, and was not lacking in the confidence department. "I'm international now, man. Cold calls. That's where I dominate. The minute I walk in that store, I am already totally stoked and certain that I will make the sale 'cause it's all in the attitude. They don't stand a chance with me. It all boils down to PMA equals OPM."

He looked at Matt and asked, "Do you know what that is?" Matt shook his head.

"That, my friend, is the key to success and happiness in sales. Positive mental attitude equals other people's money. The essence of sales in a nutshell." He rubbed his thumb against his fingers, indicating a wad of cash, and bragged, "Candy from a baby."

Matt was feeling like a sorry excuse for a hitchhiker and reckoned that, at his sloth's pace, he would only make it to Pembroke, a scant 100 miles from Ottawa, and he didn't think there was a hostel there. He continued walking and counting dead animals on the shoulder of the road. He had counted three turtles, several birds, and something unrecognizable but which smelled bad enough to merit being counted in the miscellaneous category. And, of course, the occasional jam-packed and squishy Pamper. Then he happened upon a dead baby bird that was still warm and soft and appeared to be sleeping, but its neck was broken and its shredded wings dangled in Matt's hand. He tried to shake some life into it. Poor thing. Not yet fully fledged and already gone. Too soon from the nest? He couldn't stomach the thought of letting it get squashed by a car or pecked apart by a crow, so he stepped a few yards onto the grass and dug it a shallow grave among the ditch lilies and the Queen Anne's lace, shed a tear, and thought "Straight from the heart of a bird." He had just finished covering it up with a couple paltry scoops of clumpy soil when a van with a Coleman canoe strapped to its roof pulled over—he didn't even have his thumb out—and yelled for him to hop in, which he did, and he was greeted with a big, old howdy by a twenty-something Oklahoman with a joint the size of a cigar hanging out of his cowboy mouth and by his Oklahoman sweetheart who had red far-away eyes, a gorgeous cowgirl face, and certain other features that commanded his attention.

Matt accepted the offer of a super-jumbo stogie-joint, and the three travelers were soon engaged in conversation. The driver, Bradley, said they almost didn't see him and asked what he was doing hunched over in the weeds.

"I was burying a baby bird," he said, to which Bradley and the girl—Lynn—exclaimed in unison, "A triple B!" As it turned out, Lynn was an English major who enjoyed playing word games and picking up on accents, slang expressions, and other peculiarities of language, such as the Canadian "eh" and "aboot." Her favorite movie was "My Fair Lady," and she would listen to people talk and then calculate where they came from. Matt hated disappointing her when she guessed that he was from Pennsylvania.

He'd been buzzing along pretty good after just a few tokes when he was lulled into a smoky reverie of appreciation for the beauty of his cowgirl guide and for the freewheeling ease of her stogie-toking companion. So far he had been falling in love with every new girl or woman he met, so it was natural that Lynn became his latest love and the newest flower to come blooming in his garden of ridiculous fantasies. He also found himself wanting to emulate each man he met because each one was handsomer, smarter, funnier, stronger, and more interesting than he, not to mention luckier in love.

He hoped that he was maturing and growing cool by association. The more he traveled, the more he evolved into a living collage of the best bits of everyone he was meeting. It was a safe bet because anything was an improvement upon himself. Little by little. Piece by piece. Ride by ride. And then, in the fullness of time, the disheveled pieces might all somehow fit together into a coherent and self-assured whole. Matt Mahoney— Mosaic Man!

Bradley and Lynn brought him as far as Eau Claire, where they turned south on Route 630 to the lakes and forests of the Algonquin Provincial Park where, he said, "We're fixin' to spend a few days roughing it."

*Not to mention*, Matt fantasized as he gave Lynn a final envious gawk, *a shitload of wilderness tent sex.*

Matt blushed when Lynn smiled at him and said, "Good luck, honey."

It was already near twilight and Matt knew that Sudbury was out of the question. North Bay, thirty miles away, became his new destination. And then—Ah! Good luck! A ride with an older local couple materialized. The man wore a rumpled felt fedora and resembled Kurt Vonnegut. Matt got in and said, "Hi. How are you?" The man smirked and quipped, "Pretty good, I'm told." His wife, used to his wisecracks, responded, "Well, then, just goes to show that you shouldn't believe everything you hear."

The man spoke in a professorial voice, telling Matt of his own hitchhiking past during his college years. "Yup. Used to go everywhere. Made good time, too. Faster than the buses. But now I don't go anywhere except the doctor's office and the supermarket. Most of the time I'm just vegetating at home, stewing in the pathetic inactivity of my late middle age."

His lifelong dream was to ride cross-country on horseback.

"After all," he said, "it's not where you end up. It's how you get there."

His wife said that it was a lame-brain idea, and no matter how he got there, he would be doing it alone, and she wouldn't guarantee she'd still be home when he got back.

"That's all right," he replied. "I'll pick somebody up along the way. My very own Sacajawea."

"Oh yeah?" she sparred. "And how would an ugly old fuddy-duddy like you ever be able to satisfy some cute young Sacajawea?"

"Well, honey. As they say, the older the fiddle, the sweeter the tune."

He gave Matt one of those man-to-man approval-seeking glances and Matt gave his best-guess approximation of a responsive man-to-man nod.

She rolled her eyes. "Don't encourage him. He loves an audience. Believe me, I've heard it all before, and he knows my opinion."

And it was strange, because halfway through the conversation Matt started having a déjà vu experience and knew in advance that the man's glance was coming and could have quoted his wife's response. He guided his way through several more seconds of precognition before slipping back into the mystery of real time, wishing there was a way to stay on that wavelength and know everything just before it happened.

*So it goes*, thought Matt.

Just to get the final quip, the man asked his wife, "Have you ever noticed that whenever I have an idea, your first assumption is always that I don't know what the hell I'm talking about?"

Their eyes met, she nodded, "That's because you don't," and they both settled into well-worn self-satisfied grins.

They dropped him off in the outskirts of North Bay at the very edge of a dying day, during those fleeting moments of a late evening when you can track the path of the sun as it crashes slow-motion into the horizon and, second by second, sinks out of view and, in the space of a song or two on the radio, the scarlet sky goes from dusk to dark. Thick clouds hushed any rumor of moonlight, and the unlit, residential, tree-lined streets were as quiet as a crypt except for some unusual crunchy sounds that accentuated each step he took.

A kid zoomed up to him on a bike with a banana seat and tassels on the ends of the handlebars and came to a dare-devilish stop, almost toppling over as he skidded in a broad swath.

"Hey—where are you going?"

Joey was puny of build but large of spirit. He had a toothy grin and bruised knees, presumably from reckless bicycling mishaps, and prefaced all of his questions with "Hey." "Hey—where are you from?" Joey told him there was a meeting place in North Bay where hitchhikers could catch a ride to the hostel, which was a few miles outside of town. "But we better hurry up 'cause I'm not sure how late it runs." Matt put all his faith in the youthful scout and accompanied him onward.

Joey chattered on and on about his family and about school as though North Bay were the center of the known universe, the very bellybutton of creation. He told Matt about the Dionne quintuplets who had been born not far from North Bay and said they were "world famous all over the whole wide world." Matt had never heard of them before and assumed that Joey's mouth was being steered by his imagination.

The crunchy sounds grew louder and deeper and crunchier with each step. Joey must have noticed but didn't say anything. "What is that I'm stepping on?" Matt asked. "Acorns or something?"

"No. That's the shads." Joey's voice was incredulous, as though Matt must be an idiot to ask such a question.

"What's that?"

"The shads. Those are these big flying bugs. They're all over the place. That's what these sounds are. You're stepping on the shads."

Matt bent over, reached down into the darkness, and with dainty fingertips he picked one up for a closer inspection and tossed it down as if it were on fire. It was a large ugly insect with long papery wings. There were lumpy brown piles of them on the sidewalks and the streets, and Matt felt like he was walking into the opening frames of a cheap horror flick from the 1950s: "The Invasion of the Man-Eating Shads!"

"Oh man! That is gross. Where do they come from? Why are there so many?"

Joey didn't have all the answers but said that the fish in Lake Nipissing fed off these shads and this was the feeding season.

Matt's bicycle escort delivered him to a community building where a tribe of travelers was milling around, talking and smoking and studying maps while waiting for the last shuttle. Backpacks and sleeping bags cluttered the doorway and the curbside. The side of the building, which was lit upward from the ground by spotlights, was entirely covered with ugly shads, a living crawling carpet that fascinated Matt as if it were a natural wonder of the world unfolding right there before his eyes. When he got over his initial repulsion, it was actually quite beautiful.

Joey had to go home and said he was already in trouble for being late.

Matt yelled, "Hey Joey?"

"Hey what?"

"You're a cool kid."

He beamed a broad grin, shouted "thanks," and pulled a wheelie on his bike as he sped off with shad carcasses popping and exploding beneath his tires like cracker balls.

The hostel was bustling with the typical strange brew of characters. Quite atypically, there was also a busload of Boy Scout church group campers whose bus had broken down. It was their once-in-a-lifetime luxury of being able to stay up late, drink coffee, and rub elbows with leather-clad motorcycle road warriors adorned with skull-and-crossbones tattoos and with bearded hippie guys sporting braided ponytails that fell past their shoulders and with provocatively bouncy hippie girls in floppy hats and moccasins. The scouts foraged for sticks and played fetch with an assortment of well-traveled hippie dogs wearing bandanas and sporting names like Magellan and Quasimodo and a three-legged Irish setter named Eileen. When another dog named Jagger started humping Eileen, she fell over and a boy scout, looking at the aroused aggressor, shouted, "Hey look! His lipstick is hanging out."

Then, much to Matt's surprise, he looks through a hallway and into the kitchen and sees Maureen sitting at the table eating a bowl of Cheerios and wearing cut-off jeans and a loose-fitting tie-dyed blouse with a rainbow-colored peace sign embroidered on the back. She is the very essence of gypsy desirability. Captivated by her transplendent beauty and her graceful ways, he thinks her name and she swivels telepathically in his direction and captures his glance. Her eyes light up as she skips over and gives him a big wide-armed hug and makes him feel like a celebrity in front of all the little kids.

"It's good to see you, Matt. I was wondering how you were doing. I never got to see you this morning." He hadn't said goodbye for fear of appearing too forward.

"Yeah. I was wondering about you, too. This is great. Such a great coincidence."

She smiles at him and when their eyes meet he averts his shy gaze and silently thanks all the motorists who didn't bring him to Sudbury. His heart was spilling over with happiness at seeing her again and at the thrill of hearing her call him by his name.

They sat in the kitchen gabbing and joking with everyone who passed through and played funny games with the kids. Matt pretended this were his kitchen and she were his wife and these people were all their family and friends and neighbors and they were all having a terrific time basking in his hospitality and in Maureen's goodness.

*Ah yes*, he thought, *I am both wholly and holy under this hypnotic spell.*

One blonde five-year-old kid came to the table and, for no apparent reason, said, "Not posta smoke dope 'roun here."

Not to be outdone, his younger brother bragged, "I have a rash on my penis."

A down-and-dirty bad-ass biker with an eye patch joined the kitchen chatter for a while and told his bad-ass stories about the Georgia judge who dismissed charges against him, saying, "Well, as long as you're white and ain't never killed nobody white, I don't see why you can't go" and about the dude he had to mess up for insulting his old lady and, even worse, his bike. The wanna-be outlaw, knowing he had a gullible audience, attempted to sum himself up: "Did you ever think that, well, you're so mean for so long and then you try to be nice—but it just don't work?" He was a well-rehearsed scoundrel. Matt respected him for avoiding obscenities while entertaining the peanut-gallery of saucer-eyed scouts who congregated around him in awestruck admiration.

The Boy Scout church group campers were running around like pirates, playing games with the travelers, flirting with the hippie girls, enamored by their gypsy-princess ways, and marveling wide-eyed at the wild semi-true tales of the open road. They were having the time of their lives, but it was not the kind of time the Boy Scout church group leaders had planned for them to have or wished to have to explain to the Boy Scout church group parents. In order to avoid the travesty of allowing the boys to have an even greater and more memorable time, the leader herded them to bed before any irreparable fun was had.

Matt and Maureen sat alone in the kitchen for a while. He wanted to take her hand or put his arm around her but was too timid, afraid that if he went one step too far, he would shatter the illusion he had created from the silk and sunlight of her presence. Hers was a contagious energy, and he knew it was she, not he, who had generated the effusive kitchen scene and that she was the magnet that attracted everyone and the fuse that animated them. It was wonderful to have been a part of it, a genuine home-away-from-home atmosphere. He wished his own home could have been more like that, but his parents never spoke to one another and used the kids as go-betweens to convey messages, like couriers to the generals of opposing armies during a bloody civil war.

*"Tell your father his dinner is on the table," Mrs. Mahoney would say to Matt with unconcealed resentment. Or, on payday, returning home from his teaching, Professor Mahoney would hand him an envelope and say with detectable disdain, "Give this to your mother." There was an unyielding tension, a taut spring, that Matt feared to provoke. It spun around the oppressive presence of his brooding father, floating silently through the hallways and up and down the flights of stairs or occupying his seat of command in his rocker in front of the TV, watching Walter Cronkite, his tumbler of bourbon in hand, the ice cubes melting and clinking at each sip.*

*But no one ever talked about it. Matt sometimes wondered if maybe it was all his own fault or it was all a figment of his imagination and, in reality, his father was an all-American Ward Cleaver "Father-of-the-Year" dad. Maybe he, Matt, was just a spoiled ingrate, too blind and pampered with privilege to appreciate his own good fortune.*

*It was only after his father's death that Matt noted, with a secretive burden of shame, that the house, the halls, and the kitchen had all been liberated from the suffocating airs that haunted them for so long. The civil war was over. There would be no more walking on egg shells. It was as if, in life, Professor Mahoney had been the ghost, and only with his death had the house been freed of the strange spell. A haunting in reverse. It was more than Matt could comprehend intellectually or reconcile emotionally. But here, in the color wheel of Maureen's company, and with the steady flow of engaging visitors, he experienced, perhaps for the first time, the joy of a kitchen in full glory.*

Matt grew sluggish and could not keep pace with the conversation. He wished there were a special device that could assemble all the fragments of his thoughts and ideas and turn them into stimulating and clever conversation the way Uncle Jim Fisk would turn a five-year-old's squiggle into a portrait or a landscape, a device that bypassed his self-censoring and second-guessing and god-awful powers of speech. Such a device would have been useful right then and there with Maureen.

He tried to sustain the gladdened spirit of the evening for as long as possible, but when the silences grew awkward and the yawns outnumbered the syllables, they said goodnight and went to their separate quarters. Matt lay in his sleeping bag, surrounded by dozens of peacefully snoring Boy Scout church group campers and a couple of bad-ass bikers, and thought to himself, *Mr. and Mrs. Matt and Maureen Mahoney. Aha—a quintuple M!*

# CHAPTER IX

Matt and Maureen headed out separately but made plans to see each other that night at the Sault St. Marie hostel. He wanted to ask her to hitch with him but was afraid that she would either say "yes" just to be polite or would say "no" and disappoint him, so he acted as if he didn't care one way or the other about seeing her again. He could no longer stand the heartache of loving or even just liking someone else so much more than he was loved in return.

He took an early shuttle to the road, but there were already more than ten hitchers out there brandishing hastily inscribed cardboard signs, advertising destinations. One was eating a tuna sandwich as her boyfriend, wearing a Dylanesque harmonica holder, was screeching out his best effort at some sweet blues. Another was leaning against the guardrail, scooping tobacco from a leather pouch and rolling a cigarette, singing, "One toke over the line, sweet Jesus." Several others were huddled together, studying maps, sharing jokes and tall travelers' tales, and acting mature and roadworthy. One took a jar of chunky peanut butter from her rucksack and passed it around. Everybody took a spoonful and for a minute the group went mute as they chewed and swallowed the gooey globs. The jar was followed by an aluminum canteen from which liberal swigs were enjoyed by all. One guy looked at it and, before taking a big gulp, in an impression of W. C. Fields, said, "Water? Never touch the stuff. Fish fuck in it."

Matt disapproved of the competitive greed for rides among all the thumb hounds when they were clustered together as a ride-starved gang on an entrance ramp. As a purist who saw the open road as a way of life and hitchhiking as a spiritual practice, he savored the pacifying open-aired creativity of thought that possessed him while walking in daydreams to nowhere. He was a bit snobby about that. "The beauty is in the walking," he had read. "We are betrayed by destinations."

Rather than assume the posture in last place on the ramp, where getting picked up was long odds, he sauntered past the string of stationary thumbs, still dislodging peanuts from his molars, and disappeared down the road and into the far country as though the hope of getting a ride was the last thing on his mind. As long as he was walking he was making progress. Besides, walking across the country had always been one of his ambitions. The solitary serenity of being the happy-go-lucky vagabond summoned by the call of an endless highway was, for Matt, a much-welcomed pardon from the rigors of life's realities. On a more practical level, experience had taught him that drivers who had denied a lift to the throng at the ramp might be more inclined to take pity on a lone goose stranded out on an empty stretch of road as a sort of wilderness rescue.

A ride should come in its own time and should not be begged for or forced. There was, after all, a time-honored hitchhikers' "Code of the Road" as well as an ancient tradition of hospitality governing the sacred relationship between a host and a traveling stranger. For Matt, begging rides was parasitic and sullied the sanctity of hitchhiking, which was about much more than getting from "Point A" to "Point B." It was not about destinations. It was about entering the abstract natural flow of all creation without disturbing the current. It was about honoring the laws of predestation and allowing life around you to happen of its own accord. It was about navigating the contours of the great everywhere and mapping its roads and meeting its people. It was about getting lost in thought and unstuck in time. It was about forgetting who you thought you were in order to discover who you truly are. Greatest of all, it was about shedding your skin and falling in love with life and becoming a part of the world as it dances seductively around you, inviting you to be its partner.

He often enjoyed the time between rides even more than the rides themselves. The meditative walking. The easing of inner tensions.

If he was cruising along on a well-greased and freewheeling train of thought or surfing on a fluid stream of consciousness, he was sometimes able to detach himself from the dynamics of his own lunacy and observe his convoluted thoughts from without, as from a weather plane above the eye of a hurricane, and to watch without judgment as those thoughts spin and suck and agonize, as though they belonged to some other mixed-up kid. To just watch them. And he watches himself watching them and the more detached he grows, the more he starts to feel restored to the true nature of whoever he is, his unfettered higher self, the self he had been before the advent of the unraveling that had launched his emotional odyssey and had made an enemy of his mind. Then, when the air of contentedness overcomes him, all the good thoughts start hatching and the big bag of fireworks starts going off all at once in a fiery barrage, and he begins to feel normal again as all the tight-wound coils spring free and all heaven breaks loose in a celebratory symphony of exploding firecracker ideas and theories. One thought leads to another, and everything associates and do-si-dos around, and he starts to feel more confident and, who knows, maybe things will work out okay after all. It's all just an inside job, right? And then he can laugh at himself and his torturous ordeal as the self-ordained semi-chivalrous would-be Arthurian knight, praying and swooning to the blessed virgin women of the world, so chaste, so chased, and his debilitating Mother Mary awe, his ill-conceived reverence, and the half self-imposed restraint.

Now it was all just stubbornness and fear and lonesome trances, and there was nothing Arthurian in this idiotic abstinence-by-default, and all his thwarted desires become madness, and longings become fierce cravings. But not here on this deserted highway, no, not now; he actually felt excellent at this precise moment despite all the scurrilous thoughts that continued to weave around in his head. Why couldn't he just be the person he had been with Helen instead of the weird substitute he had become in her absence, and where had that other person gone to, and why this excruciating drought, this interminable ice age, with all the fumbles and fiascoes?

Except, of course, like a spring thaw, he had fallen in love with Liza, beautiful Liza, at Brant Community College, her long, frizzy hair falling forward like a magnificent mane through which she would peek at him as if through slightly parted curtains and smile beatifically like a secret partner. Who knows? It could possibly have worked out with her. That sweep of exhilaration was certainly there. When he held her and inhaled the strawberry scent of her fair hair, he felt alive for the first time since Helen. By then, though, he was so fucked up and wallowing in his self-piteous mire that he had forgotten how to act or how to honor his affections and couldn't even quite recall now if he had ever told her he loved her, though he did, or how it had ended, or who broke up with whom. Maybe it just fizzled away—except he remembered reaching what he called his Fahrenheit 451 point of spontaneous emotional combustion when all his affections went up in flames like banned books, all that wasted romantic potential smoldering away in a pile of glowing ashes. He had even written Liza a poem, a love poem like those he had written for Helen, inspired as he watched her whirl and twirl with abandon among her eclectic ensemble of friends on a frenetic dance floor to the tribal beat of a mediocre band on an otherwise ordinary Saturday night. He had structured the poem so the first letter of each line, when spelled out, said "Watching Liza Dance," and he even remembered how it started: "While I stood and like a leaf as autumn crisped and tipped its breath with crazy threats and self-infliction's handsome wounds adorned my mood." Well, okay, not exactly like his Helen poems—more wary, more angsty—but it spoke of love, and he thought it was pretty good, and Liza seemed to think so, too. The New Yorker, however, less so. She had told him one time, frustrated by his gloomy disposition, "Oh, Matt. The world is filled with angels, but all you see are demons," which, he thought at the time, sounded a bit melodramatic, but she gazed into his eyes with nothing but love and looked so poised and earnest, so heartbreakingly sincere, as if this were a farewell address after that final straw, and, oh well, there is no need to dwell on that anymore, his bewildering self-defeating lapses of love, his mutinous betrayal of all his true emotions, and his shame and devastating self-consciousness was more than he could bear so just forget about it and Quick! Snap back! No misery thoughts. No. Not now.

And so on and so forth as he walks past a tumbling waterfall and watches a kingdom of ants building a hill, a pyramid for their ant pharaoh, a grain-by-grain civilization so doomed on the side of the road, just like his decrepit brick house in the slums of heaven, his mud hovel. Aren't we all just as doomed on our own roadsides? There's a fresh rainy fragrance in the air, kind of minty, and his skin feels vibrant and ionized, if that is the right word, and everything, really everything, is just fine right now, just fine at this single simple moment, this brilliant second. He feels at peace even with all of his wild-assed thoughts and it's little by little, step by step, ride by ride, keep your thumb out and stay tuned, keep reading the wind and working the rudder. For he is now the noble and mighty Matthew A. Mahoney, the eternal hobo, master of all he surveys, free of demons at last, and so on and so forth, with spiraling paper airplanes of transcendent thought gliding the invisible currents of his skull until a van crashes through the fragile structure of his roving mental meanderings and pulls over to give him a ride as all the paper airplanes whiz away and dissolve into the clouds of someone else's imagination.

In the van were two girls and a guy from New York City who had stayed at North Bay the night before. They were going to the Soo, 270 miles, and then heading south into Michigan on Route 75. Matt inhaled the familiar aroma as soon as he got in, and the door had hardly shut before the torched joint was all aglow between his lips, and everybody was predicting with certainty that marijuana would be legal in ten years max.

Sitting beside Matt was a dark-skinned Italianesque girl. It soon dawned on him that the driver and his girlfriend were trying with blunt innuendos to match them up. The idea was appealing except that he was hoping to meet up with Maureen at the Soo that evening and didn't want to botch up his chances. The matter was quickly settled when the girl stifled the innuendos with a staunch silence and even made a sour facial expression, not meant for Matt to see, indicating the unpleasantness of the suggestion.

Matt pretended he hadn't decoded their less-than-cryptic comments, and he was relieved when the subject was changed. Still, the sense of rejection and self-revulsion settled inside him like a rotten wad of bad memories. It spoiled his high—he even refused the next joint—and forced him to bury himself beneath that remote, unembraceable detachment of self that he so detested but could not deflect. Then, to make matters worse, a favorite old song from his Helenic period menaced him through the speakers:

*Whatever happened to Tuesday and so slow*
*Going down the old mine with a transistor radio*
*Standing in the sunlight laughing*
*Hiding behind a rainbow's wall*
*Slipping and sliding*
*All along the waterfall with you*
*My brown-eyed girl*
*You, my brown-eyed girl*

All those old love songs that used to make him happy now just resonated with the vibrational frequencies of his inexpressible sorrows and gave them wings. There were some he couldn't listen to without sinking into one of his old man's Eugene O'Neill depressions: "Your name and mine inside a heart upon a wall / Still finds a way to haunt me though they're so small." That one was his big kryptonite, but sometimes almost any old song would do.

*Like father, like son*, he lamented as he began withering away. Bye, bye, New Matt.

Welcome home, Weird Matt.

They went through Sudbury and passed signs that boasted about "The Big Nickel," a huge smokestack at a nearby nickel mine. They then stretched at a rest stop where squirrels ate right out of his hand. The fumes from a nearby pulp mill pervaded the atmosphere with the putrid stench of a million farts. Between Sudbury and the Soo, the

130

curse of obsessive introspection overtook Matt's mind, and he fell into the grip of a morose, self-pitiful mood, absorbing dysfunction as if he were bathing in it. He withdrew into muteness, somber thoughts and a brooding, intent listening. His axis had shifted, and everything had gone all off kilter. The voices of radio DJs and newscasters lulled his mind into a trance in which he could hear, loud and clear, the imperceptible gulps of air they took to refill their lungs before spewing out their words, as if speech itself were a primitive struggle and language an ineffective form of communication. He nearly screamed at them through the radio to stop their gulping and shut up. Simple words of everyday use began to sound foreign and devoid of meaning. Everything became babble. Context evaporated. Words died and became so artificial and arbitrary that there was no longer any logical link between any word and its meaning.

Matt was losing his grip on that link, and his mind was drifting toward a universe of abstractions, a wordless chaos of thought, as with someone who is deaf from birth or like a caveman's mind might have been before the invasion of speech, before thoughts and ideas were caged by words, before letters and alphabets and crude utterances made slaves of men's minds and everyone existed within the pure listening silence of uncivilized non-verbal thoughts. Nothing meant anything. The alphabet disintegrated into a random collection of meaningless symbols and sounds. Why should this particular stick-figure shape be called "A" and why should it be pronounced as "A"? And why is it first? Is everything arbitrary? Who decided such things, and what gave them the nerve or the right to do that? Words had become his enemy, his assassin. If he could only escape the world of words and seek asylum in a preverbal paradise, maybe the purity of his intentions would mean something. Maybe he would not cringe with embarrassment during his nightly gauntlet of bloody self-review. It was all becoming so confusing, all those evil and murderous words clogging up his head, as the van kept on grinding westward.

When the mad impulse to be completely alone consumed him and his thoughts got scrambled in a hail of mental static, he nearly asked to be dropped off in the middle of nowhere onto Route 68 at Espanola, planning to use the improbable pretense that he wanted to hitch down to Manitoulin, which, based on a review of his map, appeared to be an island of no hostels and few roads, towns, or inhabitants. And he with no tent. Instead, he kept his mouth shut, feeling like a nondescript nobody, all absurd and ugly and undesirable, and tolerated the claustrophobic discomfort of the van. He had to get away from this girl who, he was certain, was sickened by the thought of kissing him.

He thought of Carla. He had kissed her just once, one humid summer night, sitting in a dugout at the athletic fields. He had clung to the belief that the touch of her lips would seal the deal, just as it had happened with Helen, and then—presto!—romantic enchantment, and it would be that brand-new happy-together love feeling all over again. He was waiting for the wow, but the wow never came. It was, alas, not a joint endeavor. She neither resisted nor encouraged him. All he got was a lackluster dry-lipped response and an uncomfortable silent aftermath. There were no bells and no whistles. It was just a fool's charade. Her hands remained at rest upon her knees and did not reach to caress his shoulders or the back of his head to pull him closer, deeper. And she did not poise herself for an encore. She just sat there, frozen, with a downcast gaze. She didn't even close her eyes or lose a single breath. It was nothing like Helen, with her full reciprocal embrace and her ready lips. He got the feeling that, with Carla, for as much and as long as he had been anticipating their first-ever kiss, she had been dreading it in equal measures. But still, despite her clear message, he persisted, drowning in hope. He simply could not metabolize her indifference.

For the duration of the ride he stewed in the dismal image of himself as "Weird Matt," the goofball kid who was so awkward around girls that his affections for them did not even deserve consideration. Weird Matt, the self-imagined object of ridicule who self-sabotaged each reasonable romantic opportunity with his ignorant babbling and his inability to make that all-important first move, tripping over his feet with his jealous insecurities and his preoccupation with his own inadequacies. He was the paralytic Romeo who worshiped women from afar but did not, would not, could not approach them for fear of being booted off the balcony of his childish longings.

There was also his laundry list of girls linked to regrettable encounters, such as Deanna at The Bronze Bell (he froze and did not speak to her, and she took and then let go of his hand and walked away without saying anything), Marlene at Westland University (they talked for a long time, she smiled and laughed with him, she gave him a big come-on, he ignored or fumbled it, and she sidled away and found someone more receptive), Jan at the Elton John concert in Saratoga (she made advances and whispered in his ear, and then he spurned her with an air of disinterest and said he had to leave), and Sue at The College Inn (he wrote her one of his ill-conceived late-night pour-your-whole-heart-out letters which succeeded only in scaring her away and making him look strange and unstable), and finally the English prostitute Maggie, staying in the room next to his at the cheap Earls Court B&B in London, whose flirty spirit invited him over for a freebie but, no, he couldn't do it, even as she removed her bra in front of him, relieving it of its precious cargo, smiling with engaging eyes, and he just stood there unresponsive, an insignificant little pill bug. Despite the admonishments of his flummoxed brain shouting at him, reminding him that you cannot violate the willing! And to every other humiliating memory of failure embodied in the face of every girl he had desired so badly. Each episode just another sequel in his catastrophic comedy of errors. He had wanted them all, but his actions, or lack thereof, betrayed that desire. Why, then, all this self-sabotage? Now, to make matters even more pathetic, he realized that his utter failure was not from a lack of opportunity. It was from a cowardly lack of nerve.

It was two in the afternoon when he sprang from the prison of the van just outside Sault St. Marie. *Ah. Freedom at last*, he thought, as though the source of his emotional frenzy were lodged in the van disguised as a girl who was disinterested in his kiss. He got directions at a gas station and began to walk and walk and walk off the deep, deep, simmering blues, but it was too little, too late. Those blues were already in him, embedded and engorged like a blob of bloated ticks. He decided that, ultimately, way down within, he despised people, even though he may have admired them at first. Worst of all, despite whatever good first impression he might have made, it would soon wear thin and they would all eventually despise him in return. He was okay in small doses only. Then it all gets depressing and futile and he would just want to disappear and never talk to anybody again, ever. He wished he had the courage to do that one thing that would solve all things.

*Fuck! I thought I left this stupid shit behind. I would have a lot more fun if I didn't have to bring me along.* But even way out there, in the remote expanse of that interminable Canadian province, he was getting the old hometown squeeze, and he began to squirm within the confines of his Old Matt skin as his daymare took hold. He felt a tremor. "It found me," he whispered aloud, as he tripped over the fault line and the derangement settled in and took over as if it had discovered its own living room.

Without warning, there It was, behind him and above his shoulder. The Watcher with Its lidless, infrared gargoyle eyes piercing straight through all his New Matt bullshit, licking Its parched green lips with Its slimy prehensile tongue, hungry and on the prowl, saying "Fuck you, asshole," and cackling with pleasure as Matt succumbed to a fit of fear and crumbled into a defeated heap. His chest pounded and his ruptured heart began racing and his breath came to him in feeble and shallow grabs. A whirring helicopter roar plugged up his ears and made sensible thought impossible. His skull swelled to bursting with a turbulence of roiling blood that was erupting like lava throughout his brain. It was heart attack time again.

Everything hit him all at once, and a tempest swept through all his defenses, leaving him rudderless, and he wanted nothing other than to be transported back to the security of his home, to be in his kitchen watching TV and eating a home-cooked meal with his mother, instead of sailing out here on the wild current of some godforsaken disorbital path, struggling to strike a balance between his two competing homesicknesses: the sickness of being home and the sickness of being away from home. When he left home he hadn't planned to stray this far away, and until this moment the impact of his distance had not yet registered. He had been unwise to venture alone across the borderlands and beyond the frontier of his umbilical hometown orbit. He could feel the tension of all the miles behind him stretching, stretching, stretching the cord like a slingshot until it was ready to snap and launch him away to wherever such unguided missiles crash-land. He sat locked within a dark space, blind to everything, spiders crawling in his hair and cobwebs glued across his face, afraid and fearing death—but, no, not yet ready for that.

Low-flying planes from a local airport roared above him, soaring to and from places unknown, gliding just beyond his reach. Song lyrics parachuted into his ears with a cargo of potent melancholia:

> *In the early morning rain*
> *With a dollar in my hand*
> *With an aching in my heart*
> *And my pockets full of sand*
> *I'm a long way from home*
> *And I miss my loved ones so*
> *In the early morning rain*
> *With no place to go*

Though it was neither early morning nor raining, he sobbed in spasms with the forlorn lyric looping in his brain. He dug a wishbone from his pack, snapped it in two as he made a wish, and let the sobs flourish unabashed because he was a stranger stranded on a barren stretch of highway out there in East Bumfuck, Ontario, and there was no one nearby to witness the spectacle he had become.

It was pathetic at first. There he was, helpless as a worm, but once he surrendered to the fit that filled him, he recognized it as a great-great-grandchild of an old tantrum, still writhing and wanting its way like a barely buried baby bird that still clung to life. He floated above himself and studied the symptoms of his illness as if he were his own patient.

*The last attack that had been this bad was in January in New York City. He had hitched there by himself to see* Modern Times *at the Lincoln Center, the Charlie Chaplin classic and the last great movie of the silent era, the mute era. The simple humanity of the little tramp and the poignant sadness of the film resonated with Matt's own loneliness and epic sense of helplessness. When he exited the theater into the cold labyrinth of the streets of Manhattan, he became the little tramp, poetically adrift among the uncaring multitudes. He walked all the way to Greenwich Village, and with each step he sank deeper into the panicky existential quicksand that always swallowed him whole. The other pedestrians became alien and threatening. His thoughts began to warp. He was far from home and trapped inside an evil metropolis. His heart began to pound out of control, ready to burst open from an unidentifiable internal pressure. His chest was heaving and sinking as he started to run down the street through the crowd to get away, from what he did not know, from within, from without, he could not tell. He was convinced he was going to die and thought that maybe someone had poisoned his popcorn or coke at the movie and it had already worked its way into his bloodstream and it was too late to do anything about it. He thought everyone was staring at him, laughing at him, ridiculing him, following him, as if they were all in cahoots, and he ran away from anyone who happened to look at him. He escaped to the safety of a subway, got out in the Bronx, and walked to an entrance ramp of the Major Deegan Expressway and hitched back home overnight, crawling into his bed at dawn before his mother woke up. As always, after he recuperated, he felt ashamed and pretended it hadn't happened.*

Now, heading west alone, he wondered how he could have been so foolish. What was he trying to prove? He was certain he was setting himself up for another ambush that would detonate his heart. With all his false-alarm heart attack scares, he felt he had become a parody of Fred Sanford, shouting, "It's the big one! Hear that, Elizabeth? I'm coming to join you, Honey!"

Out on this far-flung Ontario highway, he cried for longer than he could ever remember crying. It all thrashed through him in gusts and waves, and when it was over he felt depleted and relieved, like a marathon runner collapsing at the finish line. His homesickness and anxiety had vanished. His heart was again calm and strong. His mind was refreshed and alert, back on kilter. He had crossed the Rubicon and was no longer afraid. All that remained was a profound silence. He was cleansed by tears.

Matt took a dip in the lake beside the hostel and then toweled his hair without brushing it. He liked the way it dried into an almost-Afro, like Bob Dylan on the cover of *Blonde on Blonde*, but longer. A guy on a motorcycle pulled up, removed his helmet and shades, and dismounted. In his fringed buckskin jacket, he was a cross between the Marlboro Man and a hip Dennis Hopper "Easy Rider" biker. He walked right up to Matt and introduced himself.

"Hi. My name is Leo."

"Hi. I'm Matt. Matt Mahoney."

"Nice to meetcha, Matt. Man. I feel like I've been running a jackhammer all day. My body is quaking and my ass is killing me. My teeth hurt. And, oh man, I have to take an epic piss. I'm backed up like the Grand Coulee Dam, man." He gripped Matt's flimsy hand, gave it a manly pump, and explained that he had just come non-stop from Thunder Bay on his way home to Ottawa.

Leo excused himself to take his epic piss, and when he returned Matt asked him why he didn't stay at Wawa and shorten his riding day by about 150 miles.

"I was gonna do that but the hostel was a bummer. You'd think it was a refugee camp the way they all gathered around my bike, asking me for rides. I told them I was going to the store and I would be right back and then I just took off. *Very* strange. Besides, I'm more seat-of-my-pants than plan-in-advance, so here I am."

Leo was over six feet tall and armed with a good-natured smile—not your stereotypical macho-man biker, though he had the size to fit that profile. He was more inclined to mellowing out, listening to music, and getting stoned with friends. He played bass guitar in a "psychedelic acid-rock-and-blues garage band," a "cool little combo" called The Nightowls.

"I'm left-handed. I play a Hofner, like McCartney. I'm barely competent. I play guitar a bit too. But all those upside-down and backward left-handed chords got confusing and I never got my own guitar. So I gave up on that and just stuck with the bass. I wish I were as good at it as much as I dig it. How about you?"

"Yeah. Kind of. I mess around on the guitar."

"Are you in a band?"

"No. I used to be. Lasted about two weeks. I'm not good enough. I'm mediocre at best. As they say, 'Practice makes mediocre.'"

"Hey, man. Don't let that stop you. Most people can't tell the difference. And by 'most people,' I am referring to your female fans. What was the name of your band?"

"The Electromagnetic Garbage Can Covers." Matt scratched at the knots in his scraggly beard as Leo erupted into a round of good-natured laughter. He felt his status elevated by his near proximity and the air of mutual camaraderie with someone as cool as Leo. They threw the Frisbee around for a while and then each wandered off in a different direction, humming tunes.

Maureen showed up as planned, and Matt teased her that he had reached the hostel quicker than she did. She teased back.

"That's 'cause you've got nicer legs than I do."

That was, quite obviously, not true. He blushed and became absorbed by the perfection of her legs, so smooth and bronze, and couldn't resist the teasing image of running the palm of his hand across the bulge of her muscular calf and up to the tender inside of her mid-thigh and to the frayed threads of her cut-off jeans.

As the late Ontario sunset ripened through its final purple throes and the striated fire in the western horizon went black with ashes, Matt and Maureen walked by the lake looking at the stars and talking about dreams, about journeys taken and those that still awaited.

"Dreams," she said, "are all pieces to the puzzle of who we truly are. The more we study them, the more we discover our missing pieces and the better we can understand ourselves. Sometimes when I'm in the middle of a vivid dream, I realize that I'm asleep and that none of this is real. Who knows? Maybe I'm dreaming now and you're just part of my dream."

"Or maybe," Matt said, "we're together because we're both dreaming the same dream from different places."

Soon they were lying down in the cool silky grass, gazing up into the luminous star-studded northern sky, enveloped by the sounds and smells of the dark Canadian universe. The air was a pleasant blend of onion and mint and wet organic decay. Matt's nostrils tingled. A melodious choir of crickets chirped and twittered from every angle. Chubby bullfrogs bellowed from their shallow muddy berths like slimy Buddhas. Bats swooped overhead, their silhouetted shadows flapping against a moonlit canopy. Mosquitoes buzzed around their ears and dive-bombed onto their moistened skin, drilling for an untapped pool of warm blood.

"What's your favorite constellation?" Maureen asked, mesmerized by the dome of stars twinkling in the wide heavens above them like millions of Earthbound headlights. Her tone was intimate. He was nervous and pleased.

"I'm not sure I have a favorite." He didn't want to sound wishy-washy so he dug deeper. "Probably the Pleiades. Or Orion, because my brother Rory is definitely Orion."

"What is so definitely Orion about him?"

"Orion is supposed to be a great hunter. Handsome and strong. It makes me think of him." He got sidetracked by worried thoughts about Rory. "What about you? What's your favorite constellation?"

"I don't actually have a favorite. But my favorite star is the North Star." She scanned the heavens and pointed. "See? There it is. When I was a kid, my father—he's very outdoorsy—taught me how to use a compass and how to identify the Big and Little Dippers and the North Star and lots of the constellations and planets. He told me that no matter what happened, he would always be my North Star. I thought he was so cool when he said that. I remember that I gave him a big hug and a kiss and told him that I loved him. I remember how happy he looked when I did that. And he's kept his word because I've always been able to depend on him, even though we've had our battles and I've been a bit of a wild child. Now, every time I look up and locate the North Star, I think of that moment and—wham!—I'm back home with my father. He's always able to find the happiness in me." A smile crept up upon her face as she sang in a whisper, "And I can't find my way home."

"Are you with him now?"·

She looked at Matt, pleased by his question, and replied, "Of course."

Neither spoke for a thirty-second eternity as they each sank into vastly different fatherly reveries. Matt tried to identify the few other constellations he could remember and then let his gaze dissolve into the expansive yellow sea of the full moon.

He said, "You know, people are always talking about the man in the moon. No matter how hard I look, I've never been able to actually see an image of a man up there."

"You're kidding?"

"No. I've tried. I've had people describe it to me and I think I see what they mean. But I can't ever be certain."

"How about now?" she asked. "Can't you see a face up there?" The moon could not have been larger or brighter nor its features more distinct.

"Nope. I mean, I kinda see one, but it would be dishonest to say that I see a face. It would be a leap of faith that I can't get myself to make."

He had hoped she would agree with him and, together, they could scoff at such a notion. But instead she described where the eyes were, the shape of the face, the direction it was looking and where all those features were imprinted on the yellow disc above them and said, "It's right there all the time. Plain as day. Maybe you don't want to see it. Sometimes you've just got to allow yourself to fill in the blanks. Think of it as abstract art. You've got to use your imagination." She sounded so kind, as if she were trying to heal some wound within him.

Matt explained, "I remember once, in second grade, our teacher, Mrs. Baldwin, was teaching us about the different kinds of clouds and she asked if anybody had ever seen clouds that looked like cotton balls. Everybody shouted 'yes' and raised their hands except for me. I was hoping she wouldn't notice me, but she did. She asked me directly and I told her 'no' because I didn't want to lie. She held up the class and got a book out, one of those big science books for kids, and showed me pictures of the kinds of clouds she was talking about and asked me again. For the life of me, the clouds did not look like cotton balls. They just looked like clouds. But I got so flustered and embarrassed that I lied just to get it over with. That's when I learned it was better to keep my mouth shut and go along with the crowd. Now, here I am again, only this time it's the man in the moon."

Maureen laughed. "Has that been bothering you all these years? Relax, Matt. Just let go and relax. It's no big deal. That was years ago. You're funny. Sometimes you're so easy going, you have a great sense of humor, and you don't seem to have a care in the world. But other times you're so serious, like the weight of the world is on your shoulders. If you were really just a guy who followed the crowd, you wouldn't be here now, hundreds of miles from home, laying in the grass with an underage Michigan runaway who straps a knife to her leg. You'd be home, working a summer job between semesters at college, and I'd be all by myself, sitting back there at the hostel, all lonely and bored, writing a letter or a postcard to somebody or other, because I didn't have anybody to talk to. That's not you. You are different than you think you are." She punched him playfully on the arm and looked right at him with dreamy eyes and an inviting smile. "Will the real Matt please stand up?"

He cringed with embarrassment and regretted bringing up the subject. "Guilty as charged," he said, and forced a weak laugh. "Just call me Atlas." In an effort to regain his footing, Matt said, "In the grand scheme of things, we're all just insignificant little specks. Just look at all those stars, billions of miles from here. None of this matters. It's hardly even real. Someday this will all be gone, and none of it will have made any difference."

Maureen perked up, propped herself on an elbow, looked him in the eye and said, "It's amazing that you just said that. I said the exact same thing to my father just a few months ago. He smiled at me and put his hands on my shoulders and rested his forehead against mine and said, just barely more than a whisper, he told me, 'You're a smart kid. I know what you mean, and I guess it's true.' He said he used to believe that, too—until I came along. He said that I was so tiny and helpless in my mother's arms and that, looking at me, all he could feel was pure love and that it filled his heart and soul and the whole hospital room. That's when he realized that everything matters, every little thing. Because we don't live in the grand scheme. We can ponder it, but we live in the minutiae, in the here and now, where everything matters and everyone is important. He said that he had been the center of his universe before I was born. Then, in a split-second, the Earth shifted and everything revolved around me and that it would always be his job to protect me. Then he said that there's nothing we can do about the grand scheme. It's out of our hands. All we can do is try to manage the here and now."

She was still smiling into his eyes. He didn't know what to say, managing only, "You've got a pretty cool father."

They both lay back on the grass. No one spoke. He could hear the pounding drumbeat of his heart. From the corner of his eye he saw Maureen's chest rising and sinking with each long wave of breath as her hand inched so close to his that he could feel the warmth of her flesh. He resisted the temptation to turn his head toward her out of sheer fear and the impending panic of what might happen if their eyes met. He hated that he was so serious and that there was a glitch inside him that wouldn't let him see the man in the moon or those cotton ball clouds, wouldn't let him relax in the comfort of his dreams, wouldn't let him fill in the blanks, and wouldn't release its grip and let him roll over and put his arms around her and kiss her and feel the smooth of her skin, though the whole unfathomable cosmos was telling him that now was the time to do that. Something in him knew she would let him touch her, that she was just then moistening her tongue and wetting her lips for his and was adjusting the cradle of her low center of gravity to receive the full weight of his body upon hers with warm welcoming arms.

But he dared not. He couldn't break loose. His stars had turned against him. Rigor mortis had set in, and he could not move. Maybe she would perceive his fear and sense how badly he wanted her and would take his   hand, place it upon her, and ask him, please, to kiss her. He would obey her command. But he knew he would not do it on his own. He would not, could not make that first forbidden move. So he just lay there, lamenting all his missing puzzle pieces. The only voice he heard was the one repeating the same old mantra over and over in his head: *It's wrong. It's wrong. Too pure. Too perfect. Maybe should not touch.*

Matt, ever the obedient Catholic school second grader, heeded that voice, though he could hear Maureen breathing beside him, summoning him. As the night grew late, he watched himself let the opportunity fizzle. As they trudged back to the hostel and to their separate dorms and dreams, he felt like a little boy, the tiniest of specks, plodding ineffectually and absurdly beside a full-grown woman. Maureen was heading to Michigan the next morning to be reunited with her family, so Matt knew he had blown an ideal chance, his last chance to cross with her into that next more intimate dimension of friendship. If she asked him to come with her he would have said "yes" without hesitation. But that did not happen, and Matt made no such suggestion. Though he had fallen far short of his great expectations, he tried convincing himself that it was a sort of consolation prize to at least have spent so much time with her because he was sure that in this emotionally greedy and cutthroat world, the demand for such companionship was considerable. Even he knew, though, that was a bullshit excuse and he was getting sick and tired of consolation prizes and of his own wimpy cowardice and half-assed rationalizations for not taking any initiative to test the depths of Maureen's affections for him.

The lights were still on in the men's dorm, which was filled with sleeping bags arranged in parallel rows on the floor. Matt situated himself next to Leo, who was staring at a dog-eared paperback.

"Where have *you* been?" Leo queried with a sly grin.

"I was walking around the lake with Maureen." He tried to sound matter-of-fact.

"You dirty dog. I knew there was something goin' on between you two."

"Yeah. I wish." Matt was pleasantly embarrassed.

"What do you mean, you wish? Couldn't you see the way she was looking at you? She was all yours, man. She was into you. I could see the sparks."

Matt knew that guys say those kinds of things all the time, whether or not it's true, just to make each other feel good.

"Right. In my dreams."

"I tell ya. She was sending all the right signals. The vibes were strong. She digs you, man. Couldn't you feel it? Or are you too much of a gentleman? A real prince. Don't want to take advantage of a helpless maiden."

"I admit it. I choked, man. I had the perfect chance and I chickened out. As for helpless, did you see that knife she carries?" Funny thing, he thought, that it wasn't so bad when he was able to talk about it. The stewing didn't sink in and he could almost, just about almost, see the humor in his farcical dilemma.

As the room settled down and the lights were dimmed, all the sleepyhead vagabonds began to doze off. Leo started telling Matt about different places he'd been.

"It might be out of the way, but you've got to go up to Edmonton for Klondike Days and the pancake breakfast. It's a celebration. A huge party, man. And, best of all, it's free."

As it turned out, Leo admitted that he hadn't himself attended the Klondike Days but had heard about it from others who had also heard about it, and it appealed to his imagination. He was a second cousin once removed from the actual experience.

"A free breakfast? Pancakes? Anything else?"

"Yeah. Sausage, eggs, juice. Standard fare. You name it."

"Sounds fantastic. I'll be there!"

Hitchhikers love free stuff. It fits in with the philosophy of thrift and the science of day-to-day, hand-to-mouth existence that is so dear to their hearts. It was a no-brainer. He would go to Edmonton for the free pancake breakfast and for nothing else, even though it was hundreds of miles out of his way.

They started talking about Eskimos and favorite movies and continued to talk even after the lights went out. It reminded Matt of when he was in grade school and shared a bedroom with Rory. They would have pillow fights at night, jumping back and forth on their twin beds like junior warriors in training, knocking each other down and taking turns playing dead and then miraculously resurrecting themselves for another bout in a world of laughter and how they whispered and giggled and joked around in the dark long after they were given several ultimatums from their mother.

Matt and Leo had been hushed a few times but continued talking in low, whispered tones. Their whispers, however, were amplified by the brittle silence of the room. Finally, when Leo declared in a gruff and poorly muffled sing-songy voice, "I'm a Neanderthal man. You're a Neanderthal girl. Let's make Neanderthal love in this Neanderthal world," someone yelped, "Will you please shut up so that us *Homo sapiens* can sleep!"

They obeyed like reprimanded children, snorting and suppressing giggles. Soon, they too were chasing sleep down that winding corridor of consciousness, slipping toward its weird threshold and to that man-in-the-moon land of soft caresses and jigsaw puzzle dreams. Just before that steel door slammed shut, Matt heard the dwindling echo of Leo's voice from the depths of his own corridor: "Hey Matt. You awake? Don't let me forget to tell you. *The Naked Prey*. Great movie." Leo's voice trailed off into semi-syllables and then faded away, resurfacing for a final drowsy moment as he mumbled, "Dodging spears, man. I'm just dodging spears."

# CHAPTER X

It was a bittersweet goodbye scene. Matt, as usual, grew too attached too soon despite his pledges to claim the emotional upper hand and maintain his hip role as the aloof loner he aspired to become. Leo gave Matt his address and wrote out his name so that the O in Osmen was fashioned as a peace sign. He flashed that universal hippie signal, the two-fingered one, with his right hand and said, "Peace, man" and then revved east on his bike, anxious to get back home to his bass and his band.

Matt and Maureen exchanged addresses and vows that they would write. As they said a hurried goodbye, all his secret lovesick emotions were scurrying about, praying for a last-minute reprieve and cursing Matt for his slipshod performance the previous evening and for doing nothing to prevent their premature demise.

He had rehearsed saying, "Why don't we spend another day here, check out the town, and take another walk by the lake after dinner?" Her answer would determine his future. Still, he said nothing and left the option of a final say to her.

"It was nice to meet you, Matt. Three hostels in three days. It was great, but I suppose this is it. Stay in touch."

Then, as moisture bathes his eyes, she kisses him lightly on the cheek and gets into the back seat of the car that brings her to Michigan and to her North Star father. He is perplexed for wanting to tell her he loves her, though he barely knows her, and mouths the words, but she is not looking. As the car pulls away, she turns and stares at him, into and through and beyond his eyes, and instead of waving she presses her open palm against the rear window. Matt can feel her warmth even as the distance grows greater. He raises his open palm in her direction, and the heat and energy of their splayed hands connects and bridges the void between them, bringing them together, and he thinks, "Sail on, silver girl," which, even at the time, feels corny but real nonetheless. Then he makes two fists, punches both thighs, and watches as she fades from view, and he wishes he had just one more day and one more chance. And above him the blue sky was dotted with cotton ball clouds, but his head was hung downward and he could not see them.

*Ah yes*, he thinks, *crushed in flight by time's tight vise. Or is it vice?*

The great advantage of the vagrant hostel-hitching lifestyle was that before Matt had time to dive into a deep mope of self-loathing and depression at the departure of one friend, a new one always emerged over the horizon. He met Ray at the hitching spot on the highway and, though they had been standing apart, the gap closed as they shouted conversation back and forth. He was tall and solid, a big-bicepped, Hollywood-handsome, James Garner type. Matt, on the other hand, had been compared to the homely likes of Prince Charles, Gary Lewis, and Frank Zappa, none of whom had ever been accused of being handsome. Ray carried a golf club and played his cards close to the vest, answering only, "West," when asked where he was going. They were soon hitching together, throwing pebbles into an empty ant-infested bean can they found in the scrub bushes and then placing the can on a roadside post and using it for target practice.

The morning grew dark as herds of clouds stampeded like buffalo across the sky. Just as they reached their breaking point and bullets of rain began exploding all around them, George from Pittsburgh pulled over in a VW bug and rescued the boys.

"Welcome aboard my horizontal terrestrial transportation module, gentlemen. I call it the Enterprise, and I will be your captain on this journey."

Long-legged Ray called first dibs on the front seat. Matt scrunched himself in the back beside all the baggage. The boys rejoiced to learn that George could take them all the way to Thunder Bay, which meant that they had beaten the Wawa curse. George got his stash out of the glove compartment and asked Matt and Ray if they wouldn't mind rolling a supply of bombers for the transplanetary trek through the Lake Superior universe.

"Might as well get that out of the way now. We won't want to do it after we get wasted. Or we won't be able to because we'll be wasted in the wasteland."

George was enjoying the easy rider camaraderie and the uninhibited respite from the pressure of his studies as a math major at college and was both discovering and inventing himself in a freewheeling non-academic classroom of another sort. He was magnanimous with his stash as well as with a pouch of delicious bologna and ham salad sandwiches and ice-cold soft drinks he kept in a cooler in the cubbyhole space behind the back seat.

"I am constantly finding interesting number combinations on my odometer. Just before you guys got in it was at 126,126 and I thought that, for that one mile, until the last six turned into a seven, I was skating on that configuration. I think the Enterprise was also digging the symmetry of its mileage."

Matt's deft fingers produced tight little numbers that burned evenly all the way down to the roach end. Rolling joints in a moving vehicle required more skill than if he were sitting at a table in someone's apartment with the gatefold album cover to *The Allman Brothers: Live At Fillmore East* wide open as a flat surface for separating the leafy substance from the seeds and stems and then sprinkling it into a single gummed sheet of E-Z Wider or Zig-Zag rolling papers. It required even more skill to produce the same result from an opened baggy on his lap in the cramped quarters of the back seat of a tiny car bumping along the highway during a wild storm. Matt was proud that the quality of his joints compared favorably to those Ray had rolled.

After they finished the first joint and snorted up the smoke from the roach that Matt roasted between two flaming match heads, Ray said, "This is some powerful weed. I am already toasted."

"Yeah. Primo shit. Oh, I forgot to tell you. It's opiated."

"Opiated! Oh shit!"

*Matt had smoked opiated hash in the basement of a friend's house one summer evening when he was seventeen. It was so potent that one of them swore he saw a ghost drift past the doorway and through a wall. Then he and his friends got lost during the routine five-minute drive to Bromski's, the bar where they hung out with their fake IDs before they were eighteen and old enough to drink. They managed to find the bar only after meandering for half an hour through the suddenly foreign streets of their own town, making wrong turns and arguing over the directions. Starry-eyed and laughing, they entered the garish carnival atmosphere of the bar and fought back against the assaultive glare of ceiling lights and the jack-hammer anarchy of juke box music, which blended with the droning buzz and babble of dozens of high-pitched cartoon-character conversations. Matt spent the next half hour, or so it seemed, hiding in a protective transparent bubble of pure energy in a corner seat as John Bonham hurled hundreds of drumsticks at him from within the heart of the jukebox goddess where the magically miniaturized members of Led Zeppelin were performing "Whole Lotta Love" and trying to break out of their glassed-in confinement with the sheer volume and force of their song. Within the twisty realm of his contorted mind, Matt was afraid the band would break free of the juke and that the rowdy crowd would step on them and squash them into the floor boards. He was warning the tottering patrons to be careful. The song was everlasting. At times he mistook the primitive drumbeat for his own heartbeat and couldn't tell which was louder or faster. He remained in the corner, ass glued to the chair, fending off drumsticks, until his hunger got the best of him and food became a matter of utmost urgency.*

*The driver, Waggy Taylor, was too stoned to drive, and besides, he couldn't remember where he had put his car keys.*

*"I'm not sure, man. I either locked them in the car to keep them safe or else I might have flushed them down the toilet. 'Cause I am pretty sure I had them when we drove over here." Waggy had become a simpleton.*

*Matt and the rest of the boys, succumbing to a severe munchies craving and knowing they would have to walk someplace if they wanted food, huddled at their table and unanimously decided that the closest place to eat was Carroll's Drive-In, a fast-food burger joint just north of New Holland, about three or four miles away by road but only a mile or so, maybe even less, if they cut straight across the unknown terrain of the abandoned stud farm between Bromski's and Carroll's. As they exited the bar, the bartender called to them, "Don't slip on the ice." It was August.*

*In their opiated stupor they convinced themselves that it would be an easy hike, fifteen minutes tops, and that they'd be back before their jukebox quarters kicked in. Thus, they embarked on an epic quest for cheeseburgers and fought their way, stumbling and falling through a dense forest of untrimmed overgrowth and undergrowth and in-between growth. Matt surged onward, channeling Humphrey Bogart in* The African Queen. *There were bushy ravines and hillocks, surprise ponds and puddles and mucky swamps, razor-sharp prickers and woodchuck holes, and reptiles and amphibians and hosts of other obstacles. They emerged an hour and a half later, filthy and soaking and covered in burrs and stinking like a cesspool, just as Carroll's was closing. They bought a few stale cheeseburgers and grabbed a lift back to Bromski's with a friend who laughed at their story and said, "You guys are totally boned, man. Phew, nice stench. Have you got any more of that shit? This town has been, like, completely dry lately."*

With that experience as his only opiated precedent, he was worried that the unfamiliar wilderness surroundings, the company of unproven strangers and the crammed backseat quarters of the Enterprise would be catalyzed into a paranoid and unsafe high. George started imitating Captain Kirk, talking in that stunted self-important William Shatner voice about star dates and unexplored galaxies and the ever-present threat of Romulan attack. Then Ray turned into Rod Serling.

"You're entering another dimension. A dimension not only of sight and of sound but of mind." The eerie stereo effect of their stoned impersonations from the front seat, on top of his rubberized perceptions, started playing tricks with his head, and for a few moments he thought that George was playing a Star Trek/Twilight Zone tape and that George and Ray were mouthing along with a recorded script and that their performances had both been somehow rehearsed beforehand just for Matt's amusement.

They had gone through a couple of heavy-duty joints and were all well into the ozone when the capricious sky turned crucifixion-day black and dumped out everything it had. Electric javelins struck the earth all around them. Large hailstones poured down by the millions, shattering against the tiny module so hard that Matt first thought it was a meteor shower, which, at the time, appeared to be a reasonable theory. The disorienting chaos of the hailstorm coupled with the mind-bending effects of the super-potent grass made all things seem possible and a good many of them probable. His befuddlement heightened when he couldn't find Thunder Bay on his map of Ontario, and he was convinced that they were lost on some wretched back road of this Canadian twilight zone. He pored over the map, tracing his finger along his route. No matter how many times he re-examined it, Thunder Bay was still nowhere to be found. It had somehow vanished from the face of the Earth. He finally figured it out: he was being kidnapped!

"Let me out! Let me out! Let me out!"

Through his own layers of fog, Ray somehow managed to catch on to why Matt was freaking out. "Relax, man. We're okay. We're not lost. I've been on this road before. I know exactly where we are. Give me that map." He looked it over for about 30 seconds and laughed. "No wonder. This is an old map. Thunder Bay didn't exist when it was made. These two cities here, Port Arthur and Fort William, they were combined a few years ago and renamed Thunder Bay."

Matt wasn't sure whether to believe him or not. How could they expect him to be so gullible? It sounded fishy. He still felt like he was behind enemy lines. How could two cities just disappear and a new one pop up out of nowhere? And what happened to all the people?

Ray showed him George's "Texaco Road Atlas," which identified Thunder Bay in bold highlights. Matt accepted the explanation but for a while continued to suspect that Ray and George, the masterminds behind his kidnapping, were in cahoots or were goofing on him. Luckily, his paranoia soon dissipated and he settled back into his seat in the Enterprise as it hurtled through outer space. For a while he rested within the twin rhythms of the windshield wipers and the music of the 8-track tape player as they sympathized with Matt's heart into a synchronized beat, singing, "I see a bad moon arisin' / I see trouble on the way."

Perhaps it was due to damage caused by the meteor shower or they had taken a few Romulan hits or maybe the Enterprise was being crippled by the Wawa anti-energy force field, but the VW was straining and chugging over the sloshy road as the rain continued to pour and the sky invented new shades of charcoal gray. George said, "Where's Scotty when you need him?"

Matt said, "Where's Tates when you need him?"

Ray said, "I don't know who Tates is but I think the battery's on the fritz." They turned off the highway and drove past a huge statue of a goose on the outside of town. George located the hostel as if the coordinates had been programmed into the Enterprise control panel. The vessel docked in the sloppy unpaved parking area and George turned off the ignition. When he tried to re-start the car, all he got was a stuttering series of weak clicks and then nothing.

The hostel was a dreary and cheerless sight, a desolation row encampment of drenched tents floating in a swampy field of mud. Disheartened hippie campers appeared from gloomy tent openings like disenfranchised souls in a hitchhiker's purgatory, their ponchos soaked through and clinging to their frumpy shoulders. Jeans and T-shirts and pullovers and socks hung dripping from a futile clothesline. This was no joyous celebratory Woodstock mud fest. No. This was a joyless Mudville.

The air was wringing wet, and, in the rush of cold wind that lashed its tail through the campground, Matt succumbed to a fit of shivers, which was quelled when he put on his denim jacket. He looked around and thought the Wawa outpost could be a fine place to spend a few days in pleasant weather, though it was more primitive than other hostels.

Ray shrugged and shook his head. "So much for not getting stuck in Wawa."

He and George were both car savvy and agreed that with a new battery they could make it to Thunder Bay where the alternator could be replaced. Unfortunately, they would have to spend the night marooned in the muck and mire of the cursed Wawa hostel.

Congregations of bedraggled travelers conspired in shabby tents, plotting their escape while drinking hot tea or coffee or spooning steamy soup from bowls held closely cupped to warm their hands. Ray worked the crowd and found a local kid who knew where they could buy a battery, but he was on a bicycle and they would have to trust him with the money. The kid made a couple of calls, collected the funds from George, with Ray and Matt chipping in, and beat it on his bike, hoping to get back before sunset. With his black poncho flapping behind him as he sliced a wet trail and whizzed into the distance, he was the very image of a runt Batman set off for Gotham on an urgent mission.

George and Ray and Matt stuck together like the Cartwright boys and ended up in the smoky haze of a large tent with a tribe of sorry souls sitting around a Coleman lantern telling tall tales and sad stories and passing around cheap wine and damp joints as the flickering light cast dancing shadows upon the dripping canvas. The wind was howling overhead through the trees and whistling madly through the cracks and nooks of the campground. A guy in a black top hat who seemed to be the ringmaster held the lantern beneath his face, gave an evil leer, and said, "Welcome to Hell."

Matt's taste in wine began and ended with Boone's Farm Apple, Strawberry Hill, and Annie Green Springs with maybe a quart of Ripple or Bali Hai every now and then. He looked suspiciously at the leather wineskin when it came his way. The dark figure beside him said, "Don't worry, man. It's not electric." George lit up one of his head blasters and added it to the mix of joints circulating the tent, which was filled with an intoxicating blend of smoky aromas.

A couple of dogs began sniffing and humping each other. A long-haired kid cultivating a wry Lennonesque look called for his dog: "Bilbo. Over here."

George laughed because he did not seem to know who Bilbo was and thought the kid said "Dildo." Matt laughed because he somehow knew that George thought the kid said "dildo" and Matt didn't want to explain who Bilbo was. Ray laughed because George, who didn't understand why Matt was laughing at him, had a stoned half-bemused cockeyed look on his face. The Lennonesque kid started laughing because he thought Matt and his friends were laughing at the humping dogs, and soon the whole tent exploded in a keg of laughter with everybody laughing for different reasons.

Everybody eventually started talking about where they were from and where they were going. There was a goofy straw hat that got passed around and placed onto the head of whichever person was speaking. One barefoot kid spoke up.

"I'm from down by Owen Sound and I was minding my own business and getting drunk with my friends, eh?, and I guess I might have overdid it and I must've passed out, 'cause the next thing I know, I'm on a bus pulling into Wawa 500 miles from home. No shoes, no jacket, no money, and no idea how I got here or how I'm supposed to get home, eh? When I find out who did this, and I have a good idea who it was, it's gonna be karma time."

Another kid named Randy spoke up. He was from Wawa and was with his girlfriend, Meadow, who he said was from the Mission.

"We've been trying to run away for the last three days. Getting up. Going to the highway and just about begging for a ride. People who know us drive by, beep at us, and laugh. It's embarrassing. Everybody in town knows we're trying to run away, and they thinks it's a big joke. Pretty bad when you can't even run away from home."

A long-necked ribby kid from California who claimed to be nineteen but didn't even look old enough to drive said, "My old man searched my room and found my bong and a marble bag full of other incriminating stuff and grounded me for the next twenty years, so I took off. I raided his dresser, stole fifty bucks and here I am—and I've still got about twenty bucks left."

"Where are you headed?"

"I want to get as far away from home as possible."

"Halifax?" someone asked.

"Or St. Johns. That's farther than Halifax."

"Are you sure?"

Dirty, wet, wrinkled, ripped, and poorly folded road maps appeared from everywhere. Mileage charts were consulted. Measurements were made by scrawny travelers well-skilled in the art of map reading. The consensus was that St. Johns, Newfoundland, was the farthest, but it was so isolated that some insisted that it wasn't accessible by thumb, in which case Glace Bay, Nova Scotia, was the next farthest.

"Okay. Then that's where I'm heading. One of those two places."

A gangly shirtless kid from British Columbia spoke up: "At least you left on your own. I got kicked out rather unexpectedly"—he enunciated "unexpectedly"—"when my father came home rather unexpectedly"—again enunciated—"and found me bare-assed with my girlfriend—in his bed."

"He was just jealous, man."

"It was a matter of time. I must admit, I was a rabble-rouser and did have a tendency to go out of my way to piss him off. He always told me that I had a bad attitude. He'd say things like," he pushed out his chest and imitated his father, "'You have a way of pushing my automatic piss-off button' and 'It's easier hammering nails into cement than trying to talk sense to you.' But then the straw that put the icing on the cake was when I called him by his first name. He always goes by his middle name because he hates his first name. I said, 'Relax, Dexter. It's all cool.' Man. He was steaming mad. His eyes nearly popped out of his head. That's when he blew his stack and totally flaked out. I had it out with him, and now he's got it in for me. It was ferocious, man. Our little skirmish rapidly escalated to an all-out war. We got in this colossal screaming match where, for the first time ever, he flew off the handle and got all ramniferous, and I thought he was gonna beat the fire out of me, but all he done was run his gums, so I said to him real defiant and dramatic, trying to pull off my best James Dean, 'You can beat me up but you can't beat me down,' and I stormed out of the house. It sounded cool at the time but now it sounds pretty stupid. And shit, I couldn't go back in after that. So I flew the coop and here I am."

"No, man. That *was* cool."

Then a quivering voice arose and a girl in the back stood up with her hand raised, as if she was in school, and said, "I always get made fun of because I'm overweight. Even boys who were chubbier than me laughed at me and teased me, calling me 'Chubbs' and 'Chunks' and 'Tub o' Lard.' I told my parents, but they were never able to help. Even my dad would tell me I needed to lose weight so they would stop picking on me. He said I would have more self-esteem if I weren't so fat. It was as if he was siding with the kids at school. I tried to lose weight but it never worked. It's harder than people think. So I just gave up." She was fighting back a monsoon of tears. A boy next to her scooted over and gave her a gentle two-armed hug.

Another girl in a floppy leather hat with peace sign embroidery and a wide brim casting a second shadow over an already shadowed face said, "I had bad acne when I was in high school. We had a European history class and all the kids in the class started calling me "Mary, Queen of Spots" because my name is Mary and they all thought that was very funny. Pretty soon that became my nickname and everyone in school started calling me that, even a lot of my friends. Every fucking day! They'd shorten it to "Spotty" or "Spots," as if it were my real name. It was unbearable. I ended up quitting school and moving out to live with my father in St. Catherine's where I got a job and made new friends. I wasn't a very good student, anyway."

Ray whispered to Matt, "My mom and dad are my best friends. We all go fishing and play golf together. My home life was perfect, and high school was the best time of my life. Should I tell them that?"

"No. Save that for another time."

"That's what I thought. I'm going out to see where bicycle boy is. It's already dark, and I hope he didn't run off with our money." Ray disappeared through the flap and into the stormy night.

It may have been a side effect of the daylong marathon buzz or maybe all the stifled impulses in his boxed-up dungeon of useless regrets recognized its twin in the dispirited mass of mud dwellers around him, so when the straw hat made its way to his head, Matt talked a blue streak:

"Geez, I'm not sure what to say. Had a crazy ride up here, through a meteor shower, on the Enterprise with Captain Kirk at the wheel and Rod Serling riding shotgun and got sucked into the magnetic Wawa force field and now, here we are, sitting around getting drunk and stoned and telling our sad tales of woe in a stinking tent in a miserable marsh in the middle of nowhere and all I can think about is an old girlfriend. Man, it's been years. Lifetimes ago. But in some ways it was just yesterday. We were inseparable, and for over a year it was one of those happy-ever-after fairy-tale love stories until something came over me and I just destroyed the whole thing. I think I was trying to prove something, but I can't remember what it was. I might have been trying to impress my friends, to show them I wasn't wrapped around her pinky or some other fake reason. But I liked being wrapped around her pinky. I was so confused at the time, teenage wasteland kind of stuff. So I broke up with her and then totally discarded her as if she were just an insignificant thing. I think I turned into a different person, a real-life Jekyll-and-Hyde. I didn't know what the hell I was doing. Part of me figured we would get back together in a month or so anyway. It's all a blur now. But I sent her a break-up note and I said such terrible things. I didn't even have the decency to do it in person. I was so cavalier about it and didn't even realize at the time that it was a real, uh, well, you know, douchebag way to do it. It was so mean. I was so mean. Everything else in my life, at school and at home, was caving in on me, so I might as well destroy the one good thing that's left. So I did it. I cut myself loose as though I was being liberated, as though I knew it couldn't last forever so I might as well just get it over with now. I have regretted that note from the moment I sent it. And then, afterward, I was too ashamed to face my words. Or to face her. I had gotten so depressed about other things in my life that I ended up taking it out on her. And then before I knew it, my whole life fell apart for a slew of different reasons, complicated reasons, and there were so many stumbling blocks and I didn't know how to avoid them, they just suddenly appeared, beyond my control, and in the course of just a few months, everything unraveled. I realize now that I had become self-destructive and was my own worst enemy. I went from being an "A" student to flunking out of school and running away from home, and I think a lot of it had to do with my father. I loved him and hated him at the same time. I had such mixed feelings because people in town seemed to think he was something special because he was a popular professor at a nearby college and that I was lucky being Professor Mahoney's son. They said that I was his spitting image, as if I should be proud of that. It was like we had a reputation to keep up. But nobody knew my family was in the midst of a big civil war. Or maybe everyone knew. But I couldn't understand how he could be this great guy to everyone else in town, always friendly and in good spirits in public, so generous and kind, and then, by the time he got home, in private, he was all used up and would hardly even talk to me, which I could deal with when I was still with my girlfriend because she was like an anesthesia, she numbed my pain, and, you know, we were so innocent. When I was with her, everything else disappeared, and I was happy just holding her hand and taking long walks at night and we never ran out of things to say. Sometimes just being together with the right person is all you need to survive. It was so perfect. She was always happy and fun to be with and she treated me like gold. And I'll never forget this, the first time I told her I loved her. Oh man. We were just fifteen and I was so scared and nervous because I had never said that to anyone ever, not even my parents, and I could hardly get my voice to work, but I couldn't hold it back anymore, it wanted to explode out of me, and I thought it was this monumental announcement that would change the course of history, and I was afraid that I would come out and say it to her hoping for fireworks but that she wouldn't say anything back to me so I held it in for weeks but I did it anyway. I took a big risk, and, in a nervous and thin whisper so soft that I was afraid she didn't even hear me, I said "I love you, Helen" and held my breath and immediately regretted it because I knew she wouldn't say it back to me but she didn't even hesitate and she said—God, I can still hear her saying it, it's still echoing in my head, when she said 'I love you too, Matt' and she sounded so relieved and so certain, as if she had been waiting to say it for a long time too, and my whole mind and body went numb with elation and all tingly and overflowing with happiness and we were both so relieved that we started to laugh and I could tell without question in the way that she said it that she meant it as much as I did, and we were standing there on a dark path behind the high school, and the air was moist and the grass was wet and squishy and smelled like sweet onions and we had our arms around each other and I have never in my life ever felt as close to another human being as I did at that moment, and it was so tender because, at that moment, we had merged into a single person, and I had a kind of epiphany and realized 'Yes. *This* is what love is all about." And I understood for the first time that love is a real thing. I could feel it growing inside me. It was like magic. So huge and glorious and filled with happy surprises, so dramatic and romantic and symphonic, so epic. And for the first time in my life I knew for sure that at least one person on Earth loved me, and suddenly nothing else mattered, everything else disappeared and the Earth shifted, the whole Earth, and it was just me and her in that field. We were Adam and Eve in the Garden of Eden, floating together in this huge bubble of love, so safe and strong together, and I wanted to shout my 'I love you' for the entire world to hear, and I figured that there must have been a time when my parents felt this exact same way, that they must have loved each other at some point, and that the sad thing about this overwhelming feeling of love is that it can't last forever and that the bubble always ends up getting popped, and then there you are, back down on Earth wondering what the hell happened and feeling foolish for getting so swept away by your emotions. So I developed the idea in my mind that love is doomed from the start. But with Helen it felt possible that we could have beaten the odds because when two people really love each other, no matter how young they are, there's a force that lifts them above themselves and all their petty circumstances, and it changes who they are and turns their fears into courage and unites them in a way that makes anything seem possible, and protects them from harm, and it's precious and pure and that's how... that's how," he suppressed a weepy sniffle, "that's how I know it was a true thing. Because I felt that, together, we were powerful and strong, and I remember thinking proudly, "I am going to be with this girl forever.' But then after we broke up, and I was by myself, I felt so weak and helpless. So empty. But my idiotic pride wouldn't let me admit my mistake and beg forgiveness. I mistook that notion for weakness. And that's why I am stuck in this perpetual downward spiral. Because I destroyed a true thing. Intentionally. And there's nothing I can do now to change it. I can't believe what an asshole I was! How could I not have realized what I was doing? But as they say, you can't unscramble an egg. A good person would have acted better than I did. I thought I knew everything. But I knew nothing. And now, even after all these years, I keep coming back to her in my mind. She was the only person who ever really knew me and accepted me and loved me for who I was, whether I was cool or not, and I was always my best around her, and I didn't have to pretend anything. It was just so easy, so natural, that I took her for granted and then let her go, thinking that love would always be right there for the grasping, and that it was no big deal. As the song goes, 'I threw it all away.' I was a better person back then, with Helen, before everything unraveled. I didn't understand what was happening to me. And I still don't. Man, I wish I had a time machine. Nobody ever told me that at such a young age I could make decisions that would haunt me my whole life. Anyway, without Helen, my protective force field was destroyed, the anesthesia was taken away, and the pain returned greater than ever, and I went downhill so fast and was bombarded by all those depressing things that bothered me at home. The magic was gone. It was all mostly about my father. He was a quiet man, all full of thoughts. When I was little, I idolized him and thought he was a great genius who knew all the answers to everything, and I was so proud to be his son. But as I got older, things changed, and he stopped paying attention to me and I couldn't ever figure out what I had done to drive him away. He was never mean. He never hit me or yelled at me. But that was just it; he never *did* anything. He never talked to me. Sometimes he didn't even answer me when I talked to him. He'd come home and sit in front of the TV watching Walter Cronkite with his bourbon in one hand and a book or newspaper in the other and hardly ever said anything to anybody. He might as well have been a ghost sleepwalking throughout the house. And I kept thinking, there's no way he's gonna just sit there and remain silent and do nothing while I'm falling apart right before his very eyes. If he loves me he's gonna notice that I'm having a breakdown and crumbling into pieces, and he'll catch me before I stumble over the rim of whatever emotional ledge I was standing on and crash-land and shatter into a big broken heap. I mean, he's got to, that's what fathers are for. I don't know, maybe I did it just to instigate him. Or maybe I was testing him. But eventually I couldn't take it any more. I couldn't cope with all the bullshit in my head, and I couldn't face another day at school, living in fear of being called on and looking like a fool, never knowing the answer because I never did my homework and wasn't able to pay attention in class, and I was so scared and alienated, way out on the edge of some universe that was spinning out of control. So I ran away from home, totaled his car, took a bus to New York City, and spent the day wandering around Greenwich Village. I imagined it to be a hippie promised land and that something would materialize out of thin air and I would automatically find new best friends who would rescue me and give me a place to hide until I grew up. But then I got caught by the cops when I went back to the Port Authority. They sent me back home that very same day on a late night bus. Man, that was one hell of a day. It was Valentine's Day. Couldn't even run away right. And, my old man, he never once put his arm around me or looked me in the eye to ask if I was all right or if there was anything he could do. He never said anything about it. Nothing. Never. Not a single word. I couldn't believe it. He didn't even care or didn't even know. A stranger would have shown more compassion. As far as he was concerned, I was that tree that fell in the forest and nobody heard it. I realize now that I was just screaming out for help because I was so scared. Man—all these things were so long ago. I don't understand why it all still bothers me so much or why I'm spilling out my guts to all you guys. But I can't help it. Then I dropped out of school. I was flunking out anyway because no matter how hard I tried, I couldn't concentrate enough to pay attention in class. So I went to live with my sister and her family in Connecticut. That was the best thing that could have happened. Just being away from it all made such a big difference. Before I left I thought I was going crazy. I mean, for real. Everything seemed so hopeless. My thoughts were so warped, so depressed. My mind was out of control, so obsessed with all kinds of fears and thoughts about suicide and death. I was so embarrassed by what I had turned into and what I had done, but after about a week in Connecticut I started feeling better, more normal, and I figured that it might not have all been my fault. I was finally breathing clean air for the first time in ages—maybe ever. And my sister and her husband were amazing. Man—they saved my ass. Without them ever realizing it, they walked me away from the ledge where I was standing, ready to jump or fall, and back to safety. They treated me special even though I was such a weird screwed-up kid and an odd-ball. It was so different living in a house with a family where everybody talked to each other and joked and laughed and went places together and there weren't any deep dark secrets taking up the space. My brother-in-law was a real

dad to his son, talking with him and treating him like a little man. He
was so proud of the little guy. He gave him piggyback rides, carted
him around the neighborhood in a red wagon, talked to him in a funny
Donald Duck voice, fell asleep with him on the couch, all tangled
together, hugging each other, so happy and comfortable. You could tell
he loved him. At first it seemed strange, but then it dawned on me that
that's how dads are supposed to be. And my nephew, man, he was my
therapy. He was just a kid, just learning how to talk, and that's when I
first understood the importance of being an uncle because here was
this incredible little guy who thought I was something special and so I
had something to live up to, and it was my obligation not to disappoint
this kid no matter how messed up I thought I was inside, and I had to
at least pretend for his sake that I had it all together. The overall effect
of that was that when I was with him, my whole world became
simplified and fun because all I had to do in life was try to make him
happy, and that was easy because he was already happy, and I could let
everything else disappear, and I could be happy, too, and forget about
all that other stuff and have a blast hanging out with this perfect two-
year-old kid and listening to him say words for the first time, learning
to call me by name, wanting me to tuck him in at night and give him a
hug and kiss, telling him he loved me, laughing and joking around
and, you know, there's nothing—absolutely nothing!—as beautiful as
a child playing and laughing and having fun and being happy 'cause
there's no reason not to be happy 'cause at that age they're still honest-
to-God angels in a make-believe world where everybody loves
everybody else and nothing bad ever happens and, man, they really
saved me and made me appreciate how important it is to be part of a
family. So I decided that when I went back home I was going to get to
know my father, try to break through whatever was making him so
miserable and distant, and talk to him and get to know him again, both
as a father and as a person, and to have him get to know me, too, and
I started to feel sorry for him but didn't know why but it was like he
was a wounded giant and everybody was afraid to help him. So
anyway, I left Connecticut and got back home in the middle of June,

and before I mustered up the courage to do anything, a week or so later he died totally unexpectedly in his sleep. I blew it, man. Lost my nerve. I don't know. Maybe I never would have said anything, but I hardly even had a chance. I had planned all kinds of great things to say to him, to make it easy for him, and I started thinking that maybe all this time he's been waiting for me to come to him to start the ball rolling and maybe he saw himself in me and was as mixed-up and frustrated and frozen and depressed inside as I was and maybe somehow we had both come to hate ourselves so much that it got in the way of everything else in our lives and it was strange for me to be thinking of my father as nothing more than just another unhappy person, and all I wanted was for everyone to get along and be nice to each other. But anyway, I got back home on Father's Day of all days. He didn't even seem to realize that I'd been gone for four months. Then, a week later, he was dead. But then, after he died, all the tension in the house dissolved, and I felt guilty because it was so much easier being there without him around, and when the shock wore off I actually felt better after he died, and I would go to bed at night praying that I was not happy that my father died and feeling like that kid in that story, living in a house full of whispers about secrets that everyone knew but no one would talk about out loud, and maybe I was the one who should have died, and I started thinking—oh, shit, man, who cares what I was thinking. I don't even know that kid anymore. That kid is dead. He died when he sent that note. Damn. I guess I've been rattling on. It must be somebody else's turn by now."

And the straw hat was passed on.

Matt worried that he had made an ass out of himself by going on and on, dumping out his vault of miseries to a soggy assortment of stoned strangers. Maybe he should have kept his mouth shut! But something in his near stream-of-consciousness confessional monologue opened up the door for some darker testimonials. As the gusting wind continued to howl and growl and whine and big trees screeched and bent outside like giant sea monsters and the straw hat found a fresh head to charm, a quiet hollow-eyed girl who had been hiding in the shadowy background spoke up in a bland, emotionless monotone, drained of all anger or hatred, about how her father had died and, when her mother remarried, her stepfather began molesting her when she was eleven, and her mother either refused to believe her or else just wouldn't do anything to make it stop. It continued until she was old enough to get the courage to run away, so on her sixteenth birthday she set herself loose in the world, and she'd been on her own since then and she still never felt as though anyone other than her dead father had ever loved her, and she blamed herself and didn't believe anyone ever would love her and the wind and the rain were hammering against the canvas roof with an impetuous staccato rhythm and the moldy tent was sagging and leaking and its ropes and stakes were straining and creaking against the huff and puff and baying of the furious storm, and the drenched roof was lifting, and the Coleman lantern was near to flickering out and the wine and the joints were all gone and everyone was still stoned or drunk or both. All of a sudden, a massive punch of straight line winds threw the tent up and over and all around, and before they knew what hit them, everyone was crawling out from under the heavy soaking tent, dripping in mud, including Matt and George, and though Matt had never been in a tornado or a hurricane, he thought it must be similar to this. Then Ray beamed aboard and said, "Let's get outta here. Bicycle Boy showed up and helped me put in the new battery. The Enterprise is back in action."

The muck slurped and sucked at their feet as they did a high-stepping dash through the lashing rain, dodging downed limbs across the swampy lot to the re-energized VW where a fourth figure begged George for a lift and got in the back next to Matt who did not recognize, until they launched past the towering Wawa goose statue flapping its metallic wings in the ominous crackle and flash of violent lightning, that the huddled shape quivering beside him was the runaway girl who had been raped by her stepfather. Matt cloaked her and shielded her as best he could with his denim jacket over her chest and shoulders and was so tempted to put his arm around her and tell her he loved her because, at that moment, he did love her without even needing to know her. But he didn't tell her. He didn't utter a word. He just couldn't get himself to do it.

# CHAPTER XI

If not for the capsized tent and the sobering slap of mud and the wet wind which shocked him back into his senses, Matt may have been content to stay at Wawa, sucking indolently on joints and soaking his throat with a steady stream of mind-numbing wine, and maybe teaming up with a wandering gypsy-girl from some faraway foreign land. Thanks to the adrenalized confusion of the storm, he and the other boys sprang to action and took turns driving all night long through the jet-black western Ontario forests while the waif-girl slept beside him in the back seat like a ravaged refugee. The dim flashlight beams of the Enterprise headlights carved small holes through the heavy sheets of pelting rain and just managed to faintly illuminate a gleaming path along the desolate seal-skin highway, as if from a spaceship returning to Earth after an epic extraplanetary mission. The wiper blades, making sloshy slaps and punctuated rhythms, were going crazy in their effort to fend off the gushing assault as flashes of horizontal lightning set the sky momentarily ablaze and shattered the invisible nighttime into millions of shards of pulverized glass.

Dawn crept in upon them, and the magnified warmth of the morning sun absorbed into their damp clothing and the pores of their grimy skin. It was the first day of the rest of their lives. They'd been temporarily snared but had shaken free of the Wawa curse and had escaped the calamitous Wawa hostel massacre. Now Thunder Bay lay ahead in the golden sunlight, their very own Emerald City, safely beyond the menace of the sleepytime poppy fields and the flying monkey forest. Everything now feels brand-new and opening up in slow motion. Matt sings in a whisper-voice, "I feel real loose like a long neck goose. Oh baby that's a what ah like." He is just loud enough to rouse the girl-child sleeping beside him. He reads her face as it nudges and stirs. Then she yawns awake, unfolding and stretching herself back to life, and says to Matt, "Where are we?"

"We're coming into Thunder Bay."

"Already? Oh, that's perfect." Her voice is a purr.

"Where are you going?"

"Oh, I'm not sure," she says in a dream whisper, "I'm just following the butterflies." She smiles and cuddles herself up like a sleepy little girl, resting against Matt's shoulder. "But for now, Thunder Bay will be just fine. Anywhere in Thunder Bay."

She removes the night from her eyes and pulls herself up into a ball with both arms belted around her knees. She has already turned beautiful and looks cozy as a kitten as she rocks with a satisfied smile and says, like a rescued princess, "Thanks you guys."

They found the building just as the first risers were emerging for an early start. Everybody got out, stretched their limbs, and squinted against the sunlight. The hostel was a skating arena filled with sleeping bags and backpacks and guitars. A colorful mosaic of waking kids wriggled and slept on the rink floor, like a Jackson Pollack painting squirming to life.

The warden let them take showers at no charge. Matt turned the knob to full blast and let the hot jolt pummel his flesh and turn it splotchy red as he lathered himself up with twice as much shampoo and soap as he needed. Balled up in the corner of his stall was a little brown spider, drenched and powerless against the tide that would soon wash him down the drain. It reminded Matt of his father, who had once stopped him from killing a mosquito that landed on the kitchen table, explaining that it was a living creature with a brain and heart and nervous system, and that mosquitoes had inhabited the Earth long before human beings and will outlive us as well. The whole time the old man spoke he never raised his archer's eyes from the pages of whatever novel he was consumed by at the time. When he was done speaking, he retreated back into his cold and sacred cave of thought as though Matt weren't even there anymore, but it permanently altered the way Matt thought about insects. He was certain, back then, that his father must be a genius, and so his sage declarations carried weight, even after so many years. Matt aimed the blast away from the spider and, when he was done, brought it outside and laid it on the grass where it unbundled its legs and sprang back to life among the green blades and the clover.

"Live long and prosper," Matt said.

Everyone reassembled, fresh and clean. The girl, nobody ever did get her name, hugged them all and headed down the street like she knew where she was going, bopping to some merry tune inside her head. The glow of morning sunlight enveloped her in a golden bubble as she disappeared toward the city, and Matt pictured her dancing down the sidewalk like an angel in the midst of a soft swarm of monarch butterflies all leading her to that safe sanctuary where she would never again be hurt.

George left to find a garage where someone could check out his car before he headed down to Minnesota. Ray and Matt stuck together to continue west, recharged by the sudsy cleansing but frazzled by sleep deprivation and over-indulgence. They made it to the west road and planted themselves at a convenient spot. There wasn't much traffic, and what little there was had no interest in hitchhikers.

Neither boy knew for certain which day it was.

"I don't get it. This is *the* Trans-Canada Highway. Anyone traveling west has to go on this road. Anyone in all of Canada who is going west would have to drive right past us. We are here at the funnel on *the* main Canadian thoroughfare and nothing is happening. Doesn't anyone in Canada travel?"

Ray got out his wedge and practiced his agile swing, chipping pebbles, cans, and other roadside objects onto the smooth surface of his imaginary green.

"My dad taught me to golf as soon as I was old enough to hold a club. He got me a kid-sized set of clubs and let me tee off with him, and then wherever his ball landed I'd get to take my next swing. When he made it to the green, he'd let me putt until I got it in. He'd tell me, 'Drive for show. Chip and putt for dough.' He said that there was no vacation in the world as peaceful as a day of eighteen holes at any golf course. This is his wedge. He gave it to me to take on the trip, but I had to promise to return it. He wanted to make sure I was coming back. How about you? Are you a golfer?"

"No. Other than miniature golf, which doesn't really count. I wasn't even very good at that. I've golfed on a real course just twice. It felt pointless, knocking a little white ball around and trying to get it into a hole. Couldn't get into it."

Matt immediately regretted his swift and trite dismissal of a sport that was so vital to Ray. He thought he must have sounded conceited and wondered if maybe he was conceited without ever having realized it. The real reason he didn't continue to play golf was because it was more difficult than he expected, and he was discouraged by all his whiffs, slices, and shanks in front of his friends and the other impatient golfers who were being held up behind him. He had overheard one of them complaining about beginners, and Matt, feeling ever the loser, decided it wasn't worth the hassle.

"Do you play chess?" Ray blew off Matt's comment. Matt nodded. "To me golf is like chess. It's a game of nerves, willpower, and concentration. It's just you, playing against the lay of the land, the wind, and yourself. You can be your own worst enemy in golf. You oughta try it sometime. Once you get into it, you'll get over feeling silly. It's a lot of fun. And it'll test you. As my dad says, 'It takes balls to play golf.'"

Matt grew quiet. How different would his life have been if his father had taught him to play golf—or anything for that matter—like Ray's father. He admired the casual and certain affection in Ray's voice when he said, "my Dad." You could hear the capital D and how he took pride in quoting him with a devoted respect. Matt felt hypocritical and insincere at the thought of calling his father "my Dad." It sounded too familiar. Too palsy-walsy. For Matt it was always "my father." Lowercase all the way. After all, as far as Matt was concerned, he had always been more of a "Professor" than a dad or a father.

*When Matt was in the sixth grade, he made a new friend, Chuck, who invited him over to his house to play after school one afternoon. They were shooting baskets, playing around the world, and having a good time when Chuck's father came out and joined them. He goofed around, playing keep away with the boys, dribbling the ball between his legs and taking long distance hook shots. Oddly, Chuck welcomed his father's antics and even encouraged him with whoops and cheers. It upset Matt to see a grown man playing like a kid with his son, so he made up an excuse to go home because he was too uncomfortable to enjoy himself anymore.*

*"What a weird man," he thought, unable to get the images out of his head. A so-called father frolicking about. It wasn't until he lay in bed that night, bewildered and disturbed, that he figured it out, that it was jealousy that caused his discomfort, that he was afraid he might end up liking someone else's father more than his own, and he swore never to go to Chuck's house again because it gave him unhappy thoughts about his own father and caused him to examine thoughts he would rather ignore.*

They walked a couple miles to a shopping center and bought a quart of chocolate milk, cheese, honey, an orange, and two ham salad sandwiches. They got a ride to Kakabeka Falls and, as they continued to wave their unlucky thumbs, had a lengthy discussion about every hitchhiker's fantasy ride. Such a ride, trimmed to its explosion of adolescent hormonal essentials, involves being picked up by a beautiful woman with whom you end up having a full-blown romantic encounter. Matt had never come close. Ray, however, had lived that fantasy.

"It was awesome. My theory in life is that our best moments are completely unplanned and unpredictable. I was hitching down the road and there was a girl whose car was broken down and pulled off to the side with the hood up. Man, she was gorgeous and—" he indicated with cupped hands that she had large breasts—"well, I messed around with her engine for about half an hour and got it going. I got all greasy and dirty. I even cut my thumb open by accident. We were headed the same direction and she was only ten miles from her apartment. She offered to let me come in, get a Band-Aid, and wash up before I headed back on the road. I could care less about the grease, and the cut wasn't all that bad. I'm used to being greasy. But, naturally, I knew I had to say yes. Well, we went into the apartment, and she showed me where the bathroom was. I went in to wash my hands and then she snuck in behind me and I see her in the mirror and she pressed herself against me, her you-know-whats squished right into my back, and looked at me in the mirror and said, 'The moon is in Scorpio,' and I said, 'I have no idea what that means but it sounds sexy,' and she whispered in my ear, 'Oh yeah. Now it's time for me to work on *your* engine. Tit for tat, so to speak.' Totally blew my mind. In about two minutes we were showering together and on the couch and in the bed. She couldn't get enough, and I'm going, 'Whoa, baby, slow down, you're wearing me out.' She was phenomenal and had the most incredible body and I kept saying to myself, 'Thank you God, thank you Dad, for teaching me how to work on cars.' I ended up staying with her for the next few days, and it was a nonstop marathon. I sowed a lot of wild oats that week. We even had nicknames for each other. She called me her Muffin Man 'cause I, you know…, well, let's just say I have a taste for muffins. And I called her the Wild Woman of Horneo. And get a load of this: when I left, she apologized for delaying me, thanked me for fixing her car, and paid for my bus ticket home. I felt like a damn gigolo. I've still got a hard-on over that one. She totally ravished me, man. It was one hell of a ride— in every sense," he smirked, "and proof positive that all the best things in life come totally out of the blue, unplanned and unpredictable but absolutely perfect."

Even the ever-cool Ray was struck giddy by the memory of his once-in-a-lifetime ride. Matt wished he were more like Ray: strong-armed and tall, the brawny build, the swashbuckling good looks, and the universally likable personality. The capital "D" Dad. Knows how to fix cars. A "can do" guy who has real fantasy rides rather than having to dream about them his whole life. A guy like that has it made and doesn't have to beg, grovel, or pray for female affections. Ray was a real travelin' man.

Matt shook his head and said, with comic deference, "Ray. You are my hero." But even though he admired Ray, Matt couldn't help but despise him a bit for being so good looking and having such a great upper-case relationship with his father. Maybe it was just jealousy because life was too easy for him.

*Any girl in her right mind would prefer him to me.* All that effortless charisma, the adventurous good looks, the self-confidence, the girls with their approving eyes and their come-hither smiles. Standing next to Ray, Matt felt ripped off and angry and awestruck all at once.

Whatever superpowers Ray might have had over women, they did not have any effect on his hitching. By late afternoon, after a full day on the road and no sleep the night before, they were still only a stone's throw beyond Thunder Bay. Ray gave up and hoofed it back to town to catch a bus home to Calgary. His parting words were, "Remember. If you see a girl broken down on the side of the road, even if you don't know what you're doing, fake it, pretend you're a real grease monkey. She won't know the difference and will be just as appreciative either way. But make sure you get greasy. Works like a charm."

Matt stuck it out alone and started walking away from civilization, back into the wilderness where he belonged, onward toward Pluto. He saw a caterpillar inching across the road. He picked it up and placed it back in the safety of the grass, away from the certain death of automobile tires. But, as if according to a million-year-old instinct, a rigid and unalterable grand design, it reoriented itself toward the road, oblivious to its danger, its fate, and once again blundered deathward. He repeated this exercise several times, each time with the same disappointing result. He even brought it to the other side of the road and dropped it in the weeds. Still, the stubborn creature squirmed around and persisted with its suicide march. Apparently, the little guy was predestined to cross the road, regardless of the direction. Maybe just for the smooth warmth of its surface. As Matt continued to trod westward, he thought, "There are things that cannot be saved and courses that cannot be changed," referring to both the caterpillar and himself.

He got a ride that dropped him off a little farther into nowhere— just far enough to seal his fate for the night but not far enough to deliver him to anything resembling a destination.

He said hello to a passing bicyclist. "Where you headed?"

"Halifax," the cyclist replied, as if it were a quick spin down the road and he would be there by nightfall.

"Good luck."

A freight train passed by. Matt waved. The conductor saluted him and tooted his whistle. One of the boxcars was latched open and filled with a bunch of Kerouac kids, wide-eyed dreamers headed to the mythical west, some to fulfill an undefined destiny and some simply because it was a place to go and was far away from home. They returned his wave and flashed him the peace sign en masse.

He kept walking out of sheer stubbornness. Flocks of birds circled and swooped overhead and disappeared into the deep green clutch of the forest. He could hear hundreds of them trilling from their hidden lairs, and he joined in by playing what his friend, Dave, called the hand flute. He locked his hands together and blew through his paralleled thumbs into the cavern of his cupped palms to create a shrill resonant whistle in response to the chorus of plaintive warbles. Dicky Brier had taught him to whistle that way in the sixth grade, and Matt had practiced at it as if it were a classical instrument. He continued whistling as he walked. He was sure he would be stuck in the woods overnight because no one in Canada was going west. They were all at home drinking beer and watching hockey.

Absorbed in such thoughts, he caught the glint of something in the bushes, and, when he investigated, discovered a large hand-painted plywood sign saying, "Winnipeg—Please!" Matt objected to using signs. It was beneath his dignity as a serious hitchhiker to stoop to advertising himself in such an undistinguished manner. The only exception to his no-sign rule was a hitchhiker he once saw in Albany at the Northway exit of The New York State Thruway, where traffic could be going either north or south, east or west. He was a monkish little man with a thick black beard and intense Rasputin eyes. He was holding a sign that had only a question mark on it. That was a cool sign, an anti-sign sign, the sign of a pilgrim, and Matt respected a man so free as to not care where he was going, a man whose destination was anywhere and everywhere.

Desperate for a ride, Matt broke his own rule and held the sign up like a billboard. To his astonishment, the first vehicle that came by, yet another VW bus, pulled over and welcomed him aboard. He considered taking the bespelled sign with him. Instead, he returned it to its original location in order that its good juju could benefit the next frustrated hitchhiker caught out in the wasteland.

Nancy and Jeff were from Charlotte, North Carolina. They weren't married, at least not yet. He loved Nancy's accent and felt good inside when she said she always wanted to go to Vermont, placing the emphasis on the Ver. When she started asking Matt questions about himself, Jeff intervened on his behalf:

"Maybe he doesn't want to tell us his whole life story, Nancy." But she persisted, saying that everybody has a story worth telling, and she was always interested in bringing out that story in each new person she met.

"We're all worth our stories, honey."

Matt didn't mind and felt obligated to reveal tidbits about himself to strangers who extended to him their special brand of trust and unconditional kindness. He sketched out the relevant superficial account of his self-described "measly uneventful existence." Nancy expressed sympathy for the "dead father" aspect of his life. He reassured her that he didn't mind talking about it but did not go into any of the details he had disclosed in the washed-out Wawa tent.

They reciprocated. Jeff was a dreamer with ideas floating around inside his head like loose kites. He led with his heart and his winning smile. Though Nancy seemed enamored of Jeff's flights of fancy, she nonetheless tended to the practical realities. She held and guided Jeff's string with her feet firmly planted on Earth. Matt was touched by the loving nature of their partnership and wondered if he would ever become somebody deserving of being looked up to and whether anyone would ever volunteer to guide his wild kites.

Jeff reveled in educating his Yankee passenger with his stockpile of funny stories about his rural relatives "from the hills and hollers." He had a saying for everything. He told Matt, "If you ever see somebody with their zipper down, tell them their violin case is open and it's nothing to fiddle with."

Nancy shook her head like a disapproving mother and said, "Don't mind him. It's just his hillbilly alter ego. He's going all shucks, dang and golly on ya. You'd think he just fell off the turnip truck."

Matt smiled and let his gaze drift through the trees to the beckoning horizon. The dusky evening sky was all-ablaze in a fiery pastel glow that summoned all those tired old emotions from his deep well of bittersweet memories. All of life suddenly seemed immensely sad way out there in the Canadian hinterlands in that Carolina van with such a wonderful lovebird couple, and he thought, *Ah—the sky's on fire. I'm dyin', ain't I?*

Nancy, likewise captivated by the beauty of the setting sun, rested her head against Jack's shoulder and said, "You know, honey? Every time I think, 'That's the most beautiful sunset ever.' And you know what? Every time it is."

Before it got too late, and there was still time and light, they settled into a rest area where there was more than enough grass to set up a two-person tent and cook dinner on their compact gas stove amid the mad chaotic chirping of an orchestra of twilight peepers chanting and flirting and signaling all around them from thousands of invisible perches. Spaghettios, instant mashed potatoes, and peas were all more delicious than could ever be imagined. After dinner, Nancy said, "Popcorn?"

Jeff nodded and said, "Yeah. We might could do that." And as the chirping soared and droned, Jeff whipped out his Zippo lighter, conjured a mini-bonfire, and popped some Jiffy Pop in the dark and even had some butter from their cooler to melt on it. He looked like a sorcerer, his face illuminated by flames against a pitch-black background, the frenzied popping sounding like Fourth of July fireworks. At evening's end Jeff said, as Nancy again rolled her eyes, "It's time to piss on the fire and call in the dogs."

Matt wished he knew how to express his appreciation. He recited multiple versions of thank yous over and over in his mind but couldn't come up with one that sounded just right and couldn't find the courage to give it a shot.

He slept on the grass beside the bus, swatting at occasional mosquitoes as he stared without eyes into the unfathomable hypnotic sea of stars glittering within a night sky that was polished to a high sheen, grinning with unprompted joy and with gladdened thoughts of Nancy visiting Ver'mont.

# CHAPTER XII

The next day brought the same old Matt into a brand-new time zone, a new province, and a new hostel. The lakes and forests of never-ending Ontario gave way to the bright expansive sprawl of the Manitoban plains as if it were a new planet. Nancy and Jeff went out of their way to drop him off at the hostel in Winnipeg before they dipped south into the Dakotas. They completed the routine goodbye ritual with an exchange of addresses, optimistic vows to stay in touch, and the final handshakes and hugs that tied up the loose strings to these ephemeral alliances and gave them the official stamp of approval. Jeff even gave Matt the addresses of his parents and some friends in California in case he ended up in their area. After the departure of his most recent new best friends, Matt went through his typical post-parting blues. His loneliness made him think of home. He hadn't talked with his mother since Ottawa, which had only been a few days but was already an ancient memory. He loved hearing her voice.

"Where are you?" she asked. He heard one part exasperation and two parts relief.

"I'm in Winnipeg."

"Where is that?"

"It's in Manitoba. In the Canadian Midwest. Right above North Dakota." As he said it, he felt a shiver, realizing that he was such a long long way from home. She was taking notes in order to chart his progress on a Canadian road map she ordered through AAA.

"Do you have enough money?"

"Yes, I'm fine. These hostels are great. They're all clean and have plenty of room and cost only fifty cents a night. And they feed you. I haven't spent much money. Some food during the day, some postcards, stamps."

"I got your postcard, and Mrs. Black and Mrs. Piersall both called to say they'd gotten cards. They were happy to hear from you." Both Mrs. B and Mrs. P had been second mothers to Matt because they always welcomed him with such hospitality and, for a short spell, he had even lived at each of their homes.

"Yeah. I sent out a bunch of cards."

Mrs. Mahoney wasn't one for small talk, especially if it was on her nickel, so the conversation cruised to its natural conclusion.

"Now Matthew. You behave yourself and stay out of trouble."

He laughed. "Okay Ma, I promise. I be good boy."

"I'm serious. You know how this worries me so."

"I know. I know. But I'm okay. I promise." He wished she wouldn't worry so much and that she had more faith in his ability to take care of himself.

At the sound of the hang-up click, as a distant emptiness set in, Matt pondered the miracle of telephones and smiled inside as he visualized his mother sitting at the kitchen table reciting the two commandments she had instilled in him since he was little: 1) Always pay your bills, and 2) Never go into other people's refrigerators.

He lay low and stayed in for the rest of the day, intending to spend the next couple of days exploring Winnipeg. He napped, wrote letters and cards, and finished reading *The Dharma Bums*.

The hostel was great in that it stayed open during the day but not so great in that it didn't serve any meals. At dinnertime he walked to a nearby diner, The Over Easy Cafe, slid onto the shiny red vinyl seat of a booth, sacrificed a couple quarters into the miniature juke box mounted at the end of the table, and splurged on a tuna sandwich (he had been craving tuna fish), some fries (no meal is complete without fries—the greasier the better), and a coke (ice-cold, lots of cubes). He took a couple grape jelly packets and spread the jelly on the sandwich (there was no maple syrup).

The waitress had greeted him with an affectionate smile and a welcoming "Hello there, Hon," which made him feel right at home and ready to eat. A couple other customers went out of their way to wave at him and say, "Hey there. What d'ya know?" or "How's it goin' there?"

*Man*, he thought, *this must be the world's most friendliest diner*, intentionally doubling up on the superlative. He noticed while nibbling a French fry that he was experiencing life in superlatives. The tuna sandwich, for example, was definitely the best tuna sandwich he had ever tasted. And the coke—*my God!*—was the most refreshing drink ever. And each individual fry was better than the one before. His tongue was reveling in a renaissance of taste and having a field day with the excitement of flavor. His buds were popping.

The cast of characters he'd met so far were the kindest, funniest, prettiest, handsomest, and smartest people he could possibly have met on this entire Earth. Likewise for the places he'd been. Even Wawa. Matt would not have changed a thing about Wawa because, if he did, he would not have met the beautiful butterfly girl who bummed a ride to Thunder Bay. And he would not be here, now, at this most excellent of all diners. So he finished his unparalleled meal with an unparalleled air of contentment, left a fifty-cent tip and went to the cash register to pay.

The waitress smiled and said, "I could've sworn that you was Mark Olsen. You could be his twin."

A bell jingled as someone walked into the diner. The waitress called out.

"Hey, Jerry. Who does this guy remind you of?"

Jerry looked at Matt and said without hesitation, "Mark Olsen." A woman in a booth said, "I thought he was Mark Olsen." Matt was laughing. "Who the hell is Mark Olsen?"

"Oh, he's a certain someone who lives around here." Her eyes twinkled.

"Well, if you want, I'll be Mark Olsen. Do I wanna be Mark Olsen?"

He didn't realize until after he said it that it sounded like he was flirting. He was proud of himself but half expected that she would rebuke him with a cutting remark.

She gives him a sly look, perhaps even inviting, softens her voice, and says, "Well now, cowboy. It could be that there's a lotta fellas who'd like to be Mark Olsen. It's just that you're the only one could pass for him."

She hands him his change and he is transfixed by a tender tingling sensation as her fingertips brush and linger against his quivering palm.

As he turned and reached for the door, everybody waved goodbye and said, "So long, Mark." He returned, uncharacteristically cheerful, in search of his next best friend, all the while imagining how it would feel to be Mark Olsen.

There was a kid at the hostel who was one of those inside scoopers who embraced every crackpot theory that came his way as though it were an indisputable counter-cultural dose of clandestine truth. He was telling everybody how the CIA had murdered Jimi Hendrix, Janis Joplin, and Jim Morrison because they had too much control over young minds and, after Woodstock, Nixon was afraid that there would be a youth revolution that would overthrow the government. He was nice enough but was the kind of person that nobody takes seriously or wants to be around that much. Blame it on the bullshit factor. Matt contemplated whether that was how people thought about him: a nice guy but not much of a shelf life.

Projecting his voice with profound intent, the kid spoke: "Get this. They all died in questionable circumstances or supposively accidental deaths. Jimi and Jops, man. They were too powerful. They had to be killed."

A slouchy guy in the corner gave an amused smirk, rolled his eyes and said, "That's a crock of hogwash, dude."

The inside-scooper kid, unfamiliar with the expression, flashed a mystified look and said, "Huh?"

A girl with long pigtails and granny glasses and a handmade necklace of multi-colored love beads and miniature seashells said that a psychic told her that in a former life she had been Joan of Arc. Matt was puzzled as to why everyone who believed in reincarnation had always been someone famous in a past life rather than the regular schmuck they are now.

One girl said, "In my next life, I want to be a butterfly."

Another said, "All I know is that, when I die, I want to go to heaven and be an angel."

Matt looked at her, so pert and huggable, and thought it might be cool to say, "You already are an angel," but was afraid she would scoff it off as a corny come-on, so he chickened out.

One well-intentioned guy misread the ambience and joked, "When I die, I want to come back as a dildo." The feminine disgust was palpable. Matt, having sometimes been the victim of his own misguided sense of humor, suppressed a laugh, not wanting to draw the ire of the fairer sex, but he sympathized with the poor kid, who shrank into the corner like a leper.

Someone else claimed to be able to astral project in his dreams, saying that he always ended up in foreign rooms with strangers who were dressed in odd attire but who couldn't see him or sense him.

"It's cool but scary, too. I'm trying to learn how to control it so I can communicate with them. But I don't think they speak English. Sometimes I get the feeling I'm in France during Napoleon's time. And one time I think I saw Beethoven. Kinda weirded me out."

Kids started talking about where they were from and what made their town special. Pigtail girl said she was from Meadville, Pennsylvania. "That's where the zipper was invented," she bragged.

Then, a guy in thick glasses with either an odd accent or a speech impediment, who said he was from Moncton, New Brunswick, said "Gordie Drillon's from my town." All the Americans responded in a chorus, "Who's Gordie Drillon?"

After someone else chirped in that The Guess Who were from right here in Winnipeg and that his parents were friends with Randy

Bachman's parents, Matt, rarely one to assert himself, half-blurted, "Doug Kirkland is from my town." Then, when he added that his mother had gone to high school with him and that his aunt had taught the famous actor in kindergarten, one kid said, "bullshit" beneath a muffled cough, and everyone laughed. A warm flush reddened Matt's cheeks, but he did not defend himself and wished he had kept his mouth shut.

Topics continued to drift in and out and when they landed on religion, the CIA conspiracy kid started going on about how hip Jesus was. "He knew what was happening. And you know he had to be tripping when he was wandering in the desert getting high on poppies and herb, man. And rapping with all his disciples on the mountain. Jesus was the very first freak. The first hippie."

Matt's mind drifted into a flurry of drowsy semi-poetic musings. *"All the untapped wonders of the universe, here and now espoused / Life on limbs and breaking boughs / Campfires in the dead of winter's freezing gloom / Lava lamps and murky bongs in a blacklit room / Do our lives have meaning? Are we more than just a dream? / Or are we all just tiny particles lost in a grander scheme?"*

*What the hell is that supposed to mean?* Matt questioned, amused by his peculiar thoughts. *Oh, there is so much of which we know so little and so little of which we know so much. The rest is just make-believe.*

# CHAPTER XIII

When Matt learned that the hostel didn't provide safe storage for his gear during the day, he abandoned his plan to spend the day in Winnipeg and at first light hit the westward road. His first light being later than others', there were several hitchhikers already congregated at the crowded hitching spot on the highway entrance ramp. A guy from Renfrew shared his cheese and crackers with Matt and a couple kids from Oshawa, Ontario. A while later, one of the Oshawa kids ran up to Matt and gave him some pineapple rings and apologized that it was all they had.

Around noon he got a ride in a converted laundry truck with two merry pranksters from Niagara Falls, Ontario. They had already loaded themselves up with five other hitchers, most of whom Matt recognized from the hostel. As usual, he was welcomed by the customary aroma and was forthwith offered a toke.

Everyone was stoned. One guy said, as he reached over to pass Matt the joint, "Man. My arm is so heavy. Have you ever thought about how heavy your arm is?"

"Hey man, like, why do they call it stoned?" one guy queried aloud. "It actually feels more, I don't know, fluffy?"

Another said, "It's just 'cause, you know, when you get high, you're into a different trip, man, a totally new consciousness and your senses are finely tuned and, like, a hamburger isn't really a hamburger anymore and you don't really know what anything really is because you're a whole 'nother person and, in a way, uh, it's, uh… shit, I forget what I was trying to say but I had it there for a second but then it got all slippery."

Everybody started to laugh and sing together in a lopsided refrain, "No I would not feel so all alone. Everybody must get stoned."

Yet another said, as if it were part of an ongoing conversation, "Do you think that dogs wish they had hands?"

Another, who had been resting against a rolled-up sleeping bag with his eyes closed and who hadn't yet said anything, blurted out, "Eyeballs. Man. How is it that eyeballs can see? It makes no sense. It's a miracle."

A minute later, in the middle of emphasizing an important point about dogs' eyeballs, one of the kids lost his train of thought and said, "I just noticed something. My socks don't match."

Sure enough, one was black and the other was navy blue. That was all it took to switch channels away from dogs' eyeballs and onto the phenomenon of mismatched socks.

Another guy said, "That's okay. Wearing socks that match just perpetuates the false impression that things make sense and that there is order and logic in this world."

"Yeah," said yet another philosopher in training, "it's just conforming to a preconceived corporate image of how everyone should look and dress. It stifles creativity. Like coloring only between the lines."

"Free the socks, man! I say, free the socks!" The kid threw his fisted arm up in a mock Black Panther power salute. "For now on when I do my laundry, I'm gonna match my socks in whatever order they come out. I'll close my eyes so I'm not being consciously influenced by the color. It'll be more natural that way. No prejudice."

"Right on! I say free the socks. Right now—let's free the fucking socks!"

Those who had socks on—Matt didn't—took them off and threw them in a pile. Then, one by one, each person, with eyes closed, picked out a pair of socks and put them on. Of the five hitchers involved, none ended up with a matched pair. One of them rolled back and raised up his nonconformist feet and announced, "I'm gonna let my freak flag fly."

They brainstormed about starting a "North American Free the Socks Day," to be jointly celebrated in the U.S. and Canada. Citizens of both nations would observe by proudly wearing socks that didn't match, the louder the contrast, the better. Various manners of celebration were bandied about as the idea fired their collective imaginations. The original "free the socks" proponent argued against the holiday idea because it would be a sellout that would institutionalize the movement and kill its spirit.

"You can't institutionalize the revolution because then it's not the revolution anymore, it's the system. It's gotta be grassroots. From the ground up. We don't want to impose it upon the people."

Another guy who hadn't been saying much said, "Free the feet, man. Goddamn. All these socks smell like crap. Or did somebody fart in here?"

And that was about all it took to put an early end to the "North American Free the Socks Day" movement and to change the channel of conversation to yet another new round of enjoyable nonsense.

Matt closed his eyes, rested his head against his sleeping bag, and listened as his ubiquitous theme song played on the radio. That cheerful wisp of a song continued following him around and chanting itself in his head:

*And climbing to the top*
*I'd throw myself off*
*In an effort to make it clear to whoever*
*What it's like when you're shattered*

Well, that may be one way to do it. Carbon monoxide would be much more polite. No muss, no fuss. But that was just a remote possibility at the moment. He was actually feeling quite good, quite optimistic, about things, about himself. He started thinking about all his nieces and nephews and how they looked up to him and would never be able to understand if he did something like that. It wasn't an uncle kind of thing to do.

After a couple hours the driver told Matt that the truck was overloaded and he would have to get out at Brandon. Last in, first out. He didn't mind. It was still early enough to get a ride to Regina. Regina. He wasn't sure if it was pronounced to rhyme with "cantina" or if the "i" was pronounced long, as in "vagina." He decided to avoid potential embarrassment and use the "cantina" rhyme, unless someone told him otherwise.

Prospects appeared bleak. He took his place at the end of a line of discouraged hitchers. There was a Quebecois hitcher deep into his second day of trying to get out of town. "First Wawa. Now this," he said. He told Matt there was a "hospital for crazy people" nearby, aiming an index finger at his own ear and making rapid circular motions, and said that drivers in the area were warned not to pick up hitchhikers for fear that they might be self-furloughed lunatics. For several hours he stood there, battling the tedium, attempting to increase his chances for a ride by assuming certain lucky stances or doleful expressions or keeping a superstitious count on cars and, at random intervals, sending telepathic messages to the approaching motorists instructing them to stop.

"You will stop. You will give me a ride. You will look like Ann-Margret in *Carnal Knowledge*.

When he lost faith in his psychic ability to end his no-ride slump, he figured it was just another desperate form of praying to an unlistening or nonexistent God, so he surrendered his fate to the fickle will of the open highway and began walking out into the western vastness.

As he walked past two other hitchhikers, they all started talking. "Standing still drives me crazy," Matt said. "I'd rather keep walking until I get a ride."

"Why don't you hold on a while? Give it another hour. If we don't get rides we can hop a train out of town tonight. I know where the freight yard is."

It sounded good, so Matt reclaimed his place in line and delved back into the practice of using self-crafted psychic abstractions to procure a ride like a luckless fisherman experimenting with new bait.

After another hour when all three of them were still wagging their thumbs to no avail, Matt joined up with Mike from Halifax and Wayne from Toronto. They left the highway, crossed over the Assiniboine River ("Hey, I've got a bone in my ass," Mike announced) and entered Brandon.

Wayne was the leader of the two. He spoke with savvy certainty without seeking approval. Mike was Wayne's aide-de-camp. He was tentative and always gauged Wayne's opinion before committing to his own. They had hopped freights twice before.

"Here's what we do. We go to the railroad yard and talk with one of the brakemen. Tell him where we're going and ask him if there's a freight going out soon. If there is, he'll let us know where it's going and when it's leaving."

"I don't know," said Matt. "What if he calls the cops or the Mounties or whoever? Or puts us on a train going to Hudson Bay? I thought we were supposed to be sneaky about it."

"It's worked so far," Wayne said. "The brakemen don't care. I'll explain to them that we've been trying to get out of town and we've been stuck on the road all day. With the last freight I hopped, the guard even picked out a car for us to ride in and gave us a couple peanut butter and jam sandwiches. I'll do the talking and we'll see what happens."

"The brakeman. Is that a guy who works on the train or a guy who works at the railroad yard?" Matt asked. If he was going to be an honest-to-God freight hopper, he wanted to be sure he had his terminology straight.

"Whatever. I'll talk to whoever it is that's working at the station."

"Maybe he's called a brakeman because it's his job to break our necks if we try to hop on one of his trains." Matt didn't get the laugh he wanted.

The railroad yard was easy to find in such a small town, and sure enough, there was a man walking around the tracks, checking up on the vacant freight cars parked on the pull-off tracks. The boys loitered on the platform of the deserted station with their packs and bags in a clump, trying not to look conspicuous.

"Okay. Here goes nuttin'." Wayne ambled over to talk with the man in charge. There was a handshake—good sign. Some questionable headshakes—not such a good sign. Some finger-pointing toward town—not such a good sign. A final handshake—a very good sign.

"Okay. Here's what's happening. He doesn't care if we jump the next freighter west. It's going to be a couple hours and it will take us to Regina overnight." Matt noted the long "i." "But I had to promise that we won't hang around here until then and that we won't damage anything, write our names on any boxcar walls, or do anything stupid like going to the bathroom or starting campfires to get warm in the boxcar at night, 'cause he could get in trouble and lose his job. He said it'll be cold. And—oh yeah—we've got to be careful not to lock ourselves in the boxcar. If the door closes we won't be able to get out."

Fair enough. This wasn't the Zipper but what the hell. All freight trains are pretty much the same, and hopping one in Manitoba in the seventies could be as adventurous and daring as it was for Kerouac in California in the fifties. Matt slapped Wayne on the back. "Good going. This is gonna be fun."

They bought snacks at a neighborhood store and played Frisbee in a field. Mike said that Frisbee was the official sport of hippies, hitchhikers, and hostelers and would become an Olympic event as soon as pot was legalized, thus proving that smoking pot is not a necessary precursor to ridiculous ideas. Wayne gave him a funny look and said, "Mike, that made absolutely no sense at all."

Matt guzzled down a pint of ice-cold chocolate milk. Everyone discussed their travel plans, compared hostel experiences, and shed bits of light on their lives. All three were college dropouts. Matt told them that he flunked out after one semester at the local community college.

"I got up early and hitched to school every day to give my mother the impression I was attending classes, but after about two weeks all I did was hang out in the cafeteria, shooting the shit and getting high out in the parking lot with my friends. I got busted when my grades arrived in the mail in December. My mother opened it up. Naturally,

I flunked everything. She was more disappointed than pissed. I felt bad, but after that, at least I didn't have to get up early any more and pretend to be a college student, though I did miss the fun times in the cafeteria. I would've gotten an A+ if I was graded on that."

Mike said, "Yeah. I didn't last long, either. I was mostly interested in balling chicks and getting high. Man, the only thing I passed in college was gas." He laughed harder at his own joke than the others did.

Wayne had completed a year and a half of undergraduate studies before he screwed up the courage to tell his parents he had no desire to inherit the family pharmacy started by his grandfather.

"My dad surprised the heck out of me. I thought he would have a fit. But instead he apologized and said he didn't mean to pressure me. For the first time ever we sat down and talked about what I really want to do rather than what I'm supposed to do. When it became obvious that the university was a supreme waste of my time and his money, I dropped out with his blessing. He told me he just wants me to be happy. Now I'm supposedly finding myself. If you find me, let me know, 'cause I have no clue who I am or what I want to do when I grow up." He accentuated the last two words, making quotation marks with the index and middle fingers of both hands.

Matt said, "When I grow up, I wanna be a kid again."

"A-fuckin-men to that," quipped Mike.


When it grew dark, they went back to the yard, checked in with Mr. Railroad Man, and jumped into an empty CPR boxcar. They waited a while and then, after a few false starts and a burst of clanking, banging, and jostling, the boys whooped it up in celebration of the fact that they were underway and Mike shouted, "Let's abandon Brandon."

The romantic allure of hopping freights is unceremoniously dispelled by the monotony and jackboned discomfort of the real-life experience of riding in a boxcar. As they picked up speed, the rush of wind through the open door swept up the debris that remained settled on the floor from its previous load and created funnel clouds of dusty grain particles that peppered their faces and hands and coated their ears, eyes, and hair. It went up their noses, onto their lips and tongues, and down their throats. They coughed and sneezed and itched all over. They rubbed their eyes until they were weepy and veiny and throbby red.

Regina, the next big city, was about 250 miles away. They resigned themselves to the ordeal of a fidgety and sleepless night, but despite his discomfort, Matt did feel the poetry and the clickety-clack music of the rails in the controlled rhythmic clatter of steel wheels as the freighter barreled and bellowed through the deserted wheatfield intersections and in the mournful elephant's wail of the train whistle piercing and shattering the sacred silence of the Canadian prairielands. They charged on like a rampaging dragon, devouring the sleeping sensibilities of each whistle-stop town it rumbled through and of the countryside that whizzed by invisibly but for the occasional constellation of farm lights.

Seeking comfort, the boys kept changing positions. Standing, leaning, sitting, hunkering as the jack-hammering rails vibrated in their asses and their teeth and in the echoey places of their ears. They talked about different jobs they'd had. Matt had been a paperboy for the New Holland Evening Register ("Best job I ever had"), a soda jerk ("Now I'm just a jerk"), a grunt in a newspaper distributorship ("My boss was a senile old guy who had diabetes and never washed and used to chase me around with dirty hypodermic needles"), and an assembler and forklift operator in various factories ("Now I know why they call 'em sweat shops").

Wayne had worked at his father's pharmacy ("I don't recommend working for family. The other workers all resent you because they think you get preferential treatment and then when you go home you get lectured on everything you did wrong. It's the worst of both worlds."). He had also worked at a moving company for a while ("It was a very moving experience").

Mike had worked at a greasy-spoon diner as a dishwasher and a sometimes short-order cook ("I never cooked in my life unless you count canned soup and toast. And then one day the cook doesn't show up so guess who gets promoted? Believe me, you don't wanna see what goes on in one of those kitchens"), a carpenter's assistant ("Any asshole with a hammer can do that") and a variety of odd jobs ("Odd jobs for an odd guy. Is there such a thing as an even job?").

They killed time with jokes and tales as the rails kept whizzing and rattling beneath them and the train continued conquering new land. As predicted, the boxcar got cold, and Matt had to summon the protective powers of his denim coat. Unfortunately, as the night dwindled toward morning, there was another rumbling and roaring going on along the rails of Matt's stomach and intestines. The chocolate milk he drank in Brandon not only disagreed with his innards, it was waging an all-out war. It pooled and gurgled inside him like a time bomb getting ready to detonate. He had surpassed queasy miles ago and had become a human flatulence factory. His gut started to cramp and spasm. The pains got so bad that he had a hard time concentrating well enough to engage in conversation with his new buddies. He was too busy trying not to fart loudly or let loose in his pants. He wished he could hang his sorry ass out the boxcar door and, literally, take a flying shit, and had even considered doing so.

*Ugh. Smelly belly,* he thought.

Even though he knew he was stinking up the boxcar with his putrid silent farts, neither Wayne nor Mike, God bless them, said a word. Matt felt sorry for them and ashamed of himself for being in such a mortifying predicament and for adding an olfactory discomfort to multiple aspects of the physical one. The gastric crisis came and went in wrenching waves that threatened to rip him apart and splatter his sewage upon everything. It was an inner geyser, with each wave growing more lengthy and intense and the respite between waves growing briefer. Everything was going on. Weak legs, lightheadedness, a sense of infantile desperation, and a twisted and knotted gut that creaked and growled like the rusty hinges of an old dungeon door. At one point he thought he might as well get it all over with and just go ahead and shit his pants. He could toss them out into the night and put on his other pair. That's what he would have done if he were alone. But he held on with all his might. He remembered the expression "intestinal fortitude" and wondered if that was what this was.

After an eternity, the skyline of Regina could be seen all aglow in the splendid light of the new-born morning. When the train started slowing down, Wayne said they had to jump out while it was still a distance from the station so the railroad bulls wouldn't catch them. Matt put on his backpack, grabbed his sleeping bag and, when the train seemed to be moving slowly enough, he parachuted out. Looks, however, were deceiving, and the train was going faster than it appeared. The second his feet hit the ground, his top-heavy body was flung down like a door slammed shut and he rolled and tumbled in the gravel and the broken glass and all the other debris littered beside the tracks. He ended up with a mouthful of dirt but his sleeping bag and denim coat cushioned his fall and protected him from the cuts and bruises he would otherwise have suffered. Wayne told him, "Next time, throw your stuff out first and jump out running. Makes for a smoother landing." Matt would have appreciated if Wayne had shared that helpful train-hopper's tip before his leap of faith when it would have done some good.

It was about 7 a.m. when the trio of comrade gallants found the hostel and, at long last, a toilet. Matt had been holding it since well before dawn and didn't know how much time he had before Vesuvius erupted. It was a curious phenomenon, Matt considered, that he could hold it long enough to find a toilet and then, once found, he could just barely maintain control that extra few seconds before the explosive cheek-to-seat contact. Another moment and it would be too late. With a comical stiff-legged sphincter-clenched spider walk he scurried through a door marked "Gents" and secured posthaste the privacy of a banged-up, graffiti-laden stall, unsnapping and unzipping as though his life was in the balance, and then welcomed the merciful relief as he settled his septic-tank ass onto the cold throne of the toilet seat and let the rigid shell of his flexed body fall flaccid in jubilant cannon-blasting surrender to such a gratifying release.

"Uhhhhh. The process of elimination." He closed his eyes and leaned forward, elbows rested upon his thighs, empty of all that ailed him, free of thought, content as a monk, concluding that the joy was worth the pain. He raised his head and opened his eyes to see this verse written on the door in exquisite calligraphic penmanship:

*In eternity there was a universe*
*In this universe there was a galaxy*
*In this galaxy there was a planet*
*On this planet there was a country*
*In this country there was a town*
*In this town there was a house*
*In this house there was a room*
*In this room there stood a chair*
*And on this chair was me*

The warden directed the boys to the University of Saskatchewan for breakfast and a ninety-cent shower, which was the equivalent of a spiritual purification ritual. He snorted steam and warm water in and out of his dusty nostrils, cleansing them as never before. He rinsed his eyeballs as if they were marbles in an eggcup. He shampooed his hair three times until every strand glistened and his scalp was free of all boxcar residue. He scrubbed between all his toes and fingers, beneath his nails, in his ears and in every crack and crevice of his body. As he brushed his teeth and re-dressed, he felt immaculate and sanctified, like he used to feel as a kid after confession, after penance, when he left the church in a perfect state of grace, and a bit sad because he knew the sensation would pass and he would be defiled once again, in both body and soul.

The boys spent the day exploring Regina and planned to hop another westbound freight early the following morning. They went to the Saskatchewan Museum of Natural History and then to a laundromat where they threw all their dirty clothes into one load, then to a soup kitchen, the Marion House on Halifax Street, and feasted on beef stew, donuts, and water. There was a thriving lunchtime crowd. Everyone other than Matt and his friends was an old or middle-aged American Indian. Or, Matt wondered, being in Canada, were they called Canadian Indians? He did not consider it wise to inquire.

The walls were decorated with a haphazard collection of posters and notices and other information of interest to the native community. On prominent display was a large calendar published by White Roots of Peace, Mohawk Nation, Rooseveltown, N.Y., which celebrated Indian culture by marking events of historical significance that had occurred on each date in the year. He scanned the month and read of the death of Chief Little Crow who, in 1863, was killed while picking berries by a white settler who received a twenty-five dollar bounty for his scalp, and that in 1890 the Kiowa people were forbidden to perform the Sun Dance on the Washita River, and that in 1877 Chief Joseph and the Nez Perce battled General Howard on the Clearwater River for two days. Special tribute was paid to Robert Smallboy of the Cree Nation:

In 1968, Chief Robert Smallboy fulfilled a vision of a medicine man and led 143 of his Cree people away from their Hobbema Reservation to the Kootenay Plains of west central Alberta in the Rocky Mountains. Smallboy and his people made this move because of their concern for the young and for the unborn generations yet to come. They feared the influences of white society with its disrespect for things of the Creation and felt that only by leaving this influence could they become pure people again. Today Smallboy's people—and other groups inspired similarly—live on the Kootenays in health and freedom.

—White Roots of Peace, Mohawk Nation, Rooseveltown, N.Y. 13683

*Matt pondered the sad fact that he had never before met an Indian. The only time he remembered being around them was when he was six years old and a group of Mohawks had returned to reclaim their tribal lands in Fort Catherine, a small rural community in the Iroquois Valley. They set up camp alongside Howes Creek until the authorities ran them off. One of Matt's older sisters drove him through the encampment on a drizzly gray day. Matt was disappointed that the Indians were not adorned with buckskin leather or eagle feathers or headdresses, as they were in the movies and on TV westerns, and they did not carry tomahawks or bows and arrows, they didn't have Mohawk haircuts or painted faces, did not ride horses, and were not living in teepees. They looked just as mundane as anyone he might see on the streets of New Holland. The encampment looked like a refugee shanty town of tumbledown shacks, dreary trailers, and sodden pathways. The Indians ignored them as their station wagon sloshed through on the swampy drive, but there was one man, standing taller and more purposeful than the others, who smiled at Matt, whose gaping face was pressed against the window glass, and gave him a friendly wink.*

The boys, with their long unkempt hair, sparse semi-beards, sunburnt faces, and raggy clothes, were the very image of authentic hobo travelers from faraway parts. The Indian men—oddly, there were no women—were both amused by and interested in these white strangers. Several of them glanced at the boys and laughed among themselves. Matt thought that perhaps this was an Indians-only zone and that, by daring to enter, they were violating an unposted local treaty. He got nervous when two men with serious faces came over and asked if they could join the boys at their table. Matt's tensions were eased by the polite curiosity and gentleness of the men's demeanor. One of the men took the lead: "How was your food?"

The boys, fearful of being critical, all said it was very good, nodding with emphasis in case there was any doubt. "The best food ever," they implied with their enthusiastic comments and nods.

"If you want more, you let me know. You boys look hungry and far from home." He broke into a broad smile and drummed his hands against his paunchy gut and said, "Not me. I need to eat less. Not more." His quiet friend laughed nervously.

A couple other men joined them. The most elder among them had sunken eyes, leathery sun-parched skin, and a dignified earthy aura. The others were deferential around him though he spoke sparingly through his few and broken teeth. Everyone was shaking hands and exchanging names and hellos. In the course of the conversation, in a sort of interview, Matt said that he didn't want to go to college and didn't know what he wanted to do. When he told them, upon being asked, that his father was a professor, the first man looked intently into Matt's eyes. "You need to go to school. Get an education. You don't want to be a bum like me, do you?"

Matt struggled to respond. He hated how everyone treated him as soon as they found out he was a professor's son and when they asked him, "Are you going to be a professor, too?" He hated being defined not by who he was but by who he was related to or what they thought that he should aspire to become.

*Why wouldn't I want to be like you?* Matt thought. *You've got personality. You're strong, intelligent, and worthy of emulation. You seem like an admirable man. And, after all, in a mere 30 minutes you have already shown me more kindness than my own father did over a period of years. In a fair world, maybe you would have been a professor or a doctor."*

The man pulled out a silver medallion that hung tucked in his shirt and lifted the chain over his head. "This is for you," he said, and placed it around Matt's neck as if it were a sacred relic. His eyes were clouded and damp but looked glad nonetheless. "This will protect you on your travels." It depicted an old man gripping a large staff, dressed in a toga, and with an infant, or perhaps it was an angel, on his shoulder. There was no inscription. Matt was moved but said nothing as the man smiled at him in a tender and paternal manner.

When the boys left the Marion House, they were certain they had provided that day's entertainment. But that was okay. That was the admission price for their temporary induction as honorary members of whatever tribe it was that they had just communed with.

That evening they sat around the common area swapping stories they had heard on the road. There was the one about the hitchhiker who got a ride with a truck driver carrying an open load of something or other, and the hitcher is riding on top of the load, way up there, facing backward. As the hitcher looks down the road from his high perch, a motorcyclist starts waving to him and he starts waving back. The biker starts waving more energetically at the hitcher who doesn't understand that the truck is approaching a low overpass and, well, he doesn't catch on in time and—Wham!—he is decapitated, his head flying off the truck and rolling down the highway like a grimacing coconut.

Then there were the three motorcyclists blazing down a dark, deserted highway in the middle of the night with no other traffic in sight. One of them speeds way ahead and decides to turn around and zip back toward his two friends and zoom between them. He picks up speed and zeros in on the two approaching headlights and doesn't realize until it's too late that the headlights belong not to his buddies but to a pickup truck and he is splattered like a squished bug.

Then there was the Jesus hitchhiker who had been picked up by different people at different times all over the country. He gets into the car and says nothing. After a while he starts asking the driver if he believes in Jesus and then tells him that Jesus is his salvation. Then, when the driver looks away for a split second and looks back, the mysterious hitchhiker has vanished into thin air.

Then there were the stories that Theodore "Beaver" Cleaver, from "Leave It to Beaver," was killed in Viet Nam. Someone else says, "No, it was Wally who was killed in Viet Nam. Beaver died of a heroin overdose."

Someone else says, "No, Eddie Haskell died in Viet Nam. I read it somewhere." And someone else says, "No he didn't. Eddie Haskell is Alice Cooper."

And someone else says, "What's the grossest thing ever said on TV?" To which a chorus responds, "I don't know. What's the grossest thing ever said on TV?" To which the joke teller shouts, "When June Cleaver says to her husband, 'Ward, don't you think you were a little rough on the Beaver last night?'" To which everyone howls, even the girls.

The storytelling outlasted Matt, Wayne, and Mike who all went to bed by 11 o'clock, having made half-assed arrangements with the warden to be awoken at 4 a.m. so they could hop the freighter to Calgary and Vancouver.

The wake up call never came, so instead, they rode the rails of a well-deserved deep sleep until a phantom rooster crowed Matt awake from the barnyard of a happy dream.

# CHAPTER XIV

"Ah shit!"

The golden illumination of the dingy shades proved that morning had already broken into full light. Matt jostled Wayne and Mike, who both grogged up into a slumped-over position on the edges of their creaky cots. Scratching their beards and scraping their finger nails across their scalps as if raking leaves, they stimulated thought and grumpily tended to the pinching discomforts of scrotal folding.

Wayne said, as Mike nodded in agreement, "We might as well go down there and see if there's anything we can hop. There's gotta be more than one train going west."

Matt, who had his heart set on the early freight train, let his fatigue speak on his behalf. "I'm gonna pass and catch a couple hours sleep instead."

The boys made plans to meet in Vancouver and agreed to leave messages for each other at the hostel. Mike and Wayne gathered their gear and left while everyone else still slept. Matt returned to his dreamy barnyard and slept through breakfast. He paid fifty cents for another night's stay and walked out for a second day on the town, this time as a solo act.

The sky turned gloomy and then rainy. He sought shelter in a bookstore featuring an exhibit about Louis Riel, who was portrayed as a Canadian Jesse James or Billy the Kid, a shroudy outlaw-hero who was either revered or despised, depending on who was writing the history. He skimmed through *Strange Empire* by Joseph Kinsey Howard. On the cover in bold print it read, "Martyr-Saint or Traitor?" Riel was born in 1844 into a race of people known as the Metis, a

French term meaning "mixed blood." The Metis were the offspring of the Plains' Indian women and the French, English, or Scottish men who sought solace in native female companionship as they adventured west. Riel led the Metis in uprisings against the Canadian government as it expanded its control across the plains, encroaching upon the free use of their lands. For his anti-government actions he was arrested, found guilty of treason, and hanged in Regina in 1885. His legacy has labeled him a madman and a genius, a visionary and a charlatan, patriot and traitor, prophet and antichrist.

"And I thought I had problems," mused Matt, placing the book back on the rack.

His next port of refuge was a large department store. He went inside to dodge the rain and shook himself off like a wet dog. He roamed the first floor for several minutes before taking the up escalator.

A leggy teenager in a mini-skirt caught his eye, seemed to notice him in passing, and then scurried ahead onto the escalator in a manner that piqued his curiosity. She jumped up to the fourth or fifth step above him and cast him a quick furtive glance. He entertained notions that she was flirting with him and that a promising conversation might ensue. Then, she leans across the center rail as if looking for someone. She pivots on one leg and extends the other leg out and runs one hand up her thigh and onto the soft landscape of her posterior. Matt does a startled double-take and sees that she is not wearing panties and that her charitable performance is intended solely for his viewing pleasure. "Holy shit," he thinks, "rhymes with Regina." He peers up her skimpy skirt and sees her forbidden tuft of curls as she opens her thighs and hoists herself up even farther, assuming a provocative pose to offer a panoramic view all the way north to her equator. She even looks down at him and flashes a comely smile as she again slides her hand up into her inner thigh, this time tickling her tuft. He remains fixated for the duration of the glorious ascent to the next floor, questioning whether this is meant as an invitation or merely as a display. Whichever it is, he lavishes in it and gives her a kind of standing ovation. When they reach the next floor and she turns right, he turns politely left without speaking or making eye contact.

He lost himself among shoppers in a maze of racks and mirrors, unable to purge the image of this woman revealed. Then he had a change of heart, and the emotional rupture began, causing him to reappraise this opportunity, do an about-face, and search for her. But it was too late. He looked everywhere twice, but she was gone. His two minds argued back and forth, each calling the other a hypocrite and neither in doubt. On one hand, he was pissed off at himself for being indecisive and letting her slip through his fingers. On the other, he tried to pretend he believed that he had made the right decision in turning away from her and shunning all she represented by resisting this occasion of sin and the lure of impure thoughts that had been aroused by the temptation of her flesh. *For he who loves the danger will perish in it,* he recalled. He couldn't even fool himself with that pretense, however, and he wished to hell he could strangle the obedient Catholic schoolboy within and be rid of him forever.

There was a peculiar purplish-orange tint in the air. He felt a tremor. Then, as he was moping along the sidewalk still looking for the escalator girl, hailstones the size of mothballs began pummeling the earth. They plinked and clinked and shattered rapid-fire against car roofs and hoods and windshields and slashed against storefront windows at sharp angles and pounded against his skull like pellets from a rivet gun. Everything was chaos and confusion. It sounded like popcorn popping all around him, and he imagined the city was a big container of Jiffy Pop, and it would keep popping and popping until it buried him like a moth or a flea or a spider.

As he looked up and let the bombardment punish his wicked eyes, he smelled the putrid stench of The Watcher's presence circling above him and sensed the satisfaction It took in witnessing his disintegration, so proud of It's handiwork. He folded up his mind into a defensive pugilistic crouch and felt the tying up of gloves, the tightening of fists, the injection of that certain strain of poison for which there was no antidote. At these times he would take stock and wonder why he was so far from home. Where was he going? What was he looking for? He would think of better days and ask himself why he had been so foolish. Why didn't he make things right when he could have? How had he blown the golden opportunity that had presented itself at Biagi's, all wrapped up in a bow? He hated himself all over again for that debacle and cursed himself for being so despicable and so weird for so long. And would it ever end?

*He thought about Helen and how, sometimes on lonesome summer nights or on holidays when she would be home from college, he would call her but hang up before anyone answered. Late at night when the city was asleep, he would linger in the shadows by her house and hope she would see him from a window and come running out, brazen and angry, and force him to speak and explain himself. He had written dozens of wretched lovesick poems and letters of apology, all unsent. He always carried one with him just in case he ran into her by chance. But he had no such luck. There was no epic cinematic reunion. No serendipitous midsummer-night's-dream encounters to transform the ass he had become back into the happy-ever-after boyfriend of once upon a time.*

*Then, a few weeks before beginning his journey, at 9 p.m. on a bummed-out Friday night while he stayed home hiding under his covers in a depressed sleep, the phone rang him awake.*

*"Is Matt there?" It was a woman.*

*"This is Matt." He was disoriented, still half asleep.*

*"Hi Matt. This is Helen."*

*The words jarred his brain like an electric shock. It had been lifetimes since he last heard her voice. The tone was not that of the sophomore he used to date. But the words, the endearing manner, went straight to his heart and gently strummed those rusty old chords. Did she realize that this week, on the 17th, would be the anniversary of their first date?*

*They talked for twenty minutes and it was all so effortless and relaxed, just as he imagined it would be. She was every bit as he remembered and everything snapped in place and felt as it had so long ago, as though time had collapsed and they had never been apart.* At last! Now maybe I can get back to normal! *They made plans to meet the next night at Biagi's, his favorite hangout bar. After he hung up, he lay in bed, unable to sleep, a hopeful peal of bells resonating in his head, possessed of an unbearable desire, swimming in a warm flood of awakened memories and wondering how on Earth he could survive the eternity of the next twenty-four hours until he would see her again and finally be rescued from the hell he had made of his life.*

*When he arrived at Biagi's, he didn't know whether he should sit outside so he could greet her as she arrived at the front stoop. Or would that appear too eager? Would it be better to position himself at the corner of the bar and say, "hello" as soon as she entered the dark interior? What should he do? How should he act? What should he say? Unable to decide, he just assumed his customary slouch of indifference, alone at a table. He figured that they would exchange innocuous pleasantries for a while, conduct a test run of their adult selves on one another, then he would walk her home, retracing their long-ago footsteps down the same old well-trodden streets, joining hands, and, at night's end, if he mustered up the courage and if the stars and planets were all aligned, he would ask for permission to kiss her goodnight, and then whisper, boldly, shyly, that he loved her. But it had been four years, and he was afraid she would disapprove of the grungy longhaired freak he had become. He was so nervous and frightened that he could hardly talk.*

*The bar was soon packed with the regulars. The jukebox played "Looking Into You," a B-side favorite of Matt's, which concluded with lyrics that he hoped prophesied the night's end:*

*Well I looked into the sky for my anthem*
*And the words and the music came through*
*But words and music can never touch the beauty that I've seen*
*Looking into you—and that's true*

205

*Helen arrived with two friends and elbowed her way through the crowd and was leaning against the jukebox before Matt saw her. She was more mature and womanly than the 16-year-old girl he had dated. But just as he was going to make eye contact and call her over, he was overcome by a fit of panic and fear and, before he could rise, a paralysis set in and he couldn't move or speak or even look in her direction. There was nothing he wanted more at that moment than the relief of casting away the oppressive weight of their long separation and just gazing into her eyes as he used to do. But he dared not. Something was holding him back. Maybe he had mistaken her intention and was setting himself up for a big letdown. Maybe she wasn't interested in rekindling their long-dead flame. Maybe, somehow, he would end up making a fool out of himself with his ridiculous emotions, say something stupid, fumble his lines. His mind was chattering away. It was as if that man inside his head was in full babble with The Watcher, and Weird Matt had taken control of his eyes and was looking the other way, pretending he hadn't seen her, while the Real Matt watched helplessly from within, hoping for divine intervention to break through the impasse. He sat inside his bulletproof bubble, rigid as a frightened rabbit, his mind lapsing into a scrambled fix like a man in a coma who could see, hear, and feel everything around him but was unable to react. Helen was no more than fifteen feet away, probably wondering what the hell he was doing, knowing he must have seen her, and trying to figure out what should she do in this situation.*

*The longer he sat, the more difficult it was to give up the pretense that he hadn't seen her and didn't realize that she was standing behind him, a whisper's distance, as he sat there like the Tin Man, sans oil can, looking the other way. He had painted himself into a dark corner from which there seemed no escape. There was no explanation, no logic, no reasoned voice guiding his inaction. It served no purpose and benefited no one. He had long been praying in his own inarticulate way for the very opportunity that this moment presented, and he had dreamed of this occasion as their long-overdue but joyous reunion. Given his despondency of late, it seemed that his life, quite literally, depended on it. And yet—nothing. This was not mere timidity or awkward uncertainty, nor was it a reckless ploy or calculated strategy. It was pure fear. Plain and simple. Exposed nerve-end existential fear. But of what? And why? He did not know.*

*He was terrified. Terrified by the self-destructive inertia that had assailed him. Terrified at not being able to lift a finger for something he wanted so desperately, and had waited for for so long. Something so within his reach yet which he allowed to slip away. Terrified that he watched her leave and did nothing to prevent the annihilation of his hopes and expectations, as if her departure meant nothing to him, as if he preferred his misery to her company, though a part of him died inside when the door shut behind her. This was the worst of all possible outcomes. The great promise of the evening had been wasted. She had been so near. So near that he could evoke the memory of the scent of her perfume and the aroma of her skin through the smoke and the summer sweat of the chaotic barroom. Terrified. All he had to do was turn his head. Instead, he just fell on his sword and gave up the ghost. He had no excuse. No explanation. One second she was still there. The next second—poof. She was gone. Gone for all of time. Sometimes a split second is all it takes to cement your fate. When something is over, done with, final, there is no difference between a split second and forever.*

*"Is this what it's like to be crazy?" Matt whimpered, resigned to his paralysis, as The Watcher, not magnanimous in victory, cackled maliciously at a job well done, brandished his fangs and said, "See you later, asshole" as It flew through the window and dissolved back into the bleak black sky like a million tiny bat wings.*

*He regained his mobility and left Biagi's in a state of utter disarray, grieving the loss he had brought upon himself and knowing that Helen must have thought he was playing a childish head game, intentionally ignoring her as if it were a power play or ego trip. His behavior was inexplicable, even to himself, and was contrary to all his hopes and desires. It was the defining moment of his dysfunction. And now she would return to college and tell all her girlfriends about her asshole former boyfriend back home. They would all sympathize with her and advise her to forget about him. It was obvious, even to himself, that he was a waste of time.*

*He walked to the house where Helen lived when they first met, before she moved to Sullivan Street, and stood on the sidewalk in the same spot where years earlier he had spent hundreds of hours talking and joking and laughing with her, her two younger sisters, and sometimes even her bashful younger brother. He had been emboldened by her love and was secure in the confidence that she was "the one." He tried to close his eyes and wriggle his mind back into that safe space in the weepy shelter of the old curbside trees, but it didn't work. The night was not supposed to end this way unless it was in accordance with a rigid and unalterable celestial design that demanded they not unite lest something terrible occur. There was no reason for Matt's note nor for his spurning of his own affections for Helen. She had given him a second chance and he knew there would not be another. He sobbed right there in front of Helen's old house. Selfishly. Shamefully. Pathetically. His mutinous heart was taped off like a crime scene, for he had chosen his own dark path and knew now, at the sight of his own cowardly self, that he was too far gone to be rescued by anybody, and that he was not worth the effort.*

Defeated and depleted, he returned to the hostel in the late afternoon. He had already made up his mind to leave Regina right away for Saskatoon even though he had paid to stay another night. Two rides got him away from town, and the third brought him the remaining 150 miles and delivered him to the Saskatoon hostel where he paid his fifty cents and was fed a bowl of soy bean soup, bread, and milk before he crashed into the contented amnesia of an uninterrupted dreamless sleep.

# CHAPTER XV

Matt dove headlong into a hearty breakfast of scrambled eggs, Raisin Bran, rye toast, orange juice, and milk, and then he hooked up with a prissy seventeen-year-old blond-haired Rapunzel girl named Jacqueline from Olympia, Washington. She was touring Canada on a bus pass and was insecure being on her own. Matt was happy to escort her even though he knew that, if she were at home among her peers, she would not be caught dead with a grubby hippie boy in old worn-out jeans and a rumpled t-shirt. She was a prim-and-proper Barbie Doll cheerleader with her fashionable unscuffed sneakers and stylish handbag, her pressed jeans and tightly-tucked tee shirt an ideal fit for her tear-drop bottom and her perky 40-watt top. A genuine ornament to the empire. But he had already fallen in love with her robin's-egg eyes, her perfectly coiffed waist-length mane, her precious mannerisms, and her porcelain china-doll flesh, and he didn't want to squander this opportunity to worship her close up.

"My mom and dad worry about me. They want me to see the world and become more independent before I go to college next year," she said, explaining that they drove her to Vancouver, bought her a bus pass, and set her free to visit her grandparents in Yorkton, Saskatchewan. "I have to call them every day or they get all freaked out."

They traipsed around town and ended up sitting in a park alongside the Saskatchewan River. Happy-faced couples strolled by hand-in-hand, and Matt speculated whether they were truly happy and had found "the one" or if they had settled for the two or the three or for someone barely on the charts, someone acceptable and not unpleasant to tide them over until the real "one" came along.

A pregnant mother waddled by with her toddler daughter skipping beside her. The girl sprang alive, jumping up and down and sprinting forward, shouting, "Mommy! Mommy! Look! It's Daddy!" and in a flying leap landed in her father's opened arms, gave him a joyful hug, and said, "See how pretty my dress is, Daddy?"

Matt said, "Did you see that? Wasn't that beautiful?"

Jacqueline looked puzzled and with a lackadaisical yawn answered, "See what?"

She was not used to the inconveniences of life on the road and was unable to appreciate anything outside her personal sphere. She launched into a running commentary of her many discomforts and complained so much about her aching feet and legs that Matt thought she may be expecting a piggyback ride. He might have obliged, had she asked. She whined that the previous day's storm had ruined her day and that her bus ride to Saskatoon had been hot and sticky and that she was stuck next to an irritating wrinkle-faced old immigrant lady who spoke broken English, wore foul perfume, had breath like garlic and onions, and volunteered vivid unsolicited descriptions of her bowel problems. When Matt tried to divert her attentions to something more pleasant, Jacqueline deflected his drift and, with the sheer power of her self-centered indifference, brought the conversation back to its proper orbit, which was fixed around the needs and wants of her own pampered I-me-mine universe.

Matt had noticed over the years that a girl who had at first appeared unattractive would become beautiful after he had gotten to know her better. Whenever that happened, he couldn't understand the hows and whys of such a transformation. Unfortunately for Jacqueline, the reverse was also true.

Stunned by her glamorous facade, Matt tolerated and made silent excuses for her rudeness. He nicknamed her Barbie and began resenting her because she knew she was beautiful and that her allure would provide her with undeserved advantages in life as well as an endless string of defective Kens. She would always get the front-seat window on the free ride. Nevertheless, he succumbed to envisioning her as his girlfriend and contemplated the pleasures he might discover in that role. It annoyed him that he was weak-willed enough to desire someone he disapproved of while he was snared in the trap of her apparent physical beauty.

While they were sitting on the bench, a barefooted freak carrying a stack of fliers moseyed over to them, his loyal St. Bernard lumbering beside him. He was a big guy with an all-occasion smile and shoulder-length ringlets of reddish brown hair. Matt could tell that he was a Jesus freak but was nonetheless disarmed by his gentleness, awkward sincerity, and good intentions.

"Hey there. How are you guys doin'?" He spoke in a boppy, loping tone.

"Doin' all right. How are you?" Matt replied.

Jacqueline went mute and would not even look the man in the eye.

"I'm doin' excellent, man. Yup. Just great. Just walking my dog and, you know, talking to folks about stuff."

"That is one hell of a dog. How much does he weigh?"

"Oh, whew, I don't know. About as much as I do." The beast rested his huge drooly jaw on Matt's thigh, licking his chops and looking up with weepy puppy-dog eyes.

"What's his name?" Matt massaged the muscles of his thick furry neck.

"Barabbas."

"That's a cool name. Did you name him?" Matt thought he could control the direction of the conversation by continuing to ask questions.

"Yeah. I named him that because the animal shelter was gonna put him to sleep if he didn't get adopted. I went there just looking for a Heinz 57 kind of mutt. But when I saw this guy and found out that he was on death row having his last supper, I knew what I had to do. He was just a scrawny runt back then. You could feel all his ribs sticking out. All mangy. It was sad. So that's how I got him, and under the circumstances, I thought Barabbas was the appropriate name."

"Give us Barabbas," Matt chanted, having seen the movie.

"Yeah, that's right. You know what I'm saying."

Matt made it easy for him. "You got some fliers there?"

Jacqueline still had said nothing as she examined her decorative nails. She exhaled disapprovingly, gave Matt the hairy eyeball, scrunched up her lips, and looked as though she was being forced to share a toilet with a leper.

"Yeah. I do. Here. I wanted to give you one of these." He got down on one knee and handed one each to Matt and Jacqueline, who took it but didn't look at it or him. It advertised an open invitation to learn how the love of Jesus can guarantee eternal life. In simple handwritten script it said, "Jesus is in your heart. Let us help you to find Him" and "Winning souls for Jesus." There was a poorly drawn map showing how to find the drop-in center. "It doesn't matter what religion you are," the man said. "Jesus is for everyone. Young or old. Rich or poor."

Matt thought that if all the Jesus freaks who had fought for his soul over the years had gotten an advance peek at what a ramshackle jalopy of a soul it was, they wouldn't have tried so hard. He nonetheless envied them for their peaceful air of certainty, for their obedient and selfless devotion and, most of all, for being willing to face ridicule and rejection for the sake of a belief they at least pretended to hold as true. Matt didn't think he had the courage to ignore what people thought of him and to not obsess about it at night while he was trying to sleep. Despite a cautious respect, he detested their unfailing habit of interpreting his uncertainty as a weakness and their own doubtless inflexibility as a strength. And though it was a subject in which he had a deep abiding interest, every time he tried to have an even-handed conversation or a mutual exchange of religious ideas and theories and random musings, all he got in return was a self-righteous sermon and the promise of a one-way ticket to a burning pit. They ignored his contemplations about the existence and nature of God and Jesus, about the virgin birth and the resurrection, and religion in general, refusing to even discuss them, as if they were of no consequence. Instead, they always believed they held the moral high ground and that their beliefs were indisputable facts and yours were misguided, false apprehensions. Blinded by their certainty, they were unable to even entertain the hypothetical possibility that their assumptions about salvation and heavenly rewards might be wrong and refused to examine them for flaws. They already had it all figured out. That door was shut. No need for further review. But nothing is true simply because it is fervently believed or is shouted louder or argued longer, and Matt tired of wasting his time with them. All they did was proselytize and condescend, get all fire-and-brimstoney and, like the nuns, pull out the big trump card by threatening an eternity of exquisite suffering in the flames of hell if he didn't accept Jesus as his personal savior. As far as Matt was concerned, that was the fart in the elevator.

Barabbas was a frisky emissary of good will. Matt wondered if dogs ever got depressed or were kept awake at night questioning what they had done during the day—should they have pissed on that tree or sniffed that dog's ass—and, knowing they didn't, he wished that he were less like himself and more like Barabbas. *This world would be a much better place,* he thought, *if it were run by dogs. Barabbas here would make a fine president! Certainly much better than the one we've got now.* And this long-haired pilgrim, this freak for Jesus, was a folksy spokesman, not the hard-sell huckster with whom Matt was more accustomed. So, to his surprise, Matt found himself enjoying the casual chat and was amused by Jacqueline's silent protest.

Then, with a sudden shift of heart, he slipped into a kind of epiphany and saw that it wasn't fair of him to be so critical of her, that it was shallow and arrogant to evaluate her in such crude physical terms and to be so judgmental and smug without even making an attempt to seek the substance beneath her surface. He hated being judged by others and blushed inside when he realized he was doing exactly that to Jacqueline. She was no different than he was, a young person trying to figure out how to survive in this world, seeking transformative growth, and struggling with whatever inner conflicts and whatever dreams and desires had lured her from the coddled safety and comfort of her home to this distant hostel in this foreign city with this perfect stranger. He admired the courage it must have taken for her, at such a tender age, to launch her sheltered self out into the uncertain universe of uncomfortable buses and crowded dormitories inhabited by grungy vagabonds.

*And it's a beautiful day,* he thought, *and I am sitting here on the great green grass of a great green park with a beautiful girl and, well, the more I think about it, the less her complaining bothers me, and I would really like to hug her and make her laugh and tell her that everything is going to be fine.*

*And I want to thank this Jesus-freak fellow and his biblical dog for coming over to talk with us with the noblest of intentions, and for this unexpected gift of suddenly feeling great again.*

When the guy left, he flashed them the peace sign and said, "Jesus loves you."

Matt said, "I hope so."

Jacqueline hissed through her pouty frown. "God! I thought he would never leave. You shouldn't have talked to him so much."

Matt just smiled and watched Barabbas bounding across the luxuriant green grass, dallying only to sample the fragrant bouquet of a collie's ass as he leapt toward a family of picnickers, his slobbery tongue at the ready and his barefooted master dutifully behind with fliers in hand.

Dinner was as good as a home-cooked meal. Pork chops, mashed potatoes, beans, spinach, bread, garlic breadsticks, watermelon, and Kool-Aid. Matt ate next to someone who told him to stick with the coast road, the scenic route, when he reached California.

"Pacific Highway, man, straight on down through Big Sur all the way to LA. It is definitely the coast with the most. In British Columbia, go through the Okanogan Valley down to Penticton. It might take you out of your way, depending on how your rides go, but it's worth it. And if you want, you can probably get a job picking fruit on one of the orchards. It's loaded with orchards there."

The idea of working as a migrant farmhand on an orchard in the Canadian Rockies appealed to the displaced Tom Joad refugee inside Matt. The way the kid talked about the Okanogan Valley, which Matt had never heard of before, made it sound like a mythical paradise.

Matt's next acquaintance was a fantastic kid from Toronto who had hitched by himself from Calgary after splitting up with his traveling partner. He sat next to Matt in an adjoining playground area at a picnic table with the names and hometowns of hitchhiking transients engraved in it and the dates of their visits. The kid was engaged in nervously biting his fingernails down to the knuckles. He was scared, like Jacqueline, and was battling through the growing pains of being on his own. He kept reassuring himself that going it alone was the best way to open yourself up to the many gifts of the traveling experience. Matt enjoyed the idea that the kid was looking up to him as a big brother or a road adviser, so he bolstered the kid with encouragement and good humor.

"There's nothing to worry about. You're doing great, man. And the cool thing about these hostels is that you're never alone, even if you're hitching by yourself. There's always a warm meal and a hostel full of new friends at the end of each day. We're all just one big family that changes on a daily basis."

The kid started a jittery, self-conscious conversation, excessively praising the food and seeking Matt's approval.

"It was the best chicken I ever had. I ain't gonna lie about that."

They talked about books and the kid said, "I guess I'm not much of a reader." He gave Matt an Agatha Christie mystery. "I'm almost through with it but I don't care about finishing it. Here—you can have it. It's a good book." Matt took it not because he wanted it but because the giving of the gift was important to the kid. There was something ritualistic and sacred in the offer and acceptance of a book that neither one wanted to read. Something pure that filled an abstract emptiness inside each of them.

Matt would have enjoyed sticking around and getting to know the kid better, but he had already made up his mind to leave before dark for Edmonton and the historic Klondike Days Free Pancake Breakfast. He was the midnight rambler, wandering by the half-light of a gibbous moon while the rest of the world slept. Mysterious and hip like a real travelin' man.

A ride with a carload of local kids brought him to the edge of town, and then he rode with a middle-aged man who lived in the country but worked in the city. "Eight hours at a time is about all I can take before it starts getting on my nerves. I'm a country boy."

Next was a ride to North Battleford with a late-twentyish professional who was envious of all the carefree hitchhikers on the roads. He had gone straight to college and graduated directly into a career. "My job's okay, but it would've been nice to take a year off to see the world before I get married and settle down and start having kids. That'll be a whole new ballgame."

Matt couldn't picture himself ever being responsible or mature enough to have a wife and kids or even a steady job. He had no career ambitions or plans, unless hitchhiking was a career and bumming around was a plan. He could see no further forward than to the next ride or the next night's lodging. The rest of his life was a mystery that even Agatha Christie couldn't solve.

The man went out of his way to drop Matt off at a good spot on the far side of town where his face was swarmed by a flurry of bugs for an intolerable fifteen minutes before getting a ride to Lloydminster with a man in his thirties who didn't say where he was from or where he was going.

After one of many long silences, he turned the radio down and asked Matt, "Do you have a girlfriend?"

"No. Not really." He regretted not having the nerve or foresight to lie.

"Why not?"

Matt was uncomfortable and thought the man was cautiously feeling him out but didn't want to make any direct suggestions or advances until he was sure that Matt was on board.

"I don't know. I've been unlucky. Things just haven't worked out. I haven't met the right girl yet." He tried not to emphasize the word "girl" any more than normal. Past experience told him that if the man worked up the courage to make an out-and-out proposition, Matt would get dropped off as soon as he declined the opportunity. Lloydminster was still about fifty miles away, and he didn't want to get stranded out there in the sticks.

The driver said, "Yeah. Me neither." Then he turned the radio back up, dropped the chat and ignored the buzz of tension that kept Matt alert and focused on the tunneling headlights for the remainder of the ride. When they approached Lloydminster the man said, "I'm going to stop here and get a room for the night. You're welcome to stay if you want."

Matt wasn't sure if he should be embarrassed, scared, or flattered. "No thanks. I'm gonna keep on hitching. Thanks anyway."

Before Matt could jump out of the car, the man said, "Listen. I don't mean to offend you or make you uncomfortable. I'm sorry if I did. It's so humiliating, driving around like this, but it's very difficult. Life, I mean. If anyone finds out about me, I'm dead. Or might as well be. I'm sorry."

Matt was ashamed of himself for having dismissed the humanity of this suffering soul. The man had meant him no harm, and, like Matt, was just looking for some companionship. Part of him considered making a proposal, a compromise where Matt could close his eyes and pretend that it was a woman's head bobbing rhythmically in his lap. Out of sympathy, out of curiosity, as an act of mercy. And for the pleasure. He knew it would feel good. It is the act, after all, not the gender, that delivers the eruptive sensations. *Fuck my luck*, he thought. *Why can't a woman driver make the same proposition?* Then, upon reflection, *This could have been my fantasy ride if I were so inclined. He was a nice guy and was quite good looking.* Sometimes, given his history of failure with girls, he feared that he may be homosexual and was just too much of a coward to admit it. He pondered his dilemma, uncertain why the thought of engaging in homosexual sex should bother him and, if love is what really counts, questioning why it should matter how that love is expressed and between whom.

Lloydminster was in both Saskatchewan and Alberta. According to the map, he had come 170 miles and Edmonton was another 156. He walked beyond the lights of the town and down the deserted two-laner until he reached an all-night Edward Hopper "Nighthawks" roadside café. It was close to midnight, and most of the traffic was 18-wheeled transporters, and they never picked up hitchhikers—at least not male hitchhikers. Visions of a hot and fluffy free pancake breakfast danced in his head. He planted himself in a well-lit spot at the edge of the café lot, went inside a couple times for tea and toast with strawberry jam, and about two hours later, for the first time ever, got a ride in one of those transporters that carried him through the remainder of the night and all the way to Edmonton.

# CHAPTER XVI

Matt couldn't wait to get out of the truck. Throughout the night, the jostle and bump of the nerve-wracking ride had kept him conscious enough to spoon feed the road-weary driver with a jolt of forced conversation so he wouldn't fall asleep at the wheel. Both of their heads were bobbing up and down like they were mounted on springs, repeatedly lapsing off to one side and then jerking erect with momentarily wide-awake eyes. This is what hell could be like, he supposed, an eternity of struggling against the gravity of sleep in a limbo of semi-consciousness. Matt's greatest efforts of concentration could keep his own eyelids pried open for no more than about twenty seconds at a time before they outsmarted him and eased shut with a will of their own. Meanwhile, the driver had become a crazed cartoon character with bloodshot eyes bulging out all red and throbby and on the verge of popping out of his head and splatting against the windshield like shot grapes. He snapped the cap off a palm-sized tubular vial and tossed a handful of candy-colored pills into his mouth and washed them down his throat with a belt of warm beer.

Matt was writing his obituary in the local papers: "Also dead is a dumb-ass hitchhiker from some podunk town in upstate New York who didn't have enough sense to get out of the truck before both he and the driver fell sound asleep like the idiots they must have been. His name is being withheld to avoid shame and disgrace to his family and loved ones."

Daylight arrived, and the tall buildings of Edmonton commenced glistening upon the horizon. When he was dropped off in the outskirts of town, it was like an unexpected pardon from a certain death sentence. His relief, however, was soon overcome by a mind-numbing exhaustion that left him too disoriented to string thoughts together in a meaningful pattern, as if English had become a foreign language. Like a zombie struck blind by sunlight, he bumbled the sidewalks indecisively, following a misguided intuition that he was staggering in the right direction. In reality, he simply didn't have the mental energy to convince his mushy mind to turn around. His backpack felt like it was filled with rocks, much like his head, and if he didn't soon find a place to lay down and shut his eyes, he was afraid he would keel over and end up in a hospital or jail.

Work-bound commuters scurried around him on their preoccupied paths to their bus stops, paying no attention as he weaved and mumbled garbled sentence fragments to himself. He wobbled onward in a fog and couldn't remember what city he was in. The aromatic blend of fragrant morning air and the billowing charcoal clouds of stinky bus exhaust reminded him of England, and for a split-second or two he thought he was back at Victoria Station in London. He collapsed sideways into the bushes and slid defeated to the sidewalk in a seated position. An alert lady took notice and asked if he was all right. She interrupted his delirious effort to explain himself and said, "Oh just come with me. We'll get you there." She took his hand and helped him to rise.

She escorted him to a busy corner where a flock of still-drowsy suburbanites waited in silence with briefcases and brown lunch bags. When his bus arrived, she guided him through the door and gave instructions to the driver. He felt like a child boarding the big bus on his first day of kindergarten. She waved goodbye with a loving smile and said, "Good luck, son" as though she were his own mother.

The commuters herded into the bus and took their customary seats. Matt plopped into place between two stiff figures intent on their morning papers. He slouched there in a depleted stupor, awaiting further instructions. He was dirty and smelly and felt alien and, most of all, alone. His head kept falling forward and he toppled sideways and back and forth, napping on the shoulders of the commuters beside him. They probably thought he was high and nodding out. He lapsed into a semi-comatose state during the twenty-minute ride and was revived by a stern voice and a brisk shake of his shoulder: "Wake up. This is your stop."

The bus driver loomed rubbery-faced and immense before Matt's bleary red eyes. The other passengers were looking at him, whispering their disapproval, or giggling with amusement as he came to in a salivating daze. He knew he was making a spectacle of himself but couldn't help it. He teetered from the somnolent hum of the bus to the rattling industrial clatter and hiss of the street.

He stumbled into the hostel and was registering as a cluster of the previous night's travelers were collecting their gear and readying for the road. When the warden informed him that some of the Klondike Days festivities were taking place just around the corner, Matt was artificially recharged and awakened enough to make a beeline to the breakfast bonanza he'd been dreaming about since the Soo.

Something in the notion of the free pancake breakfast had taken root in his imagination and had blossomed itself up into an overblown fantasy of utopian proportions. Throngs of happy celebrants would be indulging together on succulent mouthwatering stacks of steamy flapjacks and decadent mounds of sizzling Canadian bacon and sausage amid rivers of free-flowing maple syrup and deep-chilled pools of fresh orange juice on an extended Thanksgiving Day banquet table, and the air would tingle with the essence of honey and fresh-cut flowers. He had pictured himself returning home and bragging to all his friends about this amazing faraway celebration, and they would all be in awe of his good fortune. But, once again, he'd been sucker punched by his own gullibility and felt ridiculous when he flew there on the wings of a second wind only to discover a dreary booth where he received his free lukewarm cup of dirty-dishwater Sanka and a half of a dried-out last-night's kielbasa sandwich on a stale hot dog bun from a greasy-haired guy in a smudged-up sleeveless t-shirt, a three-day beard, and a bush of armpit hair sprouting from each side. No pancakes. No utopian throngs of joyful celebrants. And the air stank of dust and muffler fumes plus a whiff or two of fermenting perspiration. He beat a fast path back for a last minute down-to-earth feast of creamy-sweet porridge with raisins and dried prunes, which was warm and filling and gave him a homey feeling.

The entire day lay ahead of him, but he was too wasted to enjoy it. The warden refused Matt's weak plea to let him sleep in during the day while the dorms were closed but that it would be okay to rest in the reception area, so he traded in his dreams of a comfortable daytime bed and settled instead for curling up like a stray dog on the floor of a lumpy pack-filled waiting room where noisy hostelers tramped in and out all day long, dropping their bulky baggage all around and frustrating his quest for sound sleep.

His body and mind entered new unexplored territories of exhaustion, which sometimes turned surreal and hallucinatory. He was unable to maintain a coherent waking relationship with reality and felt himself slipping into a Dali-esque consciousness in which imagination superseded sense perception. At one point he found himself reciting the Green Lantern's comic book incantation, as though doing so might give him the super powers necessary to regain his strength:

*In brightest day*
*In blackest night*
*No evil shall escape my sight*
*Let those who worship evil's might*
*Beware my power—Green Lantern's light!*

He snapped back and forth in a spastic tightrope walk between the waking and sleeping worlds. In one instant he crashed into a full-blown already-in-progress dream about almost kissing a girl in the woods behind his old house and became immersed in its aroused elastic longing and, in the next instant, he catapulted back into the hostel, squinting through blurred eyes at a clock that read earlier than it did before the dream, as if time were flowing backward. And so it was. Back and forth. At one moment endeavoring to surrender himself wholeheartedly to the tantalizing promised land of sleep, and then just as restful dreams are within his grasp, they recede ever so far away ,and he reawakens into the astral surrealism of his earthbound room. At times the two worlds began merging into that hell-like living limbo where his mind could get trapped if he didn't soon fall into a sustained sleep, and he wondered again if that was what hell, or perhaps mental illness, was like: being seduced by the paranoid beliefs of a desperate mind trapped and held hostage in a frightening and detested space not of its own choosing. At his most lucid moments, he knew that all he needed was a good night's sleep on a comfortable mattress with a downy pillow and then, in the morning, a steamy shower and a stack of those pancakes he'd been fantasizing about. But in those other moments he thought he had already gone mad and that it was already too too late and that he was already too too lost.

By the time the hostel reopened at dinnertime, he had managed only a couple hours of hit-and-miss sleep, ten minutes here, fifteen minutes there, over the twisted course of the interminable day. He brushed his teeth and threw cold water on his face, ate a couple hot dogs on bread, an apple and a banana, and some sugar-infused Kool-Aid. Then he started meeting new travelers with new stories and life was good again.

There was a shy kid from Edmundston, New Brunswick, who was an expert on cartoons, knew all the theme songs, and could impersonate many of the characters.

"Behind every cartoon there is a meaning," he declared, like a prophet.

Then he met a reeky kid in highwater pants who had been kicked out of his house in Winnipeg. He was only fifteen and already filled with tales of woe.

"If it weren't for the hostels, I'd be starving in a gutter." He was glum and dazed. "I was leaving Regina and a guy said he'd take me all the way to North Battleford. And what's he do? He goes about ten miles and says he has to stop in and see an old buddy, so he drops me off in the middle of nowhere. I walk a while and finally a car stops and says he can take me to Lloydminster but then breaks down, so I end up sleeping in his backseat that night. I finally get to Lloydminster, and I was gonna stay with a friend, but I couldn't find him. So I came to Edmonton 'cause I know a girl here, and I thought I could stay at her place. But when I got there she wouldn't let me stay 'cause her sister was there and she was all fucked up over something."

There was another hosteler who looked and sounded like Mickey Rooney. He was telling stories about a dog he used to have: "Yeah, this dog wouldn't eat nothin' but steamed rice and peanut butter sandwiches. Man. You wanna see something funny? Feed your dog a peanut butter sandwich."

Later, as Matt lay in bed, searching for the peace and clarity that would grant him sleep, his mind darted back and fixed itself onto the image of the woman, the perfect stranger who had lent him her hand and had accompanied him to the bus early that morning when he was exhausted and hallucinating and heading in the wrong direction.

*It reminded him of something that happened in England. He was walking away from Speakers' Corner at Hyde Park on a Sunday afternoon when he saw a cluster of pedestrians on the broad sidewalk in front of a large department store. A filthy old bag lady dressed in torn rags had fallen and was half-sitting, propped up on one hand, unable to rise, muttering expletives at the crowd which stood there gawking as she struggled in vain, pathetic and deranged and defeated in her effort to rise to her feet. Matt wanted to help but continued on his way, condemning the passive onlookers for their indifference but doing nothing himself. A block later, he did a guilty about face and ran back to help the woman. By that time she was limping away, spitting and ranting at her distorted reflection in the storefront window. Matt's opportunity had passed forever.*

*As he went a mere two or three blocks farther down the street there was, quite incredibly, another crowd milling around another miserable old woman who had fallen and it was as if time had reversed itself and had given him that rare second chance to atone for his failure to act. The crowd watched the destitute figure as though she was the star in an amusing freak show performance. This time Matt cut a confident path straight through the apathetic spectators, got on his knees, offered his hand, and helped her rise to her feet. She gave him a look of disdain and spat at him as she shuffled away in a hail of gibberish, dragging all of her possessions in a moldy heap of old burlap bags. But it was redemption, not thanks, that he was looking for, and he knew he had done the right thing, even if it was for selfish reasons. After all, there are selfish motives behind all charitable acts and in all good deeds: the sense of moral superiority, the easing of a guilty conscience, and the assurance of a solid brick or two in your heavenly home.*

Now, recalling that incident, Matt knew that all his good intentions were meaningless and that the potential true grace of a good intention makes no difference and is not realized until it is acted upon. Otherwise it is nothing more than an unplanted seed: all potential with no results.

He thought of the countless number of disinterested commuters who had passed him by that morning as he stumbled like an idiot in his frazzled stupor. Had they entertained thoughts of doing that simple Good Samaritan deed that would have made the difference? Some, probably. But they did not. Instead they went on their urgent way and let their urgent thoughts drift to other matters, oblivious to all but their morning work bell. As far as Matt was concerned, it was not their thoughts that counted. All that counted was the single helping hand of a stranger, someone he had never met and would never see again.

He hummed himself to sleep with the tune of a favorite song:

*Oh the sisters of mercy they are not departed or gone*
*They were waiting for me when I thought that I just can't go on*
*And they brought me their comfort and later they brought*
*me this song*
*Oh I hope you run in to them, you who've been traveling so long*

# CHAPTER XVII

Matt rose early. He had a long day ahead of him. Though Calgary was only 186 miles south by the direct route on Highway 2, he had chosen a roundabout scenic route that would take him into the Rockies and through Jasper, Lake Louise, and Banff, which added more than 300 miles and an extra day or two to his journey. He didn't mind because he was impatient to see the mountains and was always happiest while on the road.

His first encounter was with an Englishman who single-handedly carved out an exception to Matt's general rule that nobody deserves to be called an asshole. As they stood beside each other in the bathroom cleaning their teeth and studying their reflections in the mirror, Matt tried to make casual small talk. Instead, the guy, imperious and erect, snapped at Matt and launched into a bombastic rant.

"Most of the bloody Americans I've met are nervous wrecks. So bloody ignorant. Always playing silly mind games and spouting their foolish drivel."

Fumbling with his leather Dopp kit, he blustered with fangs out about Americans' inability to speak proper English. It was a well-worn tirade about the general unpleasantness of the American character that he probably repeated whenever the opportunity availed itself. How Americans had no manners and treated everyone else as inferiors, a claim which, Matt had to confess, did have its merits. It occurred to Matt that the man was unintentionally describing his own self and that what we despise in others is often that which we are blind to within ourselves. It was ironic that it would be here, in far-flung western Canada, that he would be upbraided by an Englishman after having been welcomed with only kindness and generosity the entire time he spent bumming around England.

Matt wasn't sure if the man was saying these things because he knew Matt was American, and was thus was making a frontal assault, or that he thought Matt was Canadian and believed himself to be commiserating with a kindred spirit about a mutual hatred of the dreaded Yanks. The man spat out his toothpaste, stuck out his bottom lip, and sneered into the mirror at Matt's reflection as though tossing him a challenge. From his landed-gentry perch, he condescended to thinking that Americans were all shaped by the same cookie cutter and baked in the same oven. Matt felt obligated to retaliate and imagined responding with something witty. He didn't say anything, though, for fear that he might slip up and help prove the man's theory. Instead he ignored the snobby bickering and swore under his breath. But moments later he tenderized his anger by realizing that this young man, preening himself in the airs of self-presumed superiority, had once been some loving mother's sweet little boy in short corduroy trousers.

He took a bus to the westward road and hopped out into a gray drizzle. After a couple of inconsequential rides, he hit the jackpot with a ride all the way to Jasper, about 200 miles. Andrew was a hippie intellectual who Matt dubbed, "The Professor." He was driving home to Vancouver after an exploratory visit with his on-again, off-again girlfriend from his college days.

"We're still teeter-tottering and neither of us wants to be the first to jump off."

Matt explained that he was going to Calgary to visit Volker, a friend he and Boone had met in London. "It's gonna be great. Volker doesn't know I'm coming, and it'll be a good laugh to see the surprise on his face when I drop in out of the blue."

As though the topic of the day had been assigned that morning, Andrew complained that Americans were plundering the world's natural resources, implying that all Americans, by their very nature, were greedy and indifferent to the destructive effects their "rampant consumerism" was having on the world's environment. Matt despised the stigma of being American and wanted to be accepted for who he was as an individual, but he nonetheless felt obligated to throw in his American two-cents worth, and said, "As far as I can tell, there really isn't much difference between Americans and Canadians. We're pretty much the same."

Andrew gasped out a knee-jerk, "No way," but then, in deference to his American passenger, stopped short and said, "Well, maybe the people aren't much different. But the governments are."

It was a sensible compromise with neither side surrendering ground and yet managing to avoid the uncomfortable impasse. Matt pondered his growing realization that Canadians had great national pride and would defend it staunchly against any insinuation that they should be confused with their black-sheep southern cousins. Likewise, during his European visit earlier in the year, Matt had learned that America, as observed from the outside by foreigners, looks much different than as observed by its inhabitants from within, where the ugliness is less obvious.

Changing the subject, Andrew asked Matt, "Have you ever heard of 'Chariots of the Gods'?" He hadn't. Andrew explained that the book proposes the theory that aliens had visited Earth in ancient times and had assisted early civilizations with the construction of the Egyptian pyramids, Stonehenge, and the gigantic stone head statues on Easter Island, among other things. Andrew took it a step further. "What if Jesus was an alien? Or if Mary was artificially inseminated with alien sperm? Just think about it!"

The last idea appealed to Matt. He had never been quite on board with the far-fetched immaculate-conception Virgin Mary yarn. It complicated things unnecessarily and, upon new reflection, seemed a bogus and hastily crafted alibi. It just didn't pass the smell test. Matt objected to the way that poor old Joseph was always being written out of the family tree. And poor Mary, just another barefoot and pregnant little girl, a helpless pawn all tangled up in the middle of these biblical shenanigans, clueless as to all the ulterior motives at work within her and without her.

Matt applied Occam's razor and figured that Mary's was just another garden variety unwed teenaged pregnancy and that she and her budding-carpenter boyfriend concocted this fabulous story to get Joseph off the hook and save Mary from the beating she was sure to receive from her dishonored father. Their scheme worked beyond their wildest expectations and gave their unsuspecting son a legacy that took thirty-three years to fulfill. By then, given the course of the impossible-to-have-been-predicted events and the history-altering tragedy engendered by their little white lie, it was too late to set the record straight for the lie had become the "truth."

Then they discussed, "2001: A Space Odyssey" and how kids would drop acid before the movie, timing it so they would peak during the mind-blowing special effects sequence.

"Have you ever dropped acid?" Andrew asked.

"Yeah. Just a few times. But, I don't know, it started freaking me out. It was about eighty percent amazing, but the other twenty percent was what I called my acid indigestion. My heart would start beating fast and I'd get paranoid. Then I'd be bummed out for about a week afterward. It got so that I was too scared to take it anymore. How about you?" Matt didn't mention the suicidal thoughts that accompanied the coming-down phase of those trips.

"For a while I was into it. Sunshine. Purple haze. Some of that purple microdot shit. Had some interesting times. Never had a bad trip. Then I started hanging out with a different crowd and now I just smoke pot. But I don't have any on me."

*Matt liked the way his senses were honed when he was tripping. A song would last forever and he would understand the deeper meaning of the lyrics for the first time, though he had heard them dozens of times before. Even throwaway tunes sounded like top ten Billboard hits. Sometimes he even heard the conversations that took place in the studio when the song was being recorded. Or he could look in the mirror and see in his eyeball's reflection his own image making its way back into his brain to the tip end of an optic nerve from where it looked back at him with a surprised wink. And once, at 2 a.m. in Brownie's Diner with a couple of his Hill Hoods friends, he ordered a 22-ounce glass of ice-cold buttermilk with his cheeseburger and fries and was delighted to find that, with his psychedelically reconfigured tongue, it tasted like a milkshake. Flowers bloomed before his very eyes and the other diners turned into cartoon characters and everything was either hilariously funny or stupendously fascinating.*

*Each time when he started coming down, the trip would sour and he would plummet down the depression tunnel, consumed by a sublime sadness and a negative wondrousness, as if beauty and terror had been blended together into a single all-encompassing mood. Then he started thinking about heart attacks, and his experiences became nightmarish.*

*The last time he tripped was on a Halloween night at Siena College. He and his friend Buck had just started tripping and were walking across campus through the quad. They looked up and saw a room glowing in the dark from the top floor of one of the dorms. Lights were flashing and heads were bobbing through the window. Buck said, "We've got to go there."*

*They entered the building and described what they had seen to the first student they ran into. "Yeah. I know where you mean. That's the spaceship."*

*When the starry-eyed trippers knocked on the door, it cracked open. "Is this the spaceship?"*

*"Yes. Who are you?" He wore a conical wizard's cap and a spangled robe.*

*"I'm Buck and this is Matt. We're tripping and we saw your room from outside and we felt that you were calling us."*

*"I'm the Commander. Come on in. Join the party."*

*The door opened wide to a room bursting with a tribe of energetic costumed kids, tripping, dancing with abandon, and singing along with the music blasting from the stereo:*

*Nights in white satin never reaching the end*
*Letters I've written never meaning to send.*

*In the entranceway, posed elegantly before an easel, there was a black girl in a chef's hat with a painter's palette in one hand and a brush in the other. She exuded an intrinsic sensual grace. Her pupils were magnetic and round as saucers. Her teeth glowed like neon against the silken ebony of her cheeks, and her face blossomed into a Cheshire-cat smile as if, in examining Matt, she had discovered something magical.*

*"Do you speak technicolor?" Her voice was sage-like with a mellifluous African accent.*

*"What's that?"*

*"Here. Let me help you." She began dabbing her brush into the swirly pools of color on her tray and making delicate applications upon the canvas of Matt's face. "There," she said. "That's better."*

*She gave him a ceremonial hug. He felt her wet lips press against his cheek. When she released him and pulled back, her eyes were closed and her tongue was licking the blues, reds, and yellows that were dripping from her lips like a thirsty kitten at a saucer of fresh polychromatic cream.*

*The spaceship twinkled and pulsated with black lights, neon lights, lava lamps, strobe lights, and candles, and it tinkled with bells and chimes and metallic trinkets dangling from the ceiling. The atmosphere was patchouli and a blend of incense. On the wall was a large poster of Timothy Leary that said, "Turn on. Tune in. Drop out" in a psychedelic Day-Glo scrawl. The stereo blared, "It's all very lonely. You're a thousand light years from home." Matt was in a state of sensory overload and too dazzled to speak. At one point, the Commander rolled back the carpet and, with a can of lighter fluid and a Bic lighter, squirted out a pattern of flames that wriggled all around the floor like a fiery snake. Matt knew it was safe because it was the Commander and he was in control of his ship.*

*It must have gotten late. Only a few still-tripping stragglers remained, and all they could get on the TV was static. Matt was mesmerized by the chaotic blizzard of black and white particles that buzzed around the screen like a swarm of miniature bees. He stared and stared and finally realized the static was not chaotic after all. There were actual TV shows taking place, embedded and programmed into the profusion of tiny specks. It was a secret kind of programming that the networks did not tell the public about. Now that he had discovered it, it was his favorite program. He started watching these shows, kneeling there in the spaceship in front of the TV and leaning toward it as the remaining partiers gyrated all around him in slow motion. All these secret shows were, for the first time, ever so obvious and oh so spellbinding. Why couldn't anyone else see them? How could he not have known about them before? He leaned closer and closer toward the screen and then he was swallowed into it, right inside the TV itself where he floated among the particles and became one of the characters on the show he had been watching. He was riding on a unicorn and was just getting ready to take flight over a waterfall when, in the real world, he banged his head against the screen and snapped out of it. He wondered if anyone else had seen him while he was a celebrity inside the TV and hoped that they had.*

*The tide started turning when he looked at his skin and was shocked to see that each individual pore of his body was holding its breath and he had turned blue all over and would die if something didn't happen soon. Maybe he'd been infected by the static when he was in the TV. He ran in a panic from the spaceship, down the hallway, and barged into the glaring fluorescent lights and huge wall mirrors of the men's bathroom. The mirrors were mounted on opposite walls, reflecting into each other. He saw about fifty Matts of ever-diminishing sizes bouncing back and forth between all the mirrors, receding into infinity. His face was a smeared collage of feathery rainbow pigments, but during the quick sprint down the hall from the spaceship to the bathroom, his pores must have started breathing again because his pasty pale complexion was fully restored in each and every Matt he saw.*

*By that time, Buck had disappeared with the tripping hippie girl in the Jayne Mansfield costume who he had been dancing with. Matt went back to the dorm where he was staying and hunkered down in the hallway, watching a student carving out a pumpkin with a butcher's knife. It looked so much like a real head that he thought he might be witnessing a murder. The shrill sounds of the knife slicing into the pumpkin were echoing throughout the hallway. He could've sworn that he heard the pumpkin screaming, and he wanted to call the police because he thought he was next. But then the clocks were turned back an hour, and he figured that the previous hour had been just a bad dream or a hallucination and had never even happened. He struggled through dawn, unable to sleep and unable to get rid of the grotesque image of the screaming pumpkin, with all its seedy brains being dumped into a trash can.*

Matt started to realize that the clouds in the distance were not clouds at all. They were snow-capped mountains—the Canadian Rockies. A massive barricade of white peaks stood ahead of them, frowning and scowling like a fierce front line. It was breathtaking. Like a vision from the valley of a vaster planet. At first he could not fathom how anything so high in the sky could be connected to the earth. The image cracked him wide open, and he knew this whole journey had been worth it just for that view.

He jumped out of the car in Jasper and sat down on the shoulder to collect his thoughts. After about two minutes a Dodge van with Connecticut plates pulled over. A girl with flaming red hair and a face full of green freckles stuck her head out the window and asked if he was hitching, so he hopped in and joined Chas and Christina and their St. Bernard named Brandy. They were camping in the mountains and had come to Jasper for food. Christina explained that her pale complexion was extremely sensitive to bright sunlight and, in summer, her freckles turn green. "It's the Irish in me. I'm part leprechaun." Once again, Matt fell immediately in love.

They stopped at a rest area by a glacier, ate buttered buns, and tested their balance on a turquoise tongue of prehistoric ice. Brandy kept bounding forward upon the ice and then sliding back in a tottering glissade to the soggy grass with a bewildered but determined expression. Chas slipped and fell, grabbing Christina's coat sleeve and causing her to fall on top of him. They tumbled together into a kissing embrace, all laughter and joy. Matt turned his head away so they wouldn't catch his jealous stare.

They dropped him off down the road and promised to pick him up again if they saw him farther on in British Columbia. A Californian geologist, marveling at the spectacular display of rugged snow-capped mountaintops, gave him a lift to Lake Louise where rides dried up and the sunny blue sky darkened beneath an ominous thunderhead and a rumbling herd of clouds. For ten minutes the heavens erupted into a blinding deluge of warm rain and then, in the blink of an eye, it was once again a sunshiny day, and the air was fresh and minty and steamy like a sauna. In the calm and eerie afterglow of the storm, the air was electrified by the sunshine, and a golden sheen spread and sizzled upon the black asphalt like honey butter on burnt toast. Then, to Matt's wonderment, there was a full double rainbow arched like a perfect halo around the snow-capped mountain peak that towered in the pristine distance. He took it as a promising omen, reassuring him that he was on the right path and was doing the right thing and everything was going to be just fine.

Banff was a stone's throw away, but a couple hours passed with nary a nibble. Another hitcher, a Quebecois who had been there for three days, retreated to town, nicknaming Lake Louise "The Wawa of the West." Matt stuck it out, thinking, *Oh ye of little faith* because there was still enough daylight to snag a lift and make it to Banff before dark. Sure enough, he got a ride in a VW van with two guys and a girl and rejoiced, thinking he was home free. However, tthey brought him only far enough to get him good and stoned and then drop him off in the tightening jaws of the Rocky Mountain wilderness. The sun sank behind the stern peaks and the holy glow of crimson was drained from the evening sky before his eyes had a chance to adjust. The world was a black screen. The highway was deserted, and his stoned ears heard hungry bears licking their chops and growling behind every bush in the spooky darkness, politely saying, "Pass the ketchup, please."

*Oh man, I've been left in the lurch.* He reached into his pocket for his lucky French rock, palmed it for a few seconds, and said an impromptu quasi-prayer. Fear began to seep in.

Before long, a mini-Batmobile sports car with blazing fireball headlights screeched to a stop, and he was on his way to Banff with Hank, a drunk driver who thought that the posted speed limits were mandatory minimums.

Hank had to make an obligatory pit stop at a fancy reception at the Banff School of Fine Arts Faculty Club Room. He flew into the parking lot, skidded to a halt that took up three spaces, and with a drunken pretense of false camaraderie insisted that Matt accompany him to the party inside. "The hostel's too far to walk to from here. And I'll just be a minute and then I'll drive you there."

The reception was a sedate affair with a pretentious air. Once inside, Hank prowled among the coterie of well-dressed fine artists, abandoning Matt to fend for himself. The air-conditioning sent a shockwave of goosebumps across his greasy skin. Much to his dismay, the best of the finger food on the buffet table had long since been picked over by cleaner hands.

The dainty university women were mingling and chatting in closed pods. Scented waves of perfume pooled around them as, like hummingbirds, they sipped their cocktails and anointed the room with the arousal of enticing fragrances. Matt had been on the road all day and was grimy and damp and smelled like a dead turtle in his sweat-drenched t-shirt. He surveyed the array of lovely-haired women, so sexy in short tight dresses or billowy blouses with their irresistible tease of cleavage. He tried to imagine how many galaxies separated his lips from theirs. They were so far out of his league that he dared not look at them for fear of being rebuked and tossed out onto the street. But, who knows, perhaps some disillusioned half-in-the-bag sociology professor with a score to settle with her unfaithful husband, and having nothing to lose, would seek sanctuary in the untested depths of a disheveled highway bum who also had nothing to lose. At least that's what would happen in the movie version of Matt's travels.

Everyone was ignoring Hank, who was devoted to acting on his worst instincts. He went out of his way to be as cleverly offensive as possible to a few people in particular and as obnoxious as possible to all of them in general, sharpening the blade of some tired, pathetic grudge and wielding it about like a drunken sailor, caring not who he may wound. Matt thought it interesting that, in a journey so full of gracious encounters, his day would begin and end with the antics of a classic asshole.

Yet Matt couldn't help admiring Hank in an unhealthy way and for all the wrong reasons. In the freedom of his buffoonery, Hank was free to say or do anything he wanted and suffer no consequences. He dished out and was fed derision in equal helpings. No one, not even he himself, expected more.

Matt was the opposite. He could do or say nothing without suffering pangs of anxiety that he may offend someone. He always felt so alien and apprehensive, his mind petrified by the mere prospect of a conversation with a woman. He envied Hank as he demonstrated a textbook example of that fully operational asshole roaming the free range of his own asshole's habitat, not giving a flying fuck what anyone else might think of him. For Matt, it was comforting to know that there were much bigger assholes in the world than he and, for that, he could not help liking Hank at least a little.

Eventually, empty of insults and finding himself at the receiving end of an argument where an effete academic accused him of being "an idiot who can't tell the difference between sarcasm and irony," whiskey-breathed Hank somehow remembered his promise and, true to his word, chauffeured Matt up a winding mountain road to a hidden encampment of tents. There were still some late night hostelers gabbing around the weakling flames of a dying campfire. He paid his fifty cents plus twenty for breakfast and then stepped and crawled into the large snoring tent, dodging legs and arms like he was traversing a minefield, until he found a vacant space in which to collapse and shuck off his thirsty boots, having quite willingly heeded the warning not to bring any food inside because it would attract bears. It was as if the space awaited him and that his resting body had snapped perfectly into place among the contours of all the travelers around him and completed the puzzle of all the journeys of all the sleeping souls therein assembled and that, in some other plane of existence, a master puzzler was just then being congratulated on a job well done.

# CHAPTER XVIII

Breakfast among the whispering pines in the chilled and dewy Rocky Mountain morning was spiritual and contemplative. The world smelled green and newly born. Several backpackers ringed around a crackling campfire, drinking strong coffee and weak tea and rubbing off the goosebumps from their arms and legs. Matt donned his protective denim jacket, tucked his ponytail inside the back collar, and joined them, gripping a piping hot cup of aromatic peppermint tea to loosen up his creaky fingers. He sipped and inhaled the steamy menthol vapors that rose and wafted its misty fingers across his face.

Listening mid-conversation, he heard a woman say, "I know. But I just can't help it. I've always fluctuated between being a first-date charity bang and a long-term forever-relationship kind of girl. And, besides, I'm still in love with everyone I have ever been in love with. I may become disenchanted with them on a personal level, but I still love them. And then, of course, there's the sex. And that's a safer addiction than some of the drugs I had been getting into. I guess if I have to choose between feeling good and not feeling anything, I'm gonna choose feeling good. I don't know if it's a weakness or a strength. But I must admit, after a couple drinks, it has resulted in some interesting interpersonal miscalculations. Tequila makes you do funny things. Thank God for birth control!"

All the campers were rising and coming to life according to their own waking rituals. Solitary figures with blankets or unzipped sleeping bags thrown over their shoulders sat at picnic tables crouching over breakfast while reading books or immersed in sleepy meditations. Travelers' dogs spirited about, chasing squirrels and other swift forest creatures, joyfully squirting their signatures upon the abundance of trunks at their immediate disposal.

A trippy hosteler told stories about his dog, named "Dog," who once ate a half-ounce of his private stash. "From then on," he claimed, "his eyes were always red and he never barked. One time Dog brought a bag of grass into the house and dropped it at my feet. I didn't know where he got it or whose it was so I smoked it. I took him everywhere. I brought him to a rock festival and he wandered off and I never heard from him again. Yeah, man. I miss him, but I think he went off on his own trip with a new master. And I have to respect that."

It reminded Matt of a scene from the movie *Fahrenheit 451* in which, in a not-too-futuristic society, all books were banned and burned. The intellectuals had avoided imprisonment and death by fleeing to a clandestine settlement in a forest where they preserved literature by memorizing it. Matt envisioned himself as the living embodiment of all the recorded works of Bob Dylan. He could recite most of the lyrics of all his albums from beginning to end, right down to each breath and inflection, each wail and moan.

*Go ahead. Try me*, he imagined. *Did you say* Another Side of Bob Dylan, *side two, song four, verse eleven? Oh that's easy. 'All is gone, all is gone, admit it, take flight. I gagged in contradiction, tears blinding my sight. My mind it was mangled, I ran into the night, leaving all of love's ashes behind me.' Or* Bringing It All Back Home, *side one, song four, opening verse? 'My love, she speaks like silence. Without ideals or violence. She doesn't have to say she's faithful. But she's true like ice, like fire.' Next?*

There was still a sharp bite in the air when he found his way to the breakfast line and was served his first-ever bowl of granola, the last available helping. It was a new breakfast experience, and he pictured himself reborn into an edible Euell Gibbons paradise. The honey-sweetened nuts and grains gave meaning to his molars and satisfied his hunger pangs. It was a homemade concoction created by the resident headband-wearing Indian Hippie Princess with that sensuous Carly Simon vibe going on, the incredible brush-me hair, the alluring try-me eyes and, yes, even the full taste-me lips. And then, when she looked at him and smiled, the campground was suddenly awash with a King Midas flood of golden sunshine that drained the chill from all that it touched.

Calgary was an easy two-ride hitch out of the mountains and into the symmetrical grid and glittering buildings of downtown Calgary. The hostel was at the YWCA. As usual, a gang of hungry kids with rumpled road gear was already congregated outside the doorway like a pack of starved dogs. He arrived at 3 o'clock, and dinner was served an hour later, which seemed early and made him think he had his time zones mixed up. He didn't care one way or the other, though, what time it was. Or even what day, for that matter. What difference did it make?

During his Hamburg steak and mashed potatoes, a shout came from the other end of the room. "Hey—Matt! Hey—Matt! Over here! It's me. Mike." It was a pleasant shock to hear someone call his name in this faraway place. Sure enough, it was his train-hopping buddy from Halifax. "I figured you would be in Van by now. Where's Wayne?"

"That's what I was gonna ask you. I guess you haven't seen him, huh?"

"No. I've been to Saskatoon and Edmonton. Got here an hour ago from Banff. Haven't seen him. What happened? How'd you end up here?"

"We got a train from Regina that day we all overslept, but it wasn't until late in the day. We hung around the tracks all morning and afternoon, but we had to be careful. They were watching us. And then the coolest thing happened. A couple of the Indians that we met at the soup kitchen saw us hanging out by the tracks and brought over a bottle of wine for the trip. They said it would help wash the dust out of our mouths when we were riding in the boxcar. We rapped for a while, and they told us stories about their ancestors. They might've been bullshitting us. I'm not sure. Either way, it was cool. Anyway, the train we ended up taking went as far as Medicine Hat and then the car we were on got disconnected and we got caught. Man, I was scared to death. I thought we'd get beat up or arrested or something. But they were cool. To be honest, I think they just wanted to make sure that we were all right. When they were convinced we were okay, they yelled at us and said that if they saw us hanging around the yard, they'd get us arrested and sent back home. Was a trip, man."

"So, where's Wayne?"

Mike had gotten so wrapped up in his story that he forgot all about Wayne.

"Oh, yeah. We split up at Medicine Hat and said we'd meet up here or in Van. If you see him, tell him I'll meet him in Van. I'll leave him a message at the hostel."

Next on the agenda was a call to Volker, whose immigrant mother answered the phone. She managed enough English to tell Matt that Volker lived in an apartment and did not have a phone. She gave him the address, and with the help of a lady who worked at the hostel, he was able to locate the street on a city map. He liked the idea of collecting friends from around the world as a validation of their shared experiences, and he looked forward to sitting down with Volker, getting high, and talking about London. Yeah. Just like a real travelin' man.

It was a long walk, but he found the apartment, knocked on the door with irrepressible anticipation, and, when Volker answered, exclaimed with a mischievous grin, "Hey—surprise!

Volker was surprised, to say the least, and at a loss for words. It took him an awkward minute or two to remember who Matt was and, even then, couldn't pin a name to his face.

"Remember? Matt Mahoney. Me and my friend Boone met you in London." Matt's embarrassment worsened upon realizing that there were two other people in the apartment with Volker, and his knock had interrupted plans they were making. He felt asinine and wanted to run away and pretend this had never happened. He was the object in the Highlights magazine puzzle that did not fit in

TIM KELLY

the picture. How could he have been so presumptuous to show up unannounced and expect a hero's welcome?

Volker, also embarrassed, soon recovered and remembered that he had invited Matt and Boone to visit if they were ever in Calgary. On the road, such invitations are freely given and are sincere at the time, but nobody expects to be taken up on an invitation that is more a product of the exuberance of the moment than on any lasting sense of friendship. And who the hell ever goes to Calgary anyway?

"Don't stay at the hostel. Get your stuff and you can crash here. I've got to work in the morning, but we can hang out tomorrow night." Matt, however, had made up his mind in an instantaneous and stubborn manner and had already invented a story to cover his humiliation.

"I was just stopping in to say hello. I'm with some people at the hostel. I met them in Regina and they promised me a ride to the Okanogan Valley or even all the way to Van. I don't have time to hang around."

Despite the story, Matt said he'd try to meet Volker the next day, but for now, he had to get back before closing time. He knew, even as he said it, that there would be no next day with Volker. He had already decided, and the decision was irrevocable.

On the long walk back, he counted his steps for a while to divert himself from the shards of ugly misery thoughts festering in his mind. Here he was, still dragging his old hometown anvil around these foreign streets as though his journey had taken him nowhere. The pretentious would-be travelin' man was exposed for what he really is: a wimpy Mama's boy who couldn't even find a girlfriend. Always just a boy. Still just a kid. Never yet a man.

*Stumbling blocks. So many stumbling blocks. How to avoid? What to do?* He felt a tremor. Then he heard the snap and felt that sour wad fill his stomach. His mind had tripped the wire and released the parade of horribles that marched in triumph through the frontier of his under-defended brain. He could feel the sadistic gaze of The Watcher, like the eye of Sauron, burning red holes into the back of his neck. He could hear Its gleeful cackle echoing from the sewer and reverberating from the gloomy corners of the gathering night and Its drooly slobbers as It bore down on him as though he were the devil's plaything and this were the appetizer to what promised to be a buzzard's feast. He knew it was already too late to prevent the rippling in his faltering heart and the suffocating panic as his mind whirled around the drain of his private terrors. He felt the click of that switch and then he was gone. Sub-zero. Less than nothing. Incapacitated by self-loathing and preyed upon by a host of ugly things. Sometimes all it took was a fleeting, inconsequential thought, and then before he knew it, that rotten feeling roiling in the pit of his stomach devoured him. The fleeting thought that triggered his black mood would dissolve into the forgotten history of so many other hordes of bygone thoughts that had plundered him when his guard was down. And it would grow all the worse, in part because he usually couldn't remember why he was upset in the first place, and then his sullen substitute would slip behind the wheel and step on the pedal. There he would go, ever downward in a self-flagellating dive, all morose and inconsolable and unable to unzip the straitjacket that wrapped itself around him like a scaly tentacled creature, accompanied by an overpowering fear that he was dying. He could even feel his heart preparing to detonate. Chest pains. The barrage of barbed thoughts. He was a nobody who had been rudely awakened from the dream in which he had deceived himself into thinking he was a somebody. He shrank back into hiding, ashamed, deflated, frightened, back to the refuge of muteness and invisibility and then, in retaliation, he waged a fuck-everybody-and-just-leave-me-alone rebellion that has its roots in his childhood tantrums, which he could still remember.

*His mother imploring him, "Please, Matthew, talk to me. What's wrong?" And he, silent and staunch, ignoring her as his vicious tantrum rages within his uncomprehending five-year-old mind, trying to imagine what terrible thing he must have done. Why doesn't she do that something special to rescue him from such torment? She must hate him to let him suffer so. She begged him to come with her to the store. She promised him an ice cream cone, and he wanted to go with her, but his tantrum just laughed and wouldn't let him, so he refused, embedded within his fearful stubbornness, and watched helplessly, mute within his madness, mad within his muteness, as she pulled from the driveway in the family station wagon and disappeared down Merchant Hill. Then, when it was too late, the tantrum released him and allowed him to run to the window and scream, "Come back, Mommy! Please come back! I want to go with you!" He was so frightened, there, all alone with his tantrum. How could she abandon him? His tantrum, much amused, would say, "There. Are you happy now, you stupid little brat?" Then It would go away to wherever It came from, leaving him both relieved and in tears because he was scared and wanted his mother. Even then, he knew the tantrum would return. It always did. He never knew when to expect It or how long It would possess him. But when It did return, Its impact was always immediate and severe. No warning. No buildup. No aura.*

Somehow It had tracked him across Canada and had ambushed him once again, this time at Volker's door, just as he was starting to think It had lost his scent. All he could do now was concoct an antidote to straighten out the emotional contortions that were wringing his guts into knots, something to absolve him from the toxic "Repent Walpurgis" mood that infected him. He ran through the twilight streets of Calgary, made swift by fear, as thoughts of dying in a pathetic heap on this distant sidewalk taunted his mind. Maybe he would find a girl at the hostel who would grace him with her company and who would snap him out of his sulk with her kind attentions and help him find a shortcut home from exile on Pluto. To help him crawl back over the splintered grooves from the perilous reaches of the vinyl edge all the way to the hug of the spindle where he could fight against the expulsive force of his swiftly spinning universe. But he had no such luck that night. To make matters worse, he got back too late to take a shower. His last one was pounds of caked sweat ago in Regina.

But things did work out in their own way. He started talking to a flirtatious and anatomically compelling bronze-legged girl who said her name was Viola, but "ever since high-school French class, everyone calls me 'Voilá'!" She sucked in a languid cinematic drag from her Eve cigarette, struck a sultry wide-eyed "I'm up for grabs" pose, and laughed as if to say, "It is I! Voilá of the bronze thighs," as the ecstatic display of hormonal fireworks all shot off as the gang of horny boys began brawling in spirit for the privilege of her flamboyant company. She commanded her suitors like an omnipotent hippie goddess initiating a fertility ritual. She wore a tattered multi-hued skirt she had designed with strips of cloth cut from dozens of old garments and stitched together in a risque fashion with the loosely hung strips brushing apart and flashing up to her tropical regions at the gentle insistence of her sensual stride. Enamored of her vivacious bohemian allure, Matt imagined her to be a someday-famous movie star or a Wiccan enchantress. The prize of her company and, perhaps, a ticket to her high-voltage peek-a-boo thighs, went to a transparently phony but extremely virile California beach boy hippie dude who knew all the right phony lines, just a shallow Adonis who relished in the undeserved pleasures that came to him as a perk of being so handsome and muscular. *What a bore,* thought Matt, who was jealous and knew from the start that he himself hadn't stood a chance for that prize of thighs, those prized thighs, the surprise of her prized thighs. That flash of bronze. But just the sight of her made him feel better.

There was a serious little guy from Tennessee who had also missed his shower and was getting tired of hostel life. "Believe me, I need one. It's been about a week. This place has took my last quarter. I'm busted. Man, I'm so broke I can't even pay attention. Had most of my money stole in Vancouver at some dumpy hostel. Take your eyes off your stuff, and in about five seconds somebody's gonna rip it off just like that," and he tried to snap his fingers but it was a dud.

Then he told Matt about his brother who had a rare disease. "He's supposably one of only two people in the world who survived it, and the other one's dead now. Supposably died of ammonia, but it was really this disease that done it. It's been ten years or more. He took sick and they done give him up two or three times but he recouped. So I figured if it didn't get him yet, maybe he's okay 'cause he's still fuctioning pretty good. But it could come back again and get him because now he's more acceptable to getting sick because he's so weak. They keep giving him all kinds of medicines, but they don't work. They just exasperate everything, and he gets all kinds of side effects. One thing I learned from this is that it's a lot easier to give medicine than it is to take it."

"What's it called?" Matt asked.

"I can't remember. It's in Latin or some other language and has lots of syllables. When doctors have conventions about rare diseases, they always talk about him. His file is this thick—" he spaced his hands about two feet apart from each other, "and he's been in all the technical magazines and books. Yeah, my brother is famous with a lot of those doctors and scientists. Even though they all take that Democratic oath, they're more interested in studying him and talking about him rather than helping him. They're all in cahoots. They admire the problem more than the cure."

The kid in the cot next to Matt's, Lou from Locust, Pennsylvania, was on the road to recover from the heartbreak he suffered when his high school sweetheart spurned him in favor of some new guy she met at college. They talked until Matt relaxed enough to sleep. He dug a wishbone from his pack, snapped it in two and made a wish as he lay awake listening to the chorus of sleeping sounds around him, the snoring, the snorting, the tossing and turning, the rustling of sheets and sleeping bags, the high squeak and low rumble of night farts, the dreamy mumblings of restless sleepers and the escape of gaspy throat sounds, all of which had become the sweet lullaby for wayward wandering Matthew A. Mahoney as he once again took his refuge in the company of strangers.

# CHAPTER XIX

With Vancouver at such close range and crowds of hitchhikers headed that way, Matt was the early bird on the road before breakfast, but rides were scarce, and he was still a mess from his episode the night before. He ended up walking for over three hours trying to create a diversion from the batch of self-annihilating thoughts that remained. The undulating road, the whoosh of cars, the hiss and buzz of insects, the sweep of twittering birds circling against the canvas of clouds that was the sky. None of it helped. He felt worthless and scared and had that depressed feeling that curdled his stomach and clouded all his thoughts. He wished he could be more adventurous and confident and manly, like Kerouac, the guy with the girl on his arm, making novelesque friends and having profound spiritual experiences with artists and poets and mystical visionaries.

His first ride broke into his downtrodden train of thought. It was refreshing to slip into an air-conditioned car, his body cooling down and his clammy layer of sweat settling upon him like a slimy fly-paper gel. He extended his arm out the window and let the cool rush of the 60-mph breeze billow his sweat-stained sleeve and blow-dry the pit juice that was gushing from under his arm. There was a girl crunched next to him in the back seat, and though their legs and shoulders were braced together for the entire ride, they never spoke. He was smelly and sticky and couldn't think of anything to say that didn't sound lame or rehearsed, but he enjoyed the furtive arousal of the feel of the flesh of his thigh mated in sweat to the freckled flesh of her thigh. He wondered if she also enjoyed the commingling of their flesh and felt the same tingle.

It was noon when he got out of that car and continued rambling west on Highway 1. The wild-blue-yonder sky was beaming with a heavenly light. He walked beyond a string of hitchhikers, nodding, exchanging perfunctory peace signs and "How ya doin'"s and "Where ya goin'"s and acting all cool. He knelt at a stream for a drink of ice-cold Rocky Mountain water, got down on his belly, and dunked his head into the electric mountain socket of the shocking stream and rose up like Adam on the first day. He inhaled a lungful of fresh piney air and took a moment to assess the solemn vista, visually climbing to the peaks of the no-nonsense mountains surrounding him, opening his eyes as wide as possible and then shouting at the top of his puny lungs, "Holy shitballs, Batman!"

An impulsive determination to hike straight through the mountains invigorated his legs and lightened his load. Beckoned by the grand scheme, he decided that, yes, he would walk all the way to Vancouver. "Damn the bears!" was his new motto as he trekked forward with more courage than sense, sheathing away his thumb and ignoring the traffic. The birds above encouraged him and whistled him onward, and he whistled them back. He wished he could yodel, gave it a shot, and failed gloriously. Nonetheless, when summoned by the minutiae, he accepted the ride in a van with bouquets of flowers and a rainbow peace sign painted on the side.

"Want a lift?" someone sputtered. The driver, Rob, was twenty-eight and was going home to Penticton, in the Okanogan Valley. The five other people in the van were hitchhikers. Matt recognized three of them from the hostel.

Route 1 took him back to Lake Louise and then ricocheted west into the green heart of the soft, breast-like peaks too steep to climb and plunging valleys too perilous to descend. Their enormity exceeded all expectations. The van was nothing more than a microscopic pest meandering across the broad back of each mountain it traversed, rising and sinking with the relentless contours like a rowboat riding atop the swells of a wild green sea. Matt felt grander and more powerful in their midst and figured that if he had been born among these giants it would have made him more of a man.

He was gawking out the window when he noticed something odd rummaging and munching beside the road. All he could see was a bulky brown head protruding through the bushes and then a massive sweep of antlers that was camouflaged among the tree branches. It was huge. Matt didn't say a word until he realized that another kid had seen it, too.

"Did you see that?" he asked the other kid, who looked bewildered.

"Yeah," the boy replied, nodding his head.

"What was it?" Matt asked.

"I don't know. It must have been a moose."

"Yeah, that's what I thought."

"It looked like Bullwinkle."

"Yeah, that's *exactly* what I thought."

"Nice rack," the boy quipped.

The other kid, a flatlander like Matt, was also having his first mountain experience. They were both struck giddy by the novelty of seeing a moose picnicking on bushes and that they had been able to identify it by virtue of its resemblance to a cartoon character. "What's next?" the kid asked. "Yogi Bear?"

Rob reveled in his role as tour guide to this collection of hither-and-yon kids. He called his van "The Magic Bus" and spoke in what was already an outdated, late-sixties, Haight-Ashbury, mellowed-out, peace-freak hippie jargon that sounded like bad dialogue from a cheesy low-budget film. It was one of the few times Matt had ever heard someone use the word "groovy" without being facetious. Everything was "far out" or else it was a "trip," be it a capitalism trip or a vegetarian trip, an ego trip, or a power trip. Or, if it wasn't a trip, it was a "gig." There appeared to be no limit to the number of trips and gigs any cat or chick could be grooving to at any one time. He talked about his gig working at a casino in Vegas, or as he called it, "the Mecca of capitalism," where he got to meet the Righteous Brothers.

He referred to one of them by name—Matt didn't know if he meant the tall one or the short one—and said, "That cat was a real asshole. He was on a heavy celebrity trip. A sell-out. But the other one, he was pretty groovy. He knew where it was at."

Matt laughed to himself. He once thought he knew where "it" was at, but that was years ago and he had already forgotten both what and where "it" was.

When Rob turned off Highway 1 and headed south on Route 97A, everybody bailed in order to stay on the main highway. Everyone, that is, except for Matt and one other hitcher who was also taking the alternate route to Van where he had some kind of odd job lined up in some kind of ship headed some place or other. Rob stopped at a diner to, as he put it, "score some lunch," and he bought Matt a bowl of clam chowder, a glass of milk, and two slices of toast. The other rider wanted only toast and water. Matt was raving about the chowder.

"Everything tastes better in the mountains," Rob said.

"And everything tastes better when you're hungry," Matt responded.

"Right on. I can dig that."

Matt bought a few postcards to send home. One pictured a jackrabbit with antlers, identifying it as a Canadian Jackalope whose only habitat was in the Canadian Rockies. Another showed a fur-bearing trout and claimed that it was caught in the uncharted depths of Lake Superior where it evolved a thick white coat as protection against the frigid waters. Next to the postcards was a bookrack from which he bought a paperback copy of *Chariots of the Gods*.

Back on the road, The Magic Bus filled up with a new hodgepodge of hitchhikers who were homeless or wandering kids looking for work. Two of them were from eastern Canada and were chasing down their dream of working with the forestry department and making a lot of money fighting fires during the wildfire season. Some were going to pick fruit or going to Van to scout out the fishing boats. Some were doing it for the money, some for the experience, and for some, it was for both.

Descending into the lush valley of orchards was like entering into a secret Shangri-La paradise. It seemed an impossibly fertile oasis, a respite from life's cruel realities, tucked and nestled so cozy within the protective fortress of so many forbidding peaks. Matt had thought that peaches grew only in southern climates, like Georgia, and was surprised to find orchards of them thriving so far north and wondered if they would be as sweet and juicy as their southern cousins.

When they reached Penticton, everyone got out but Matt. Rob told him he could stay at his house, which was on a working orchard just outside of town, and maybe get a job picking peaches. When the last hitcher slid shut the van door, Rob and Matt continued to the orchard.

The house was a breezy white cottage with a Dutch door and creaky floorboards. Rob's dog, a Labrador retriever named Karma, greeted them in the driveway. Rob cuddled her snout, rubbed noses, and said, "Sui ar mo aghaidh," explaining that it meant, "May the sunlight brighten your day," in Irish, as taught to him by a Galway girl he was flirting with at a bar in Penticton. Matt was shown to a cot in the den. "It's not much, but it's comfortable and you've got your privacy. Make yourself at home. Tomorrow I'll see if they need any pickers. If so, you can crash here, and we'll work something out rent-wise. I'll have to discuss it with my roommate."

Matt excused himself during the first full lull in conversation to relieve himself of the epic piss he had been holding since before Bullwinkle. There was a sign on the medicine cabinet next to the bathroom mirror: "If it's yellow, let it mellow. If it's brown, flush it down." He aimed his stream against the porcelain bowl above the waterline to avoid making the loud splashy sounds that others might hear.

The roommate, Max, was at work and would be home soon. Rob explained that Max was on a sex trip and that he misused his powers to take advantage of women in order to satisfy his own primitive urges. "It's a total bummer. He's into this pagan animalistic trip and he needs to conquer every woman he meets. Sexually, that is. Pernicious intentions, man. It creates a bad vibe with me because it's a spiritual cop-out and I'm into more of a platonic love trip now. I'm building up my powers for other reasons. I don't want to waste them on sex. I'm stronger now, man. Much stronger. Pretty soon I'll have enough power to keep all of the evil away and live blissfully. True peace and love. That's the way to live. Sex complicates everything and turns people into animals. Man, you know what? I'm getting so that I prefer just rapping with chicks. Platonic love. That's where it's at."

Rob was separated from his wife and two kids, a seven-year-old boy and a two-and-a-half-year-old girl. It sounded as though he didn't see them very often, but Matt veered away from that subject. When Rob talked about his kids, his voice softened and the muscles in his face changed, but then he snapped back into his happy hippie façade. Matt was taken in by Rob's hyperkinetic gabbiness and his misguided quest for inner peace but pitied him because, beneath all the fake happiness of his hippy-trippy overflowerpowering rap, he seemed a sad and hollowed-out man.

Max showed up for a short while. He was handsome and athletic and as easygoing as Rob was worrisome. Rob's jealousy was immediately apparent. Max had a girl with him, a hitchhiker he picked up outside of town. Carol was bra-less and stunning in a scoop-necked t-shirt, tight short-shorts, and leather sandals. A beaded turquoise necklace was strung around her neck and dangling from it was a silver chain with a Scorpio pendant half-hidden within the swell and jiggle of her cleavage. It was only in profile that Matt could appreciate the fullness of her attributes, her water balloon lushness and the twin exclamation points penetrating the defenseless thin veil of her translucent top. He couldn't help but be spontaneously aroused by the surge of her every breath and found himself visualizing how she would look if freed of all apparel, which wasn't difficult considering how scanty and tight-fitting it was. He took a good long x-ray look until the image came in clear. But he left the sandals on. He liked the sandals.

"Hey, Max, this is Matt. He, uh, is gonna see if he can get a job around here and he might stay with us for a while." It sounded like he was asking for permission.

Max gave a carefree smile and extended his hand. "Welcome aboard, Matt. No problem. The mare the morrier. We run a bit of a commune here as it is, and there's always room for at least one more. Carol might be here tonight too."

Carol gazed in Matt's direction and gave him a halfhearted smile. Matt blushed because he thought she caught him trying to peek down into her t-shirt, which—he was sure she didn't realize—was humanly impossible to not do, but she was polite enough to acknowledge him with a "Hi, Matt" and a cordial handshake. Her skin was moist and warm, and he didn't want to let go.

There was an awkward energy between Rob and Max that made it uncomfortable to be with both of them at the same time. Rob resented that Max was more likable, had lots of girlfriends, and got through life without all the self-imposed torments and needless worries. Max dealt with Rob's neurotic insecurities by ignoring them and continuing to entertain women however he saw fit and get laid as often as possible. It was as if the cottage was an invisible battlefield where the haloed army of Rob's platonic love trip ideations was engaged in a pitched cataclysmic struggle for survival with the evil animalistic demons of Max's orgasm-crazed sex trip.

What it boiled down to was that Max had an appeal that radiated with his smile and his boyish charm. Girls automatically wanted him. He was spoiled for choice. He couldn't help it. It was a force of nature, magnetic and undeniable. You've either got it or you don't.

Carol threw her pack on the recliner next to a player piano that dominated one of the walls in the small family room and went to the bathroom to freshen up. She returned, all loveliness and desirability, having squeezed herself into a snug pair of denim cut-offs with a peace sign embroidered on one butt cheek and a hemp leaf on the other, and was as dazzlingly bra-less and perky as ever in a tight white top. She and Max took off for the evening, and Rob was able to relax again.

For a while, Rob and Matt carried on a normal conversation as they toked away at the hefty supply of joints Rob had stashed inside a tin container originally loaded with cough lozenges. It was odd for Matt to be able to confide in him about Helen and how he was still mourning that he had bungled the relationship so terribly, his first true love, and that lately he had been obsessing over her and didn't know what to do about it.

"Our relationship was phenomenal right up to the end. Then, out of the blue, I just broke it off. One day it was great. The next day it was over. I became an asshole and ruined my life overnight."

"Hey, don't let it bother you, man. You were sixteen, for Christ's sake. Everybody screws up their first relationship. You were just a kid learning the ropes. Falling in love and learning about relationships, man, it's all independent study. It's a normal part of growing up because it's all so new and you don't have any idea what the hell you're doing. It takes practice. Look at me. I've got a wife and two kids and I have made a royal mess out of that and I've created a lot of bad karma for myself. That's why I named my dog Karma. She was a stray and I adopted her so that I could take good care of her and start working off some of my karma now. With a vengeance, man. I don't want to wait until my next life to start working on my big payback. As for my wife, well, she's history. The vibes are too hostile. She was destroying my serenity. I gave her my heart, but, man, the bitch wanted my soul."

Matt thought it interesting that so many people he had met were hoping to achieve everlasting salvation by being kind to a dog. Matt continued. "I wrote her this spiteful breakup letter and told her— well, I don't even want to say what I said. I'm so ashamed of myself. I didn't understand what I was doing. I always thought she was so beautiful and felt happy just staring at her class picture that I carried in my wallet. Back then, I thought I was a good guy. But not anymore. I destroyed our innocence. I felt like a murderer. There's a lot of guilt there. Wakes me up at night. And now part of me thinks that I'm still in love with her, and another part thinks that I'm exaggerating how perfect it all was just because I'm so miserable right now. It's like I recovered from a long spell of amnesia and remembered her all over again. I don't know what to do. I guess the joke was on me. Speaking of karma—I'm getting what I deserve."

"Like the song says, 'Don't it always seem to go that you don't know what you've got till it's gone?' You've got to let her go, man. You're treating it like it's a tragedy of epic proportions. It's just a simple breakup. Happens all the time. Too much time has passed. You can't go back. You are trying to return to a time and place that no longer exists, to a person who is no longer the same person and whose life has changed. You tell me. Are you the same person you were back then? Can you throw yourself back into her life and expect her to trust you all over again? It will never be the same. Burn that bridge, man. If you try to barge back in now, you'll just end up creating a scene or, if she does still have feelings for you, you'll probably mess up her life all over again. You've got to move on, man. You've got to learn how to live with it for her sake—and for yours. And besides, no offense or anything, but you're like me. You're a freak. Not all chicks dig freaks."

*Interesting question*, Matt mused in silence. *Am I the same person I was back then? Before the unraveling? Before the screamin' demons and all the misery thoughts hijacked the wheel and charted their own swervy course?*

Matt was afraid that Rob was right. Or was he? It sounded like Rob's advice might have been meant more for himself, trying to accept the fact that his marriage was over and that it was time to move on. Maybe Rob was right by default, and Matt was being foolish and should wave goodbye to the past. Forget about Helen. He feared that he would remain stuck in his in-between place, forever the child, never the man, unless he could let her go. Give up his rear-view-mirror tendencies and navigate forward through the clear glass of the windshield. *Maybe I'd have fewer crashes that way.*

But he knew by the way that Helen's image tugged at his heart that he would never be able to let go and forget her until he had confessed his sins, had done penance, and had amended his life in the manner of his religious training. After all, no matter how long you live, you can only have one first love and one first kiss.

The smoke was potent so the conversation remained animated and tangential and artificially profound. Rob said that he had achieved a state of inner peace and was happy at last. "As a matter of fact, there is so much love in this house now that even the mice don't run across the floor anymore. They walk. Sometimes they come up to sleep with me. And Karma never used to come in the house because of all the evil vibes. She was an outside dog. Now even Karma can sense all the love here and always wants to come in. You know, since I've been building up so much peace and love inside me, the evil demons have been rattling their cages and trying to get back into my soul. Just the other night they were at it again, and I was tired and just didn't have the strength to keep them out, and I was totally bummed. So I put on my Indian love beads and went out and slept in my van, my love bus, to get away from all that evil. They were still trying to get at me, but I was shielded by a protective love bubble, man. I was still scared, though, and when I fell asleep, I had a dream that my wife had just stabbed a bunch of people to death and I tried to stab her but I couldn't. She said, 'I have too much power for you.' So I prayed and prayed until I gained the courage to tell her, 'You are the hate of my life' and stabbed her eyes out. Then the strangest thing happened. I woke up in a state of perfect peace and wasn't afraid anymore. I couldn't even scare myself. I went back to sleep and I had a wet dream. Man, it blew my mind. Only the second time in my life. And, you know what? It was better than sex."

*Rob's blissful declarations, despite their weirdness, reminded Matt of an experience he had one night a few years earlier. He was sitting in the dark on his bedroom floor in one of his remorseful insomniac mulls over Carla when his depression reached an all-time rock-bottom low. But then something happened. Before he had time to even contemplate it, the weight of the world lifted off his shoulders and his thoughts were immaculate and serene. It was a state of no mind, an instantaneous transformation, a sudden satori that evaporated all the layers of his dysfunction and revealed his true nature, so glorious and godly and unencumbered. He had somehow transcended the morass of all his disabling fears and frailties as if his tumultuous black sky had been raked clean of all thunderclouds to reveal a universe of heavenly sunlight. Finally! His woes had ended forever! His path was now all so simple! He just needed to let Carla go and free her from his annoying attentions and himself from the spell of his infatuation. It had long ago been obvious that she did not share his affections. If it were meant to be, it would have already happened. He could even laugh about it and was not even embarrassed by how foolish he had been or that he could have continued to persist so against such preposterous odds. Then, in wake of Carla's absence, there was, perhaps, Helen in the sunlight beneath the heavenly sky.*

*In his exhilarated state, he realized with stunning clarity that the emotionally crippled Matt who tortured himself with self-deprecation and imagined fears was just an illusion, an imposter, a fictional façade created by his dark tyrannical mind. Now, inspired by this new revelation and freed of all his inhibitions, it was like being introduced to his true self for the first time. It was now immediately and irrefutably clear that absolute happiness and joy was the natural state of being, and that nothing less was acceptable, and that the Matt whose spirit was levitating in his room was the true expression of whatever it meant for him to be a human being. He spoke it as if it were a prayer: a* human *being.*

*Stripped of all ego, he left the house at midnight to meander the empty streets of New Holland, inhabited with a giddy joy and a childlike sense of first impressions. He was, quite literally, "out" of his mind. He was his own perfect stranger. He left all that chattering Old Matt pessimism and paranoia back in his room and realized that that mind was not who he really was and, without it constantly nagging at him, everything was so beautiful! He wandered the woods in the darkness as though he were discovering a new wonderland and experiencing the genuine essence of life and the beauty of nature and the magnificence of self for the very first time. Everything was a miracle: each leaf, each blade of grass, each cricket that chirped from its invisible perch, each blazing star, each tiny speck. All of life was exalted. It was holy, and he was one with the holiness.*

*He returned home at full dawn. It had been liberating, not hating himself for a few hours, but as the ceiling of dark storm clouds refilled him, the euphoria dwindled and the same old emotionally crippled Matt returned to reclaim his subversive mind and once again inhabit his no-longer-enlightened shell, his suit of armor, as though nothing had happened. What remained, however, were seeds of hope and the unforgettable knowledge that locked somewhere inside of him there was this other true self, free of care and worry, waiting to be released if only he could find the key.*

Rob eventually talked himself out and went to bed, telling Matt, "If there's anything you want, utilize it. Certainly no one else here has control of their facilities." It was an odd thing to say because as far as Matt could tell they were the only two around.

Matt retired to the den and fell asleep. He was wakened in the middle of the night by the alarm of the screen door banging shut and the tipsy laughter of Max and Carol in the next room industriously converting the nondescript, sparsely furnished old family room into a raucous boudoir, crashing into furniture and against lamps and knocking stuff onto the floor and, in the throes of their pagan passion, tumbling onto the couch, which was thudding against the other side of Matt's wall. He heard what sounded like a body slamming against a table accompanied by a dull tinkling of ivory keys, and heard Carol giggle as Max said, "Oh fuck. That hurt." For the moment, as their General slept, the army of Rob's platonic love-trip was being clobbered by Max's fully mobilized sex demons. Matt knew that Rob's army stood no chance when, through his mind's eye, he pictured Carol's splendid breasts, free at last and springing into action as she lifted her t-shirt over her head in one fluid cross-armed sweep. And then her sensuous slither and wriggle as she unsnapped her cut-offs and stepped out of them as they dropped to reveal her tender thighs and her lovely tanned legs and landed around her delicate sandaled feet as Max accepted the purring invitation of her sweet pantiless stance. Matt listened with jealous voyeuristic ears to the careless abandon of their wrestling bodies, all paws and tongues and luscious slobber, all boozy giggles and moans and kittenish whimpers, the slippery naked scrum, the smacks of wet kissing and musical sucking sounds and muffled mouths and the entire vocabulary of pleasure being excruciatingly recited line and verse just inches away, worlds away on the other side of his thin barrier where Max's animalistic forces were having a field day. When the giggling subsided, it was replaced by heavy breathing and impassioned moaning and the rapidly accelerating symphony of singing couch springs. Other than some semi-literate murmurings, the only words Matt could hear came from Carol, cracking her crop like a skilled equestrian, commanding, "Don't stop," "Harder," and then, nearer the end, "Faster, faster, faster." Max said nothing, but it was evident from the urgency of his labored breathing, the escalating "William Tell Overture" tempo and the slapping rhythms of their colliding flesh that he was vigorously obeying each command and had been swallowed up into the welcoming folds of her warm, wet universe. It reached its pitch and then fell abruptly and mercifully silent. Then Carol growled, "Oh, Wilbur" in a Mr. Ed voice and the round of muffled laughter dissolved into a happy collapse of soft purrs and tickling squeals and slurpy kisses and satiated slumbers.

Matt, unable to withstand the agonizing temptations of such delicious torture, had joined Max and Carol in his mind for a sort of ménage á trois, closing his eyes and summoning just Carol through the wall and into his bed where he fondled and feasted upon the sweet swells and hidden valleys of her luxuriant body and caroused the soft wet wingspan of her splayed thighs, carefully pacing himself so he could gallop with her across the finish line as she erupted into that final depleted spasm of sublime release.

# CHAPTER XX

Matt rose and soon realized that Rob had no intention of helping him get a job, so after two over-easy eggs and a steamy cup of Postum, Matt hunted down the head honcho only to find that the orchard would be fine without him.

"Have you ever picked before?"

"No."

"Well, come back in a coupla weeks. I might have something for you then."

The man's voice was sharp and disinterested. Perhaps Matt's hands were too smooth or his voice too soft. Whatever the reason, he returned to the cottage, discouraged and deflated, and thus ended his would-be career as an underpaid and ill-treated migrant fruit picker.

Carol and Max were nowhere to be seen, and Rob didn't mention them. He and Rob sat around the cottage and jump-started the conversation that had stalled the night before. Rob rhapsodized about a friend of his who slithers on the floor at parties looking up women's dresses or gropes them from behind or bites them on their breasts. As he described his friend's antics, there was an approving animalistic glee in his voice that contradicted the karma-conscious peace-and-love freak Matt had been introduced to. It was as if the platonic Rob of the previous night had been body-snatched by a hedonistic demon substitute who drooled in admiration of his misogynistic friend. Of Rob, Matt thought, *Every paradise needs a fool*, and then, of himself, *And every fool needs a paradise.*

Rob talked about women with an authoritative air. "I should've listened to my old man and never gotten married in the first place.

Before I got engaged he told me I should take a good look at my girlfriend's mother and ask myself, 'Would I ever want to sleep with that?' because that's what she'll look like in about twenty years. I thought it was true love that would last a lifetime, and I thought that getting married meant I would get laid every night. Her mother was pretty hot for an older woman, so I thought it was worth the gamble. Probably the worst decision of my life. And, believe me, I've had some doozies. But, sheeit. It only took about five years. She went downhill fast, man. Very uncool. Things went sour. Once burned. But relationships are difficult for me 'cause I'm on a rejection trip. Usually I won't even notice if a girl is flirting with me. I am not equipped with that radar. There was one chick, man. She came on so strong that even I noticed it, so it must've been like a neon sign to everybody else. But I was slow on the uptake and thoroughly blew it 'cause, you know, the flirting scene is not my gig. Besides, you and me, we're just the sidekicks. Nobody wants to fuck the sidekick."

Matt, who identified with Rob's rejection-trip mentality and his bewilderment with the art of flirting, said "I watch guys come on to girls, and the whole time I'm thinking how transparent and superficial it looks and that no girl with any common sense would actually fall for that bullshit. But it works for them and, in a way, I think it's the obviousness that makes it work. I think women are just as shallow and sleazy as we are. I think that flirting only works if they're already attracted to you. It wouldn't work for me. I've never figured out how to make that kind of connection. It's a mystery."

"You know it. That whole sex trip. Like you said, women are a mystery, man."

Matt nodded in agreement but thought, *No, man, that's not what I meant*, and aimed his thoughts inward.

It was 1:30 when Rob dropped Matt off in Penticton, flashed him the peace sign, and said, "Sui ar mo aghaidh." Rob put up a thin façade, pretending he was sorry to see Matt leave so soon, but Matt could sense the palpable relief in Rob's demeanor and was glad when the van door slammed shut and The Magic Bus, with its cargo of prefabricated love and peace vibes, disappeared around the corner.

After finding that the hostel was already full for the night, he went to a shop and bought some postcards. He addressed one to "Raphaelo's—Home of the World Famous Hot Fudge" and wrote: "Dear V-Man, No to Halifax. Yes to Vancouver. Ruminations have been deep. Thinking cap in full operational mode. We're all just stuck in the grooves of this vast vinyl universe. It's crazy out here on Pluto. (248 years to revolve around the sun.) It's much safer at the spindle. (Mercury only takes 87 days.)"

To another friend, he wrote: "Dear B. L., Am still waiting for my fantasy ride with the Montana Wildhack of my dreams. Have had numerous offers, of course, but none up to my standards. They begged but I remained firm, so to speak. Say hello to the Captain. Your friend, Antennae Jimmy."

His final card read, "Dear Mrs. Black: Here I am again. The mountains are even more beautiful than they look in the postcard. When I get back I'll stop over and challenge you to a game of Perquackey (sp?). Oswh tsurbe igdno? Say hi to Mr. Black. Love, Matt."

He finished with his postcards, toured the town, and found a drop-in center called "His Place," run by Jesus people. There was a rickety card table with a plate of free Oreos and a glass pitcher filled with Kool-Aid. Beside a slumpy old couch was a bookcase stocked with a comprehensive selection of born-again Christian literature. Jesus was illustrated as a Hollywood-handsome hippie with long blondish hair, gently braiding flowers in a golden meadow with a cluster of equally blondish and blissfully innocent Caucasian children gathered about him like cherubs. In reality, Matt figured Jesus would have been swarthy with a nappy black Afro and coal black eight-ball eyes rather than those sweet baby blues. More Omar Sharif than Jeff Chandler, though not as handsome.

Matt changed into shorts and a wrinkled t-shirt and played the house guitar for a while in a meeting room with a watercolor poster that said, "Welcome to Jesusville." It was a relaxed space, and everyone was courteous and kind. Someone even complimented him on his finger-picking style as he played "House of the Rising Sun" and asked him, "Could you show me how you do that with your thumb?" Matt was flattered. "I'm not really that good. I wish I was as good at it as much as I like it

He spoke with a Jewish guy who, with his thick plastic pick, was combing the tangled shock of russet hair he called his Jewfro. He had spent a couple years at a monastery in Kentucky and was now an itinerant preacher spreading the gospel and praising his Savior's name.

"Now I'm just a wandering Jew," he told Matt.

"I guess that makes me a roamin' Catholic," Matt quipped, pleased with his wordplay but not sure if his new friend had detected it.

"Imagine that. A Jewish Jesus freak. It freaks my parents out, that's for sure. But what can I say? I love Jesus. He is my savior. He lived the perfect life and then died on an old rugged cross. I love praying to Jesus and giving thanks to Jesus for all the blessings I'm receiving and for the plentiful fruits of this valley. This place, with all its orchards, is like a Garden of Eden, an earthly sanctuary for Jesus. You should stick around for a while. We could hang out."

Matt wondered if Jesus freaks got extra credit every time they mentioned their savior by name. He thanked the man for the invitation, and if it weren't for the prerequisite Jesus avowals, he might have taken him up on it, but he didn't want to take advantage of such freely given hospitality under false pretenses or mistaken apprehensions. And Matt, who had always been gullible, was afraid he might be lulled by such kindness into falling for the eternal salvation rap and end up pontificating upon the same half-baked propaganda he was so tired of hearing from others and would find himself proselytizing disapproving strangers on the touristy streets and in the parks of such a fair city as Penticton.

"Sorry, man. I've got to get going. But good luck."

"Yeah. I'm sorry, too. I don't want to be pushy because I know it turns people off. But I believe I have an obligation to share my faith. I hope you understand. Here. Take this and read it every now and then. Or if you don't want it, pass it on to someone else. Good luck to you and, remember, Jesus loves you and God is watching over you." He handed Matt a prayer card that read,

> *My Lord God, I have no idea where I am going.*
> *I do not see the road ahead of me.*
> *I cannot know for certain where it will end.*
> *Nor do I really know myself, and the fact that*
> *I think that I am following your will does not*
> *mean that I am actually doing so. But I believe*
> *that the desire to please you does in fact please you.*
> *And I hope I have that desire in all that I am doing.*
> *I hope that I will never do anything apart from that desire. And I*
> *know that if I do this you will lead me by the right road though I*
> *may know nothing about it. Therefore will I trust you always though*
> *I may seem*
> *to be lost and in the shadow of death.*
> *I will not fear, for you are ever with me,*
> *and you will never leave me*
> *to face my perils alone.*

Matt had nothing against Jesus, but he didn't buy into the "Jesus loves you" and "God is watching over you" business. He didn't feel comfortable with the idea that God was such a voyeuristic and all-powerful Big Brother. He wanted more privacy than that, and he thought that both a firm belief or disbelief in God required blind faith in something that could never be either proven or refuted. Flip sides of the same silly coin. He was tired of trying to discuss it with people who had no respect for his opinions or points of view. And what difference should it make if Jesus was divine or human? What does that even have to do with it? That was just a distraction, a technicality. If Jesus had had any say in these matters, Matt thought he would have preferred slipping in without making a big stir, doing his work, sowing his seeds, and then making a tidy, unobtrusive exit after his seeds had taken root. Matt thought that the true importance of Jesus was in following his example and obeying his cardinal rule that we should all love one another. It's so simple! But everybody wants to complicate everything and argue about insignificant details that don't matter. Why can't they see that their beliefs are just opinions? And what value is anyone's opinion on such an unknowable matter as the existence of God or the divinity of Jesus? Or whose God is the true God? Whose church is the right church? It was like a multiple choice quiz in which everyone disagrees on the correct answer. It was nothing more than an ancient dead-ended cleverness contest sponsored by power-hungry religious zealots competing to see who could manipulate the most people into believing their own completely fabricated myth above all the other completely fabricated myths just in order to enrich themselves and acquire power. It both puzzled him and pissed him off. Everybody thinks they know everything, but in reality, nobody knows anything. Why doesn't everyone admit that it's all just a guessing game, a crap shoot, pure speculation—and that we are all as ridiculous as mice arguing whether the moon, which they all agree is composed of cheese, is Camembert or Swiss. Imagine such mouse crusades.

Here's what Matt really thought about God, whoever he or she or it may be: Matt's God or Gods neither loved him nor hated him. They weren't even aware of his existence. They were just bundles of energy and light surging forth like fountains with gifts of love and wisdom and the possibility of miracles, and they didn't give a shit if you believed in them or availed yourself of any of it. They were as indifferent as a well to be dipped from or an orchard to be plucked. They did not threaten you with punishments nor did they promise you rewards. They didn't belittle nor did they praise. And unlike the God of Matt's upbringing, they were generous with their fruit. They had more important things to worry about than the selfish prayers and petty doings of such an insignificant planet as this. They were all about the grand scheme and didn't bother themselves with the minutiae. In a way, Matt didn't even care if there was a God, as long as it would just leave him to his own devices.

It was a long sweaty walk out of town on a congested two-laner before he found a good spot where cars could pull over. Across the road was a deserted beach. He sat down to rest and remembered a dream he'd had the night before in which he was walking through a peach orchard looking for a job. The air was redolent with the sweet fragrance of ripe fruit dangling in bunches from the trees. When he found the owner, he was surprised to recognize him as Frankie, Vinny's dead brother, the boy from New Holland with the cerebral palsy disease. In the dream he was very much alive and he was strong and handsome and appeared to have not only been cured but was, in fact, a prime specimen of physical fitness.

"Frankie! What the hell are you doin' here?"

"Just working. Picking some fresh peaches for the store. Dad can't do it anymore so I've taken over the orchard." He was contagiously cheerful. The dream version of Penticton, as it turned out, was in upstate New York, north of New Holland, in the foothills of the Adirondack Mountains. It was comforting for Matt to know that he was no longer thousands of miles from home and could commute to work if Frankie hired him at the orchard.

"Man. I can't believe it. You look amazing."

"Yeah. Thanks, Matt. I finally got over all that stuff. Came through with flying colors, man. Hey—watch this." Frankie sprang into a cartwheel and a back flip, stuck the landing, and said, "Ta da!"

Matt said, "Wow. I wish I could do that," and then, "I'm sorry, but when you were sick, I think I might've laughed at you sometimes. I was just a dumb kid. I didn't know any better."

Frankie laughed. "Don't worry about it. You didn't mean anything. Everybody laughed at me. I got used to it. And it made me stronger."

Then there was one of those Bergman movie time-and-place dream switches, and Matt found himself standing on the A.L. Henderson High School auditorium stage with Frankie at his side. They were dressed in glittery Roy Rogers cowboy clothes with fancy leather fringes, playing guitars and singing a stomping version of "Travelin' Man" to an adoring audience of screaming teenaged girls.

Between verses, Frankie stepped forward and played a sizzling guitar solo, and the girls screamed even louder and he smiled and started shuffling his feet with rat-a-tat steps, his nimble toes defying gravity and balance. Then, from the wings, a diminutive girl in a fleecy cowgirl-style outfit pirouetted onto the stage. At first, Matt thought it was a miniature Helen, but when she turned around, he recognized the doll-faced ballerina as Esmerelda. The fans all cheered. An announcer introduced her: "Ladies and Gentlemen. Give a welcoming hand for the one and only Queen Esmerelda as she does the dipsy-doodle."

In the dream, Queen Esmerelda had shape-shifted into a glamorous, intelligent woman who, as it turned out, was also a world-famous dancer. She sang to the audience in a growly Mr. Ed voice:

> *Namby-pamby*
> *Dilly-dally*
> *Hunky-dory do*
> *Huggy-kissy*
> *Lovey-dovey*
> *All the whole night through*

But somehow she was also whispering right into Matt's ears, "Sometimes we become what we become just so willy-nilly, like it or lump it, for reasons beyond our comprehension and control." Then she whisked away behind the curtains like a twister in tap shoes.

Matt, stunned by Esmerelda's performance, thought, "Man. All these things I never knew. Or did I?" and then the dream dissolved into a fog, and Matt woke up in an unfamiliar room, disoriented, homesick, and sad to realize that none of it was real.

About an hour later, a VW with California plates stopped and two girls jumped out. "Sorry. No room for a ride, but here are some apricots." They handed Matt about a dozen juicy ones, which he gobbled up in a minute or two.

After another while, two hitchhikers walked up to him. He recognized them from Rob's van. All three of them climbed a fence and went swimming in the lake. Matt shared his shampoo with them and they all went in deep enough to take off their clothes and have a proper wash. Matt, typically pale and pasty, was proud of the golden tan he had cultivated since taking to the road, and he took pleasure in the nature boy freedom of splashing around in the lake, naked as a jaybird, in plain view of the highway.

They were climbing back over the fence in their wet shorts and bare feet and their dripping long hair when a pickup truck with an extended produce-hauling trailer stopped to pick up two other hitchhikers. Matt yelled, "Hey, do you have room for three more?" Sure enough, they were hailed into the back of the truck where there were about two dozen crates full of just-picked apricots and peaches being delivered to local markets.

After a short ride to Route 3, Matt and two teenaged runaways from Vancouver got off and headed toward Princeton. He was white and she was either Eskimo or Indian. Matt couldn't tell which and did not want to ask for fear that she would think he thought it made a difference and was making a racist white-guy judgment. They hitched together till about 1 a.m. before splitting up. On the western outskirts of Princeton, Matt found an outpost café glowing in its own radiant halo. He went in and had a hot cup of generic tea and two orders of rye toast with strawberry jelly. When he finished licking the final few crumbs from his mustache and beard, he cursed his stupidity when he realized that for the same amount of money he could have had pancakes. He'd been craving them since before Edmonton. The residual pangs of disappointment over the non-existent free pancake breakfast at The Klondike Days still tugged at his appetite and, standing alone on the side of this hopeless stretch of road in the middle of a lonely night, he could smell the melted butter as it swirled and blended into the gooey pool of maple syrup on the tall stack of steamy pancakes that had been frying in his mind since his craving began.

At 2:30, just as he had accepted the verdict of being condemned to spending the remainder of the night half-snoozing in the bushes, an 18-wheeled transport truck bore down upon him with its air brakes screeching. It had a shiny silver grille the size of a garage door, which was painted to look like a saber-toothed tiger, snarling at all oncoming traffic and devouring the empty highway and everything else in its path. The steel letters that identified the make of the truck had been rearranged to read, "DORF." He climbed up into the cab and threw his pack in the back.

In an exaggerated faux-cowpoke accent, the driver said "Howdy pardner. Where ya headed? Vancouver?"

Matt nodded, "Yup."

"That's a big can-do, good buddy." He extended a fleshy jumbo-sized hand and said, "My name's Arn. What's yours?" And in a matter of minutes, Matt found himself on a harrowing roller-coaster ride through the invisible nighttime mountains with yet another speedy-eyed and narcoleptic truck driver.

High beams burned out a tunnel of light into the curvy pitch-dark screen of wilderness before him. The driver negotiated the rise and fall of the bends and switches with a determination that was dwindling against the ascending power of his exhaustion, saying, "I think a snake made this road" and "This road is crookeder than a dog's hind leg." Arn struggled, reddening his cheeks with brute-force slaps, yelling, "Oh baby! We're rolling now" at the top of his lungs and glaring at Matt with droopy eyes, cranking the radio to a full blast of irritating static because the crummy thing was too weak to pick anything up, and opening the window, sticking his head out and yelping with a mad grin, "Watch out, motherfuckers, 'cause I'm comin' to getcha" as the night bugs gnashed against his teeth. At one point, Matt had to grab the steering wheel and yell to awaken Arn when his head dropped and his hands slipped from their grip.

They barreled down to the Hope Slide where, according to the driver, a mountain had collapsed and buried fourteen people.

"Missed a Greyhound bus by less than a minute," Arn said.

Matt got out several miles east of Vancouver in the dawn's pearly light feeling as worthless and depleted and disoriented as he had the morning he arrived in Edmonton. Arn had reached the turnoff for the warehouse where he was delivering a load of frozen chicken. He yawned and growled like a grizzly as he stretched his arms to a full wingspan.

"I have to wait a couple hours for the place to open before I can unload. I'll try to nap 'til then." As Matt jumped from the cab of the Dorfmobile, Arn said, "Didn't mean to scare you back there, Matt. Thanks for keeping me awake—and alive."

"No problem. Thanks for the lift, Arn."

Matt swore off any further nocturnal hitching because, in addition to the threat it posed to his continued existence, it left him too wasted to function, threw him way out of whack, and destroyed his consciousness for the whole next day.

He got little rides into the city from commuters either returning home from the graveyard shift or else having the misfortune of needing to rise at that god-awful hour for an early day's work. There was something spiritual about arriving into the mystery of a large unknown city and walking alone on an empty sidewalk just as its skyscrapers are being illuminated by the earliest spill of sunlight over the mountains as its streets are awakening to the first wave of human commerce and the chill of night is still in the air and all green things are dripping in dew. He felt empty and senseless and totally fulfilled and enlightened at the same moment.

Matt watched garbage men as they dumped trash into their trucks and then carelessly tossed the aluminum cans back onto the sidewalk in a loud clatter. His father had once told him, "It doesn't matter what you do in life. What matters is that you do your best to do it well." Then he told Matt the story of the garbageman who always placed the cans quietly onto the sidewalk so as not to awaken anyone and who, in rainy weather, turned the cans upside down to keep the insides dry.

"Take pride in whatever you do. Every job has its dignity," his father concluded before drifting away to that other place, the silent lost habitat of his thoughts where Matt no longer existed.

270

At 7:10 Matt made a collect call home where it was three hours later. Rory answered the phone, still half-immersed in dreams. After negotiating with the operator, who he initially called "Babe," mistaking her for his girlfriend, Rory accepted the charges.

"Where are you?"

"I just got into Vancouver. I hitched all night. Been here a couple hours."

"Man, you've gone a long ways. I heard you've been hopping freight trains."

"Yeah. I shouldn't have said anything about that. How's Mom?"

"She's okay, but she's worried about you. Every time she sees that commercial, the one about 'It's 10:30. Do you know where your kids are?' she gets upset and turns off the TV."

"I wish they'd take that goddamn commercial off the air. All it does is scare people."

"When you coming home?"

"I don't know. I'm gonna go down the coast into California. Go through the Redwoods. Go to San Francisco and down through Big Sur to Los Angeles. And then I'll head east, straight across the country through the Grand Canyon and back home."

"Sounds like fun. How's your money holding out?"

"Not bad. I don't have to spend much up here, staying and eating at the hostels. But I'm not sure how it's gonna work out when I get back to the states. We'll see."

"You getting lucky with any of those free-loving hippie chicks?"

"Oh yeah. They're all over the place. I've got a couple of them waiting for me right now."

Rory laughed. "Hey—guess what? I saw the Cricket Man and he was asking about you. I told him you were walking cross-country and he believed me. I asked him how long he thought it would take you to walk to California He scratched his head, looked at his watch, and said, 'About thirty-five days'. The Cricket Man—he's a riot."

"He can't help it. He's probably never been outside of New Holland. As far as he knows, California is just past Mananaugua."

"I was just goofin' on him, having a laugh. He thought it was funny, too."

"Have you seen anybody else?"

"Yeah. Tates stopped over yesterday. Gail was with him. They sat around and played Yahtzee with Mom. Mom loves it when they visit. He came over 'cause he got a postcard from you, said something about getting a ride with Rod Serling and William Shatner. He wanted to show it to Mom 'cause he knew she was worried and he thought it would make her feel better. He was joking around and got Gail laughing. You know how it is with Gail. Once she starts laughing she can't stop, and it gets everybody else laughing. It was pretty funny. It really cheered Mom up."

After some more small talk, Matt said, "I better get going. This is costing Mom a fortune. Tell her I'll call her back later, okay?"

"Yeah. She'll be upset that she missed you. I'll tell her."

"Thanks. I'll catch you later."

"Okay. See ya. And don't take any rides from anybody who looks like Charles Manson."

Vancouver had a network of hostels and a central office that assigned travelers to specific locations. Matt found the referral service, but it was closed until 2 p.m. So, like an authentic hobo, he curled up on the sidewalk entranceway of the office and tried to get some sleep. Other hitchhikers trickled by itching for 2 p.m. Time passed glacially, and sleep was an impossible dream.

He met a guy from New Jersey who was driving to Alaska in his beat-up old Falcon because he dreamed he received a postcard from his dead father which read, "Juneau where to go." He took it as a sign from beyond and said that everybody, even he, thought it was crazy, but he couldn't help it.

"If I don't go, I'll always wonder. The worst that can happen is that I'll get there and nothing will happen and I'll go back home. In the meantime, I'm having a fantastic summer. So who cares if I've got a crazy reason? Life is all just a gamble, isn't it?"

"Yup," said Matt. "And he who never gambles always loses."

A while later, one of his train-hopping buddies appeared at the doorway. "Hey, Wayne. How are you? Where have you been?"

"Matt! What's happening, man? Mike and I got separated a while back and we're supposed to meet here in Van. I've been looking for him."

"I saw him in Calgary a few days ago. He was looking for you. He said he'd leave a message for you here at the hostel."

"That's what I thought, but I couldn't find any messages. We didn't know there were so many different hostels. We assumed there'd be one big one for everybody. I've already been here three days, so I've gotta check out. I'm gonna sleep on the beach."

"You sure it's okay to sleep there? Can you do that? Is it safe?"

"Other people are doing it. You've just got to be careful or you'll get your stuff ripped off. As long as it doesn't rain, it should be okay."

In order to kill time, Matt walked with Wayne to check out the beach but decided in favor of a bed, a roof, and hot meals. He told Wayne he'd look out for Mike, and then he walked back to his doorway and tried to nap. When the office opened up he was sent to the Y Lodge Hostel, which, unlike the others in town, was opened all day and had no curfew. Once he settled in and celebrated the fact that he had made it to the West Coast, his system went on strike, and all he wanted to do was sink into a death-like sleep and enjoy the benefits of a sleep rebound. So he crashed in his cot, skipped dinner, and detached himself from all human contact and all worldly concerns. He had chased the sun to the end of the westward horizon, and there was no more west left. Like Lewis and Clark, like Marco Polo, he had achieved his goal. It was a thing accomplished. But he hadn't given much thought, if any, to what he would do in Vancouver once he arrived. His nomadic thoughts migrated south to San Francisco, to Big Sur, to the Grand Canyon and beyond to new horizons and to the edges of other worlds just waiting to be experienced, enjoyed, and explored.

# CHAPTER XXI

Breakfast tasted exceptionally delicious. He hadn't eaten anything since his tea and toast at the all-night café in Princeton, but now before him was a plate with three superlative slices of hot-melted-buttery-syrupy French toast, a bowl of crunchy Grape-Nuts with prunes, which tasted elegant and newly discovered, and a spiritually transformational cup of tea which was made from an ordinary run-of-the-mill bag of rot, Matt's acronym for regular old tea, such as Lipton or Tetley, but which tasted robust and specially brewed for the occasion and which reminded him of something he'd read in *The Dharma Bums* concerning the Oriental passion for tea: the first sip is joy, the second is gladness, the third is serenity, the fourth is madness, the fifth is ecstasy.

A few minutes of extra help with cleanup earned him an extra helping of food in addition to the meat pie and pastry that was handed out to everyone for daytime munching. He stayed in and slept and read and wrote all day except for a couple of afternoon hours when he went to the beach and walked around town looking for Wayne and Mike. Other than that, he was listlessly unwilling to do anything more than rev his engines in neutral.

Late in the afternoon an Australian bloke sashayed into the dorm effusing about the nude beach he'd been to all day. To quell the disbelievers, he changed his shorts and made Exhibit A of his ruby-red ass. Matt couldn't imagine himself balls-out in a public place, shriveled by embarrassment, and so he envied the carefree Aussie as he described his naked romp with a comical Aussie shtick.

"I told you, mate. Totally nude. There were tanned tits everywhere I looked and the odd donger or two. And all the young Sheilas rubbing themselves with lotion. A wanker's paradise. And there stood I, smack bang in the middle of all that glistening flesh. Couldn't keep myself down, if you know what I mean." He winked like a vaudevillian of olden times as he whistled a sunny tune and finished off with a jaunty bit of the old soft-shoe.

That evening the warden showed the movie *Hotel* on the wall in the dining room. Someone yelled out, "They oughta make a movie called *Hostel*!" Everyone laughed at the obviousness of the joke, but the best part of the evening was the cartoon before the movie. *Robot Rabbit*, a Bugs Bunny cartoon starring the voice of Mel Blanc, brought down the house and left everybody in a jovial mood. Like a family of overexcited children whose parents were allowing them to stay up past their bedtime, the hostelers begged the warden to play the cartoon again after the mediocre movie, and he obliged. They all began singing cartoon theme songs. Someone called out, "Okay, who can name the seven dwarfs?" Dopey, Grumpy, Sneezy, Happy and Sleepy all came right away but then they hit a brick wall. Others started shouting, "Stinky," "Grungy," "Pukey," "Dick Breath" and then, "Horny." Someone yelled, "Snow White was pretty sexy, so I bet they were all horny."

Everyone had a favorite character. The Road Runner. Foghorn Leghorn. The Pink Panther. Yosemite Sam. Matt's favorite was Wile E. Coyote because no matter how many times he got blown to smithereens or steamrolled into a pancake, he would be restored and show no sign of injury as if nothing had happened. And no matter how many times he had been thwarted in his quest to snare the Road Runner, such failures never stopped him from launching a new and vigorous pursuit. *Just like me*, Matt thought, *and my cartoonish pursuit of Carla*. No matter how many cliffs of failed expectations he'd tumbled over or how many times he'd been flattened by rejection or had his infatuation blow up in his face like emotional dynamite, he had never given up and was still none the wiser. Deep down inside he knew that in some disastrous way, his own chances of success were no better than the coyote's and that the same fatalistic hand was at both drawing boards. Yes. He had always been certain that he would never have her. That truth was always there, plain as day. He just never wanted to see it.

As the dorm lights were dimmed, two late stragglers swaggered back from a night of youthful debauchery. Matt heard them giggling and exercising their bragging rights with unrestrained whispers about how they had gotten stoned with a couple hippie girls on the beach and, when it got dark, had sex with them right there in the sand. They snorted and egged each other on as they described their lucky fling in lurid detail, including the itchy fact that "my nut sack is all crusty with sand." Their escapade ended when a flashlight-toting Vancouver cop spotted them in all their pagan glory, resulting in a mad grasp for undergarments and a frenzied escape into darkness, hightailing it with their scrotums and breasts a-flailing. Matt felt repulsed by the vulgar glee they took in recounting their conquests and their self-congratulatory back-slapping because he knew that those girls meant nothing to them. And yet, eavesdropping through the curtain from that other place within himself, his other self knew that his disapproval masked the fact that he was jealous and wished that it had been him.

# CHAPTER XXII

With another lazy day behind him and a good night's sleep under his belt, Matt was recharged. He had already wasted two lethargic days and had made no friends among the hostelers, thanks to an antisocial apathy that had lulled him into submission. Usually such an emotional withdrawal was a symptom of his depressed mind—he thought they went hand in hand—but he was not at all depressed. In fact, he was content, non-introspective, and non-self-analytical. On this entire journey, he'd had very few significant bouts with the paranoid attacks that terrorized him on a regular basis at home, where the aftereffects could afflict him for days or weeks at a time. While on the road, the attacks came and went like sudden squalls followed by a quick recovery thanks to the good company he kept, or else he dodged it artfully as he took flight ever more westward. Whatever the reason, that constant voice inside him, his traitorous shadow companion, his Watcher, his screamin' demons and that ever-present man inside his head had been mercifully quiet most of the time or had been left behind on the road, in a hostel, or a van somewhere across the great Canadian expanse or on the darkening streets of Calgary where It or they could find some new host to possess for a while. He had to keep on keeping on because the moving target is always safer than the sitting duck.

Being antisocial and lethargic was pointless without that dismal bloom of his much-cherished depression to make it all worthwhile, so he might as well do something. Besides, if he didn't get off his ass and stir something up soon, he knew that homesickness would prematurely summon him back east. So he bolstered himself up enough to make plans for the evening with two boys at the hostel. One of them, Al, was a local and had a van. He was evicted from his apartment for having too many parties and had since run out of hospitable friends. His van was all that saved him from having to sleep on the beach or in the parks. The other, Andy, was a drug-dealing hitchhiker from Arizona who had been supporting himself by dealing hash and grass to the hostelers or on the streets. He charged bargain basement prices, which covered his living expenses and also provided him with a steady private stash of good smoke. He smiled. "It's just enough to keep the street chicks interested in me."

They got stoned on Andy's hash on their way to Gastown and strolled the hip and vibrant sidewalks parading their illegal smiles. Al told Matt, "You're gonna love Gastown. It's a nonstop freak show." True enough, the street scene was energetic and alive with a colorful variety of lopsided, oddball characters. Guitar-toting street musicians, panhandling drifters, mumbling drug entrepreneurs, bare-footed hippie chicks with homemade paisley handbags and their bare-chested boyfriends in fringed buckskin vests, and a panoply of wide-eyed, stoned-out freaks and drop-outs all cavorted in full bloom. All the glorious riffraff that Vancouver had to offer. It was everything Al had promised.

They went to the Anchor Hotel Bar and had a few drinks. Matt wanted rum and coke, a favorite since he visited Spain where rum was cheap. Unfortunately, they didn't serve hard liquor, mixed drinks or wine in this bar. Just beer. Lots of it.

This was a real beer hall. Unlike American bars, like Biagi's and Bromski's, where drinkers laid claim to their tables as if they owned them, this was an open range with a roving and boisterous crowd. A free-for-all hub of booze-infused revelry where the community of celebrants young and old mingled at long wooden banquet tables, sharing drinks and stories and jokes and songs. It was possessed with that everyone-is-welcome, the-more-the-merrier, swill-your-fill spirit. Matt did his best to chug his sudsy brew with the same gusto as the guzzlers around him. A symphony of jabbering voices swelled and blended into an oceanic roar of white noise, mouths gaping and chomping like real-life Howdy Doodys, while there he sat, cowering within the protective fortress of his mute sanctuary, unable to decipher any of the babble or think of a single sentence to say to anyone. A girl in a sheer, loose-fitting summer dress danced past him and into the all-enveloping arms of her brawny boyfriend who had just entered the bar. Matt inhaled as she passed and timed it so he could enjoy the breeze of the perfume that trailed after her like a scented silk scarf.

Beside Matt sat a distinguished-looking elderly man who reminded him of his father. From the looks of the man, he didn't often say no to a drink. His face was round and jowly and upon his left cheek there was a constellation of liver spots. He raised his frothy vessel in Matt's direction, quaffed a healthy slug of his stout, and intoned, "Ah! Mother's milk."

Matt tried to imagine sitting in a bar with his father and having even just a simple conversation. He realized that he could recall only a couple instances when they had been together outside of the confines of their home. In public, Professor Mahoney was a different person than his non-communicative father at home. He was cheerful, exhibiting good humor with whomever he met, as if they all belonged to the same social organization. He was, by all appearances, beloved by all, and most of all by his students, who were mesmerized by his lectures and always greeted him with reverential smiles. Yet, despite his outgoing public persona and his convincing display of camaraderie, he had no friends that Matt was aware of. Matt could never get a handle on who his father really was. He was different things to different people. Matt sometimes wished that, instead of being Professor Mahoney's son, he had been his student.

The old man's deejay voice boomed above the loudspeakers and smashed through the bubbles of other people's private conversations. He said with authority that no one would ever sing as well as Bing Crosby except, of course, for John McCormack. Moved by the memories and the tipsy emotion and not just a little by the consumed pints, the old man stood like a politician with a raised mug and led the barroom in a rousing rendition of "Did Your Mother Come From

Ireland?" receiving uproarious acclaim from the gang of cheerful
drunks, half of whom had never heard the song before. He doffed
his cap, imbibed in a ritualistic manner, and took a sweeping bow.
When he took his seat, he smacked his lips, nodded his pint in Matt's
direction, and said, "Slainte!"

Matt, half-lapsed into a blind admiration, asked, "Do you know
'Two-Shillelagh O'Sullivan'?"

The man was amused by the question and, looking at Matt
through Alka-Seltzer eyes, said in a mocking tone, "Well now there,
laddie. May the saints preserve us. You must have a bit of the Irish in
you. Or are you just Irish by injection?"

He spoke in an inflated theatrical accent, making the most of the
eroded remnants of his Irish brogue, and placed his hand on Matt's
shoulder in a paternal fashion, in the way it had never before been
touched by his own father, and looked at him with his intent and
rheumy old eyes. But then, like his own father, the man just slipped
away without giving any answers, balancing a drink in an unsteady
hand and brushing his other across a shapely girl's ass in an act of
calculated carelessness as he tottered toward the bathroom.

"Fuck you, old man. You're nothing but a bar fly," Matt muttered
into his beer, cursing the shaky old lush camouflaged beneath the dulcet
tones and regretting that he had already grown fond of him. Uninvited
unruly thoughts swilled in his head. The scalpel. The postmortem. The
butchered corpse of regrets. The conquering disease. Stupid thoughts
like that.

"Fuck you. Fuck me. Fuck the world," he muttered again and
felt the nauseous squirm sickening his stomach beneath a blanket of
sorrow, the big raging Matt, all gagged and bound down with ropes
and chains, like Gulliver, and he's struggling to get free and, man, if he
ever gets unbound, there's no telling. There's just no telling.

*He started remembering the days when he still idolized his father
and hung on his every word. The childhood days when the old man
treated Matt like a son and was still kind and wise in fatherly ways.*

*As a boy, no more than five years old, Matt had a dread fear of the barber, and at the prospect of an impending haircut, he would yell and scream and fight his way out of the shop. He had a notion that the man would cut his ears off, an idea most likely planted in his head as a joke by an older brother or sister. His father solved the problem by bringing Matt to his own barber and reassuring him that this man was safe and gentle, a master of the scissoring arts, and would not harm him. The occasion of Matt's first visit to Pete the Barber was all the more special because he was accompanied by his father, who introduced Matt as "my son," the only time that he ever heard his father utter those words. He climbed into the big black swiveling throne without opposition and shook Pete's large caveman hand, marveling at the clumps of hair sprouting from his nostrils and ears. When he heard his father tell Pete that from now on he would be Matt's one and only barber, Matt felt like a proud and special little man, like an actual son.*

*But as Matt grew older, his father grew more distant. He would sit silently at the kitchen table late at night, brooding over some thick literary tome while the house was slumbering in shadows. Matt would tippy-toe downstairs and sit beside him at the table, watching the pages turn. His father barely acknowledged his presence as he read and tended to his fresh tumbler of bourbon, but he did not shoo him up to bed. And though it was never anything that amounted to a conversation, the silent companionship was somehow enough to convince him that his father still loved him. As the moments grew fewer and the distance grew greater, he began to wish that his father was more like his Uncle Joe, who always greeted Matt with a big squinty grin and a new joke or a riddle or a card trick.*

*Matt could no longer remember the breaking point, that critical day when he stopped visiting his father at the kitchen table because it was a fruitless endeavor to strive for his affections. What had he done to drive that man away? What he did remember was that when that critical day came and went, when Matt withdrew his affections, it was an event unmarked in any way by the silent grim man who had been its target. He hadn't even noticed.*

Matt choked down another bitter belt of beer and damned the memory of the dreaded amber contents of his father's ever-refilling tumbler, recollecting how crushed he was to find that he was not even a blip on the old man's radar. He swigged again to realize that he had to memorize and periodically recite all these unpleasantries in order to justify his anger and his sense of fatherlessness and to appease his own guilt at having such mixed feelings about his old man, both in life and in death. *It's a fucking inside job.*

Alcohol magnified the sting of his barbed introspections, but he continued swigging anyway as the hyped-up energy of the boozy barroom filled back in around him and he found himself buried in the din and howl and singing with abandon, first to "American Woman" and then to "Brandy," as the collective lungs of this human throng swelled up into a unified warlike roar.

Al and Andy were launching a charm offensive, putting the make on two Asian-looking girls, each with a garland of yellow daisies adorning the sheen of their jet-black hair. Matt thought for sure he would be left to fend for himself, but one of the girls called Al a male chauvinist pig and backed away just shy of delivering a slap after he got too anxious too soon, more offensive than charming, and made an ungentlemanly suggestion.

Andy reprimanded him with a punch to the shoulder. "Damn. Downshift, man. Just downshift! You really fumbled the keys on that one."

"What are you talking about? What keys?"

Andy, the poet of the two, said, "The keys to the knees, man. If you kept your rap cool for a few more minutes, you know where we'd be right now? Do you? We'd be out there in the van cooking up a bowl of hash and pollinating those pretty little flower girls. We'd be laid in the shade. But now we might as well just jack off in our hats." He formed an oval with his right hand and made a series of suggestive stroking motions.

Al rolled his eyes and chuckled. "Don't be such a crybaby, man. I did that because they were just teasing us, playing hard to get, so I cut to the chase. We were wasting our time. Sometimes you have to admit defeat. You are not the lady killer you think you are." Then, with a snarky leer, he said, "Tough titty said the bald headed kitty when the milk went dry."

They bantered for a few more rounds like a couple of inebriated comedians and then finished their beers, agreed that everything was copacetic, lifted their anchors, and took a woozy stroll along the trippy streets of Gastown. When Matt, whose "Maynard G. Krebs Lost Change Detector" was apparently functional in Canada, found a quarter on the sidewalk, Al said, "Consider yourself lucky. These streets are sucked clean. I bet you that quarter couldn't have been there for more than a minute or two."

They followed their ears to a street corner where a guitarist and a fiddler played lively Irish dance tunes. A scruffy gypsy girl wearing dozens of jingly bracelets on each arm wove through the crowd carrying an upside-down fur cap, imploring, "Spare change for the band?" The contagious energy of the music was made even more so when, as if in a movie, two barefooted teenaged girls with long hair and flowing skirts jump in and present their loose-limbed version of a jig which mutated charmingly into a homespun can-can frolic. Matt has never seen anything so beautiful in his life. An audience gathers and claps as the dancing duo link arms, spinning and laughing and throwing their heads back and lifting their skirts like gypsies and improvising with gravity-defying dance steps. Then, a rambunctious Little Orphan Annie girl in a flowery sun dress, who couldn't be more than four years old, squeezes her way into the clearing around the musicians and joins the older girls in a fierce frolic, inhabited by the primal pulse of the music and the tribal frolic and the spirited prompting of the crowd all rolled into one rollicking and exhilarating moment. Her red corkscrew ringlets spring up and down and around as she jumps and twirls with bewitched eyes, indifferent to the attentions of the admiring swarm around her. Matt wonders if he has ever for anything had as much enthusiasm as that whirling dervish before him and, if he did, where did it go?

She continues dancing until the performance ends. Everyone cheers, and the two barefoot figurantes lifted the girl above their heads in triumph to the ovation of the crowd, hug her, and put her back down. A woman's voice summons, "Rainbow! We're over here, honey!" and she darts and disappears into the arms of the applauding audience. Matt is transfixed, immobile, unable to cheer or applaud.

In the van on the way back, the boys torched up another bowl and made plans for a return trip to Gastown the next night. Matt said he wouldn't be joining them because he'd be leaving in the morning and returning to the land of his origin, so they drove around a little longer, just long enough to fire up a second bowl in his honor and to bless and protect him on the road.

# CHAPTER XXIII

Matt left on a full stomach, expecting a long, punishing walk through the suburbs of Vancouver on his way south into Washington. It was a dull, gray morning. The telltale puddles in the gutters and potholes were all that was left of the overnight pop-up showers. As he was walking across a bridge, a hippie girl walking the same direction, drawn to his backpack, caught up with him and asked where he was going. She was slender and had a boyish shape, but her dimpled smile revealed a sprite-like femininity.

"California."

"Wow! That's cool. Never been to California—yet. What's your name?" she inquired, as though there might be magic in his response.

"Matt. What's yours?"

"Gracie. Just moved here two weeks ago. Living with some friends. I'm from Kelowna. Do you know where that is?"

"Yeah. It's in the Okanogan valley. I went through there the other day. It was beautiful."

"Well, it's always more beautiful if you're from someplace else. Where are you from?"

"Upstate New York. A small town. New Holland. You probably never heard of it."

"Wow! You're a long way from home. New York! Yeah! I've always dreamed of going there." She elongated the word "dreamed" so that the "e" took about three seconds. "Maybe staying at a crash pad in Greenwich Village. That's a fantasy of mine. Who knows? Maybe someday."

TIM KELLY

A momentary silence and then, out of the blue, she said, "You know what, Matt? You're a nice guy. I wish more guys were nice like you."

He was flustered. "You don't even know me. For all you know I could be another Charlie Manson."

She laughed. "Yeah, right. I mean it. Sometimes you can tell right away. You're a good person. You've got a good heart."

He got quiet, almost sad. How could she know anything about his heart? "You give me too much credit," was all he could muster.

"Hey, what's wrong? Don't get all glum on me. Maybe I should keep my mouth shut. But I can't help it sometimes. I say what I feel and I go on my gut reaction. The good guys all need to be told so." She shook her head and lifted her shoulders and, without apology, said, "That's just the way I am."

"I'm sorry," he said. "I don't know what it is about me. But happy always makes me sad."

She brightened. "Well, I'm sorry to be the bearer of such bad news, but I regret to inform you that it's official—you are a good guy."

"Well so are you." He half-smiled. "I wish I were more outgoing. I'm always thinking of good things to say or do, but then I chicken out and don't act on it. Or else I say things all wrong and then regret even opening my mouth."

"Man, everybody does that. You just gotta find the right person to reach you in there and bring you out. Then it's, 'Hey everybody. Look who's here. It's Matt—the real Matt.' And then—presto!—there you are. Free at last."

"Are you always this friendly?"

"Nah. Sometimes I'm a royal bitch. But I'm having a good day today. I woke up feeling extra positive and I thought, 'I'm gonna get my sulky self out of bed, take a walk, and see what happens.' And so I took a walk, and look what happened. I met you. It's a good day all over."

"Yeah. I guess so," he replied, feeling both sadness and joy and having a hard time believing that he could have made someone else's day.

286

There was a sudden rumbling from above, and a heavy rain began to fall. They ran down the street, pelted by raindrops, and ducked into a hash house luncheonette, dripping wet and laughing as Gracie shrieked in a thin falsetto, "Help me! Help me! I'm melting." They shook off the rain and she said, "See? It's a great day."

They slid into a cushy booth in the empty diner and ordered coffee and wheat toast. Through the foggy plate glass window they watched and listened to the riveting rain, invigorated by their steamy beverages, and chatting about music. He asked, "What's your favorite song?" and immediately thought it was an inane question, like "What's your sign?"

"That's a tough one. There's so many. Let me think …," then she took a few seconds and said, "Okay. Here's one." She closed her eyes and started to sing in a silky whisper.

*Across the evening sky all the birds are leaving*
*But how can they know it's time for them to go?*
*Before the winter fire I shall still be dreaming*
*I do not count the time*
*For who knows where the time goes?*
*Who knows where the time goes?*

Matt was moved as well as relieved that he didn't have to pretend that he enjoyed her singing. He felt a deep soul connection to her, through her willingness to sing for him, and in their mutual reverence for the magnificence of this song.

"You've got a good voice. That was beautiful. I love that song, too. You should be in a band."

"I wanna be a singer. I've been writing songs for a few years, but most of them aren't very good. I can't even remember most of them."

"Sing me one," Matt said. "Come on. I wanna hear one of your songs."

"I don't know. Are you sure? I'm pretty shy about singing my own songs." But she didn't need much coaxing, and her reluctance dissolved like the sugar in his coffee.

"Tell you what. If you sing me one of your songs, I'll show you one of my poems."

287

"It's a deal. But you've got to promise not to laugh." "Promise. You too?"

"Promise."

Gracie looked around as a safety check. She closed her eyes and sang as if in the privacy of her own living room.

> *Oh I will climb the highest mountain*
> *And I will sail the widest sea*
> *To be with you my own true love*
> *My own true love with thee.*
> *And I will ride through every forest*
> *Upon a brave and noble steed*
> *To be with you my own true love*
> *My own true love with thee*
> *And should the armies come between us*
> *And should the blood flow free*
> *Oh I will lie in dreams so sweet*
> *My own true love with thee.*

Matt couldn't say much except that it was beautiful and to thank her for singing it.

"I've never sung that for anyone yet. I love English folk songs, but I didn't want to use all that "lily-white hands" and "milk-white steeds" stuff. Or that John Riley "my long-lost lover who sails the deep salt sea" stuff. Well, I kinda compromised on that. But it's not finished. It's still a work in progress."

"Well, it's already great."

"Okay. Your turn."

Matt pulled a folded sheet of paper from his wallet, opened it up and handed it to her. "Here's my poem."

"No. You have to read it to me."

"I can't do that. I thought you could just read it yourself."

"No way. Fair is fair. I *sang* you a song. Now you *read* me a poem. I wanna close my eyes and hear it through the poet's own voice. That's the only way it makes sense."

He struggled with the idea of reading the poem out loud. He had never done that before, not even with Helen, and certainly not in a public place. What if someone heard? But he didn't want to spoil the moment, so he ignored his fears and cleared his throat. "Okay. It's kind of long. But here goes."

*When i was young*
*and the girls were blouse-blooming and bursting like sunrise and*
*flowers*
*sprouting their acorn lives in a timeless forest at the world's*
*angel-ancient edge,*
*the sudden magic of spring*
*cast me wholly under its hypnotic spell*
*opening my stapled-shy eyes to the heavens*
*as my growing ears heard new songs in the soft heroic nights,*
*with girls skirts' rippling rapid pleats in a placid sea spreading tidal*
*waves of light where no sun had ever ventured as their perfume, thick*
*as honey in the April air, left my slaved senses perched*
*and buzzing quietly beside their dripping petals*
*like a bewildered bee, just aware of pollen*

*and holy under its hypnotic spell*
*i saw angels splendid and speaking my name*
*to virgin women who held me dearest in their mysterious*
*affections and the angels oh the blessed angels soared treetops to my*
*child's passions,*
*my fingers reaching strong and tiny through the silent sky, my*
*spangled notions flying sparrows*
*quick in the pigeon-slow park of my light-lunged life to the*
*breadcrumbs of my feeding curiosities*

*but all around me voices whispered rumors of dead angels*
*who, crushed in flight by time's tight vise,*
*sang their dying songs to the invisible wind*

*that blew through me unnoticed but for the cold*
*as all around me, though through some mist,*
*the perfumed flowers grew gay and free in my buzzing eyes as*
gray and sheathed i hid like a weed
*growing solemn in the forest's devil-dark corner*
*cast wholly under its cold hypnotic spell*

He was so nervous that he could hardly look up. His voice quivered and cracked, and his palms and brow were sweaty and his mouth was dry.

Gracie opened her eyes. "That was beautiful—but so sad. Can I have it? I want to be able to remember it."

"Sure. I've got it written down at home. This must be the reason I brought it with me."

"Yes. And this must be the reason I woke up feeling so positive and came out for a walk. You know, most people are put off by me, the way I barge in on them, like I did with you. Nobody takes me seriously. They think I'm a ditsy flower-child who's all unicorns and rainbows and who's happy only because she's just a shallow chatterbox. But you're different. You know what? You're the first person who has ever asked me to sing one of my songs. Can you believe that? Everybody knows that I write them, but nobody ever asks me to sing one for them. And I know you for five minutes and already here I am singing for you. Usually I feel weird around people until I know them for a long time, but I am feeling real normal around you. I think we're on the same wavelength or something. It's coming in loud and clear with you. It's a nice feeling."

It was magically quiet for a moment. Then she teased, "At first you acted like you thought I was coming on to you."

"Well, were you?" He didn't know what else to say.

"No. I wasn't. But I wasn't trying not to either."

He is penetrated by her sweetheart smile. She reaches forward and places her hands upon his. He nearly jumps at the delightful shock of her touch. The warmth of her flesh mingles with his until they melt together and there is no longer a distinction between the two. They go through two more cups of coffee and exchange addresses before it stops raining. "I better give you my parents' address in Kelowna because who knows where I'll end up."

Matt pays, leaves a fifty-cent tip, and they step outside into the purified morning air. He doesn't want the moment to end. He wants to ask her to join him, to be his lady fair, and he her gallant lover. They could hitchhike together and see the Redwoods and the Grand Canyon and everything in between and beyond. Together. Singing songs. Reciting poetry. Falling in love like the lovers in her song. Maybe she's "the one."

But he dares not. He knows, even as he considers it, that it was not written into his script and that in about a minute he'll be saying goodbye and will never see her or hear her sing again for the rest of his life. That's just the way it has to be, for better or worse. Every new friendship is its own little heartbreak.

"Thanks for everything. Especially the poem. It was great."

"Thank you, too. I'm glad we met. It's a shame that—" But she wouldn't let him finish his sentence.

"I've got an idea. Let's make this memorable." And before he even has the time to say, "It's already been memorable", she steps forward, closing her eyes and moistening her lips with her tongue, puts her arms around him, and gives him a warm wonderful kiss, pressing against him all soft and tingly, smelling of hope and fresh flowers. It was maybe a bit terrifying because it sweeps him back to the dizzying sensation of his first-ever kiss with Helen. That was the proverbial kiss worth dying for. And here, now, with Gracie, he feels the same marvelous and otherworldly out-of-body thrill he experienced with Helen, as if true love really is a matter of fate, a thing of destiny, and here he is now, in this distant city, right on time, discovering his true soul mate according to the designs of some predetermined cosmic master plan. Or then again, maybe nothing is predetermined. Maybe things happen the way they happen for no reason and you can either drift rudderless through life at the mercy of the winds around you or you can set your own sails and chart you own course to your own self-chosen destinations.

*How long has it been?* he thinks, trying to squint through clouds of drought to the dim image of the last lips to touch his. He had fantasized about kissing Gracie as he gazed at the perfect oval of her face while sitting in the diner, but the full euphoric swell of the physical touching of lips galvanizes the moment and brands it upon his heart. Kisses like this are once, or maybe twice, in a lifetime.

"That's from the real me in me to the real you in you." She giggles, a pure golden giggle, and then, in a matter of seconds, they say goodbye and drift in opposite directions, leaving Matt to fear once again that he is letting "the one" slip through his fingers. And there are church bells pealing in the distance.

This he recalls:

*One summer night, when he was fifteen and had known Helen for only two months, they snuck out of their houses after their parents went to bed, a real Romeo and Juliet midnight tryst, sans balcony. He was sure that she would chicken out and was pleased and surprised when he saw her slip across her front lawn to meet him on the sidewalk. They spent the entire night together, holding hands and strolling the vacant streets and, at the sight of headlights, ditching into the shadowy side yards to avoid capture.*

*"If my father catches me, I'm dead," Helen said with a mixed sense of dread and adventure. That she would risk her father's wrath to be with him said more than words could say and made him feel special. She smiled at him, bravely took his hand in hers, said "Let's go," and walked on, resolute and unafraid like the commander of an expedition. New and wonderful sensations bubbled up inside of him as together they explored their sleeping city and saw it with their brand-new eyes.*

*They strode along the secluded railroad tracks that led from the monolithic old factory buildings all the way to the wooded hills that rose above the East End of town and into the eerie darkness behind and above the Wigwam Restaurant. Her hand cradled in his was so gentle and warm, and his heart beat proudly and soared as if it had grown wings. By himself, he would have been frightened on these remote tracks in the middle of the night, but together it felt safe, even welcoming, as if her company made him brave and eliminated all danger.*

*The hours melted away as they made the long trek back to Helen's house, immersed in a never-lagging marathon conversation. Matt, who had always found it so difficult to talk with girls, had experienced no such difficulty with Helen. He thought it was beautiful, the way they listened to each other. He was amazed by how easily the words came and by her kind nature, her sense of humor and all the unforced laughter. She seemed to like him! They were still a new couple, still navigating the unexplored depths and shallows of their relationship. They had, so far, not touched bottom. It was an automatic rapport. And though his love-at-first-sight enchantment had been by instinct when they first met, the more he got to know her, the more his instincts were confirmed. The comfort of her company felt too good, too perfect, to be a true thing.*

*They circled around the glare of a streetlamp as they tiptoed furtively through a backyard and hid behind her neighbor's garage, both relieved to see that there were no lights on at her home. They did not know what time it was, but the ebony sky still showed no sign of dawn. In the splendid secrecy of their hiding place and the lush shelter of the nighttime shadows and the overhanging branches and the bushes and spongy grasses around them, and in the vibrant breath of that shining moment, Matt realized that everything he ever thought, hoped, or expected of love had already been exceeded.*

*"I better get in the house." She looks down and then smiles back into his eyes and says, "This was fun. I had a really good time." He senses something new in her smile and in the air around them but is unable to identify it.*

*"Me, too." He is proud and numb and transfixed by her beauty and by the intangible something just now budding somewhere inside*

*of him. He knows already that he loves her. The mere sight of her fills him with a brand-new happiness. No one has ever been so beautiful. He has never kissed a girl before and doesn't even realize that he is about to do so.*

*They face each other and are holding both hands together, square dance style, shyly, boldly, mutually incapable of speech, and sinking into an unanticipated spell. He has no idea what he is supposed to do next. He glimpses into the deep Persian Sea of her eyes and feels the electric thrill of a momentary connectedness to something inside her. She giggles, a pure golden giggle, and averts her eyes but then snaps them right back, back to his eyes, riveted, and her gaze is ever-so-slightly changed, deeper, softer, almost sad, and he feels his heart beating madly and all his crazy nervous thoughts evaporating into a new joyful kind of confusion and he realizes that he is holding his breath and that the beat of his heart is vibrating throughout every fiber of his body and quivering upon his skin.*

*Then some mysterious invisible force guides his hands to caress her slender waist as her hands, by the mercy of that same hypnotic force, glide up his trembling back to grip his shoulders and coax them toward her, with an instinctual tilting of their heads, and as their eyes close as if on cue and the space between them disappears and their lips touch for the first time, his heart somersaults, and he tumbles into the staggering depths of her kiss and the sweet fragrance and soft folds of her neck and the brand-new universe of her willing embrace. They kiss and kiss and kiss and after a dozen or so he loses all count in their flurry of kisses and he is afraid to open his eyes but opens them anyway. Helen's eyes are still shut, her face and lips expectant. He brushes his fingertips across her cheek. When her eyes open it's as if he is watching her waking from a deep sleep of happy fairytale dreaming and as their eyes meet again he is shy and embarrassed and lost for words but is emboldened by the still-fresh taste of her rosy lips and the tenderness of her penetrating gaze and the cling of her linked hands around the small of his back. He combs his fingers through her velvet hair as if sifting for gold. He kisses her cool moist forehead a dozen times, her sleepy eyelids, her flushed cheeks, the tip of her nose, exhales against her earlobe and then kisses it and laughs at the silly gestures of his overflowing affections, not even being sure if earlobes are meant to be kissed, but he just couldn't help it, and he pulls back and cradles her half-shadowed face in the palms of his hands as if she is a precious vase and says "You are so beautiful, Helen," and at the mere speaking of her name, bells start ringing in his head and an excitement ripples through him, and Helen smiles, looks boldly into his eyes and says "Not as beautiful as you," each word a pearl, which felt wonderful because he has never heard of a boy being called beautiful before, and they both laugh in relief and collapse back together, leaning against the garage, and the hugging and the hush and the whispering warmth of her breath across his ear and the kissing so serious and inexperienced at first is now so playful and confident and his helium heart soars dizzy and giddy in love's darkness, and he is still soaring and still adrift, silent and blind, throughout the enduring timelessness of this elastic night as the stars above them vanish, as they struggle valiantly against the slow but inevitable tide of rising sunlight and share their final goodbye kisses in the mystical and holy light of a new day.*

*"Hey, how did it get so light so fast?"*

*"I wish it could be nighttime forever."*

*"Me, too."*

*He lingers in her arms like a newborn baby, so warm and drowsy, and she says again and again "I really have to go" and he says "I know" and kisses her again and again and she says "No, I mean really" and kisses him again and again and he says "I know, I know" and has to tear himself free of all her magnetic loveliness so she can sneak back into her house while her parents are still sleeping.*

Two rides and he was at the border. He wasn't sure how he would fare upon his return to the indifferent U.S. with no hostel destinations to greet him each evening with a congenial hello, no disparate family of drifters to share tales, no warm meal or safe bed to comfort him at the end of each dusty day. But soldier on he must, so soldier on he did. It was a couple of lifetimes since he'd been in the states. The U.S. customs guard examined his passport and laughed because there wasn't much resemblance between the clean-cut high school senior pictured there and the grungy longhaired hitchhiker before him.

"This is you?" he asked Matt with a hint of either disbelief or disgust.

"Yes, sir."

"Do you have any rolling papers?"

"No."

"Roach clips?"

"No."

"Pipes, bongs, chillums, or drug-related paraphernalia of any sort?"

"No."

"Are you carrying any marijuana or any other illegal substances on or about your person?"

"No."

"Tell me, son. If I were to dump out that rucksack and empty your pockets, would I maybe find something you'd rather I not find?"

"No, sir. Be my guest. But watch out for the dirty socks." The man was not amused.

"Do you have anything to declare?"

Matt thought, *Yes. I just met this incredible girl—Amazing Gracie—who could very possibly be "the one," and I know I should have asked her to join me, but for reasons beyond our control, we'll never see each other again, and I'm still quite high and feeling pretty good without any of my typical weirdness because of an incredible kiss she gave me, and I am resolved, sir, that whatever you say or do, I won't let it bring me down 'cause it's only castles burning, sir.*

His audible answer: "No, sir."

The guard waved him through and said, "Get along now, son. And be careful. You're a long way from home."

His first ride on U.S. soil was in a van with a man from Vancouver who got him stoned on the way down Route 5. The driver bore a strong resemblance to Dustin Hoffman and, between deep tokes, took noticeable pride in reciting memorized lines from *The Graduate* and Mi*dnight Cowboy*, singing,

> *Orange juice on ice is nice.*
> *Orange juice on the ice.*
> *Orange juice on ice is nice.*
> *It's refreshingly cool and naturally.*
> *Break away from old habits.*
> *Take a word of advice.*
> *Serve real Florida orange juice.*
> *Orange juice on ice.*

Matt could have taken the ride all the way to Portland, but he got out at Olympia and headed to the coast road. He eventually got a lift west on Route 8 with a middle-aged man.

"Sorry I can't take you farther, but my wife'll have my hide if I don't get right back."

Then a ride to Aberdeen on Route 12 by a guy about Matt's age who worked nights at a sawmill. He pulled out a stash bag and a strange homemade folk-art pipe and they smoked a bowl of hash.

"A friend of mine made me this pipe. He's a genius when it comes to making things. Like this pipe. Now everybody's got one, and he's just about famous for being a professional pipe maker, and the cops keep trying to bust him. But here's the cool thing. The dude is straight as a poker. He doesn't even get high, man. He just digs makin' the pipes. He's part Indian or maybe even all Indian, I'm not sure, and he's totally into carving. You should see what he's working on in his barn. I have no idea how he got it there, but he's got a huge tree trunk in there, and he's carving a totem pole, man. An honest-to-God larger-than-life totem pole with all those serious-looking Indian faces, and hawks and bears. It is intense. The dude is a wizard, man."

He caught another ride out of Aberdeen, south on Route 101, the coast road, with a twentyish family-man freak driving a pickup truck. He shared about his wife and four-year-old daughter and his farm with all their chickens and a 400-square-foot garden where they grew all the organic vegetables they needed and more—including his secret spot where he grew 100 pounds of weed per year. He lit up a sample joint, which was about the size of the Hindenburg.

"May not be Acapulco Gold, but it's pretty good shit, and it's free."

"Oh, the humanity," Matt mused as the monster joint went up in flames and filled the cab with smoke.

The evening horizon was dusky gray when two girls in a Falcon station wagon with California plates picked him up. He wasn't very good company. He was so stoned and mentally stunted that he wanted only to rest his eyes. They burned daylight through the rest of Washington and, while he slept, traversed a long bridge into Oregon and all the way to just south of Newport where the girls camped for the night.

It was about 11 o'clock. Although he was tired, hungry, and wasted after a long hot day of multiple stonings, he reflexively stuck his thumb out and was promptly picked up by a VW bug eager for Frisco.

"Where you goin', man?"

"San Francisco," Matt responded, resisting the temptation to call it "Frisco."

"Hey, man, can you drive? We've been driving nonstop all day and we're not stopping 'til we get home." Three sets of tired eyes glowed nocturnally from the dark interior like a family of fugitive raccoons.

"Sure. I can drive."

He drove as far as Dunes City where he saw a sign for a camping area.

"Hey guys. I'm gonna get out here so I can hitch the coast road during the day time. I've heard it's beautiful." Everyone understood. They thanked him for his stint of service to their cause and then continued on their bleary-eyed way.

The access road to the campground was pitch black. He walked like a blind man until he reached an area that was grassy and protected by bushes. His nostrils inflated. There was a hint of skunk in the dank air.

This was the first time that he had to camp outdoors by himself. The night always felt safer if he were awake and walking and alert to the threats hidden in the unpredictable darkness. But laying down, slipping into the cocoon of his sleeping bag, vulnerable, with closed eyes, was an act of faith in the safety of the night about which he still had some doubts. Eventually his doubts were overcome by his fatigue, just enough to allow him the comfort of sleep, while still considering the possibility of bears or, at a minimum, skunks and raccoons.

# CHAPTER XXIV

Matt was awakened by a shrill shriek. He popped up like a jack-in-the-box, still asleep, his head piercing through the dome of bushes above him. He thought he was in the Adirondacks, camping with his friends at Moffat's Beach.

"Tates? Chrisbeau? Where is everybody?"

His friends were nowhere to be seen, and the tents were all gone. "What the hell's going on here?" A disoriented emptiness hollowed him out until his brain thawed and he remembered, *Ah, yes. Far away. Oregon coast.*

Some kids were squealing their tires and screeching their brakes on the pavement next to where he was sleeping. They didn't realize he was there and were driving away in a cloud of blue smoke as he emerged from his lair like a disturbed bear. The smell of burning rubber drifted across his face and stung his eyes. In the light of day, he could see that he had missed a turn for the camping area and had settled down next to a parking lot in a cul-de-sac. He figured he was a mile or so inland and was looking forward to hitching south to the next beach and having his first-ever romp in the Pacific Ocean. It took only a minute to ready himself for the road. There was an open spigot for tooth brushing and face-splashing. A tree trunk worked well enough for other morning toiletries.

*Toilet trees*, thought Matt, imagining such an orchard. *So that's where they come from. Hmm. Okay. Zipper down. Dinky out.*

As he completed the obligatory jiggleshake and zipped up his pants, he recalled the adage he had learned from another student at

Bishop Dunphey High School: "No matter how I shake and dance, the last drop's always in my pants."

Looking west through the thin array of saplings and undergrowth, he was beckoned by a barrier of sand dunes. Fighting gravity, he trudged upward with the extra stretch of muscle required to ascend against the sinking resistance of the dune, dropping to his knees and clawing with sweaty effort. He reached the peak, gasping for breath, and with a heart-pounding sigh of relief, was astonished to see the magnificent Pacific Ocean displayed before him. He inhaled the salty air until it filled his lungs. Energized by the sight of the sea and the electric shimmer cast upon it by the morning sun, he tumbled down the dune and stomped barefooted and exultant across the empty beach. Sea birds skittered about the creamy tide as, with a pointy driftwood stick, he etched into the damp sand, changing his thought mid-scrawl, "Am I am a man." He stabbed the exclamatory stick into the sand for punctuation, stripped off his clothes, and dove into the biting chill of the lapping tide of this boundless new ocean as the salt sea stung and seeped into the infected pores of his red and swollen eyelids.

His first ride was with a kid from Montana who was already carrying one hitchhiker from New York City. The hitcher was independently wealthy as a result of a settlement in the lawsuit that followed the tragic deaths of his parents in a car accident with a drunk driver when he was little. He hitched around not because he needed to but because he enjoyed it. The money was being held in trust until he turned twenty-five. He could draw certain sums each year, doled out at the discretion of a favorite uncle who was the trustee. Although the trust was bountiful with funds, he was reluctant to dip into it.

"I can't help but feel guilty using the money. I was so young when it happened. I hardly even remember them except for a photo album of family pictures and a few memories that I don't even know if they're real or if it's stuff I've made up from things I've been told and things I've seen. When they died they were just a few years older than I am now, and I was their only child, so I'm the sole beneficiary. It's a good thing that I can't get at the money. Sometimes I think I should just give it all away. I didn't understand what was happening when it all went down. I thought that, if we gave the money away, my parents could come home, and I somehow got it in my head that it was all my fault. But now that I'm older, I don't blame myself anymore. I blame God for letting it happen."

*Matt was thrust into thoughts of his own father's death. He and his friend, Beau Kingland, were the last to see Professor Mahoney alive. It was about 3 a.m. They were headed up the stairs from the basement where they had been playing pool. Matt's father had been summoned down the stairs to get a fresh bottle of Jack Daniels for the drink he was nursing while reading James Joyce at the kitchen table. It was not unexpected that the Professor, a veteran insomniac, would be awake at such an hour. Intent on his mission, Professor Mahoney did not speak to or acknowledge Matt and Beau as their shadows crossed at the landing. It was as if they were invisible. There was no detectable hint of death in the stairway.*

*Matt left for the remainder of the night and returned at noon to find out that his father was dead.*

*His mother was sitting on the couch surrounded by sullen faces. "Matthew. Come here."*

*"What's wrong Mom?" Inside he knew. But no—that could not happen. That was impossible.*

*"Your father died last night." She was swift, merciful.*

*All eyes were on him. He was in the spotlight, uncomfortable, and didn't know how to react. Everyone was studying him. All he wanted to do was disappear.*

*"I'm tired, Mom. I'm gonna go to bed," was all he said. He could react later after he figured out what was expected of him. He didn't even ask how the old man had died. It was an inconsequential question. He was just as dead no matter how it happened. He wished*

*he could have reacted differently. That he could've broken down in a hail of tears at the loss of a father who had been his tower of strength and that he would despair over how he could possibly go on without his guidance. The capital "D" Dad. Later on, when he woke up in the evening, after a fitful sleep, he still didn't react except for harboring a perverse sense of relief.*

*Matt had been completely ambushed by the death. His father had not been sick; no one anticipated it. Despite his seeming indifference, Matt sank into a state of shock. He shunned those who attempted to console him, including Helen, who sent him a sympathetic note. He disintegrated in silence and self-pity like a dying man nurturing his own disease. There was no potion to heal him or map to guide him homeward, so he dove inward and continued to wallow in an emotional coma as though he welcomed the unraveling that was tearing him into shreds.*

*He wished that he had been the one to find the body and had been able to steal one final intimate moment from the man who had eluded the yearn of his affection for so many years. But no—his father's brilliant elusiveness outlasted him and left Matt stammering in a permanent unanswered pause. He never even thought to blame God for his father's death. He never blamed God for anything. As with his earthly father, Matt's heavenly father played no role in his life and was oblivious to his needs and to the terror and anguish that had defined his existence. God had nothing to do with anything, good or bad. Matt had no one to blame but himself. For it was he himself who had been the architect of his own misfortunes, and if any potential salvation were to be his, it would come from within, not from his obedience to the demands and expectations of any hypothetical blackmailing God.*

Matt got out in Bandon and helped himself to a plastic cupful of free samples in a cheese shop. Another ride brought him all the way to Brookings, just shy of the California line. He flung his pack over his shoulder and strutted down the seaside highway feeling exceptionally road worthy and cheery and thankful to be within sprinting distance of that great and golden state. There was a spring in his step as he looked out over the glittering sea, humming along to the song in his head:

*"Strolling the hills overlooking the shore*
*I realized I've been here before*
*The shadow in the mist could've been anyone*
*I saw you comin' back to me"*

*Yup. It's just Woody, Jack and me on this never-ending ribbon of highway from the Redwood Forest to the Gulf Stream waters.*

Lost in his rambler's reveries, he failed to pay sufficient attention to the pebbly nature of the roadside until he was thrown off balance by the punch of an unseen force, and his feet went up as if he were on roller skates and his top-heavy back went down with a head-over-heels thud onto the pavement. For a stunned couple of seconds, he lay there like a flipped turtle, arms and legs waving uselessly. Embarrassed, he looked around for witnesses and, seeing none, unscrambled his limbs and lifted himself up into a cautious stance. Acting as if he had meant to fall, he laughed self-consciously and sought solace in the probability that even Woody and Jack must have had similar moments when, caught in the swell of a self-glorifying hobo daydream, they too were cut down to size by the quirky power of nature just as they started to take themselves too seriously.

Fortunately, his backpack had cushioned the impact and he was unharmed except for a bruised tailbone and a nasty gouge on the heel of his right hand. He tweezed out the tiny pebbles and lacerating particles with his fingernails and then sucked the torn flesh clean and spit out the blood in the manner he'd seen in westerns after someone had been bitten by a rattler.

In no time he got a ride over the California line into Smith River and then another ride in a 1955 GMC Carryall Van with Donna and Jack and their greyhound-shepherd mix named Jude. They were going to Ukiah. By the time they reached Crescent City, there were two more hitchhikers in the van. Marty was a short, hollow-chested would-be intellectual from New York City who wore thick wire-framed glasses and had an uncombable auburn shock of steel wool pricker bushes upon his head. He was a Kerouac kid, but more devout than Matt, and revered Kerouac's writing as though it contained inspired verse of biblical import. Charlie, from Brecksville, Ohio, was tall and broad-shouldered, had a robust woodsman's beard and a full head of sandy blonde hair sprouting like wild grass from beneath the brim of a straw hat that projected the look of an Amish farmer. He greeted Matt with a firm handshake and a beaming smile that crinkled up his face and made him look like a slimmer and more youthful Santa Claus. He didn't take anything too seriously except for his love of nature, for which he was both teacher and student. The great earth was his classroom and every trail was another lesson. The five of them bonded into a makeshift family all too well and all so soon thanks to Donna and Jack, who were the heart and soul of graciousness and hospitality. Given Matt's track record, it was no surprise that Donna's calm absorbing poise and her affectionate demeanor filled him with respectful but eager longings. In Jack, Matt could see the promise of himself fulfilled, his yielding devotions, his boyish enthusiasm and curiosity, and his unconventional blend of free-spiritedness and reverence.

"I hope you guys don't mind," Jack announced, "but we're not in any big rush here. We probably won't get any farther than Eureka tonight. We'll find a place to camp out and then, tomorrow, we're going through the redwoods. The Avenue of the Giants. Right, Donna?"

Donna nodded. "Yeah. You can all camp with us if you want if you don't mind sleeping outside the van."

"And helping with the dishes. Right, Honey?"

"Yeah. That too."

"No problem, man. That's cool. I'm into that." Marty said. "The redwoods, man. I am definitely into that."

"That'll be just fine," said a grinning Charlie, who removed his hat and segued into a discourse about the coastal redwoods and the high mountain sequoias, fascinating Matt with the depth of his knowledge and the professorial certainty with which he spoke.

305

Ever since he was a kid, Matt had fantasized about visiting the redwoods. He thought that they all grew in a single forest, like a Sherwood Forest, and that they were all just one variety.

"What's the Avenue of the Giants?" Matt asked.

Charlie readily fielded the question and pointed it out to Matt on the map.

Marty interrogated. "Isn't it obvious by its name? Avenue of the Giants? And it's in the redwood forest?" There was a whiny condescension in his voice.

"I just never heard of it. Had you?"

"No. But I knew what it was when I did hear of it."

"Sorry, man. I didn't realize I was being graded."

Jack intervened. "You'll all be blown away if you've never been in the redwoods before. Won't they, Donna?"

She nodded and smiled in a way that took Matt's mind off of the redwoods and Marty's smug know-it-all attitude and everything else other than her cool pacifying aura.


It was a lazy day bouncing along the coast and kicking sand from beach to beach with no concern for the time or anything else other than getting acquainted as they gamboled about within the context of such awe-inspiring seaside scenery. Marty and Matt were both Kerouac kids, kindred spirits with equal doses of brotherly love and sibling rivalry. Matt said that he wanted to hop The Zipper, just as Kerouac had done.

"Me too," Marty replied, "but I found out that it doesn't run anymore. But that's cool. That was his trip, man. We've gotta find our own trip."

And then, on the apocryphal account of Kerouac's writing of *On The Road*, Marty said, "He did it in one weekend. Start to finish. Didn't eat or sleep. Took a heavy dose of speed, drank a lot of coffee, and wrote it all in one flawless draft. Complete stream of consciousness. No edits. Totally Zen."

Matt replied, "I heard that before, but I find it hard to believe that a book could come out so perfect in a first draft written in one weekend. I heard it got rejected about fifty times before anyone would publish it. He must've had to do some revisions."

Marty bristled. "Man, how would you know unless you've been there, in that state of consciousness where all your thoughts and experiences are just pure and flowing out without any interference from your mind? You've got to expand your mind and then you'll see. Kerouac was an enlightened being. He was deep, man. That's how he did it."

Matt's understanding of enlightenment or Zen was rudimentary at best, and he didn't know much about Kerouac other than having read a couple of his books and that he drank himself to death. From where he sat, covered with cobwebs and locked in the thick and oppressive gloom of his own spider room, plotting against himself and grumbling about his unfulfilled desires and his squandered disfigured dreams, Matt was anything but enlightened. He was endarkened.

"I'm not saying it's not true. I'm just saying it's hard to believe." Matt didn't want to argue but also didn't want Marty to have the last quibbling word, and he wished uncharitably that the pint-sized brillo-headed gnome would try keeping his trap shut once in a while.

*Must be his New York City upbringing*, thought upstate Matt, wondering why he couldn't just let Marty have his say and leave it at that.

Marty and Charlie then started talking about yin and yang. Charlie made an off-the-cuff comment that he liked to think of the forces of nature as having a yin and yang relationship with each other. Marty, the resident expert, tugged at his whiskers and stung back, "No. No. That's all wrong. That's symbiosis. Yin and yang is different. It has to do with human consciousness and the balance in the way people interact and relate to one another. It can't be applied to nature."

Charlie, a better man than Matt, didn't push the point and let Marty have final say, though if Matt were a betting man, his money would be on Charlie. For several moments, no one said anything for fear of provoking criticism from Marty. Jack cured any hint of discord by joking, "Yin and yang. Now, they were those Siamese twins, right?"

The topic shifted to jobs and futures. Everyone agreed that suits and ties were out of the question. Marty called a suit "the straitjacket of conformity" and referred to a tie as "the noose of the establishment," and said, "Conformity sucks, man. I want to be an individual. That's why I dress and act the way I do."

Jack looked around and said, "Everybody here's got long hair and is wearing jeans, t-shirts and boots. We're *all* dressed pretty much the same."

Charlie said, "That's 'cause we're *all* individuals."

Matt said, "I don't know what I want to do. I've thought about being a professional hobo. Bum around the world. Hop trains, hitch rides. Get menial jobs here and there and then move on. Like on *The Fugitive* and *Route 66*—except I don't want to get beat up as much as they did."

Charlie said, "I want to be a ranger in a national park. The Grand Canyon or maybe Yellowstone. Or maybe a lighthouse keeper. Some sort of naturalist."

Marty said, as if reading from a hippie manual, "I want to be a writer who lives in a monastery or a commune. I want a simple life and an organic vegetable garden of my own."

Donna said, "I want to do something creative. And I want to help people. Work with children or the elderly."

Jack said, "I have no idea. But I don't want to get caught up with worrying about money or being rich. I don't want my self worth to be based on how well I can convince other people to take *their* money out of *their* pockets and put it into *mine*."

Charlie assessed and addressed the congregation, "Let's see. We've got a professional hobo, one gardening monk, one naturalist, one social worker, and one undecided anti-capitalist. No suits. No ties. And if things don't work out, Donna has to take care of us when we're old."

By the time they passed through Eureka, night was closing in and they hadn't eaten yet. The van was making a chunking sound and Jack said, "Man, something's wrong with the van."

Donna listened for a moment and said, "I think it might be a loose nut." Jack screwed up his face and said, "A loose nut?"

"Yeah," she said. "There's a loose nut behind the wheel." Everybody roared because no one suspected Donna capable of pulling off such a good joke with a straight face.

Jack was following directions to a campground and got lost on an errant side road that didn't go where it was supposed to go. He pulled into a turn-around spot beside the railroad tracks and stopped to re-check directions and also to inspect the engine.

All of a sudden, there was a blinding red light twirling behind them. A police car pulled up and a uniformed officer stepped out. *Not a single problem throughout the whole breadth of Canada,* thought Matt, *and now, here I am, just a couple days back in the U.S., minding my own business, getting busted for nothing.*

There was a collective "Oh shit!" groan from within the van. Donna angled her head backward and in a hushed voice asked, "Are any of you guys dirty?"

Everyone knew what she meant and whispered back, "No."

"Are you sure?"

"Yes."

"Then we don't have anything to worry about. Just stay in here. I'll go see what's going on." Even though no one had done anything wrong and nobody was carrying anything illegal, everyone was scared. They all had long messy hair, beards, backpacks, and all the other stereotypical features of a band of counterculture, flag and draft card and bra-burning, non-underwearing, pot-smoking, war-protesting, free-loving, draft-dodging, devil-worshiping, acid-popping, gypsy, commie, pinko, hippie freaks.

Jack, Donna, and the officer were gabbing and gesturing. The officer peered into the driver's window and aimed his flashlight into the back of the van, illuminating three nervous faces and a canine snout already drooling in anticipation of what may have seemed a perfect opportunity for a tasty treat. He went back to Jack and Donna and they continued their pantomime routine until the officer took out his pad and wrote out a ticket for Jack because his taillights weren't working properly.

"Now, you kids be careful," he said.

"Thank you, Officer. You have a good day," Jack said with his ticket waving in his hand. When Matt and the others grouched about the ticket, big-hearted Jack said, "No big deal. He was just doing his job."

Matt said, "Yeah. But Andy of Mayberry would've let you off with a warning."

"Maybe. But Barney would've thrown us all in jail," Charlie added.

Jack followed the Officer's directions to a campground at Field's Landing. Once there, Donna set up the gas stove by flashlight and, like a magician working in darkness, conjured a delicious meal of rice and vegetables in less time than was humanly possible. She set aside a saucepan of food and let it cool down for Jude, who stood watch while the two-leggeds devoured their portions.

They digested dinner and eased into the comfort of each others' company when Charlie, ever the stargazer, said, "Hey. A shooting star. I get to make a wish."

Jack held up a wishbone-shaped twig and said, "C'mon Donna. We can wish, too."

The brittle twig snapped in Jack's favor.

Donna said, "Oh dang. You win."

Jack said, "That's okay. My wish was that your wish would come true."

Marty soured the moment. "Well, then it's not going to come true because you're not supposed to tell."

Matt volunteered to wash the dishes and was assisted by both Marty and Charlie. Afterward, the thankful hitchhikers snuggled into their sleeping bags and formed a protective barrier around the van.

Everything turned serene and prayerful. A lonesome bullfrog broadcast a horny baritone groan like a foghorn into the misty darkness. Matt was still wide awake and could hear the soft rhythm of snoring sounds beside him. He strained his eyes into the black expanse of the infinite universe above as though from the crow's nest of a wayward ship. The air was crystalline and the stars were large and bright. All of creation was luminous. The sea was nearby. He could feel it.

# CHAPTER XXV

If Matt had ever felt like a member of a nomadic family of gypsies, this was the day. The three sleepers rose together with the birds, blinked drowsily against the stabbing rays of early sunlight, pulled the twigs and leaves from their hair and beards, and washed their toes in dewy clumps of grass. Donna and Jack descended from their van as if they were the reigning king and queen of the gypsies with their loyal three-man entourage and their trusty beast at their side, the bunch of them all falling somewhere between Robin Hood's Merry Men and Ken Kesey's Merry Pranksters.

Marty squeezed a meager dab of toothpaste from a travel-ravaged tube and, entertaining the notion that his enchanted tube was spontaneously regenerating itself, said, "I swear, for the last three weeks, no matter how much toothpaste I've used, there's still more." Matt joked that it was only because he hadn't really been brushing his teeth. Marty didn't see the humor, but Charlie chuckled and dribbled toothpaste into his beard.

The merry band assembled and continued on its way. As they drove down Route 101 toward the redwoods, Donna blurted out for Jack to stop. He pulled over and she said in a breathy near-whisper, "Blackberries."

Sure enough, there was a rich thicket of blackberry bushes alongside the road. It passed by Matt unnoticed, but Donna detected it with the radar of her keen eye. Everyone tumbled out of the van and began picking until their fingers and beards were all stained bluish-black and they had collected a good-sized pouch of sweet and juicy berries.

"I'll make blackberry pancakes for breakfast," she said.

*Leave it to Donna*, Matt thought. Matt was building a gallery of images around his reverential affections for Donna and her green-thumb Mother Earth goodness. He was soothed by her presence. He imagined her baking bread at home and tending an organic garden that provided all of their vegetables and herbs and that she had a heavily laden spice rack with exotic seasonings and pungent aromas drifting up from antique bottles self-labeled with esoteric names. He imagined the chattering of birdhouses and hummingbird feeders and, somewhere in her past, a proud memory of raising a rescued baby raccoon or an injured squirrel.

Farther down the road they entered the redwoods, the Avenue of the Giants, and found a piney site to camp for the day beside the waters of the Eel River. Donna fulfilled her vow and made the most delicious blackberry pancakes in the history of breakfast, topped with organic wildflower honey. She mixed up a pitcher of frozen orange juice, and Matt's tongue and tummy tingled with pleasure as the chill of the nectar soaked an icy path down his throat and numbed his brain.

"My tummy says yummy," swooned Matt as he slurped up the last of her pancakes. He told Donna about his disappointment at the Klondike Days in Edmonton and emphasized that these were the best pancakes he had ever eaten. She blushed and said, "Well, this is the Redwood Days Free Pancake Breakfast, and I'll make as many as you can eat." He could tell that she was flattered when he praised her cooking, and he felt happy inside the way she thanked him so gently and shyly.

Then, without warning, she reached over and rested her fingertips on the left side of his neck. "What's that?"

"What's what?" Matt was startled by her unexpected touch.

"That brown mark on your neck."

"Oh that. That's just a birthmark."

"I thought so. I didn't say anything at first because I thought it might be a hickey."

"Nope. Not a hickey." The suggestion made him blush.

"Can I touch it again?"

"Sure. If you want."

Donna rubbed her fingertips ever so softly upon the curious patch of skin and said, "Kissed by an angel."

*Don't I wish*, he thought, watching her lips.

"It's beautiful. It looks like a heart."

"Yeah. Some people think it's an arrow."

"No, It's definitely a heart. A big, soft, beautiful heart." She smiled at him so sweetly that he almost cried.

The brave mid-morning sun filtered through an umbrella of top-heavy redwood branches and as Matt lay on his back staring skywards it was like gazing backward in time to a point where all the Earth's treetops converged against a primeval sky and all nature was glorious and wild. He held a redwood cone, no larger than an acorn, and was awestruck that each of these giants looming above him so many stories high and so many centuries old had once been just a seed miniscule enough to cradle in the palm of his hand or crush beneath his foot. Who would have predicted the potential in something so tiny and unimpressive? He stood, dwarfed against a tree, and gave it his best approximation of a bear hug and envisioned it taking ten more of him to ring it with linked hands and give it a group hug. He pressed his cheek against the cool velvety-green fur of the trunk. He closed his eyes and listened for a heartbeat. Actually, thought he heard one. He saw an ant climbing upward in the canyons of deep grooves in the bark and wished he could be that ant just long enough to taste and smell and tread the rugged bark trail of such a majestic specimen all the way to the sunlit peak.

Everyone went swimming in the river, frolicking in its swirling current, tossing Matt's Frisbee, and making fearless diving catches in the water. Matt loved playing full-tilt Frisbee, never giving up, running and leaping like an ancient Greek Olympian and coming down with the snatched disc firmly in his grip even after he had thought it would be an impossible catch. Jude dutifully fetched sticks from the water and begged for more. Jack took out his fishing pole and cast it once into a shallow rocky pool and yanked out a rainbow trout. He showed it off for a minute and then let it wriggle free into the flow. Squinty-eyed, bespectacled Marty waxed philosophical about the Zen of Frisbees and then waded and skipped with elfin grace upon the slippery rocks to reach a boulder in the middle of the river, where he sat bare-chested and cross-legged, reading Lao Tzu as he meditated in the sun like a pale and pipsqueak Buddha in training, then falling asleep and almost splashing into the river.

Matt had tried to teach himself transcendental meditation at home after reading a book about it, but every time he attempted to empty his mind, all his worries barged in and started screamin' at him and made him so nervous that he had to take a two-hour walk just to get back down to the original baseline level of his cautiously controlled paranoia. It seemed to him that in order to be able to meditate effectively, it was necessary to have already attained the inner peace he was seeking. His rush-hour mind was so wary and dedicated to its daily regimen of anxiety and pessimistic self-reproach that it had become serenity-proof. For him, it was like letting down his guard and setting himself up for an easy attack. But he found some sort of bewitching comfort in staring at the hypnotic flow of the rippling river and noticing that there were places where the surface appeared to be a tranquil pool, placid as a sheet of glass, "no pebble tossed nor wind to blow," just still waters, but that there was an invisible deeper current that was revealed whenever the channel narrowed. He thought that maybe all of life was like that, calm surfaces and deeper invisible underlying currents and the periodic calamity of narrowing channels. And, always, the risk of drowning.

Charlie identified trees and birds by sight and sound, studied leaves and feathers, foraged and tasted edible roots, and knew everything by name. He meandered sure-footed along the river's edge and picked out rocks and held them glinting against the slanting sunlight and then positioned them back in place. He examined various holes dug into the riverbank by wild creatures and identified their tracks.

Donna found a patch of sunlight beside the river where she set out a blanket and wrote in a journal. Growing drowsy, she closed her eyes for a nap. She looked so relaxed, so angelic in the lucent quilt of sunlight and shadows that covered her as she slept to the melodic lullaby of the river lapping over rocks beneath the fairy tale skyscraper trees. Matt imagined sneaking over and, with a kiss, waking her up and then disappearing together in an idyllic valley hidden here among these redwoods. Sometimes he thought that the right person was all it would take to still his waters and budge him forward. No more Mr. In-Between. Other times he realized that he must find the peace and happiness on his own because no one like Donna would want him for long in his current emotionally precarious condition.

*The key to happiness*, thought Matt, *is to hitchhike and camp out forever with an ever-revolving series of new best friends and to run faster than the momentum of your madness and never to settle or rest long enough to let the demons track you down and trick you back into your cage.*

They gathered together and zigzagged back and forth along the Avenue of the Giants, exploring trails and then settling down at Hidden Springs State Park, which charged $3 per night for the van plus fifty cents for pets. Everyone agreed that charging for pets was a rip-off, so the hitchhikers threw in a buck each to cover the humans and they snuck Jude in.

Donna worked her dinner magic again, preparing fried potatoes with vegetables and eggs. She said, "We're mostly vegetarian, but every now and then we slip back into our old habits. But I love animals and can't justify eating them even though I do sometimes. I think God created animals to test us. Kindness to animals earns big-time points in heaven. I wish I were a better vegetarian."

"Yeah, me, too," said Matt. "I'm an on-again, off-again vegetarian. I've been mostly off-again this summer 'cause I've had to rely on eating whatever the hostels were serving. Back home I'll be good for a long time, and then it's always the delicious scent of a Big Mac that brings out the carnivore in me."

"Big Mac! How can you eat that garbage?" Marty's face was scrunched up with a sour look, as if he'd taken a big bite out of a lemon. "I'd puke if I ate one of those things. They're disgusting!"

"No they're not. They taste really good," Matt taunted.

"They may be sensually pleasing, but they're still disgusting."

"Of course they're sensually pleasing. If they weren't, nobody would eat them. What can I say? The aroma and taste hits my weak spot. I can't help it. I'm a sucker for the Golden Arches. Guilty as charged."

Matt didn't want his skirmishes with Marty to escalate into an all-out war, so now, more amused than irritated, and because he knew that Marty couldn't help but say the things he said, Matt nonetheless wished he had a Big Mac right then and there so he could make a sloppy spectacle of gobbling it down and letting the special sauce smear all over his cheeks and into his beard as though he was slurping blood from a fresh carcass.

That evening they drank fruity herb teas around a campfire amidst the flaming crackle of twigs and kindling, blinking their eyes in the smoke pluming across their faces, and reflecting on the day by telling jokes, reciting funny poems, and weaving yarns.

Matt recited a poem he'd written in Vancouver but told them that he'd read it in a hostel bathroom stall:

*When men were men*
*And women were women*
*They'd leave their caves*
*And go out swimmin'*
*But cold and wet*
*They'd quickly tire*
*And wish someone*
*Would invent fire*

Charlie spun a long-winded cowboy spine-tingler he'd heard from a ranger while camping in the Grand Canyon. It had to do with coyotes, wild horses, the vengeful ghosts of Indians killed in battle, and how it all came together to seal the fate of a disbelieving greenhorn city slicker one howling canyon night. It was too long and only half-funny but was worth it for the theatrical glee he took in the telling.

Marty read from his Lao Tzu book with profound mystical intent:

*There are three treasures which I embrace and follow closely: The first is to be kind; The second is to be simple; The third is to not put one's own importance first in the world.*

Then he leafed to another page and recited another excerpt:

*Without going out of your door, you can know the ways of the world.*
*Without looking through your window, you can see the way to heaven.*
*The farther you go, the less you know.*
*Thus, an integral being knows without going, sees without looking and accomplishes without doing.*

Donna read from Tolkien's "The Return of the King," which she was reading for a second time, and said, "This is Jack's favorite passage. He says it's about us."

*Then Faramir laughed merrily. "That is well," he said; "for I am not a king.*
*Yet I will wed with the White Lady of Rohan, if it be her will.*
*And if she will, then let us cross the River and in happier days let us dwell in fair Ithilien and there make a garden. All things will grow with joy there, if the White Lady comes."*

Jack said, as if he was snapping out of a daydream and hadn't heard what Donna said, "You should never expect more out of a person than they are capable of giving. That way you will never become disappointed or disillusioned with others."

Donna said, "I was somewhat apprehensive when we picked you guys up. I wasn't sure it was a good idea to invite you all to stay with us. But I'm glad we did. It's been like a big family camping trip, and it's been a lot of fun."

Matt felt fortified against the strange sense of burden that typically sucked him downward and inward like the gravity of an enormous planet. During times like these, when all his senses were caught up into the admiration of someone so pure of heart, he would break free and levitate above all his petty concerns and watch everything as if from above. His love for Donna grew with every syllable she uttered. There was something about her. She was able to find the happiness in everyone. Jack was a lucky man. Matt could only hope that someday he would be half as lucky and that he, too, would then make a garden with his own White Lady.

# CHAPTER XXVI

Everyone slept late except the ever-resourceful Charlie who rose at dawn to cash in on yet another beautiful morning.

"That's me," Charlie had said. "Bright-eyed. Bushy-tailed. Crack of dawn."

Left to his own devices, Matt was more of a bleary-eyed crack-of-noon kind of guy, a real Pokey Sam. But he had enjoyed sleeping outdoors beneath the articulate sky and loved waking up at the rise of the sun in the dewy grass with his head burrowed inside his sleeping bag. The rush of brisk morning air infused his lungs as he poked his head out like a turtle, took a deep breath, and opened his eyes to the celebration of sunlight that began each new day.

Today the band of gypsies would be splitting up. Jack and Donna were returning home to Ukiah. Matt would go only as far as Leggett, where Route 1 branched west off of Route 101 and began its southward course, hugging the scenic California coastline and connecting a string of lazy seaside towns stretching all the way to Los Angeles and beyond.

He got out of his sleeping bag and scratched and yawned his way into the shower stall, where faded black magic marker graffiti proclaimed, "There is no devil stronger or greater than the warrior with the right-sized sword."

He had already soaped himself up to a high gloss when his blast of hot water turned cold. "Fuck it," he stammered. "I can take it."

Just to prove the point, he staunchly withstood the shock as he shampooed his hair and forced himself to rinse it with a leisurely nonchalant spirit.

Jack rallied the troops, and they left late in the morning to finish their tour of the Avenue of the Giants, stopping here and there for this and that. Jack slammed the brakes at one point and yelled, "Turtle crossing!" as a box turtle plodded across the road at full turtle throttle with its carefree head straining for a clearer view. Donna jumped out and gave the turtle a free lift to the safety of the wet grasses on the other side of the road.

They went by a popular attraction and pulled over. It was a redwood that was so gigantic a tunnel had been carved through it. It cost a buck to drive through. The reactions were mixed. Charlie didn't object because the redwood appeared to be sturdy and in full bristle and the demonstration increased his sense of awe for these ancient wonders.

Marty saw it as a blatant symbol of man's exploitative relationship with the earth and the destructive commercialization of nature for greedy capitalistic motives. He shook his head and said, "It's not nice to fool Mother Nature, man."

Matt sensed something repugnant about the sight of this wounded giant, similar to how he felt at the Bronx Zoo observing a lethargic elephant tethered to a fat post in the middle of its open-air pen.

The debate ended when Jack said, "Hey, let's stick around and check it out. I don't think the van's gonna fit through there anyway."

Everyone walked through the tree except Marty, who refused, he said, "on Taoist principles." Even Jude walked through after first relieving himself against the irresistible trunk. Matt resisted the temptation to join Jude in this baptismal ritual. There was a nearly imaginary echo from the inside.

Charlie said, "I feel like I'm in the belly of a whale except it's not a whale."

Donna said, "I feel like a hobbit moving into a new home."

Charlie, the only one with a camera, said, "Okay everybody. Get in place. I wanna get a picture of this."

Jack and Donna stood in the sunlit archway. Matt stood shirtless behind them, his arms outstretched around their shoulders. Jude posed sideways in front of them, looking like a fierce medieval Irish wolfhound. It was the first time on this journey that Matt had had his picture taken. And at the click of the shutter he feels as though the whole world is tilting in balance and harmony from the center of this redwood tree. Something in that moment makes him realize he will always remember standing in the here-and-now hollow of this prehistoric giant with these fleeting new-found friends, and he will always look back on this isolated frame of time as evidence that, within the grand scheme of all things, his existence had meaning. It was as if the course of his entire life has led him to this perfect silver sliver of time with these perfect strangers in fulfillment of an ancient prophecy, the purpose of which he will never know.

*There was one strange memory from when Matt was seven or eight years old that felt like it must have been from a dream in some other kid's life. It was a pleasant summer evening. His parents were sitting together on the backyard patio with their arms around one another, laughing and even kissing in plain view of their children who giggled and ran around making fun of the unprecedented sight. Such peculiar behavior startled Matt. He had never seen them embrace or express affection, but it filled him with a humorous joy and a pride which reassured him with the knowledge, or at least the belief, that his parents loved each other. It made him feel safer, happier, relieved, almost loved.*

*There were some other happy memories from his early childhood. Until now, he had forgotten about them, but he could now recall his father driving him, Rory, and Elaine, "the three little ones," to Tastee Freeze, the drive-in creamy-whip ice cream store in the country just north of town. They competed for their father's attention and laughed at his corny jokes and funny faces and all the silly things he said to them. The highlight of each ride was the contest to see who would be the first to spot Tastee Freeze in the distance. And when they did, they all chanted, "I see Tastee Freeze, I see Tastee Freeze," and, in their zeal to win the contest, they all saw Tastee Freeze long before it came into view, each claiming victory. It was always declared a three-way tie. As they drove past the horse cemetery at Danforth's Stud Farm, Professor Mahoney told the children to hold their breath until they were beyond the monuments marking the horses' graves or else, when they died, they would be buried there with the horse bones. The kids loved it and held their breath as if they were underwater, their eyes bugging out and their cheeks all red and ballooned-out like blow fish until they were safely past all those monuments and past all those bones.*

*In a way, Matt felt that he had never even met his real father. He had seen the old pictures, his parents together and appearing happy, when his father was still thin and handsome like Gregory Peck, before whatever happened happened. Before the civil war that divided the family. Before the incessant disputing over which parent was to blame for the terrible shambles their marriage had become. Before their unraveling.*

*Matt knew there were two sides to every story but didn't know whose fault it was. To an extent, he didn't even care. All he knew was his own reality, his own truth, the things he himself had seen, felt and heard, who had given him comfort and love when he needed it and who had denied him again and again. He knew unflinchingly who had been true and constant in his own life. His North Star. And that was all that mattered. The rest was all nothing but sadness and regret.*

Leaving the Avenue of the Giants and the redwood forest was like waking from a timeless fantasy and returning to the dull realities of the polluted, time-weary world. It was so sad to watch the spiring trees recede in the distance behind them and feel the pure forest air being replaced with gas fumes and rancid wisps of exhaust.

Rather than taking the direct route to Ukiah, Jack followed the coast another 40 miles or so. This gave them all the respite of extra time together and postponed the inevitable parting of ways. He picked up four more hitchhikers: two girls from Iowa, a Texan, and a native Californian. They dallied at all the scenic overlooks and beaches. Charlie kept on being good ole Charlie, spotting blue herons, vultures, hawks, eucalyptus and cypress trees, doug firs, and in the foggy Greek shoreline waters, with rocks jutting out like huge deformed breasts, a pod of pelicans. Hundreds of sea birds squawked overhead, flapping and lunging and dropping their loads indiscriminately like a squadron of B-52 bombers.

Charlie said, "Man, I wish I could do that."

"Do what?" said Jack. "Soar through the sky or shit on everybody's heads?"

"Hey Charlie," asked Matt. "What happens if the baby bird won't leave the nest?"

"I guess they either get too big and fall out or else Mama Bird gives them a nudge. Baby birdy's gotta fledge so it can earn its pilot's license. They can't stay in the nest forever."

Jack put his head back and arms out and asked, "Hey Charlie. How come we don't get shit on more often?"

The ever-pragmatic Charlie pondered the phenomenon, saying, "That's an interesting question. I've often wondered that myself. Maybe it's because we don't spend enough time outdoors." Then, pinching his straw brim, he said, "But a good hat never hurts just in case."

It was early evening before the van rolled into Fort Bragg. The four new hitchers all got off in town, and the van continued just a mile or so more until Route 20 shot east across the coast ranges, back to Route 101. Matt and Charlie had decided to hitch together down along the coast. Marty was going to Ukiah with Jack and Donna. Everyone participated in the customary exchange of addresses and phone numbers and vows to stay in touch, which were all well-intentioned but which they all knew would not be kept. And, given Matt's experience with Volker in Canada, maybe it's better that way.

"Happy trails, partners," said Jack. "And farewell wherever you fare."

"See ya in Frisco," said Marty.

Everybody shook hands and gave hugs.

Donna said, "See you guys. Be careful. Stay safe."

The moment is dreaded. Matt's weirdness sets in. He feels so clumsy. There is a frozen grip around his Adam's apple. When he dares a flimsy goodbye glimpse into Donna's kindhearted eyes and feels a momentary unexpected connectedness, he is overcome by emotion and has to choke back a sob, and he finds himself crying and doesn't know why. He hopes to God she doesn't notice the watery eyeballs accompanying his sad inadequate utterance. He wants to hug her but dares not. There is so much he wants to say but cannot find the words. She has reached him at that deep and holy place, in the vacant spaces of his unspoken world. And now she will be gone for all time and will never know she has touched him and has stirred him in a way he will always remember. A person should know such things.

Charlie and Matt walked down the road and found Hidden Pines Campground. "We might as well camp out here tonight. Besides," Charlie continued, "I've hardly had a chance to use my tent. It's still light enough. We can pitch the tent and rustle up some grub." Charlie liked using the word "grub" and gave it a humorous cowboy twang.

"Yeah. Let's rustle up some grub, amigo," Matt said.

Also at the campground setting up their tent were two bikers they'd seen at scenic overlooks a couple times during the day. They all hollered at each other and made dinner plans: hot dogs over an open fire. They bought a stack of firewood for seventy-five cents and an eight-pack of hot dogs and some buns at the mom-and-pop market at the campground. They were uncertain about the firewood; it looked like redwood, but it was the only wood available, it was just a small stack, and Marty wasn't there to lay a guilt trip on them, so they looked the other way and didn't dwell on it.

The hippies and bikers joined forces and told tall tales. One thing Matt had learned over the summer was that there were few bikers who fit the Hell's Angel "Gimme Shelter" outlaw profile. Some strained to cultivate the biker persona, but Matt hadn't yet met one who fit the fearsome stereotype.

Bill was a pugnacious leather-jacketed Italian from New York City with unconvincing macho-man affectations. More Brooklyn than biker. He said things like "It shows to go you," "No bout a doubt it," "Fut the whuck," and the old stand-by, "Chuck you, Farley," as he told his locker-room-bravado jokes and hyperbolic road stories and tried harder than anyone else to be the coolest, toughest, and gruffest billy goat around the campfire. He even did the snot thing, shutting one nostril with his thumb and blowing mucus out of the other nostril, shooting it onto the ground like a marksman.

At one point, after swaggering back from taking a "picked wiss," he continued, "Back home I've got this dog, a German shepherd named Boner. He helps me work on my bike, man. You know, fetch this and fetch that. I've been teaching him to steal things for me, like oil. But he always gets the wrong weight. Now I'm trying to teach him about clutch cables."

The other biker, Dale, was just eighteen and from south of L.A. Uncontaminated by Bill's cocky disposition, he remained sensitive and easy-going, his eyes being opened wide for the first time. He was soaking it all in like a brand-new sponge. At home he had two dogs, both of them mutts he had found, named Tommy and Uncle Ernie. He was a huge fan of The Who and said that he had been reborn when he saw them perform "Tommy" while he was tripping on a tab of sunshine.

"For about three weeks after the concert I *was* The Pinball Wizard. Sent me right into obliviation. It was scary, man. But you know what? I went out and got the album and memorized the whole opera, and I realized it's just a story about a kid overcoming obstacles and remaining true to himself and refusing to lose his innocence. It's about personal salvation, man. I can definitely relate to that."

The hot dogs were speared with sticks and cooked above the licking scarlet tongues of the hardy redwood blaze. Charlie was well-skilled in this culinary campground practice and was proud of his ability to produce well-cooked dogs that were neither black nor blistered. Bill, on the other hand, made sure that he got his dog well-blistered and charcoal black before he scarfed it down. They had no condiments, but the boys nonetheless devoured their dogs, though without relish, with relish.

Charlie, still hungry, said, "I wish we had some s'mores."

"Or some Jiffy Pop," chimed in Dale.

After an hour or so of shooting the shit around the weakened glow of the redwood fire, Bill and Dale made plans to ride into Fort Bragg to check out the bar scene and paint that town red. Bill was hot to trot and expounded upon his evening's mission with a lurid string of indelicate assertions. Palming a brass hip flask, he took a nip and then lit up an unfiltered Lucky Strike, filled his lungs to capacity, and then huffed out a series of perfect smoke rings. "It's Friday night. I'm gonna take my joystick into town and see if I can catch me some snappers or grab me a juicy roast beef sandwich." He cracked his knuckles, licked his lips with a lascivious grin, and started to sing, "Nothing would be finer than to be in your vagina in the morning.

"Yup," he continued, like a shift supervisor from the euphemism factory, "The nookie brigade is on duty this evening and is ready for action. We're gonna get stroked, lubed, screwed, blewed, and tattooed." He must have meant it because he brushed his teeth and scrubbed most of the grease and grime from his face and hands and fingernails and, just to be on the safe side, he splashed a generous dose of Brut on his face, neck, and crotch and spiffied himself up into a relatively clean t-shirt before he and Dale revved off toward town like a couple of horny cowboys heading out for Miss Kitty's saloon.

Charlie told Matt some more stories about his camping experiences. Then, during a silent pause, he farted and said, "Quiet. Did you hear that?"

Matt laughed. "Yeah. I heard it."

"Did you recognize it?"

"Yes. I recognized it. It was a fart. A loud, raunchy fart." And, still laughing, "Smells like egg salad."

Charlie said, "No. That was the Great North American Barking Squirrel. They're well known in these parts. Tend to come out at night, after dinner, when campers are sitting around an open fire."

Matt managed to work up a good one.

"Hey. There's another one. Sounded like a mating call. Do they travel in pairs?"

"It's hard to tell because they're so rarely seen."

"Like leprechauns?"

"Yup. Like leprechauns," Charlie nodded with his poker face intact.

Everyone everywhere laughs at farts and loves a good fart story. On rare occasions even Matt's own mother had a fart yarn or two to tell, usually involving their dog, Eustace, though his mother, with her own inimitable notion of delicacy, insisted on calling them "stinkers." The other bodily functions were rivers and loadies.

Matt couldn't resist telling Charlie his own fart story.

"It was a few years ago. I was at a friend's house lying on the living room floor watching TV. He was sitting behind me in a cushioned recliner, and his mother and two younger sisters were on the couch. All of a sudden I felt one coming on. I could tell it was gonna be silent, so I let it slip out real slow. I figured I was safe because this was a big room and they were all the way back by the wall and I was way up front. Whatever I ate that day must have caused a lethal chemical reaction in my stomach because it was the raunchiest, heaviest one I ever cut. It actually burned on the way out. I realized right away that I made a big mistake because it smelled so bad—I could just about taste it—but I didn't say anything. I didn't think it would make it all the way back to the couch. I thought maybe it would filter down or else they'd blame it on the dog. But, instead, it just grew and got worse until it filled the room like a dead skunk. It was atomic. Honest to God, it took about ten minutes and nobody said anything and I'm thinking, man, how can this last so long and keep getting stronger? The suspense was killing me. I kept lying on the floor, afraid to move or say anything, pretending I didn't smell anything. When the stench got so bad that nobody could ignore it, one of the girls, I think it was Mary Lou, yelled "Oh my God! I can't take it anymore. Who cut one?" And with that, they all ran out of the room shrieking, even their mother, gagging and laughing at the same time. I thought they were gonna start puking, it was so bad. I still didn't want to admit it, but I was the only one who didn't run out of the room and my face was so red that they all knew it was me. Well, once I got over being embarrassed, I was kind of proud of it because everybody agreed, even their mother, that it was the best one ever. The living room was toxic for about an hour. It was ferocious, man. A legendary fart. They still talk about it."

Charlie laughed. "Yeah. Nothing like a good fart story. I bet even cavemen laughed at farts." And then, assessing the sleeping arrangements, Charlie concluded, with a devilish grin, "On second thought, maybe the tent isn't big enough for both of us."

# CHAPTER XXVII

Matt awoke in the middle of the night, startled from a hometown dream in which he was walking across the parking lot toward the front entrance to Bishop Brannan High School, which, in the dream, was perched atop a steep hill. Each step was a slow struggle of supreme effort, as if the pavement was made of sand. At the top there was a car. The driver's window was opened and a woman was calling to him, waving her arm vigorously, "Matt! Matt! I have something to tell you!" It was Helen! As he struggled nearer, a big happy smile beamed across her face. It was as if they had never broken up but had been separated for a long time due to circumstances beyond their control but which were not relevant in the dream. As he drew near the car, Helen stepped onto the pavement and, with open arms, glided toward him, and, as he readied for her embrace, the pavement gave way and the dream dissolved as dreams do just as they are about to come true. Matt lay awake, at the mercy of his guilty conscience, and then fell back to sleep, hoping to revive that doomed dream and fulfill its promise of a joyful reunion.

By the time the boys arose, the greenhouse atmosphere of the pup tent had turned it into a tropical rainforest. Their sleeping bags were drenched with condensation and perspiration and thus were spread out on picnic tables to absorb the morning sun. Dozens of newly spun spider webs lay atop the glistening grass, their gossamer nets shining silvery and silky with the dew and looking like an encampment of miniature inch-high trampolines where gymnast spiders exercised while a flurry of butterflies floated above them, illuminated like angels against the bright sky.

The boys stood barefooted in the cold shock of soaking grass, looking seaward with enlivened nostrils. Something in the aromatic blend of briny sea air and the goosebumpy breeze made Matt think, *I bet this is how Ireland smells.*

"I wonder what time it is," Matt said.

Charlie looked up at the sun, shaded his eyes with the brim of his straw hat, and, like a ship's captain, made some silent calculations.

"I bet it's about 7:15." Sure enough, when they found out the time a few minutes later, Charlie had been right. Pleasure and self-satisfaction lit up his face. "Whaddya know? I must be synchronized."

The snappers must not have been biting in Fort Bragg because Bill and Dale both crawled out of their tent as lonesome as ever.

"It was a bummer, man. Just a bunch of scags and cock teasers," Bill said in typical crass fashion. Dale just grinned. By all appearances, the town's hue had remained unchanged, though Matt noticed that since the previous evening a nasty-looking, barely concealed bruise had blossomed at the tender juncture of Dale's neck and shoulder. They loaded their gear and readied for the road. The routine goodbyes were recited and they roared out of sight down Route 1 like a couple of still-horny easy riders. Charlie and Matt waited for their bags to dry as much as possible and then revved up their thumbs and caught a ride to Mendocino in a beat-up Chevelle. Behind the wheel was a fifty-two-year-old chain-smoking, unemployed lumberjack with a corrugated face and a greasy old San Francisco Giants ball cap. In a blistering ten-minute seemingly speed-induced monologue, he rambled on in a broken voice about lost jobs and wasted opportunities but mostly about his troubled relationship with his ex-wife and three estranged children who wanted nothing to do with him. Matt once again marveled at the ease with which some people spilled their guts out to total strangers, and he figured it was the safety of anonymity that freed their tongues.

"I admit it. I made a lot of mistakes. I went right when I shoulda gone left. And I went up when I shoulda gone down. It's like baseball. You've got winning seasons and losing seasons. Sometimes you commit a few errors and sometimes you make that phenomenal

Willie Mays basket catch. Sometimes you're stuck in the dugout and sometimes you get sent back down to the minors until you've cleaned up your game. I can't claim that I've ever been an MVP, but we've had some all-star years. Then we went into a slump, and now, here I am. I got traded, man. But I wasn't entirely reliable for all the shit that went down in my marriage. She was about as bad as me. She struck out as much as I did. But the kids, man. They only heard her side of the story. Shit. I wish I knew as much now as I thought I knew when I was twenty."

They sought breakfast in Mendocino at The Sea Gull, where they were not disappointed. They were welcomed by the aroma of bacon and fresh-brewed coffee. The diner was a lavish gallery of driftwood, conches, lobster traps, and other seaside artifacts. There was a display of exotic butterflies in a rustic frame, their colorful angel wings muted with age and pinned beneath glass. Charlie was in heaven, studying each item and asking the self-conscious teenaged waitress questions she tolerated politely but then dismissed, saying, "I don't have no idea. I've only been here a month or so."

It was the best breakfast Matt had eaten in a long, long time, maybe ever. Fresh-off-the-griddle buttermilk wheat cakes, so fluffy and buttery and syrupy that he squealed and moaned like a puppy dog out of sheer mouthwatering joy, accompanied by toast, strawberry jam, and a blissful cup of generic tea poured from an old battle-scarred Brown Betty tea pot.

Next to them sat a mangy twenty-year-old orphan-looking kid with raccoon eyes, a self-professed tramp who shunned all worldly possessions and lived a hermit's life in the mountains with neither hut nor tent nor even barrel to live in. His clothes were tattered and earthy, and his hair was matted into tight ringlets. He paid for his breakfast with 116 pennies, his entire savings.

"I don't wear clothes when I'm in the mountains, but I have to be careful. One time I accidentally wandered too close to town and got arrested. A lady who saw me started making up some kind of weird sexual allocations against me. The cops were okay, I guess, 'cause they dropped the charges, but they didn't dig where I was coming from, my naked-in-nature trip. It's an ancient trip, man. The Greeks dug it. I'm just not into society and buildings and working a job I don't want just to make money to buy things I don't need from people I don't like and who don't like me. I just want to be myself. Naked in nature. That's what I'm all about. It's my trip, man."

"What do you do when it rains?" Charlie asked.

"I get wet," he mumbled self-evidently into his coffee mug.

They walked on, enamored by the small-town tranquility, imagining what unanticipated treasures it might hold. Matt wished he were an artist with a bohemian loft overlooking the majestic Mendocino coast. "But you never know," he said. "It looks like one of those towns in an Alfred Hitchcock movie or a *Twilight Zone* episode. Everything is okay on the surface, but watch out. *The Invasion of the Body Snatchers* was in a town like this. So was *The Birds*."

But they encountered no such menace on that fine morning. Rather, to Matt's delight, Charlie drew his attention to a side yard and a fragrant profusion of fuchsia and jasmine shrubs where a congregation of hummingbirds zipped and flittered about as they breakfasted upon the sea-dampened bouquet of drooping blossoms.

Traffic was sparse and local. That meant they could expect short infrequent rides and plenty of in-between time for talking and walking and watching and listening. This was the perfect place for all of those things, and Charlie was the best of all possible traveling companions with his mellow, inquisitive temperament and not a shred of moodiness.

They got a ride to the junction of Route 1 and Route 28 in a vintage VW bug and then tramped onward across a bridge where rogue breezes tousled their hair and all of life was panoramic and oceanic. The winds swirled against the wide-open seaside rockscape and the breathtaking beauty of the coastal hills as the frothy tide churned angrily below them. Suddenly, they heard an Irish penny whistle melody lilting magically from nowhere, with no one and no thing near them that could account for the dulcet rush of tones that danced around them. They spun around and the tune changed. They spun back and it changed again, as if an invisible sea nymph was teasing them, luring them to the rocks with her own rapturous whistling. After a bewildering minute or two they discovered that the music was caused by the wind running across a row of holes in the frame of Charlie's backpack.

"Hey! I've got an enchanted pack frame," he said with his big squinty grin.

Though the air was clear at ground level, a gray ceiling of fog rolled in over the Pacific and gave the seaside hills an eerie netherworld atmosphere. Matt knew that God must be a poet to have created such sea fog and mystical hills and the charm of evanescent music out of thin air. Captivated by the view, Charlie got his camera out and said, "Hold on a second. This is too incredible to pass up." He scoped out the best perspective and took a series of shots, swiveling his body just enough with each snap of the camera so that each successive picture began where the previous one ended, with as little overlap as possible.

"I did this at the Grand Canyon," he said. "When you match them all together, you've got one of those professional National Geographic 360 degree spreads. You should see it."

A northbound car drove past them and came to an abrupt halt. A girl with a backpack got out, said "Thanks a bunch," waved goodbye to the driver, and started running toward them, waving and shouting. When she got close enough to see them clearly, she stopped dead in her tracks and, looking at Charlie with an incredulous wide-eyed gaze, her mouth a perfect oval, gushed out, "Holy mackerel! Ohmigosh! This is outta sight! I don't believe it! This is amazing! I am freakin' flabbergasted! I thought you were a friend of mine from Oregon. I'm hitching there to see him now. You could be him except for the glasses. Wow, this is incredible. I am freaking out."

Jerry Anne was a natural actress, a flamboyant full-bodied communicator who accentuated every sentiment with robust gestures and animated doe-eyed expressions as though she herself was amazed by everything she said. Her effervescent happiness was contagious. Such a parade of tell-tale expressions was foreign to Matt, who had pretty much one expression for all of his emotions.

She took out her camera so Matt, who was jealous of all the attention being heaped on Charlie, could take a picture of her and Charlie together.

"Take off your hat and glasses. We gotta have the full effect. He is gonna absolutely flip out when he sees this. I mean it. You guys could be twins." Matt flashed on Mark Olsen in Winnipeg and figured everyone has at least one twin somewhere in the world.

She headed back north and, being an attractive female, got a ride with the third car that passed by, while Matt and Charlie continued to wag their homely thumbs in a southerly direction. As they waited, a logging truck passed by with its only cargo being a single redwood trunk, large enough by itself to constitute a full load. Charlie shook his head in disgust.

Next was a ride to Elk with a black man driving a van. He brightened up when Matt said he was from upstate New York.

"Whereabouts?"

"Oh, a small town. You probably never heard of it."

"Try me."

"Have you ever heard of New Holland? It's about—" But the driver didn't give Matt a chance to finish.

"I know it well. The carpet mills. Rossi's Bar and Grill."

Matt was taken aback, as though his hometown was a secretive place that ceased to exist simply because he had left it so far behind. It turned out that the man used to live in Schenectady when his father was an adjunct at Union College before taking an associate-professorship position at Howard University.

"No kidding? My father graduated from Union in the thirties and my sister is going there now." Matt didn't mention that his father had also been a professor, but at Millington University, and it was conceivable that their fathers might have known one another.

"Your sister? It's an all-male college." He was skeptical.

"Not anymore. They started admitting girls a couple years ago. She'll be in the first four-year graduating class. They've had some transfers who've graduated but not a full four-year class yet."

"Yeah. That's cool."

They joked about the statue of Chester A. Arthur, the former president who was a Union grad back in the 1850s. The statue has him poised with an outstretching arm and an upturned palm. It's been a long-standing frat prank to hang things, such as bras and panties, from the President's hand as if he's making a peace offering to some frat boys.

"Yeah," the man said. "I heard that one time somebody stole a mannequin, put a noose around its neck, and hung it there. Dressed it up in street clothes and made it look real. Somebody called an ambulance because it looked like a student had committed suicide. I think it was around Halloween. Or maybe around finals."

"Have you been back to New Holland in the last few years?"

"No, man. Not since we moved in the mid-sixties. Not much reason to go back."

"Well, New Holland's going through some serious changes. All the factories are closing down and moving south, and a lot of historic old buildings are getting torn down so they can build a mall and supposedly modernize the city. Downtown is about half gone so far. And so is the classic old-fashioned train station. Replaced it with a useless building about the size of an outhouse. I couldn't believe they would actually do it until it was already done, and then you realize, holy shit, the building is gone forever and that you're dealing with people who don't give a shit about what they're doing. Pathetic. Proves that sometimes you shouldn't trust the people you trust."

"Tell me about it. I've lived in a few different places. That shit is happening all over the country. So-called urban renewal. People making a lot of money off that. It's the profit motive. Sorry to hear about it, man."

Four rides and they'd only gone about twenty miles, but the drivers had been interesting and the scenery astounding, so it had not been a waste of time. And he enjoyed the leisurely "we'll-get-there-when-we-get-there" freedom of spirit and the sense of having squirmed free of time's daily grind. Then, before he knew it, they were in a van with a woman named Dorothy and a hitchhiker named Sean. Dorothy's dog, a tail-thumping cocker spaniel, panted out the window with ears flapping and teeth bared like a front grille. "What's your dog's name?" Matt asked.

Dorothy smiled. "Toto." Everybody laughed but it was true.

Charlie said, "I don't think we're in Kansas anymore."

Everyone got out at the Manchester flea market where Dorothy was volunteering at a non-profit ceramics booth. For a half hour, Matt and Charlie looked around at a jumble of homemade crafts, odds and ends, used books, and other flea market stuff. For ten cents, Matt bought a used copy of *The Golden Apples of the Sun.* He stuffed it into his rucksack, pulled out the Agatha Christie mystery he had received from the jittery kid in Canada, and gave it to the plump lady at the book table. Her upper arm jiggled as she reached for it. Matt's heart was gladdened when she said, "Hmmm. I may just have to read this myself."

Another couple rides brought them to a place called "The Sea Ranch." They stood in the torrential drizzle and chill of a soupy sea fog that wrapped around them like a soggy quilt until a ride in a Chevy Van delivered them to Richmond, just outside Frisco, arriving about 10:30 at night.

Matt took advantage of a nearby phone booth to call his mother and hoped the three-hour time difference wouldn't be a problem. The phone rang once.

"Hello?" Her voice was nervous. Late night calls usually bore bad news. The operator spoke and the charges were accepted. It was not surprising that Mrs. Mahoney would be up at 1:30 a.m, still sitting in the kitchen, crocheting and reading and watching TV. Rory was probably still out.

"Hey Ma, how are you?"

"Matthew, where are you? I've been beside myself with worry."

"I kept meaning to call but I haven't been around too many phones for the last week. Did you get my card?"

"Yes. Otherwise I would have really been worried to death. Where on earth are you?"

"I'm in San Francisco. Just got in. I'm with another hitchhiker I met a few days ago and I'll be staying with him. He's got friends out here. You'd love this guy. He reminds me of Tates, but with less hair."

"When will you be home?"

"I don't know. I'll be here for one or two nights. Then I'm going south along the coast to Los Angeles. After that I'm going back east by way of the Grand Canyon. Three weeks. A month." Then she told him about some friends of his who had been in a car accident. Though none had been injured, it nonetheless trained her thoughts on grim possibilities and validated her worry habit.

"You be careful who you ride with," she cautioned. "There are a lot of crazy people out there. You know how much I worry."

"Don't worry. I'm being careful. Honest."

"Oh, I almost forgot. Patrick will be in San Francisco this coming weekend. It has to do with law school. If you're there you'll have to get together." Matt's brother was a law student and had one more year of night classes before graduating.

"No. I'll be in Los Angeles by then. Hey—I don't wanna run up your phone bill. I'm glad you were awake. I'll be in touch."

At the cold click, his mother was once again 3000 miles away, and his silent "I love you" nosedived to the earth somewhere above the Oakland Hills.

A ride with a tattooed biker girl in a rusty old jalopy with a stained-glass pentagram dangling from the rear view mirror brought them to Berkeley. At least that's where they thought they were. They thumbed all night through some seedy neighborhoods where multi-racial strings of slum-goddess hookers giggled at them and didn't even bother to ask, except for one who grinned at Charlie, did a suggestive little shimmy that drew a bull's eye around her crotch, and said in a seductive tone, "Hey lumberjack. You want a job?" Matt chuckled. Charlie blushed. She was sexy, but her voice was rough, and Matt thought she might have had an Adam's apple and a five o'clock shadow. The public display of so much forbidden flesh reminded him of the red light district along the canals of Amsterdam, where the scarlet women of easy virtue lounged on saggy couches in chintzy lingerie, exposing their breasts in the gaudy dim-lit showcase windows. A netherworld of urban grit and bargain-basement glitz. He felt both lust and disgust. Attraction and repulsion. Drawn both toward and away from such an occasion of sin. He was both ends of the magnet at the same time.

At 5 a.m. they found a Greyhound bus station on San Pablo Ave. They boarded for Martinez at 6 and had a two-hour layover in Richmond where they got Styrofoam cups of hot chocolate and a half dozen donuts at a Doggie Diner. In the front of the diner, mounted on a pole, stood a garish statuesque head of a long-eared, bow-tied dachshund with a shit-eating grin on its face.

The morning air had lost all its teeth by the time they arrived in Martinez. They tramped through town to Clementine Avenue and to the elegant hospitality of one Mrs. Constance Hartwell, a gray-haired widow who reminded Matt of a refined and educated Granny Clampett. She had a smile that was all honey and happiness and a kitchen that smelled like home. Though Charlie's arrival was anticipated, Matt came as an unannounced bonus. Without a moment's pause or trace of displeasure, she graciously adjusted her hostess calculations to accommodate for the surprised guest like a mother birthing unexpected twins.

"Well look at what the cat dragged in! You boys must be famished. Both of you—get yourselves in here and let me fix you a good breakfast."

As soon as Charlie got his bulky pack off, she said, "Let me give you a hug, young man. It is so good to see you. My goodness! You must be plum tuckered. How long have you had that beard? You look like a lumberjack, for goodness sake. How *have* you been?" Apparently, Charlie's lumberjack vibe was not confined to hookers.

She wrapped her toothpick arms around Charlie's redwood trunk and he reciprocated like the domesticated grizzly bear he was, embracing gently lest he accidentally crush her. A feisty miniature brown dachshund charged from another room, her nose and paws smudged with dirt, ricocheted against everyone's legs and wriggled in hyperactive circles, licking everything in sight and squirting excited piss squiggles onto the floor.

"Now Lady, calm down, you rascal you. Have you found that mole yet? Now stop your barking. Don't be in such a tizzy. It's only Charlie. You know Charlie, don't you?" After a spirited round of petting and belly rubbing, Lady downshifted and resumed her normal occupation of scouring the rug and the linoleum floor with her tongue, scrounging for tasty morsels.

"Oh Lady," said Mrs. Hartwell, "Stop the licky licky."

The boys set their gear in the sunroom and rested in a near daze until they heard, "C'mon boys. Breakfast is ready. Take your seat. It's time to eat."

Mrs. Hartwell's kitchen was a tidy celebration of color and daylight. The morning sun flooded through the parted curtains and sprayed dozens of multicolored diamonds upon the dinette set and the simple white porcelain vase from which a bouquet of fresh-cut garden flowers erupted into a riot of color. The famished boys soon devoured their eggs ("sunny side up, please"), bacon ("I like it burned"), English muffins with orange marmalade, orange juice, and a piping hot cup of coffee. Matt had just finished licking his plate clean and then it was, "Here. Try one of these. It's a Santa Rosa plum," and Matt slobbered down the juiciest, sweetest plum he had ever eaten.

Mrs. Hartwell had already planned an afternoon outing to the historic adobe home of Ygnacio Martinez and the adjacent home of John Muir, a Scottish immigrant who became a famous American naturalist. Charlie and Mrs. Hartwell were alarmed that Matt had never even heard of John Muir. Matt, who consider himself well-informed, was embarrassed but eager to learn as much as he could on the tour. The Muir home was decorated with period furniture that was varnished to a high gloss and a collection of other artifacts from days gone by. A step into the home was a leap backward in time. Matt studied all the exhibits so he could fill in the gaps of what he should have already known, as if preparing for a quiz.

They feasted on a picnic of chicken, potato salad, pickles, lemonade and Screamin' Yellow Zonkers, which seemed somehow incongruous in the dainty hands of Mrs. Hartwell. Matt saw his first orange tree, picked a damson berry, and listened to conversations about bay trees, eucalyptus trees, and birds and flowers of all varieties and descriptions. A renegade band of squirrels pillaged the grounds and scurried away with whatever edible treasures they could find. Mrs. Hartwell tossed off a handful of Zonkers, as if on the sly, and said, "They're very crafty at getting food."

Later, Mrs. Hartwell's son, Peter, showed up and went through the reunion ritual with Charlie, throwing his arms around him with an effusive bear-hugging sincerity. With all the how-have-you-beens and the you-look-greats behind them, Peter said, "Come on. Let's go for a drive." Mrs. Hartwell agreed. "You boys go for a ride. You've got a lot of catching up to do. And you can show Matt around, too. I need to rest my feet. I'm worn to a frazzle. I'm not as young as I used to be. But then again, who is?"

Matt was too brain dead to enjoy the reunion tour with Charlie and Peter and hoped that his sluggishness was not mistaken for rudeness. Besides, he was the square peg in the round hole of their rekindling friendship. He couldn't keep his eyes open and had no geographic sense of where they were driving. Matt, the veteran insomniac who prided himself on being able to get by on little sleep, passed out from exhaustion and didn't wake until they pulled in to Mrs. Hartwell's driveway. Charlie, on the other hand, was alert and enjoying the benefits of a second wind. Afterward, Matt vaguely remembered something about Walnut Creek and then overlooking a bay at a massive naval depot clogged with a disarrayed and mismatched fleet of old mothballed destroyers, troop ships, and aircraft carriers.

Peter headed back home to San Francisco. "I'll see you guys in a couple days and give you the grand tour. You'll love it."

With Peter gone, Mrs. Hartwell said, "Okay, boys. You just relax. I'll make you some dinner." She puttered around the kitchen, looked at the clock and said, "Time for my medicine. Ever since my surgery it seems I can't get by without this pill or that one. Take my pills to cure my ills."

*Matt thought of his mother's surgery so many years earlier. At that time, the word "cancer" was never spoken in the household except in hushed and secretive whispers among the grownups who protected him from harsh truths. Cancer meant death. When she returned home, her gouged body was so weak and ravaged that it frightened him. No one, not even his father, that distinguished man of letters, explained what was happening or consoled him as he sought to understand what was wrong with his mother. Was she dying? He didn't know and was afraid to ask.*

*She recovered in the living room, her beaten frame sunken into a hospital bed equipped with a pulley to raise herself, slowly and painfully, into a sitting position. He learned courage as he studied her and weighed her pain with each encounter. But she never complained, and he, so happy for her return, quickly learned to honor her convalescence with silence, obedience, and invisibility.*

*After a week or two, Mrs. Mahoney mustered up the courage and, in her own delicate but matter-of-fact manner, explained what had happened. "Matthew, has anyone talked to you about why I was in the hospital?"*

*"No. Nobody said anything. I just know you had an operation."*

*"Well, I was very sick and the doctor had to cut one of my boobies off."*

*He was silent, surprised. A slight blush reddened his cheeks. He certainly didn't see that one coming. Why would a doctor have to do that?*

*"Are you going to be okay?" He didn't want to talk about boobies with his mother.*

*"Yes. I'm going to be fine. But it's going to take a while for me to gain my strength back. They had to take all the muscle out of my arm. I have to do a lot of exercises, but I should be okay in time."*

*He didn't like "should." It created room for doubt. It created a possibility of "would not." He trudged away curious, but too embarrassed to ask, which booby had they taken.*

*Descriptions of human anatomy in the Mahoney household consisted of dinkies, hinders, and boobies. Despite the multiplicity of girls in the family, there was no word for that other female part. And though it was humorous the way Mrs. Mahoney told Matt about her operation, even at that tender age he knew that his mother was deeply troubled that he might somehow think less of her for being a one-booby mother in a two-booby world.*

That night it was more potato salad, canned mixed fruit, lemonade, and charming conversation with lonely, wonderful, and dignified old Constance Hartwell who got rid of her television set when her husband died and always kept the radio tuned to the classical station.

# CHAPTER XXVIII

Mrs. Hartwell let the boys sleep until 10:30, Charlie in the guest room and Matt on the floor in the sunroom. He, the self-professed night owl, was no stranger to late sleep-ins. Charlie, ever the early bird, felt the need to offer an apology, but Mrs. Hartwell didn't mind and had prepared their morning meal while they slept and allowed them the luxury of being gently lured to the kitchen table by the    sizzling skillet and the irresistible aroma of a sumptuous breakfast of bacon, eggs, muffins, homemade non-yeast bread, jelly, orange juice, and coffee. And, not to mention, a healthy dose of licky-licky from Lady, who bounded upon Matt and slathered his face with gobs of doggy drool as he lay in his sleeping bag.

*I hope you haven't been licking anything gross*, thought Matt.

Lady lay snoring upon the linoleum, coiled within a rectangular patch of sunlight, practicing flatulence and basking in her doggy dreams and making half-muted barky sounds as if she were chasing a dream rabbit down an Alice-in-Wonderland hole.

"Ah, there's a love," cooed Mrs. Hartwell. "My little Lady always finds the hot spot."

The day's itinerary pivoted around a hike to the peak of Mt. Diablo. Mrs. Hartwell prepared a lunch and gingerly placed everything into a frayed picnic basket, which was already filled with the cherished memories of a long history of bygone family picnics which she spoke of with such a melancholy fondness that Matt felt deprived for having to say he had never once gone on a family picnic. When the basket was packed with practiced precision, she closed its woven lid and announced, "Onions. Pickles. Lettuce go."

They pulled into the parking lot and began their ascent of a well-marked trail to the 3,849-foot summit. "It's a lovely day for a hike," said Mrs. Hartwell, perhaps recalling past hikes on days not quite so lovely. She was a hardy soul who welcomed the boys for the companionship as well as the opportunities for hiking and picnicking, which were so dear to her durable heart. Though by appearance she was a mere slip of a woman, she demonstrated her intrepid spirit by keeping pace and making it to the top in full breath and nary a complaint.

Gazing out across the vast, wild vista, Mrs. Hartwell rested her head against Charlie's shoulder and put her arm around his waist, perhaps to steady herself against the dizzying height, saying, "Oh, gracious. I will never tire of this view."

On the way back down, they picnicked at Juniper Picnic Grounds, visited by species of birds that Matt had never before noticed. He had a way of thinking that most birds were just robins or sparrows, give or take the odd cardinal or red-winged black bird. Charlie pointed one out and asked, "Do you know what that one is?"

Matt recognized it. "Yes. That one I know. It's a blue jay."

"Nope. It's a scrub jay. And there're also stellar jays. The blue jay is an eastern bird."

Mrs. Hartwell and Charlie were peering through binoculars, admiring plumage, identifying the hawks and buzzards soaring overhead in lazy circles.

"How can you tell the difference, say, between a hawk and an eagle?" Matt asked. Even as Charlie began describing their distinctive features, their predatory habits and their swooping and soaring patterns of flight, Matt glided into a reverie. He daydreamed that if he hung out with Charlie for a few months he might become a naturalist himself and could dazzle his friends and family with everything he'd learned on the road and he could rest at night in the comfort of knowing something useful and worthwhile. He could impress his nieces and nephews with lessons about pin-tailed hawks and golden eagles, the Doug firs, eucalyptus and bay trees, the redwoods, both the coastals and the sequoias, Santa Rosa plums, pancakes with fresh-picked blackberries and honey topping, quotations from Lao Tzu and John Muir, and, for a dose of comic relief, a few yarns of the Great North American Barking Squirrel. He wanted to be a man with personality, a funny teller of tall tales around a campfire in a dark canyon on an eerie black night as coyotes howled on jagged ledges, silhouetted against a full moon. The bearded trail guide who could navigate by compass or stars who knew the weather before it hit just by flaring his nostrils in a passing breeze or by reading the flight of the birds. A man who understood the language of the hiss of the snake and the lonely croon of the gray wolf and who, at the end of a long day on the dusty trail, could fix up some tasty grub over a fire he had built without matches.

It was 7 o'clock by the time they finished their hike and drove back to Martinez. The indefatigable Mrs. Hartwell wasted no time slapping a couple pounds of burgers onto the stove, scooping out copious amounts of her essential potato salad, and, for dessert, preparing bowls of sliced peaches on vanilla ice cream, all topped with a mountain of whipped cream.

"And we can't forget Lady," she said, tossing a chunk of hamburger to the floor where the ever-expectant badger hound was already slurping at her leaky butt gland like a messy-faced kid with an ice cream cone on a hot summer day.

Mrs. Hartwell reminded Matt of his mother, her greathearted air of personal dignity and, at the end of a busy day, the way she would relax and deliver her aches and pains to the sanctuary of her faded floral sofa, reading by the light of her ornate bronze table lamp with the fringed lampshade, content in her widowed domain, submitting to the merciful solitude of another evening, surrendering and sinking into the cozy cushion of memories and images that make her both happy and sad at the same time.

*He thought of his father and all his frailties. The surreal powerlessness of viewing the cold corpse at the funeral home and the trauma of being abruptly fatherless and the shock that it seemed to make no difference. And of the troubling dreams of his corpse, spastically attempting to rise from his casket as dreaming Matt gaped in horror, frozen, unable to help.*

*He thought of the time when he was fourteen and his father had fallen to the floor while rising from his living room chair and how he, Matt, had been alarmed and had run to his assistance with an extended hand.*

*"Here. Are you all right? Let me help you up."*

*His father, wedged between the chair and the wall, refusing Matt's help and insisting that he was okay, but what Matt recalled most was the feeble look and the flush of embarrassment from a man who was too proud and remote to accept his own son's helping hand.*

*Matt remembered their last kiss. As a young boy, he used to kiss his mother on the cheek and his father on the forehead each night at bedtime and his father would say, "Nighter, Nighter, Mr. Schneider." At some forgotten time for some forgotten reason, the bedtime kisses between father and son became fewer and further between until the day the ritual lapsed altogether. Then one night as he, Matt, was going to bed, he absentmindedly pressed his lips against his father's forehead, unintentionally resurrecting the long-ignored habit. Both were stunned as they stared into the unfamiliar landscape of each others' eyes with confused expressions and a painful recognition of the unbridgeable chasm that now separated them. Matt had hoped this minor slip would stir to life the vestige of love buried within his old man's heart. He had to believe that, beneath the debris of disappointments and regrets, there was a shiny lock-box of paternal love waiting to be rediscovered and sprung wide open. Otherwise he might as well disown and distance himself forever from this shell of a man posing as his father. He was surprised by the resurgence of hope created by this single accidental token of affection, and he reprimanded himself for the weakness of caring. He wanted to be there, ready and waiting, if his father woke from whatever kind of coma he was in. But he did not want to beg.*

*Nothing ever came of the incident, and Matt knew that his father had forgotten it by morning. "Why," he asked himself, "is a mother's love so presumed and taken for granted while a father's love has to be fought for and earned?"*

*Now, in Mrs. Hartwell's radiant presence, Matt pondered the intricacies and secrets of her marital relationship and hoped that Mr. Hartwell had been the good and loving man she deserved.*

The Hartwell's home was decorated with souvenirs. There was an old yellowed card on the fireplace mantle. Inside it said, "My Dear Wife: As we grow older together, I'm finding that I want to please you not out of obligation but because I love you. Happy Mother's Day. Your Loving Husband." On living room shelves were dozens of family pictures chronicling the evolution of their relationship, their optimistic smiles, and the sequence of scenic vistas as their backdrop. Though the fragile-boned white-haired figure before him, resting peacefully in her comfy chair with Lady curled up on her lap, bore no resemblance to the fresh-faced girl in the wedding dress who stood framed in tarnished silver on the end table, locked in a perpetual embrace with her dashing husband, Matt saw upon closer examination that the eyes were the same, unchanged across the decades, and that the sparkle had not dimmed and was still all aglow like a bright beacon from the attic window of a lonely old house.

"Growing older," she told Matt in a delicate whisper, "is like snow falling gently."

Matt faded first. After saying goodnight to Mrs. Hartwell, who announced that she was "too pooped to pop," he paused on his way to the sun room just long enough to give her a light kiss on her forehead and say, "Nighter, nighter. Thanks for everything."

*As he lay on his sleeping bag enjoying the joyful chorus of tree-frog and cricket songs being performed in Mrs. Hartwell's garden, Matt's mind drifted to Helen and to the soirée they attended at the end of their sophomore year at Bishop Brannan. He, in his cranberry double-breasted suit with the stiff clip-on tie and a boutonniere pinned to his lapel, looking somewhat less dashing than Mr. Hartwell on his wedding day, but overall not bad for an awkward sixteen-year-old. And Helen, of course, appearing lovely and bridely in her sleeveless white gown and holding in her white-gloved hands the corsage that Matt's mother had selected. They entered the gym, which had been transformed for the evening into a glittering Shangri-La. Banners proclaiming the night's theme hung from the walls as the song "Love is Blue" blared from the tinny speakers and echoed in the twilight. He felt out of his element in such a formal atmosphere but was reassured when Helen took his hand and smiled at him, mouthing the words, "I love you." He slipped his hand free so he could place it around her waist and pull her closer.*

*They took their seats at a round banquet table with three other Cinderella and Prince Charming couples, all gorgeous and dapper in their elegant attire. As the night wore on, Matt felt himself retreating into an insecure bubble, wishing he were a better partner and believing that Helen would be happier with any of the other, more handsome boys at the prom. He surveyed the competition and wondered how she could ever truly love him. She always said she did and always treated him lovingly. She listened compassionately when he shared with her his conflicting emotions about his father, wrapping her arms tenderly around him in a warm caress and comforting him with loving reassurances that succeeded in making him feel better, and whispering in his ear, "Don't worry. It'll be all right. I'm here for you."*

*But, as seeds of doubt took root in his mind, he was struck by an unfounded jealousy and a wave of fear. How could he ever know for sure that she didn't secretly prefer some other boy to him, someone else who might even be in this very same room at this very same time,*

349

*within sight and reach? Were they maybe exchanging undetected furtive glances, right there, under his nose, when he wasn't looking?*

*"Are you okay?" she asked.*

*"I'm fine. Why?"*

*"I don't know. You're so quiet. Are you having a good time?"*

*"Yeah. I'm having a great time." He smiled unconvincingly.*

*"You seem preoccupied, like you're thinking about something else. Are you sure you're okay?" She squeezed his hand and examined his face.*

*"I'm fine. I'm sorry. Do you want to dance?"*

*A slow song created a diversion from their conversation, and they melted together into the anonymity of the crowded dance floor where he hung his head upon her shoulder, pressed his cheek against the warmth of her cheek, and felt calm again. He distanced himself at arm's length and gazed into her eyes. She smiled. It felt good. It felt right. He loved her and knew that she loved him. It was tangible. But once the doubt and the irrational fear entered his mind, with its army of ugly thoughts, he didn't know how to get rid of it.*

# CHAPTER XXIX

After two full days of hiking and sightseeing, both the boys and Mrs. Hartwell needed a day of rest. "It does me a world of good," she told them, "getting out of the house and stretching these tired old legs, especially with such delightful company, but I'm not as spry as I used to be."

Matt updated his journal and wrote letters and postcards to friends and family back home. He explored the yard and garden, dodging the mole holes and the deep trenches that had been engineered by Lady in her dogged pursuit of the little rodent. He admired the high-bobbing sunflowers that cast huge lollipop shadows upon the grass as well as the houses and feeders and baths that invited the mingling commerce of birds of many feathers. One in particular—Matt imagined it to be a thrush—swooped into a bath, did a frenzied jig, splashed water into a mini-geyser, and flew off with drippy wings.

He rested atop his sleeping bag, melted into an epiphanal reverie, and wrote a fairy tale.

## THE GIANT WHO LIVED IN A CAVE

### I

Once upon a time there was a giant who lived in a cave. He had not always been a giant, and he had not always lived in a cave. In fact, he was once a king who lived upon a high hill in a great and golden castle with his beautiful queen and their 23 perfect children.

In those days the King would return home each evening after spreading good will throughout his happy realm. Whenever he walked through the castle gates, all his children would jump into his arms and demand silly stories and funny faces and cheerful sing-along songs. The King would always oblige them because, as much as all his children loved him, he loved all of them even more.

One sunny day in early May, the King was in the forest beyond his castle at the foot of a mountain when he noticed water trickling through the cracks of a mossy cliff wall. At first he thought it was rainwater oozing through the damp earth, but then he heard a bubbling sound and realized that it was coming from a fresh spring.

He filled his crystal traveling goblet with the seeping waters. There was an amber hue and a peaty aroma, but the taste was bitter so he spat it out. Then, after it soaked into his tongue, it delivered a rather pleasant sensation. He filled up his goblet one more time and risked another taste. This time he took a big swigging mouthful and let it tingle all through the inside of his mouth and down his dusty throat and into the hollow of his stomach. It radiated throughout his body. His first thought was to bottle it up to share with everyone, for such was his custom. But he changed his mind and chose to keep it all for himself for the time being.

As the months passed, the King spent more and more time in the forest away from his beautiful Queen and his 23 perfect children, lured by his mysterious potion to the privacy of the mountains, or down to his secret chamber where he stored a reserve supply in little brown jugs for quick relief in times of dire need. The more he drank, the more he wanted. He no longer had time to tell his silly stories or make funny faces or sing his cheerful sing-along songs, and he didn't seem to notice that his 23 perfect children no longer greeted him with laughter or leapt into his arms. For when he indulged in the solitary pleasure of his favorite pastime, his thoughts danced merrily through his head, and he had nary a care and all appeared right in his world.

The Queen was beside herself with worry. What was she to do? The King would rarely come home and his 23 perfect children were all sad because they missed their father. Some blamed their mother and claimed she drove him away with unreasonable demands. Others blamed their father for neglecting his Queen and doting instead on the sacred elixir that had stolen his affections and left his family fatherless. He, however, was the King, and with his title came certain privileges, so no one dared question his decisions. No one, that is, except the Queen. One night, the angry Queen smashed all the King's little brown jugs that were stored in the secret chamber and left the shattered debris on the floor in a swampy puddle as evidence of her displeasure.

The Queen's protest infuriated the King. How dare she defy him so? But he said nothing. In retaliation, he left her a hateful note condemning her for giving him no choice but to abandon her and their 23 perfect children forever. He stormed from the castle and sought refuge in the solitude of the deep, dark forest. When he reached his secret fount, however, he felt doubly cursed, for the spring had gone dry. All that remained was a dampness that coated the rock wall like a cool perspiration.

In despair, the King took his heaviest axe to the rocks and, after grunting and groaning and heaving, he was pleased to see the rocks give way to a tiny entrance into a large cave. He rejoiced because his efforts were rewarded with the merry sound of trickling waters echoing from the craggy recesses within. He clawed and shimmied through the narrow tunnel and was very proud of himself when he plopped into a big domed room filled with many oddly shaped boulders and crystalline rock formations. Most impressive of all was that the high-vaulted cavern was illuminated with an eerie greenish phosphorescence that emanated from a well in the middle of his hidden lair. To the King's delight, his prized amber fluid was bubbling from the well and spilling over into tinkling rivulets that disappeared through the crevices in the cavern floor.

He scrambled to the well and hugged it with joy. If this were not perfect enough, there at the well was a two-handled jewel-encrusted goblet just waiting to be dipped. When it was dipped, it glowed like a torch because each jewel shone like a star. As the King drank, he was transfixed by the swirling and twirling kaleidoscope of colors that danced across the perspiring ceiling and walls of his new sanctuary.

The King loved his cave, for it was inaccessible and so huge that it protected him from his many tiresome responsibilities. He loved his goblet, for even when its ruby rim was overflowing, it sat ever so lightly in his hand and glistened hypnotically. And he loved his well, for it nourished all his wants and never ebbed even an inch no matter how much of it he drank.

Sometimes, the King would kneel beside the well in a position of prayer and lean forward with lips pursed for a sip as if giving it the sweetest of kisses, just as he had first kissed his beautiful Queen. He would never forget that first kiss. There she was, in her courting gown and garland of scented flowers, the loveliest woman in the kingdom and most certainly in the whole wide world. Then he would relax back to the floor, bewitched by the spectrum of rainbow patterns cast about the cave by his goblet, oblivious to the ancient spell that had been cast upon these waters by an evil giant so many hundreds of generations ago.

II

An Old Giant named Bortig had lived in this land many centuries before it was a kingdom, when giants still ruled the earth. Bortig's mother was a witch goddess and His father a dragon king. It was the last age of the giants. He had grown strong on the flesh of men, and His thundering footsteps shook the earth and sent villagers stampeding into the forests, the marshes, and the many hidden nooks and crannies too tiny for the Giant's clumsy fingers. Neither the most powerful wizards nor the bravest warriors could defeat His wickedness though many had been devoured in valiant efforts to free the people from His ruthless tyranny.

The Old Giant was happy in His wicked ways, for He had no warmth of heart, no measure of compassion, and neither knew nor cared for love or kindness. All He had was a repugnant and limitless love of flesh. But even giants grow older and weaker, and in the inevitability of time there came a day when Bortig's waning strength could no longer match the strength of the wizards' incantations or the prowess in battle of the rising might of the hordes of revenge-minded men. The monstrous Old Giant stood His ground well, and in a final flourish sent many men to their graves, scattering their desiccated remains across the bloodied glen. When He was finally struck by the right-sized sword and fell to the earth in a thundering crash, there was a great feast and celebration.

Bortig's head was mounted on a pike. The remains of His butchered body were thrown into the well, which had been filled with oil and set aflame like a fissure from hell. A brave warrior dined upon His liver. Then came the final observance in which the Chieftains each stabbed a burning sword into the Old Giant's silent heart. A wizard then threw the heart into the raging inferno for the conflagration and condemned it to hell and damnation for eternity.

As the heart was still ablaze, an anguished warrior, overcome by agony because his own wife and children had been served upon Bortig's banquet table, began to laugh nervously, and the laughter spread among the throng despite the wizards' urgent orders to stop.

Suddenly, the burning heart began beating like a war drum and a voice boomed: "Rejoice not, you fools!" All eyes tracked the voice to the well and to Bortig's gruesome piked head. Its eyes had opened and Its mouth was set in a grotesque charred grin as It shouted, "Whoever drinks from this well shall be cursed, for my body and my blood shall poison its waters forevermore, and I shall devour your children and your children's children from within. I will live forever and murder them all with my undefeated will."

As he took His last breath and perished a second time, the Old Giant cast a spell of forgetfulness over the villagers so they would remember nothing of His vile words and would partake of the sensually pleasing flavor of the waters brimming over the stone lips of the well, which itself was transformed by the Old Giant's death spell into a perfect fount with its own special two-handled jewel-encrusted goblet with which to sip the dreadful poison.

The villagers, having no memory of that which they had just witnessed, all wandered in a state of befuddlement as if being roused from a fit of sleepwalking. They beheld the sight of the well with wonder and began to drink freely of its waters, just as Bortig had predicted. There was, however, one wizard whose memory remained untainted because his powers had shielded him from the amnesiac effects. He chased them all back to their villages, but he could not undo what Bortig had wrought, nor could he destroy the well, nor plug the ever-brimming tide of polluted waters. Instead he summoned the full thread and drip of his powers and brought a harsh reckoning upon that place and caused a great storm of boulders to shower from the sky and bury the well beneath a mountain of stone in an inaccessible tomb where none could fall victim to the irresistible lure of the evil well and its fouled waters.

When that shower of stone ceased, the sky cleared and turned a magnificent blue, and the mountain rose like a proud monument to the death of the treacherous Old Giant. The act was blessed because there were swarms of butterflies in flight around the mountaintop like a fluttering crown. Overhead there was a halo of promise and renewal, a double rainbow that glowed phosphorescent deep into that first night as if to announce and baptize the newly forged mountain.

As an untold number of centuries passed by, the mountain grew lush with greenery and wildlife and a bountiful harvest of butterflies that flitted all around. There flourished a forest of redwood trees that were taller and older and stronger than any other trees in this kingdom or in any kingdoms known through all of recorded time. No one ever knew of the Old Giant's curse or of the entombed well, for all memories had been washed clean. No one knew—except the one wizard, who died ruing the knowledge that the well still bubbled and that the curse still lived on in its deep vault of stone.

III

As the King succumbed to the powers of the poisoned well, his mind twisted and his thirst became all-consuming. He did not realize until it was too late that he had gone too far, that his note was too cruel, his behavior too extreme, and that there was no returning to his beautiful Queen and his 23 perfect children, for a collapse of rocks had sealed the passageway. He would sometimes hear the sorrowful cry of his Queen or one of his children from beyond his stone prison, calling his name and begging him to come home. At first he would not answer, out of sheer stubbornness. But soon, though he tried, he could not even muster the strength of voice to do anything but send a booming echo that thundered within his cave and drove him mad but did not leak a single wisp of sound to the outside world. It was as though, even in life, he was dead to himself and to all others.

The waters turned a dull gray, and the glimmer of his precious goblet dimmed until it glowed no more and the jewels were just stones. He was left alone in darkness with no one to console him except his own defeated thoughts. Most frightening of all was that he began to grow and grow, taller and broader, until his precious goblet was no more than a thimble in his bulky hands, and his kingly attire tore into shreds and tatters and was unable to conceal his disfigured nakedness. As Bortig's spirit infected the King's mind and body, he grew and grew until he filled the cave and his head scraped against the rugged ceiling. He could barely double himself over to dip his thimble-goblet into the well, and it no longer satisfied him because no more than a drop would soak into his tongue, leaving none to trickle down his dry throat or quench the ache in his stomach.

The ancient curse attacked the King like a virus and brought alive in his mind the transplanted memories of the Old Giant's murderous deeds, which had been proud memories for Bortig himself but which, to the poor deformed King, were nightmares that robbed him of all sleep and put him into a state of perpetual misery.

357

The King realized his errant ways but could not escape the cave. The Old Giant's rancid waters were now his only nourishment. Though, for the time being, it kept him from dying, it did not allow him to live. It merely prolonged his existence, which had become miserable and devoid of love or joy or even simple happiness. He yearned for his beautiful Queen and his 23 perfect children, and his heart ached because he knew that they must hate him for abandoning them and his kingdom.

He grew feeble with self-pity and bitter remorse. Death would take him soon, he knew, he hoped, but he could not hasten its call. On his last day, though he did not know it was to be his last, he rose to a full stance as his rusty joints creaked open, and he fit his head into the highest nook of the stone ceiling and reached out his arms to their full span and with his head tilted back he shouted out deliriously, "Am I am a man" and budged himself from his stupor just enough to fall into a choking fit of tears. Each tear could fill a bucket, and there was no end to them, for they had been stored inside him for so long. They were not tears of pity for himself or his tragic foolishness nor were they tears of rage at his soon and certain death. They were tears of love for his beautiful Queen and his 23 perfect children. And he imagined them all in their vast reception hall, assembled before their fireplace as if for a wedding or some other celebratory banquet, and he recited their names in a sweet prayer of remembrance, and for one final moment he was whole again for the love of them.

## THE END

# CHAPTER XXX

Though they rose at 7, the boys offered no resistance to the temptation of yet another of Mrs. Hartwell's breakfasts to fuel themselves up for a day of rigorous exploration at Muir Woods. Heaping their plates, she repeated the old adage: "Eat breakfast like a king. Lunch like a prince. And dinner like a pauper." They didn't leave until 9:30, and it was 11 before they arrived at the woods with Charlie at the wheel of Mrs. Hartwell's powder-blue Chevy Nova.

Muir Woods was as Charlie had promised: an enchanted place that did not appear to be of this time or of this earth. Displayed inside the entranceway was a cross-section of a massive redwood trunk. It was polished and inscribed upon in order to delineate the growth rings in a chronological context. The tree was "born" in 909 A.D., not old by redwood standards. There were live specimens more than double its age still thriving in the forest, collecting annual rings like steadfast senior citizens competing for longevity. The tree had grown like a proud prince in a lost kingdom, oblivious to the ravages of man for more than a millennium. So many centuries of summers bound and wound together in one extraordinary wooden tablet of time. Its rings chronicled the Battle of Hastings, the signing of the Magna Carta, the "discovery" of the New World, the colonization and independence of America, and all things subsequent until that final day in 1930 when an enterprising woodsman took a saw to it so it could be converted into dressers or reduced to ashes in so many fireplaces.

There was an older couple blocking the gate to the trail. The man was huge in height and width and grossly overweight. He braced his ponderous bulk against his walker and lost himself in temporary awe, eyes skyward. His wife saw the boys approaching and said, "Tiny—they want to get through."

Tiny snapped back to Earth and said with a kind, sad smile, "Oh, sorry boys. I'm a bit of a redwood myself."

Muir Woods reminded Matt of his own woods back home, lush and green, though this was much grander, and he felt his old trail-blazing urges being reawakened by crisp leaves and delicate branches being crushed by boots, by the rustle of leaping squirrels, and by the mingling aroma of mosses and decaying leaves and trees felled by bullying winds. Charlie was back in his element, "stalking the wild asparagus" and tramping through what he called, quoting John Muir, "the university of the wilderness."

"This is all old-growth forest. Beautiful coastal redwoods. The tallest of all living things."

"What's that mean—old growth," asked the student.

"That means that it has never been logged. But it would've been logged long ago if it weren't for John Muir."

They walked the shady trails through generations of trees, craning their necks like dwarf tourists, gazing up into the towering chiaroscuro tangle of dizzying treetops, which shielded them from the streaming opulence of sunlight that penetrated through only the uppermost canopy of overhanging limbs and cast long, shadowy crisscrossing patterns down upon the cool, damp earth. They fondled the bulbous burls that bulged from branches and trunks like huge goiters, tasted the airborne particles of decaying bark, and took in the musty aroma of the moist carpet of composting leaves squishing beneath their feet. All of it, this flourishing multi-sensual forest experience, blended together and stirred within Matt the remnants of grainy childhood memories of being by himself exploring the creek and trails in the wonderland of his wooded backyard.

Charlie continued the redwood lecture he had begun at the Avenue of the Giants. Some of the coastals were over 350 feet high and more than 2000 years old.

"Yeah. That's the kind we saw before and the kind we've got here. Some of these trees were here when Christ was crucified. But the sequoias, they're even older and more stout. They can get to be 3000 years old. They're all up in the mountains, up in the Sierras, in the colder, higher altitudes."

Matt ran his fingertips across the corrugated ridges of bark that felt like a petrified elephant's hide and trod a balancing act upon the gigantic root structures that were coiled into a gnarled and woven knot-work design that clutched around big rocks and tendrilled into and out of the Earth like mythological sea serpents. He marveled at the natural shelters created within the rotted-out trunks of redwoods still standing strong and spiring hundreds of feet high, each its own private chapel. The lowest branches didn't even begin until well beyond the full height of the other trees. Mossy green girths with sturdy outgrowths of shelf fungi braced upon them, and the dense thickets and broad blades of ferns in hidden grottoes gave the woods a prehistoric aura. And the twin-trunked trees with barky upside-down crotches and redwood legs spread wide to the sky like a willing partner.

The air was a bouquet of sweet fragrances. "Ah—that's the bay laurel," Charlie said, inhaling through finely tuned nostrils. He found a leaf and crumpled it between his thumb and forefinger for Matt to sniff. Matt closed his eyes to savor the lifting scent.

They walked through a dense profusion of fronds in a shady grove where the atmosphere was chilled and breezy, raising patterns of goosebumps onto their bare arms and then, moments after, stepped into a golden oasis where the goosebumps were chased away. It was eerie and quiet, a land for hobbits and angry fairy queens and enchanted princesses and vigilant knights embarked on selfless and heroic quests.

"How could anyone cut down one of these trees?" Charlie mused aloud. "For Christmas, my dad always buys those potted live trees with the root balls. We decorate them in the house and then we plant them in the backyard in the springtime. We've got a whole row of 'em back there. It's Christmas all year round," he concluded with his wrinkly grin.

The boys had been so eager to lose themselves among the giant trees that they neglected to pick up a trail map. They wandered intuitively throughout the pristine forest, sometimes in circles, sometimes up steep hills into the universe of sunshine and then back into the shady redwood netherworld. Though they proved that intuition is not always the best guide, it was impossible to take a wrong turn in a such a fairy-tale forest. Following a less-frequented trail, they climbed to a hostel built by Germans, the original hostelers, in 1912. It overlooked the woods and afforded a commanding bird's-eye view of the treetops and beyond. Inspired by such beauty, Charlie tossed his head back and yodeled, "littleoldaladywho."

There was a woman caretaker living there who instructed them on the history of the hostel and gave them a map of the trails. They then meandered upon another network of trails and discovered a restaurant indicated on the map. It, too, was built by Germans in 1912.

"We should've packed a lunch."

"Yeah. If Mrs. Hartwell were here, we'd have a picnic basket full of stuff."

"Yup. And plenty of potato salad."

They both gave a fond laugh because it seemed that, for Mrs. Hartwell, no meal was complete without an ample portion of her homemade potato salad.

They rested at an outdoor table. Charlie bought a sandwich, but Matt got only a coke because he was conserving his meager funds. The coke was refreshing, but man, that sandwich looked mighty good.

They re-looped into another part of the woods and found the main trail where they met a French girl from just north of Nancy, a city in northeastern France. She was spending two months touring the U.S. by bus and thumb and had already been to the Grand Canyon.

"Oh yes. It is so very beauty-full. You must go there." Matt had always had an infatuation with foreign accents. They sounded so intelligent and sexy, regardless of nationality. So mesmerizing. He mentally recited what he could remember of his conversational French from grade school. "Je voudrais te presenter mon ami Jacques," "Ou est la biblioteque," and "Fermez la bouche." But he didn't try any of it on her for fear that she would think he was trivializing her language. He didn't want to be the arrogant American she would ridicule to her girlfriends when she returned home to France, so he fermezed his bouche and wallowed in the pleasure of the seductive musical tones of her voice until she continued on her way. They wound around a few more trails and were still marveling when they returned to the furnace of their sun-baked car, pulled out of the parking lot, and once again said goodbye to a forest of redwoods.

It was evening when they arrived at the Wilson Street apartment of Peter Hartwell and his wife, Nizoni, a full-blooded Navajo.

"You finally made it. Man, I thought you got lost or something." Peter was thrilled to see his friend again. "You're spending the night, right? I mean, my mother said you could keep the car as long as you need it."

Nizoni, demure and contented behind dark native eyes, had a jet-black ponytail that hung down to the back of her thighs. She treated Matt kindly and spoke with him in a calm and direct manner. She was clearly more at ease listening than speaking and avoided saying anything about herself. Matt admired her quiet ways.

"Where are you from?" she asked, and "How long do you plan to be on the road?" She did not hurry his responses and was attentive in a way that made him feel that his answers mattered, especially when she asked about his family.

"Can I see your medal?" she asked, indicating the chain around his neck.

"Oh this," he said, holding it out to her.

She studied it and said, "It's very nice. Silver. It's a Saint Christopher medal."

"What does that mean?"

"Saint Christopher is the patron saint for travelers. You didn't know that?"

"No. I'm just wearing it because a guy in Canada gave it to me. I don't usually wear jewelry, but it was a gift so I made an exception. I didn't know it had any significance." He chose not to describe the Canadian man as an Indian, even though he knew that would make his story more interesting.

"It is a very generous gift."

A shaggy orange cat came out of hiding, massaged herself against Nizoni's calf, and then sprang onto her lap and made a squeaky-toy sound that was like nothing Matt had ever heard from a cat. "Mosi has a meow impediment," Nizoni explained. Then, addressing the tufted clump of fur that had taken residence upon her lap, she said, "Mosi, this is Matt. He is our guest. No scratching." She cradled Mosi like a baby and leaned forward so Matt could become better acquainted. Mosi bristled her whiskers and proffered her stiffened tail, assumed a regal sphinx-likes pose, demanding adoration, and paid no attention to Nizoni or Matt. "Oh look. She's so impurrious," said Nizoni, quite satisfied with her pun. "Look, Matt," said Nizoni, as the cat plied Nizoni's thighs with her paws, "Mosi is kneading bread."

Before long, Peter broke out the pipe, tamped it up with a pungent wad of rich sweet-scented weed, and everybody got stoned. Their appetites led them to a nearby Vietnamese restaurant. Matt couldn't afford the extravagance of going out to eat, even at such an inexpensive place, but the pot had keened up his appetite and there was no way to graciously bow out. He went along, kept his second thoughts to himself, and enjoyed the fragrant orgy of spicy sauces and hot heapings of rice, sweet-and-sour chicken, egg rolls, and Chinese tea in steamy little cups with no handles. This was exotic for Matt because there were no Chinese restaurants in New Holland, and he had eaten Chinese food only a couple of times in his life.

"Do you know why Chinese teacups have no handles?" Peter asked.

Charlie and Matt examined each other's faces, not certain whether to expect an explanation or a punch line, and both said, "No."

"The Chinese are very practical. They know that, if the teacup is too hot to hold, the tea will be too hot to drink."

"That makes sense," nodded Matt, storing that fact away in his library of interesting snippets to be repeated on future occasions. He tested the side of his cup with his fingertips and then carefully manipulated chopsticks in public for the first time, saying, "Here goes nuttin'."

Of Nizoni, Peter boasted, "Man, she is so good with chopsticks she can even eat soup with them." Nizoni blushed but said nothing.

Peter and Nizoni ate adeptly and chatted with the heavily accented Vietnamese waitress who knew them as regulars. Charlie wasn't having much luck with the rice, so he went the barbaric route and asked for silverware, which was provided with an amused expression. Matt studied the waitress's face, her movements, and the intensity of her alert eyes as she placed the serving bowl in the middle of the table. He had never met anyone from Vietnam and wished he could read her thoughts and understand who she was within. He contemplated whether he should feel guilty for being an American and, though he tried to convince himself that he should not, he did anyway.

The check arrived on a tip plate with four fortune cookies. "Hey, everybody, don't forget your fortune cookie," Peter announced. "But you have to eat the cookie before you read the fortune or else it won't come true." Matt cracked open the brittle shell and pulled out the thin strip of paper, which advised, "It's not over when you are defeated. It's over when you quit." But he forgot to eat the cookie first.

Peter insisted on paying for dinner. Matt protested but caved in because he was worried about going broke in some backwater southwestern desert town while the breadth of the continent still separated him from his own home bed. He didn't want everyone to think he was a cheapskate who was hanging around just so he could continue sponging off Charlie's friends. He was starting to worry that he had worn out his welcome and that Charlie was too polite to say anything. He winced because he knew that once those kinds of thoughts entered his head, they would pretty much set up house and get louder and run rampant until they started screamin' for attention.

Matt lay in bed, engrossed by the staccato ticking of the moon-faced Big Ben alarm clock staring at him from the nightstand. Car lights and nighttime street sounds seeped through the sun-bleached curtains of a half-opened window. There was a thud at his feet. Mosi floated up and curled herself beside Matt's shoulder and nuzzled her nose against his ear, purring steadily like a mechanical toy. If he didn't know any better, Matt would've thought that Mosi was trying to comfort him, telling him to relax, that she would be his pillow, and that everything was going to be okay.

# CHAPTER XXXI

Peter called in sick and, after a communal breakfast buzz, the boys were out on the town. They spent a few hours flitting around Fisherman's Wharf in the patchouli air among the poets, mimes, musicians, and other artists festooned in hippie regalia performing and collecting tips in an open air street carnival. There was a legless black man in a wheelchair wearing a t-shirt emblazoned in rainbow script with "I Am Whole In My Soul." A Vietnam vet in drab-green fatigues and a bullet-riddled military helmet stood on a crate wearing a U.S. flag around his waist and black skull-and-crossbones armbands around both tattooed biceps. He was protesting the war with free-form poetry, punctuated with the occasional mantra, "We're all just meat, waiting for the kill. Hamburger on the wartime grill," while his girlfriend sat lotused beside him, banging away on red, white, and blue bongos. Bald-headed devotees with polka-dotted foreheads chanted "Hare Krishna," rang brass bells, shook tambourines, and performed blissful marionette dances in their baggy orange robes, handing out tulips and free literature to the passersby.

There was an assortment of old ferryboats and sailing vessels tethered to the docks, and in the bay seals flipped and flopped and barked or spread out languidly upon the rocks like portly nudists. They rode up steep hills in cable cars and went to the legendary City Lights Book Store, which felt no different than any other halfway decent bookstore. Peter drove them down the steepest, curviest street Matt had ever seen. It was a tight series of hairpin curves so tortuous that it seemed to exist exclusively for the puzzlement of tourists. They strolled through Golden Gate Park.

Matt was surprised by how expansive it was and by the buffalo that grazed there. He smiled and nodded hello to a young hippie mother sitting on a beach blanket, cradling and breast-feeding an infant child, singing, "Everything is gonna be fine. Everything is gonna be fine. Cause you're a little baby, cute as a bug. And everything is gonna be fine." Above them, squirrels and chipmunks were skittering through the cypress and eucalyptus trees, and having a very important conversation in a language Matt didn't understand, when, suddenly, an acorn dropped onto his head, startling his senses and triggering memories.

"Gotta watch out for those things," Charlie cautioned. "They can pack a wallop."

Peter picked up Nizoni after work and they all went to dinner at a Mexican restaurant where Matt had his first-ever authentic dinner of tacos and corn tortillas and a tasty cup of some kind of hot chocolate concoction that was perfect as an after-dinner taco tamer. Peter paid once again, and Matt once again got that queasy parasite feeling.

Before bed, Matt told Charlie he would be leaving the next day, heading south through Big Sur and Los Angeles and then east to the Grand Canyon. He thought about the universe, about Pluto and Mercury, and how the planets all revolve around the sun with precise and predictable symmetry in the immutable grooves of their own celestial paths. The more he thought about it, the more it seemed that a record album should just explode into a million pieces from the pressure and tension of trying to maintain equilibrium and structural integrity as it spun wildly around on the turntable at so many different speeds, all at the same time. His mind fixated on an image of his *Highway 61 Revisited* album buckling up like it had been hit by an earthquake and was splintering on his turntable, the needle and tone arm bouncing erratically and gouging through the vinyl as black shards shot through the room like a shower of shrapnel. And there he was at the outer edge, out there on Pluto, screaming, "How does it feel? To be on your own. No direction home. A complete unknown. Like a rolling stone," hanging on for dear life and afraid of being ejected beyond the farthest grooves and set forever adrift into that doomed and frozen void of lifeless space, forever beyond all hope and human contact. He couldn't get that image out of his head no matter how hard he tried to think of other things. It was definitely time to go.

# CHAPTER XXXII

When Matt woke up he realized he would be heading east, not south, to go back home, not to the Grand Canyon. He did not gradually grow weary of the road. It was a swift death. He had read the wind and was working his rudder and putting his faith in the process. His hometown was whistling him back: "Come home, Matthew. All is well. All is forgiven."

Since entering the Redwoods of Northern California, Matt had struck an effortless balance between the grand scheme of things and the rough-and-tumble minutiae of his daily grind. A kind of existential compromise. But he had rested too long in San Francisco and had allowed his homesickness to overtake him. It was just another sign of his weakness. He yearned to break free of all emotional attachments and never get homesick, but the homeward tug was yanking him back into the safe perimeter of his umbilical orbit. That cord hadn't broken after all. and Matt's inner hamster realized he was still running in circles, though on a larger wheel and in a larger cage, but still getting nowhere. Now that he'd made up his mind, nothing could delay his desire for a speedy return. The decision was immutable. It was time to go home.

Charlie was disappointed, and Matt felt that his travelin' man status had been demoted a few notches. "What happened? I thought you were determined to see the Grand Canyon. You can't miss it."

"I don't know. Just kinda changed my mind. Spur of the moment. Besides, I'm getting low on money and I don't wanna end up broke in Arizona."

Peter, who was skipping yet another day of work, said, "Well, before you head out, let's take a drive through the Haight. We haven't been there yet. No trip to San Francisco is complete without at least seeing it."

Driving through Haight-Ashbury, Peter said, "It's not what it used to be. All the cool hippie head shops have gone out of business or gotten commercial. Now everybody is conforming to non-conformity, and the groups can't hang out on the street or in the park anymore 'cause they've all gotten so famous. They've moved into mansions or out on big farms or ranches. Now there are tour buses with foreigners and tourists from all over the country poking their heads out of the windows and taking pictures of other tourists thinking that they are genuine Frisco hippies. Most of the true hippies are gone to communes up north or down to Big Sur or who knows where else. But it's still fun to come down here and check out the scene every now and then, despite all the fake commercial hippie bullshit that's moved in."

Matt looked at the street sign at the intersection of Haight and Ashbury Streets and thought it was no different than Merchant and River Streets at home. He was scanning the pedestrian traffic when he saw a familiar halo of reddish-brown hair popping up through the wrinkled rainbows of a tie-dyed tee shirt, looking like a real-life Mr. Natural.

"Hey! It's Marty!"

Sure enough, there he was, bopping like a daisy down the street as if he were a native. Charlie said, "Peter—stop the car. We know that guy."

A big happy, goofy grin overpowered Marty's typically indifferent face when eye contact was established.

"Hey—what're you guys doin'? Man, this is far out! I never thought I'd see you guys again."

"We've been in town a few days. Went to Muir Woods. Did some sightseeing."

"Yeah—and I'm getting ready to head back east. Goin' back home."

"What happened? I thought you were going to the Grand Canyon?"

Marty got in the car and they drove to a nearby park where everybody practiced their stories for the next hour or so. He explained, "I spent a couple nights with Jack and Donna and then they drove me part way to Frisco, to a small town, Geyserville or Geezerville, or something. From there I got an easy lift to town, and I met a bunch of freaks in the park who let me crash with them. They're not charging me anything as long as I buy my own food and don't steal their dope. It's cool. They're all into meditation and vegetarianism. Right up my alley, man. Actually, that's how I met them. I was sitting in the lotus position underneath a tree in the park and I had my eyes closed and I was all mellow and blissed out and one of their dogs jumped on me, knocked me over, and started licking my face. Then suddenly this family of freaks is standing around me laughing. It was fate or something."

Marty and Charlie exchanged numbers and made plans to get together over the next couple of days. When they dropped Marty off at the intersection of Haight and Ashbury, he flashed everybody the peace sign with his right hand and waved with the other. It was a hippie moment for the ages.

It was 2:30 on a sunny Friday afternoon when Matt got out of the car on an entrance ramp to the Bay Bridge and said his patently clumsy goodbye to Charlie and Peter. Charlie bade him good luck and said, "Let's keep in touch," and seemed to mean it. To Peter, Matt said, "Thanks for everything. And be sure to thank your mother. She was incredible. And thanks for both of those meals. They were …" and he made an Italian or French gesture with the tips of his fingers bunched together at his mouth and then, with a kiss, blowing them open, meaning to indicate that the meals were either "magnifico" or "magnifique." But Peter didn't understand what the hell Matt was doing, so his flimsy attempt at a cool goodbye and thank you did not quite get through and, instead, ended up looking foolish. Then, in a matter of seconds, he was alone with all of San Francisco behind him and the rest of America beckoning from across the bridge and beyond.

# PART THREE

We have to stumble through so much dirt and humbug before we
reach home. And we have no one to guide us. Our only guide is our
homesickness.
—Herman Hesse, *Steppenwolf*

# CHAPTER XXXIII

## The Homebound Man

The travelin' man and the homebound man are two fundamentally different creatures, forever at battle with one another for the soul and the spirit of the man they inhabit. For the travelin' man the road is both a servant, which obediently delivers him to all longed-for places, and a master, which commands him onward with irresistible tales of distant destinations and offers of new fast friends at every crossroad and turn. It is a thing of adventure and danger and freedom. Most of all it is a thing which offers love with perfect strangers and a kind of unpredictable fulfillment that can never be found at any hometown place.

The homebound man is impatient and weary of the road and is deaf to the beckoning call of all places save that one, and though the travelin' man may win many a traveling battle, it is the homebound man who is always victorious in the end because even the most nomadic soul has a secret desire for the peace and security of home. And so it was now for Matt, whose passion to map the great everywhere had been eclipsed by another passion and another hunger.

For Matt, the road now offered a singular promise and led to one place only and to the sublime comfort of sleeping in the clouds of his own hometown bed and to the presence of his unwavering mother and her home-cooked meals and the creature comforts that all wandering folk secretly yearn for. To his fast friends and all the familiar places that both charmed and haunted him. Just the word itself, "Home," now had an Odyssean aura that rang mythological like "Shangri-La" or

"Valhalla." It was a mighty and sacred word, spoken with reverence. The road was now devoid of glory, it was just a means to an end, to deliver him to that hallowed destination. Side roads now led nowhere. That great nowhere. Distant horizons were a distraction unless they were in the direct line of his homeward vision. His wanderlust, his coast-road town-hopping scenic-route curiosity, his tireless traveler's quests, his infatuation with the world of hostels and campgrounds and perfect strangers, the allure of the otherworldly grandeur of nature's magnificent wonders, and the ever-revolving cast of fellow travelers, had all been murdered by his homesick heart and replaced with a manic single-minded compulsion to be home. To be repentant, reborn. He was the prodigal returning to the place he could never forsake. Back from the edges of his erratic Plutonic orbit to the humdrum and security of his hometown spindle. If he could have transported himself home with a click of his heels, he would've done so with no second thoughts. For all practical purposes, his journey was over. He was no longer the aspiring travelin' man. No longer the lone-wolf adventurer. No more Jack. No more Woody, at least for now. While he slept, he had been transformed overnight into the homebound boy, the homesick son questing only for those things he already knew, for the non-adventurous mundane routines, for all those things he had once feared and sought to escape in terrified desperation. All that remained was the ordeal of a 3000-mile homestretch trek over mountains and deserts and the perpetual prairies, plains, and pastures and, at journey's end, to the sanctuary of his own lush valley, all of which was a minor detail, a nuisance.

## A Late Night Ride

Matt got off to a rocky start, discovering after a few moments that he had lost his maps or left them at Peter's place. Hours later, after two meager rides, he was all sweaty and still stuck somewhere around Oakland, feeling misdirected and marooned by the last driver, who promised to drop him off at a good spot. He was supposed to be on Interstate 80 East, but none of the signs in the knot of freeways weaving around him mentioned Interstate 80 or gave him a hint of which direction he should be heading on this multi-laned fiasco of cloverleaf on-and-off ramps. For the first time on his journey, he was lost.

When he abandoned all hope of getting a ride that would take him somewhere he wanted to go and he faced the unpleasant possibility of spending the night in the confusion of this inhospitable urban sprawl with the skid-row winos and the junked-out down-and-outers, he asked directions at a nearby convenience store. The attendant was an Asian girl with a heartwarming smile. She was intrigued by Matt's backpack and sleeping bag and expressed a sisterly concern when he told her how far he was going. She gave him a free coke and directed him to the nearest bus station.

"The police might pick you up around here. This is a lousy place for hitchhikers."

Matt was surprised by her perfect English and then ashamed when, upon noticing her glossy, oversized plastic name tag announcing "I'm Susan – Gold Star Employee of the Month," he realized that, despite her features, she was every bit as American as he was.

Matt gave up, swallowed his pride, and purchased a ticket at the Greyhound station in Hayward just as the ruby sun disappeared into the concrete. He found out that he had not even been heading in the right direction. Oops. Wrong Way Corrigan.

A late and lonely bus ride took him to Sacramento.

*In the meditative darkness of the bus, Matt stared at and through the transparency of his reflection on the window and thought of a song his father taught him when he was a child:*

> *Chip chip a little horse*
> *Chip chip again, sir*
> *How many miles to Dublin town?*
> *Four score and ten, sir*
> *Will I be there by candlelight?*

*Yes and back again, sir*
*Chip chip a little horse*
*Chip chip again, sir*

*They sang the song together like a cabaret act, taking turns and singing alternate lines as if they were engaged in a musical conversation. Matt's young heart swelled from the glee and whimsy of the song, and he even noticed a prideful and playful grin on his father's face. He recalled the visible pleasure his father took in watching* Sing Along With Mitch *as the family sat around the TV set and followed the bouncing ball with everyone singing along to sunny tunes such as "Don't Fence Me In" and "I'm Looking Over A Four-Leaf Clover." He missed that father. The one he could hug. The one he could kiss. The one he could love.*

*In later years, Matt's father slipped into that same old satisfied grin, playing peekaboo, singing silly songs, and making funny faces as his adoring grandchildren competed for his attention, chattering away in his direction and climbing into his welcoming lap, and calling him by his self-baptized alter-ego nickname, "Big Daddio," which he had modified in beatnik fashion from Big Daddy, the Burl Ives character in* Cat on a Hot Tin Roof. *Matt smiled at the thought, pleased that his father loved the grandchildren, but was stung by the intangible and tragic sadness of that memory because, somehow, now, it made no sense. Somewhere along the line, the old man had lost all his funny faces and had forgotten all his silly songs.*

He strained to see his father's features in his reflection in the bus window, but all family resemblances had been buried beneath his beard and long hair. The spitting image was long gone. There was no hint of recognition, neither in his own swollen red eyes nor in the reflected window-eyes as they stared to and through each other, either inward and into the prison of his own skull or out of the bus, into the depths of the black soul of the California night. There was a frozen moment when he and his reflection could read each others' minds and they were both thinking the same things: "Who am I?" and "What is wrong with me?" and "Is there any end to this nightmare?"

*This late-night ride to Sacramento reminded Matt of that other lonely and frigid late-night bus ride home from New York City during his first junior year of high school at Bishop Brannan. He was sixteen and had run away from home. He got caught at the Port Authority in Manhattan where an apprehending officer bullied, ridiculed, and threatened him to a state of choked-back tears. They sent him home that night on a miserable three-hour Trailways bus ride from which he could have escaped at any stop if he wasn't so vacant and numbed by an illogical and unexplainable sense of helplessness. Like he had been set adrift in the middle of the ocean, in a row boat with no oars, just hoping to be rescued by some random vessel. He did not then nor did he now understand the whys and hows of the depths of the depression that consumed him. There was no making sense of it or plotting a new course. It was who he was. It was as if his life had reached its end.*

*It had been about four years since that other night, but it felt like several lifetimes ago. Returning home on that other night, that winter's night in New York, on that frigid doomsday bus, so frightened because he didn't recognize the reflection of the stranger staring back at him from the black void of the icy bus window, his heart so sad, so empty, his eyes burning with tears that would not flow, so confused because he didn't understand what was happening to him and how he could have fallen into such a downward spiral, and how just a few months earlier he had been in love and happily dating Helen and all things seemed right in his world and his future looked certain. And now he dwelt in shame because he had been so cruel to Helen. And, for his mother, his running away had caused so much alarm, he had let her down, suffocated her with worry, and he did not think he could face her without erupting into a wail of sobs and tears. He didn't want to do that. He didn't want to feel anything back then. He was already so mixed-up and isolated that he dreaded the dawn of each new day. Most of all he felt just plain pathetic as a failed runaway being sent back home with his tail between his legs. To make matters worse, he was met at the bus station in Schenectady and driven home by Brother Delaney, the principal at Bishop Dunphy High School, who didn't even like him and who had scoffed at him while mocking his hair and humiliating him in the front office in front of the high-school staff and students, sarcastically suggesting that maybe he should apply for admission into the all-girl Our Lady of Grace High School, the sister school to Bishop Dunphey.*

*"With your long hair you could be one of the girls. You could wear a skirt. You'd like that wouldn't you, Master Mahoney. Or should I say Miss Mahoney?" His cold steel Vatican eyes fixed to Matt's unrepentant eyes in a riveting glare. "You are a disgrace to this school. I don't want to see you again until you've cut your hair and are worthy of walking these halls."*

*But on that sad long-ago night, at that late hour, when the easily disgusted Brother picked Matt up among the snowbanks of the Trailways station in Schenectady, he exercised uncharacteristic self-restraint and kept his harsh Catholic judgments and his prefabricated outrage to himself as he delivered Matt's spiritless remains to his parents. And though Matt knew he should have been appreciative for the ride, he resisted any such temptation. He had hoped his mother would meet him at the station so that, if he cried, no one else would witness his failure of tears. He couldn't help but despise the mere presence of Brother Delaney and everything he represented, and this pretense of coming to his rescue, and Matt cursed the fucking asshole and wished he had just minded his own goddamn business.*

## Fucking Gort

He descended from the bus in downtown Sacramento where he was relieved to be free of San Francisco's gravitational field. He tramped through the dormant city at 2 a.m., too determined to be tired, and got a ride clear into the Sierras and over Emigrant Pass and the infamous Donner Pass to Truckee with a thirtyish man going to work the weekend for time-and-a-half OT. His car kept overheating from the strain of the climb, forcing him to pull over onto the roadside and let it cool down a couple of times because there were no service areas open in the middle of the night along that deserted stretch of steep mountain highway. The driver kept saying, "It's the thermostat. I knew I shoulda replaced it. Fuckin' thermostat," and, "If I don't get there in time they'll take off without me and this will all be just one big waste of time," and he kept apologizing to Matt for his language while chugging gulps of Pepto-Bismol from a flamingo-pink bottle. But Matt wasn't upset. At least he knew where he was, he knew he was heading in the right direction, and every mile they grunted up the rugged breast of the mountain brought him one mile closer to a hot home-cooked meal and the warmth of his own bed.

The world around him was wrapped in a cloak of darkness. When the sunlight began lapping and spilling over the high peaks ahead of him, the formless void through which he journeyed was gradually revealed, as if in a slowly developing Polaroid photograph, and all the invisible and shadowy figures of night were magically transformed into an exquisite landscape of precipitous peaks and daunting depths of luscious evergreen valleys and plummeting ravines.

When he got out at Truckee in the first full light of a high-mountains morning, he felt like a long lost Cartwright brother returning home to Pa and Hop Sing and the rest of the cowpokes at the Ponderosa. But no sooner did the old theme song start booming and resonating through the pines and twanging around the ranges inside his head than he got transported to yet another world with a joy ride down the back side of the Sierras and into the desertlands of Reno.

"Yessiree! I've made up for my lost time in whoever-heard-of-Hayward anyway and I can already smell the eggs and bacon in the kitchen and I can hear Eustace gruntin' and snortin' and fartin' at the back door and Mom is calling me awake, 'Matthew Anthony, you're breakfast is still hot. Get down here this instant or you'll be late for work,' and the desert here looks hospitable enough and, well, it should be an easy straight shot over this flat-as-a-pancake state 'cause, hell, there ain't any alternate routes to consider."

So he ambled through Reno and Sparks, confident and excited as all get-out at the prospect of traversing this much-fabled state. He reached an Interstate 80 on-ramp on the east side of Sparks where there were four other dog-faced hitchers brooding among themselves and looking like a sorry lot of refugees at a frontier border crossing.

"Pretty grim, man. Just wastin' my time, swattin' flies. Spent last night here, and it's not looking much better today. But it's still early. I don't know if this is a shitty spot or people just don't pick up hitchhikers around here." He was a thoughtful-looking goateed man with dark baggy eyes and a few wrinkles grooved into his sun-beaten cheeks and was dressed a bit more suave than your typical road rat. He was heading to Denver. His partner was lazing in the grass with his back propped against his pack, listening to a transistor radio and chewing on a plastic straw with the visor of a "Mile High City" cap shading his eyes, which were hidden behind a shiny pair of reflective shades. He had a patient shit-eating grin on his face that reminded Matt of Paul Newman in *Cool Hand Luke*.

"Wake me up when the gorgeous blonde nymphomaniac in the convertible T-Bird gets here."

The other two hitchers carried no gear and were toothpick-thin and dressed in ill-fitting clothes. When Matt asked where they were going, one answered, "As far away from Modesto as possible."

Matt planted himself at the end of the line, but before anybody got even a nibble, a trooper pulled up with lights flashing. A steel-jawed, granite-faced uniformed Goliath in a wide-brimmed trooper hat, impenetrable sunglasses, and a stern Clutch Cargo mouth got out and sauntered toward them with hands robotically attached to his hips. He resembled a humorless Mr. Clean in uniform.

Matt gasped, "Whew! It's a fucking Gort. Klaatu berada nicto." He shuddered when it aimed its mechanical index finger and motioned for them to approach. At close range, Matt could see hundreds of gravity-defying beads of glistening sweat advertising heat across the broad billboard that was his forehead.

"Okay, boys. I'm here to tell you that it is illegal to hitchhike within the city limits and you *are* within the city limits. I could arrest you all right now but I am not going to do that. Here's what you need to do. You need to walk out of town a couple miles, and you'll find a rest area to set down your belongings and stick your thumb out. It is hotter than Satan's toenails out there, but there's water and shade and it's a better spot than where you are right now and nobody will bother you. Now, you'll all be free to leave as soon as you show me some ID."

Everybody started yanking out wallets from their pockets or digging into their backpacks. The officer scrutinized the documents and conducted little quizzes. He just grimaced and shook his head when he examined the photo in Matt's passport. Everyone passed until he got to one of the kids from Modesto.

"I don't got no ID."

"How old are you?"

"Nineteen. Going on twenty."

"What's your date of birth?"

"August 12th."

"What year?"

"Uh, 19, uh, 53"

"What year?"

"Uh, I mean, 52."

"You don't know what year you were born?"

"Hey, I'm just nervous, that's all."

"You're nervous because you're lying to me. I'm going to have to take you in. It's for your own safety. The rest of you can leave. And I mean leave. Now you. Son. You need to get into the back seat of my vehicle. And I don't want any monkey business or I will have to cuff you and I would rather not have to do that. Do you understand?"

Nobody said anything. The kid's face was contorted with the scaredest and sorriest trapped-animal eyes Matt had ever seen. His friend didn't say anything until the trooper left.

"Shit, man. This is a raw deal. His parents are gonna have a basket case. They're gonna blow like Mount Rushmore. They'll kill him if they send him home. I mean absolutely totally whip his ass inside out. This is all my fault. Shoulda got him a fake ID before we left."

"Wasn't your fault. There was nothing you could do. If you tried anything, your ass would be right there with his and that wouldn't have done any good."

"Yeah, but still …"

## A Foul Disorderly Rant

Everybody split up. The Modesto kid walked over to a row of strip-mall shops to make a phone call and figure out how to rescue his shell-shocked friend. The other two hitchers took Gort's advice and dissolved into the heat. Matt walked back into town with freight trains on his mind. One final road-warrior tale to tell. He found the railroad yards and got into a conversation with a couple of sun-ravaged hungover nickel and dimers in moth-eaten t-shirts who were educated as to the behavior of the trains. Through visibly rotten teeth they told him he was in luck because an eastbound freight was getting ready to leave.

"Don't you get on there without any water. Those cars are like ovens. And they don't call it a desert for nothing."

He scrounged through a rusty old trash can and found an acceptably clean half-gallon jug, which he rinsed out and filled with tepid water from a grimy gas station hose. The winos knew a worker in the freight yard and got a semi-official okay for Matt to sneak into an empty boxcar. It was all so well-timed and effortless. Matt could tell that fate was smiling upon him and that his decision had been wise, had made up for his bus ride, and had boosted his travelin' man status back up a few notches. And when the train chugged out of town and into the scorching immensity of Nevada, with him inside his own steel-wheeled suite, he knew that the hobo life was the life for him. But he was perplexed as to how it was that he had strayed so far off the conventional path that led most high-school grads directly into college or into jobs or into relationships or into something, just anything. Most of his friends were pursuing their studies or were recently graduated and starting careers that would define them in life, or they were already in a forever relationship that would lead to marriage and children and mature responsibilities. They were actualizing their potential while he frittered his away. Just a wasted seed. For that he envied them and wished he possessed something certain, a special skill, a true potential that would guide him forward, away from the embarrassment of all his nagging insecurities.

*What happened? Maybe I could have been a professional ballplayer or track star or mathematician. Where did I go wrong? Of all the girls or women in the world who I could possibly be with right now, why am I all alone and with no prospects? And of all the millions of places to be on this wobbly orb at this precise moment, how did I end up here? In this smelly sweat factory of a boxcar? In this sweltering desert? All by myself?*

It worried him that he felt as at home right then and there, all alone, in his dirty hotbox freight car, as he did on his own couch in his own living room. He feared that, after a mere week back home, when the novelty of its comforts had worn off, the anxiety and the fears would find him easy prey once again. In his current confines, Matt wasn't able to expand his mind and ponder his predicament in the context of the grand scheme of things, nor could he take solace in the belief that his journey was anything other than a manifestation of his incompetence as a human being. He was the insignificant speck whose existence was meaningless and whose death would not alter anyone's course in life.

He thought of Helen and tortured himself with thoughts about where he would be right now if he had only walked over to her that night at Biagi's and said, "Hi Helen. It's good to see you." That's all it would have taken to prevent the travesty that befell him and the full course of poisonous emotions that followed. His brain was trapped within a maze of "what ifs." What if he had never sent that break-up note? What if he and Helen had crossed paths on one of his solitary late night pilgrimages through the streets of New Holland? What if he weren't such a coward and had called her on the phone to explain himself or had written her a letter of apology? Why oh why had he left everything to chance? Why did he remain so stubbornly resigned to his helplessness? What was he protecting? What was he afraid of? How could he be so fearful of someone who had always been so kind, so forgiving? Maybe it was just that he felt undeserving. Or was he afraid to confront his shame? At the same time, he realized that the outcome at Biagi's was probably to her benefit, that in his present state of mind he was too much of a mess to be any good to anyone, much less as a trustworthy half of a meaningful adult relationship. So he was only half regretful, believing that Helen had rightfully moved on and had found someone else, someone more mature and more desirable. Someone who had a future and who would never treat her as callously as he had done. Someone with fewer missing puzzle pieces.

But he couldn't help getting bogged down in memories of his prelapsarian world, his Helenic period, through such a haze of years. Memories of walking her home after school with a mountain of her books in his arms, she in her emerald-green Catholic-school blazer and matching pleated skirt. Or strolling homeward after the Friday night dance at Columbian Hall, after the basketball game at Bishop Brannan High, after a movie downtown at the Tryon theater, or after a night of nothing more than just being together, for that was satisfying in and of itself, walking around, hand-in-hand, talking and laughing. They would linger inside each convenient cove of darkness, postponing as long as possible the inevitable end to their night of companionship. Such simple pleasures now seemed so precious and rare, and he hated himself for having grown complacent and taking her for granted and throwing it all by the wayside for no discernible reason. Now, years later, here he was, sacrificing himself for a cause no one believed in, not even himself, and feigning contentment at being the apparently happy tramp on his own erratic path and in his private mansion on wheels, rolling to who knows where, who knows when, and who the hell knows why. And all he could think at that moment was, "I am not the person I wanted to become."

*Maybe*, Matt thought, *there's a parallel universe with a parallel me who never sent that note and where no catastrophic night at Biagi's ever occurred.* A universe where he had played his cards well, had never dropped out of high school and had gone to college like most of his friends, and where he and parallel Helen were still a couple enjoying their break from classes, working summer jobs, saving pocket change for the coming semester, and, in the meantime, still lazily strolling the dark New Holland avenues on the scenic City Hall route home after a movie. He envied parallel Matt's blissful ignorance of earthbound Matt's misfortunes and wished he had parallel Matt's sound judgment and his reverence for the sanctity of a true thing.

He settled into his rumbling nest, soothed by the raw beauty of the barren landscape. He sang, with a cracking not-quite falsetto:

> *I've been to the desert on a horse with no name*
> *It feels good to come in from the rain*
> *In the desert you can remember your name*
> *'Cause there ain't no one for to give you no pain*

Although he liked the song, the lyrics never made much sense, and he wondered if they meant anything at all. And that last line. Was he getting pain? Or was he getting no pain? Sometimes he wondered if anything made any sense or if the true meaning of anything ever made much difference. Maybe everything just means whatever you want it to mean.

His head was swirling from fatigue, so he retreated to the dark end of the car, cushioned the floor with his sleeping bag, and folded up his denim jacket for a pillow. Scrawled in faded magic marker on the gritty boxcar wall in decorative cursive script and embellished with flowers and rainbows within a large heart-shaped design was this:

> *Everyone is a no one*
> *Until they have been a someone*
> *To someone else.*
> *Then they become a someone*
> *Who is part of everyone who had been a no one*
> *Before a someone came into their life.*
> *When I am a no one*
> *I do not recognize a someone else*
> *And I forget about everyone.*
> *When I am a someone*
> *I recognize that there is a someone else*
> *And I remember everyone*
> *And, in them, I see myself.*
> *Gizmo C.*

He tumbled into dreams about roller coasters and redwood trees with houses built into the interwoven tangles of their upper limbs and with stairways and elevators and escalators running inside their industrial strength trunks and of an elaborate network of underground tunnels and compounds inhabited by a lost civilization of people with special powers. The tunnels led to a shortcut portal, which opened into the basement of his old house in New Holland. In the dream he still lived there and he could see his father, back from the dead, playing pool with Mickey Mantle and John Glenn, chalking up his cue with an open-hearted grin and wearing the cap he'd gotten in Ireland shortly before he died. Upon seeing Matt, the old man flashed a welcoming smile and summoned him through a transparency in the basement wall, waving, his book in hand, and calling, "Matthew. Come here, son. I've got something important I have to tell you." Matt reached for the knob to the secret door and was about to pull it open to greet his father, his capital D "Dad," and receive his important message. But then, instead, it became the door to the spider room, and at the first creak of the rusty hinge, a black vacuumous force sucked him through an icy-cold threshold and tossed him free-falling into a dark room thick with daddy-long-legs spiders and matted-up piles of webs that covered him from head to toe and wrapped around his face and seeped into his mouth. He was just about to try to scream and die of a heart attack when the train stopped with a screech and plucked him from his dream, yanking him away from the dreaded spider room and from his father and from his home.

He awoke in a drooly stupor. The boxcar was stifling. He was dizzy and disoriented and basted in sweat and had no idea how long he'd been sleeping. It could have been ten minutes or three hours. The sun was still high. Outside there was nothing but the blazing extra-terrestrial landscape, a grove of pricker bushes and a steep gully beside the tracks. He took a big belt of warm water and then splashed his face to wash away the greasy layer of soot and grime that coated it. His eyes were red and itchy and watery. His t-shirt and long pants, which he was still wearing from the night before, were soaked, and his skin and body hair tingled and itched, and he smelled like a dirty dishrag.

Remembering the trapped infantile discomfort of his train ride in Canada, he decided to cop a squat in the bushes. Seeing that there were no leafy branches and, not having any toilet paper, he got his pair of underwear from his pack and concluded that, under these circumstances, they would do just fine and he would be forgiven this tiny bit of littering.

He chuckled. *Mom was right. It's always good to have a clean pair of underwear. You never know when they may come in handy.*

He didn't really have to go but figured it was better to be safe than sorry. After looking both ways, he hopped out with his underwear and coat in hand. His coat would shield his arms from thorns and prickers as he wormed his way through the thicket to a safe and private shelter.

The perfect spot was a short bustle around a pebbly slide to a clearing hidden from view by the bushes. He squeezed through the undergrowth and, once there, he scrutinized the ground for snakes, dropped his pants to his ankles, and assumed the position. He gave it the old college try but did not get the desired results.

"C'mon now, baby. You can do it," he thought. "I'll thank myself later."

But in the middle of a promising effort, he heard a shocking sound. The train made a clanky noise and was inching forward. "Oh, shit," he muttered and jumped up to run to the train, immediately falling flat because his ankles were shackled by his dropped drawers. As he lumbered through the bushes tugging up his pants, he fell again, but this time he tripped topsy-turvy down to the bottom of the gully, bruising his bare ass and thighs because he hadn't been able to get his pants up. He scrambled up the hill as best he could, but it was too late. The train was slowly shrinking and melting against the steamy horizon.

"Goddamn mother fucking no good son of a bitching cock sucking train!" he shouted at the top of his lungs, waving helplessly from halfway up the hill with his pants halfway down his legs. A sickening sensation soured his stomach. Everything he owned was on the train except the clothes he was wearing and the underwear he still held in his hand. In his pants pockets he had three wrinkled-up dollar bills and sixty-three cents in change, his lucky French rock, a receipt for his bus ticket, a tiny redwood cone for his niece, Sam, and some folded-up pieces of paper with notes and unfinished poems and names and addresses scribbled on them. Dangling ironically around his neck was his St. Christopher medal.

*Oh man. What am I gonna do now? I have no water. No map—not that it would be of any use out here. No sleeping bag. No clothes. And no clue where I am. I've really been left in the lurch this time.*

The angle of his shadow implied that it was noon. He saw nothing but train tracks disappearing into a shimmery terrain. He considered walking back toward Reno, but for all he knew, that could be a fifty-mile walk or more. He reasoned that the tracks would be parallel to the highway but didn't know if they would be to the north or south of it. He didn't want to arbitrarily choose a direction to trudge through the open country in search of civilization. What if he went the wrong way? There was nothing to climb to survey the area for roads. He couldn't hear any traffic. At this point it was all speculation. He didn't know how long he could take the punishment of this one-hundred-plus-degree oven without water or a hat to protect his head. He was already weak with hunger and half-senseless with exhaustion from lack of sleep and didn't know how long he could maintain whatever still remained of his composure. The safest bet would be to follow the tracks eastward and hope for an intersecting road or another train, which he could flag down. Or maybe he would come within sight of the highway and he could start hitching again, as if nothing had happened. He didn't want to spend a night in the desert because he'd been told he might attract rattlesnakes seeking the warmth of his body. Also, according to *Have Gun, Will Travel* and *The Rebel*, his favorite childhood TV westerns, he knew that nighttime desert temperatures could plunge and turn frigid. He didn't know if that was true but wasn't interested in finding out.

He walked on the ties for a while but fell into the involuntary mental habit of counting each tie as he stepped on it. When that became obsessive, he switched to walking on the rails where there was nothing to count except that he continued counting each step anyway, which became just as bothersome, and he kept losing his balance and losing his count. He started trying to recite the lyrics to songs and that became frustrating because he couldn't remember so many of the lyrics to the songs that were popping into his head and because so many of the lyrics he could remember sounded silly without the music.

He fell prey to a diabolical form of psychological self-torture when he fixated on the chorus to "Sugar Sugar" by The Archies as it repeated itself over and over thousands of times, and he couldn't get it out of his head until he landed on a new song and chanted, "War— what is it good for? Absolutely nothing! Say it again," but he couldn't remember any other lyrics to it and got caught in the loop, singing it repeatedly, with every "good God y'all" and every grunt included. In the face of his own abject stupidity and his grand delusions of becoming a man of the road he grew frustrated, angry, and mortally disgusted by his mere existence.

"Shit. I'm no travelin' man. Who am I trying to kid? I'm just a fucking sewer tomato."

The sun's rays stabbed down like daggers, and the top of his head was getting scorched so he put his underwear over his head to block the bombardment of heat, styling it so the waistband went across the hairline on his forehead and the ass part was pulled back over the top of his head and the leg holes hung in back with his ponytail pouring out through one of the legs. The underwear helped but he still felt as though his head was baking in a kiln and that his brain would melt like a lump of wax and dribble out his ear holes and he'd turn into a babbling idiot chasing watery mirages across the hot coals of the indifferent terrain and that the vultures would be first in line to find him after he had collapsed, dehydrated and deluded, and had slipped mercifully into an oblivious unconsciousness.

He lapsed into a foul disorderly rant about lost opportunities, angry recollections, wasted potential, foolish decisions, emasculating encounters, ignorant comments, and all the other ugly things that flailed against the walls of his mind. Girlfriends. Misery thoughts. Excruciating longings. Sex and fear and self-loathing. His pervasive mediocrity. Missed kisses. School. Nuns and priests. College. Wasted time. Track. Baseball. And Helen! Helen! Helen!

He recalled the crushing disappointment and his crestfallen sense of shame for not making the cut for the Little Leagues and the belief that he would never be good enough, never, not for anything, even though he had hit the ball well at tryouts and had fielded better than most of the other kids. How, instead, he was relegated to what they insultingly called the "Grasshopper League," which was not so much a league as it was a designation of failure. Didn't even wear uniforms. And how he let it destroy all his baseball aspirations and big-league fantasies.

*Shit! If I couldn't even make the Little League, how could I have ever expected to make the majors? But I was good, man. Why didn't anyone notice? Those assholes. Those motherfucking assholes. They never even gave me a chance.*

The rails went on and on and on monotonously, dissolving into the vaporous haze of the horizon and his rant eventually evaporated. At times he imagined he was standing still and that the rails moving beneath him were a treadmill because he wasn't making any progress and the barren far-off mountains were as distant as when he began. And at other times he imagined that he was being thrashed about at the far edge of an album that was spinning out of control, way out there on Pluto, and that he was clawing and scratching and making desperate grabs for a hold on the slippery vinyl grooves, trying to make it back across the bleak wasteland of the solar system, accelerating rapidly through meteor showers, comet tails, and asteroid belts to the safe center of the spindle where he could rise and assume a safe stance.

*It's the little decisions that kill us*, Matt thought. *Leaving thirty seconds early just in time to get run over by the car that would have missed you if you had left on time. Considering it, but then not cutting that piece of steak in half and then choking to death because it is just a bit too large. Or, in my case, dying like a bum in the desert for wanting to take that dump that I didn't even need to take.*

Finally, in what felt like the discovery of the century, he came upon a dusty road intersecting the tracks. If he didn't get away from those rails he'd go crazy, so he decided to flip a coin, like either heads or tails, to let him know if he should go north or south. It came up heads, rhymed with dead, so he flipped it two more times until he got tails, rhymed with rails, and so he blundered on in the direction he wanted to go anyway and thought of that last gulp of water he'd taken on the train and wished he'd gulped down just a swallow more and maybe there'd be an improbable phone booth out here on this crossing and this wasn't such a good road and maybe he should stick with the tracks but, no, he'd walk up a ways to see if there's anything up there, maybe a town or even just a house, because he could always come back to the tracks if there weren't and he kept bumbling on and on beneath the jeering sun until he doubted that he had enough strength left to make it back to the tracks even if he did turn around.

He kept trudging and trudging, slower and sloppier and weaker, wilting lower and lower with each staggering step. It was still light out, but the dwindling sun was dropping and he was drooping, and man, this had to have been the longest day of his life, and *Oh, I am so little and so lost,* and by this time he put his denim jacket over his head to shield him from the torture of this heat and his festering thoughts were starting to get all dizzy and fragmented and spastic like they had been cut free of whatever anchor held them in place and kept them from jerking loose and drifting right out of his head and into the sky like cartoon speech balloons and he was pretty worried because he was starting to feel weak and his mind was getting so sloppy and rubbery and it was starting to get dark outside and he knew how fast the sun could get to setting around this time of day and he continued to worry for a good while longer and his legs were feeling all funny and it was weird because he couldn't work up any spit in his mouth and he began to despair for fear that he would die with a parched tongue out there in the killing inferno and he hoped only that he would be dead before the coyotes and buzzards began feasting upon his sun-baked remains and before the insects started crawling into his eyes and nose and ears and mouth or whatever other holes they might find tasty, and he lapsed again, though he had sworn that he would never do so, into a forlorn "Please God" episode in which he promised to be good and to pray and go to church for the rest of his life if he could just get a sign that somebody up there was listening and to please rescue him from such a pathetic and embarrassing death and he recited the "Our Father" and, as he did so, began to confuse "God the Father" with his own father and he forgot which one he was trying to talk with but it hardly mattered because neither one had ever listened to him before but he finished the prayer anyway and began mumbling, "Bless me, Father, for I have sinned," but then he stopped and in a rage that came over him like a seizure, though it produced nothing more than a weak croak squeezed through a sandpaper throat, he stammered aloud,

"No! I refuse to beg any longer. It is not I who have sinned. You have sinned. You have forsaken me. And I will not confess to you or anyone for things I have not done. I refuse to beg forgiveness for sins I have not committed. No! You'll get no penance from me! Now it is I who demand that you beg me for my forgiveness," and his mind lunged into a vengeful fury against the higher powers of his life, screaming at the man inside his head about all the fathers who had refused to show him the signs he deserved and he then recoiled against the absurdity of his rage until he was waging a battle against himself, trying to claim his flagging soul before it left him though he did not know it well enough to recognize it, and screaming into the ruptured emptiness of his sizzling skull, "I love you! I hate you! I'm glad you're dead! I want you back! I refuse to be my father's son. I reject this image. I am not my father's son," and he wept though he had no tears left to cry and when he grew too delirious for further thought and only bitter rasping remained, he gasped, "Fuck you! You son of a bitch!" but wasn't sure if he was cursing at God or at his own father because by that time they had been blended together into one form, one single target for his bleeding contempt, and he started to think it was all useless and he might as well just give up. Or maybe he could lay down on the side of the road, take a nap, or maybe even sleep through the night, and wake up rested and sane again in the morning.

He felt a tremor. Then, before he had a chance to analyze that thought, there came the snap and the slip as, from high above, he heard a banshee cry. There came a silent flapping of immense black wings as an enveloping shadow settled over him. There It was, hovering like a kestrel before the kill. A lethal stench blew into his face as The Watcher in all It's hideous Grim-Reaper majesty charged upon him and flew circles around his cloaked head and then landed before him in an open-winged vampire stance. This time It was a man-sized vulture with a ragged beak and bits of shredded flesh dangling down like worms on a fisherman's hook. It cackled, "The old man's getting to you now, isn't he? It shouldn't surprise you to know that we were well-acquainted, your old man and me. He was a late arrival but such a fine student. He resisted for a while but he just loved that dark glow. Just like you. Who do you think gave it to you? I don't visit just anyone. Consider yourself special. Yes," he hissed. "From a young age. Late at night when you couldn't sleep, I comforted you. And who do you think nursed you through your silent moods and your tantrums? And that note to Helen. Who do you think guided your pen? Each word so precise, so carefully chosen. So fucking perfect. Bullseye. And your father. I welcomed him at his end. Before I lifted him above my head and threw him to the floor, he hugged me and made me promise to watch over you. Yes. Well, you can forget about him. He never gave a fuck about you anyway. You knew that. That's why you hated him. You're just a fucking Judas, which, in my world, is a compliment of the highest order. You and your asinine 'chip chip a little horse' bullshit. He thought you were just a stupid asshole kid and he hated that song and he hated you and your annoying whining and he wished in his heart that you had never even been born." A sudden transfiguration cast the shadow of Matt's father's face upon the face of this dark apparition like a grotesque mask, and when it spoke again, it was with the grim tones of the old man's voice. "But the way you treated Helen at Biagi's that night really made the old man proud. You really socked it to the bitch, didn't you? Put a big smile on his dead face. You exceeded all expectations. A superb performance. You received wonderful reviews. Spittin' image all the way. Just a chip chip off the old block. By the time you came around he was sick of kids. And you can forget about Helen and your stupid fucking parallel universe and all your "grand-scheme-of-things" bullshit. Welcome to your own shit show of an existence and your fuck-up of a life. This is all there is, asshole. I am your grand scheme. And Helen can't even stand the thought of you anymore. You're just a waste of time. You have certainly proven that. You've got a hole in your soul. Sick in the head. Nothing's ever gonna change that. All your sniveling bullshit about wanting to be a good person. To be so fucking full of grace. Never gonna happen. Do you want to know why you don't have a girlfriend? It's because you're an asshole. A gay fucking asshole. And nobody wants an asshole for a boyfriend. And I'm always gonna be right here to remind you of that, watching your every move, just like your old man wanted me to do. Just watching and waiting. Keeping you in line. I'll be that ten-ton anvil shackled to both your ankles. That dark shroud covering your eyes. Fumbling the keys. That's all you've ever done and all you ever will do. And all your stupid little comments. Might as well just rip out your fucking tongue, you ignorant little Henry boy. It's all just stumbling block after stumbling block. With your tail between your legs, crawling back into your pissy little hamster cage. You might as well get it over with once and for all. Because I've got you now. It's just Me and you, you little shit. Cellmates in your own little spider room. And it's never gonna get any better. Welcome to your here-and-now. Have a seat. Get comfortable." It approached with Its yellow teeth and Its leathery wings closing around him in a bleak rapture and Its infra-red gargoyle eyes and Its harping laughter and Its breath like rotting flesh and he was too weak to run and there was nowhere to escape to anyway and that relentless crimson sun had already evaporated beyond the Earth's edge and it had grown so dark and so he gave up and dropped to his knees, defeated and depleted, assessing the carnage, and crying and begging as he disintegrated beneath this predatory demon, "Please! Either kill me or leave me alone," his breath labored, his heart maimed and pounding, and he knelt with his head hanging forward like a disobedient servant at the mercy of his wicked and all-mighty lord and master, conquered by fear, sobbing through shut and trembling eyelids, all red, swollen and crusty, begging "please, please" and afraid to look up at the horrid sight looming above him, or rise for fear of meeting the fate he now welcomed and he waited, wavering from exhaustion, but nothing happened. Waiting for his heart to explode and deliver him the overdue deathblow that would bring an end to this long day's journey. And then his palpitating heart turned eerily calm and unafraid, his breath now steady, but still waiting and even willing to give up the ghost and be taken. He had just convinced himself to fall over onto his side to take a nap, just a quick one, he was so tired, when he heard a clunky rattle—he hadn't heard any noises except for some low-flying jets and the drone of insect sounds ever since the train chugged away from him—and now a growling whirlwind came up behind him and swept him up in a cloud of dust and a blast of heavenly light. Matt looked up into the blinding glare and thought he saw a pair of great white wings spread open above him and that he was being borne away by an angel. Instead, when the dust cleared, there appeared before him, like a gift from the anonymous God, a pickup truck with its high beams illuminating his woeful face. The driver got out and took him by the hand, dropped the tailgate, and helped him climb into the truck bed, which took every remaining bit of his energy, and he sat down among a group of Indians who stared at him but said nothing and when he took his jacket off his head all the little kids started laughing and he didn't know why until he remembered that he was still wearing his underwear over his head and so he started laughing too and tried to speak in a full sentence but all that came out was a single word, "water," spoken as a statement not as a question.

One of the kids offered him a slug from a G. I. Joe canteen half-filled with metallic sun-warmed water that soaked into his cracked lips and tongue like they were dried-out sponges. He could feel the path the water took as it flooded against the roof of his mouth, behind his tongue and down his sandpaper throat like fine wine into the arid gulch of his stomach. He took a second slug and let it fill up his mouth as he swished it around and felt the dry insides of his cheeks saturate and replenish with moisture. His lips were coated with sand, and it must have looked like he was wearing grainy light-brown lipstick. As he laughed at the thought of the sight of himself, he noticed that his cheeks and eyelids hurt.

He was with the Indians for a long time before they reached the Interstate and headed east. It was the strangest ride ever. Nobody spoke the entire time or asked him where he was going or told him where they were going. It was like he wasn't even there. They arrived at a rest area on the Interstate where the Indian driver went over to talk to a man in another car and then came up to Matt and said, "He can give you a ride to Winnemucca." Matt realized that the driver had felt duty-bound to deliver him into safe white hands. No ambulance could have done better. He watched the truck turn back onto the highway and return in the direction it had come. He waved, and the G.I. Joe kid waved back with his canteen swinging in the air like a pendulum. Matt smiled and looked for the North Star in the lovely black sky that was brimming with the twinkling of a million other stars, and he felt content and at peace with the universe.

## Blouse Buttons

Matt's ride to Winnemucca was with a guy named Ed from Prineville, Oregon. He was out on an aimless drive, neglecting all his adult responsibilities back home after having a heated squabble with his wife who had accused him of being unfaithful.

"It was a real bummer. We'd been arguing quite a bit and, well, I wouldn't mind so much if it was all tit for tat. But lately it's all been just tat. We'd be okay if my mother-in-law would keep her nose out of our business. She's a busybody. She called me a scoundrel. Can you believe that? Who even uses that word anymore? She's the one who starts all this accusatin' stuff." He started singing the old song, "Worst person I know. Mother-in-law. Mother-in-law," and then laughed it all off as if it were of no importance.

Ed had a cooler filled with ice-cold soft drinks. Matt found a Coke and savored each frigid swallow and realized, mid-sip, that despite his long history of thinking about suicide and death, he didn't really want to die. He would rather just get unstuck and be happy. He was tired of all the absurd inner turmoil that filled his life with so much melodramatic misery.

"That Indian guy said he found you stumbling around, lost and delirious on a dirt road, and thought I should take you to a hospital. You're pretty lucky. There are some weird desert rats out there. Any crazy old stranger could've picked you up."

"I've been pretty lucky with strangers so far. They've all been perfect strangers."

"If you want, I can take you to an emergency room to get checked out. There must be one in Winnemucca."

"No. I'll be all right. I'm just dehydrated. Got a little too much sun. But this Coke is hitting the spot. Best Coke I've ever had. Without question."

"A *little* too much sun? I'd say that's an understatement. It only takes a few hours before you end up with a barbecued brain. What the hell were you doing there in the first place? Making like Jesus in the desert? He said that where he picked you up you could have wandered for days without finding the interstate."

Matt gave him the whole story, underwear and all. Ed apologized for laughing, saying, "I guess it's okay to laugh since you got out of it okay, except for a sunburned face and some wounded pride. And, who knows, those underwear might have saved your life."

Matt was embarrassed but also somewhat proud as though his brief bout with peril had made him more of a man. "Where are you headed?" he asked.

Ed said, "I'm going to spend the night in Winnemucca at a KOA campground. Then I'm heading back home. My wife told me to get lost. So I did. I ended up in Reno. I thought it would be all winner, winner, chicken dinner. But instead it was all loser, loser, drunken boozer. Blew a week's pay, mighta lost my job. I've done enough damage. It's time to get back home, change my evil ways, and reconciliate. How about you? Where are you going?"

"Going home to New York. Upstate New York."

"Whereabouts upstate?"

"A small town. You probably never heard of it. New Holland."

Ed's eyes lit up. "You're kidding? Yeah—I've heard of New Holland. Ever since I was a kid."

"What do you mean? You have some relatives there?"

"No. When I was a kid I used to be into all the typical bang-bang-shoot-em-up cowboys and Indians stuff. And I had a collection of cap guns. They were toy Colt-45 Six Shooters with imitation ivory handles with designs that made them look authentic. And they were pretty solid for a toy gun. You could put a roll of caps in there and start shooting away, killing all the Indians."

"I'm glad you didn't kill the one that just saved my life."

Ed flinched, realizing he may have put his foot in his mouth. "Sorry, man. I didn't mean it the way it sounded. I dig Indians. I really do. But, anyway, on the guns it said that they were made in New Holland, New York at Regent Enterprises. I always remembered that. And when I was a kid I wanted to go to that toy gun factory. It was my dream when I was, like, seven years old. I drove my parents nuts with that. You woulda thought it was Disneyland or something."

About halfway through the spiel, Matt had anticipated what Ed was getting at. "Well, guess what? I used to work there."

"Where? At Regent Enterprises?"

"Oh yeah. Bet your fuckin' bippy. Last year for about two months. I used to make those guns. I grew up in New Holland and never even knew we had a toy gun factory in town until I got the job. It's weird, man. You living so far away and knowing all about it and me being just down the street my whole life and having no idea. But, believe me, it's no Disneyland. You're lucky you didn't get to visit it when you were a kid. You would have been disillusioned."

"No kidding? What was it like?"

"Let's just say it lived up to its reputation as a sweatshop. I worked in what I called the lava pit for a while. They had huge cauldrons filled with molten metal that we scooped out with heavy-duty ladles and poured into molds, and they didn't give you any protective clothing for your face or your arms, just some gloves because the ladles get so hot. I worked with an old Italian guy who barely spoke English and he thought he had the best job in the world because he got all the overtime he could handle. He always said 'Good pay. Time and a half.' And he'd laugh and scoop out some more of that stuff. He'd been doing it for years. His arms and hands were covered with bizarre-looking scars from where that lava had splattered on him while he was pouring it out. Didn't bother him at all. He was proud of the scars. He had been through some bad times in Italy during the war and had lost everything. He felt privileged to be in America and be able to have a steady job so he could buy his own house and support his family. He had a daughter in college, and you'd think she was Einstein the way he bragged about her. Bragged about all his kids all the time. I admired him because he loved his family and his life and his work and he was always happy. I couldn't even understand half of what he said, but you could tell he was proud of them. And he never complained about anything. I always felt better around him. I bet he was a great father.

"I worked in the spray room, too. That's where those white plastic grips get spray painted with black paint to give them that cool-looking inlay pattern. The ventilation never worked, so the air is permeated with thousands of black molecules and they don't give you a face mask or anything. At the end of the day I'd go home and blow my nose for about a half hour and all kinds of black stuff would come out.

"The other fun thing was glue time. When the guns were assembled, they'd get hung onto these big racks and rolled in to the spray room and get sprayed with a glue coating. Same thing. No ventilation. No masks. You'd get glue in your hair, up your nose, on your eyelids, everywhere. Certain workers always volunteered for that duty. They'd get so high they had to go right home afterward, but they got paid for the full day. Everybody thought it was pretty funny."

Matt worried that he had been monopolizing the conversation. *

"Yeah," said Ed. "It's always freaky when you find out how things are made or where they come from. I saw this report on TV. They had a hidden camera in this meat packing plant and they showed how hot dogs are made. I haven't had one since then. You'd be grossed out by all the crap that goes into one of those things."

They entered Winnemucca and settled at a campground where Ed spread out his sleeping bag across a mattress of grass and Matt curled up in the back seat. He closed his eyes and saw shooting stars streaking across the back of his eyelids. Throughout the uncomfortable headachy night, he obsessed over his now-comic despair of the previous day and was only able to grab start-and-stop snatches of sleep. Just before waking, he had a dream that he was standing naked in knee-deep water in a bay that was filled with battleships and sailboats. Clenched in his right fist was a map of the world, and upon his head he was wearing his life-saving underwear. There were crowds of people everywhere, and he was trying to get everyone's attention to announce a bicycle race back to New Holland. The older people in the crowd were disgusted by his nakedness, which he himself barely noticed. They all stopped their conversations and looked his way. Several of his friends were standing near him, quarreling among themselves about which roads they should take. Everyone had a different, better route to propose and a different, better map to prove it. It was a moment of monumental importance. The multitude of spectators swarmed around him where he stood, still naked, against a thick post with ropes and shackles dangling from it. When there was total silence and all eyes and ears were upon him, he held up his map and declared like a prophet, behind a spontaneously appearing rostrum, "The pyre of the old and stern is liquiding," and then he woke up.

The best feature about the campground was the hot showers. Matt was a new man with his freshly shampooed hair and every pore of his flesh scrubbed clean of all residue. After he finished lathering himself up and rinsing the suds from his body, he turned off the hot water and let the cold water shock his gleaming skin and brace it against the sweltering heat of the coming day. His cheeks were sunburned a bright lobster-red-orange neon hue but his beard had protected much of the rest of his face. His eyes retained his garden-variety red and swollen characteristics, and in the mirror he appeared to be a bloodshot Gabby Hayes impersonator. His ass and thighs were decorated with scrapes and black-and-blue marks, and he still had a nagging infected sore on the heel of his hand from his roadside stumble in Oregon and a headache from the day before when he swore he could hear fluids bubbling around his parboiled brain.

They ate breakfast at a diner on the main strip in town. Ed wasn't all that good looking, but he knew how to sweet talk women and had a semi-irresistible charm that made up for his unspectacular looks. He had his rap down pat. The waitress, a bouncy brunette with one too many blouse buttons undone, was exceptionally considerate when it came to leaning over the table for the viewing pleasure of the customers. She was quite well-assembled. On the soft upper swell of her right breast, beside a name tag pinned to the lapel of her revealing server's uniform, was a tattoo of a rose. She was classic American. If she were a car, she would be a bright red custom-pinstriped '57 Chevy convertible with fuzzy dice hung around the rear view and just enough miles on her chassis to guarantee a reliable ride.

She stretched in front of them to sponge down the crumbs and spills.

"It certainly is a lovely day," Ed said, without any attempt at subtlety.

She smiled and snapped her chewing gum, "I'll take that as a compliment." Ed took a long gander and then looked her right in the eyes and grinned. "And well you should, Rosie."

"You boys aren't from around here, are you?"

"No," Ed said, "Us *men* are just passing through, enjoying the scenery."

When Ed winked at her, Matt didn't know whether he should be embarrassed or proud of his audacity.

After she scribbled down their order and delivered it to the kitchen, Ed said, "Damn, man. Nice begonias." He rolled his eyes upward, sighed rapturously and exhaled, "Succulent, man. Just fucking succulent. My hornometer is in the full-tilt boing position. Goddamn! You know, women are so much more complicated than men. We're simple. All it takes is some cleavage and we turn into horny little puppy dogs. They've got us trained, that's for sure. In some ways that's good. But when it's not good, that's bad. That's when we blow it. And, man, I'm tired of blowing it. I better stop all my reckless gallivanting and get back to my wife before I start thinking with the wrong head."

"I think it's too late for that," Matt said.

"Yeah. I've lost all discipline. I don't even need to be tempted anymore. I need more willpower. When I get home she's gonna want to nail my nuts to a stump and push me over backward. Not much to lose at this point."

"What you need is won't-power," said Matt in an attempt to be clever.

The sparring between Ed and the waitress continued throughout Matt's fluffy French toast and burned sausage patties. No matter what Ed said, Rosie was always one step ahead of him, leaning just enough to keep him aroused and guarantee a generous tip.

"Man," Ed said. "My rap is usually much cooler than this. I gotta admit. I am intimidated. She's way out of my league. I am worshiping at her pedestal." Ed, still calculating from his wrong head, left a note on a paper napkin as a final volley: "Dear Rosie: I apologize for drooling while I was staring down your blouse. Thank you for turning breakfast into a such a great mammary, oops, I mean memory."

Matt laughed and threw down a dollar bill for a tip. Ed vetoed Matt's offering. "Save it, man. You're gonna need that on the road." He handed the dollar back to Matt and replaced it with a fin, designed to exceed Rosie's most optimistic expectations. "She earned it," he said with a crooked smile.

They waited in the car while she read the note and swiveled her head around until she caught Ed giving her a confident sailor's salute. She waved back and, in the classiest and sexiest move Matt had ever seen, stood erect to accentuate the prominence of her breasts, slipped the bill into the soft paradise of her blouse and blew him a kiss.

It was like a scene out of a movie. Ed knew he'd been trumped. "Damn! I would love to be able to wriggle my way into that sweet thing," he moaned, forgetting his previous vow. "Sometimes I just can't help myself." Then, affecting a Maverick-like drawl, he said "But as my pappy told me onest upon a time, 'It's a bad man that brings out the best in a good woman.'"

• "A-fuckin-men to that," quipped Matt, who felt immediately ridiculous for saying it.

They stopped at a gas station and, for thirty-five cents, Matt bought a triple-A map of the western states from the proprietor, Mr. Phil Stewart, who took the time to give them a local history lesson and told them to read the book *Life Among The Piutes: Their Wrongs And Claims* written by Sarah Winnemucca Hopkins, the daughter of the great Indian chief after whom the city was named.

"Yessir, boys. This is the kind of history they don't teach you in school."

The morning was slim pickings when Ed dropped Matt off at the edge of town and drove north on Route 95 toward southeastern Oregon.

"Here you go, buddy. You be careful out there. Get your ass home safe and stay out of the goddamn desert." He handed Matt a five-dollar bill and a jug of ice water. "It'll stay cool for a while. And you, you stay cool, too."

"Thanks a lot, man. Come and visit me in New Holland. I'll take you on a grand tour of the Regent factory. Maybe you can get a job there. Good overtime, and all the glue you can sniff."

"I'm there," he said. And then he wasn't.

## Not Debbie

Matt assumed his hitchhiker's stance at the city limits, gazed down the highway, marveled at the massive outcroppings of pure-white monumental clouds sailing across the sea of the otherwise azure sky, and accepted the challenge. Though he was tempted, he stood his ground and resisted the urge to saunter into the unforgiving waves of heat that filled the arid desert like an invisible dry ocean. Without his pack and bag, he felt naked and vulnerable. He had no identification other than his own memory. His wallet, which contained souvenirs from England, some Cadbury candy bar wrappers, wise sayings torn from the side panels of English matchboxes, cardboard tickets from the London underground, and a frayed piece of Egyptian paper currency just in case he somehow made it there, was now history. His passport, with his comically outdated photograph, was also gone.

*That's okay. That's not who I am anymore anyway.*

Also gone was his notebook with all his would-be poetic tidbits, his collection of curious words, his new fairy tale, the journal he'd kept faithfully all summer containing the names and addresses of all the friends he'd made along the road, the keepsakes and postcards tucked between the notebook's pages, the eucalyptus and bay leaves and a handful of redwood cones, and the remaining wishbones he had been saving for special occasions such as this. And the prayer card that promised that he would never face his perils all alone. And, alas, even his trusty old Wham-O Frisbee. Everything was gone, unintentionally bequeathed to whichever toothless hobo or waylaid hippie next set up house in that dusty old boxcar. But he was neither scared nor worried, despite being broke, stranded, and nearly a continent away from home. He knew that all he had to do was keep on sticking out his thumb, and he would make it home just as quickly as if he hadn't lost anything. And if he so chose, he was confident that he could continue hitching for the rest of his days with no money or home or worldly possessions. In either case, he would be fine. Everything would work itself out. In a strange way, by losing everything, he had gained something new. He felt freer than ever before, as if someone had somehow adjusted down the intensity knob to the gravity of his personal burdens. As if, had he put his mind to it, he could have flown home.

He thought his prayers had been answered when, after a few minutes, a car swung onto the shoulder ahead of him. Just as he reached for the back door handle, the driver gunned his engine and screeched away, spewing pebbles and dust, as a peal of raucous laughter through the open windows proclaimed their practical joke a rip-roaring success. It was nearly evening before his real ride arrived and he slid his sweaty self into the front seat of an air-conditioned Buick Skylark with a woman named Deborah—"Not Debbie," she instructed—who was returning home to Salt Lake City. The right side of her face was discolored by a purplish-blue blemish. He couldn't tell if it was a severe sunburn, maybe a rash, or perhaps even a birthmark.

Deborah was distant. Matt tried putting his hitchhiker's small talk skills to use and ease the taut non-conversational space between them, but given his historic insecurity with women, he found it challenging to think of anything clever or compelling to say to get the ball rolling. Everything sounded so lame. He tried telling her about John Muir, but she was non-responsive, so he busied himself by studying the surroundings, looking for signs of wildlife, but detecting nothing much more than the inquisitive heads of little critters popping up from their tunnels like furry periscopes.

"Are they prairie dogs?"

She raised her shoulders but said nothing.

"I was surprised," he said. "I thought Nevada was supposed to be flat, but it's actually a series of mountain ranges, one after the other." He was using his new map as a conversational aid.

"The one we're climbing now is Emigrant Pass. 6114 feet. That's funny. I just went over an Emigrant Pass in California too."

"Oh, really? She was mildly piqued within a rigid and businesslike shell.

"Yeah. And the next one is Pequop Summit. That one's 6967 feet high. That's the highest one. But it's about a hundred miles away. Almost to Utah."

"That's interesting."

"Yeah. And these mountains. I've never seen these kinds of mountains before. They're nothing like the Canadian Rockies or the Sierras or the Adirondacks. That's where I'm from. The Adirondacks. I'm used to mountains that have lots of trees and lakes where you go camping and swimming. These are more like lunar mountains or something. This is a whole 'nother world."

"That's true."

Just as he was giving up for fear of being a nuisance, Deborah mercifully eased the pressure, telling him that she worked for the phone company in Salt Lake City and was returning home after visiting her father in Carson City, where he worked as a dealer in a casino. Her parents separated when she was a teenager and she hadn't seen much of him until recently.

"He was getting older and started thinking about his life, and out of the blue he called me one day and said he wanted to see me. I was indifferent. Didn't care one way or the other. I had no feelings left. And part of me didn't want to make it too easy for him. After all, he just vanished one day with some new girlfriend and started up a new life of his own that didn't include me. So why should I include him? He never called or anything, and then, without warning, after about ten years, I'm supposed to be all forgiving and I-love-you-daddy-daddy just because he finally grew a conscience and decided he wanted to see me? He could tell that I didn't care whether I saw him or not. Well, he started crying on the phone and apologizing to me for not being a good father and started telling me that he always loved me and he wouldn't bother me again if I didn't want to see him. It made me feel good to hear him cry. I actually smiled and almost laughed out loud. I know that's terrible. I was glad he was hurt. But then something changed inside me, and I wanted to see him, but I didn't want to get duped into loving him only to have him disappear again. So I got his phone number and told him that I'd think about it. That was mean of me, I know, but I couldn't help it. I wanted him to have to suffer like I did. I was gonna wait two weeks, make him sweat and worry for a while. I figured that I had waited for years and years. A couple weeks wouldn't kill him. Well, after a week I called him and we got together, and it was great. I'd forgotten what a great guy he was. It was hard to start calling him "Dad" again, but I did. I found out that my mother had been lying to me about him, that he *did* call and she always told him that I didn't want to talk to him or see him anymore, and he believed her. He even took her back to court to try to see me when I was a teenager, and she never told me. After a while he gave up. He said there was a court order, and he'd be arrested if he tried to contact me. He even showed me his court file. Can you believe that? He still had the fucking file! I had to rethink my history. I realized that it wasn't his fault. All that anger for nothing. Even then, I had gotten so used to blaming him for everything that I didn't want to forgive him too soon. But then I decided to start fresh and leave the past alone, and things have worked out good so far. Now my mother. That's a different story. I was very p.o.'d at her. I still can't believe that she did that to him—and to me!"

Matt, who was tiring of the dead-father sympathy ploy, nonetheless spoke of the old man and the assortment of regrets he'd lived with since his death. Deborah said, "We can't change the facts of our life. We can only accept them and adjust to them. Besides, most of what we think are facts are just bad theories. I don't think anybody ever knows what's really going on, but nobody ever wants to admit it. It's all screwed up. You think you know what you think you know, but you don't ever really know what you think you know. I wasted a lot of time and energy blaming my father for everything that was wrong in my life and everything I thought he had done. Years of theories down the drain. A lot of misdirected anger. My whole fucking life has been one big lie. Still, I figured if he had been a more together person, I wouldn't have had so many problems of my own. But I found out that he still blames his father for his problems, and, who knows, his father probably blamed his father, too. It's got to stop somewhere or else the blame just keeps going back further and further until we all might just as well pin everything on that idiot, Adam. 'Cause he must've started this ridiculous blame game. Who knows why things happen? And why does everything always have to be someone's fault? I realized that there comes a time when you've got to stand on your own two feet and stop blaming everybody else for your own misfortunes."

Matt said, "Does that include nuns?" He was only half-kidding.

The evening sky was all shimmery and rosy as they approached Silver Zone Pass and "Peaceful Easy Feeling" by The Eagles came on the radio, with the opening lines:

> *I like the way your sparkling earrings lay*
> *Against your skin so brown*
> *And I want to sleep with you in the desert tonight*
> *With a billion stars all around*

Deborah looked out at the stark moonscape and said, "I've never slept in the desert. Have you?" She gave him an almost grin and an off-center glance, eyes hidden behind shades that were no longer necessary.

"No. I never have, either. Almost had to last night." He'd already told her about his train-hopping fiasco and he winced when she told him that his dalliance with death was a "cute" story.

"I wonder what it would be like?" Even Matt could hear the invitation in her voice. It did not give him a peaceful or easy feeling.

"I don't know. I was told there are a lot of snakes out there." (*Damn*, he thought. *What a fucking stupid thing to say. What the hell is wrong with me?*)

"Oh, yeah. I guess that could be dangerous."

Deborah's comment had taken him by surprise and his mind, as usual, pursued the path of most resistance as he was overtaken by the curse of obsessive introspection. Was it a thinly disguised suggestion or was it just a casual passing comment? Either way, Matt worried that his dismissive response might have sounded rude and off-putting, but he couldn't think of anything else to say on such short notice. He wondered whether his knee-jerk brush-off would instead have been a warm welcome if she didn't have the facial blemish. Might he have been receptive to her suggestion if she was more conventionally attractive, or was it simply his inordinate fear of the female touch that triggered his response? Either reason was equally sad and frustrating for the "New Matt" who was desperate to transform his "Old Matt" stumbling blocks into stepping stones. And as the moment passed and the song ended, his inarticulate heart sank, and he was overcome by an unbearable impulse to run his hand across her shoulder and to place his palm upon her face, to lightly massage her blemish with his fingertips and kiss her gently on her mottled cheek and tell her she was beautiful.

It was all so confusing. The desire and the fear. The strait jacket of guilt-ridden shame that immobilized him whenever he was stirred by romantic longings. Crazy, frantic thoughts always ricocheting inside his skull, unable to break free. No way to silence or control them. Fucking nuns and priests! And the goddamn Virgin Mary! Those paragons of sexless virtue! That unassailable pedestal! It ruined everything! Always! Too pure? Too perfect? It was as if he thought that, by fumbling each and every romantic opportunity with each and every object of his affection, he was maintaining a virtuous moral standard, he was remodeling his heavenly home, and that he must resist all temptation and he must honor all the Virgin Marys of the world, because a transgression against any one of them is a transgression against all of them and against the Holy Mother herself, and he must never, never, never waiver, or take such an indecent liberty until and unless he found "the one" who was divinely preordained to welcome his advances. "The One." You never knew where or when she might pop up. But when it came down to it, he could not deny that he was just another shallow guy tracking the feminine scent and obeying his ancient Neanderthal instincts, looking for a pretty package, and that the only thing holding him back was not morality but fear. He was no abstaining saint. No moral standard bearer. It was all just fear, plain and simple. He was petrified by the prospect of making that first move and by the paralyzing specter of rejection. He was no more chivalrous or virtuous than every other run-of-the-mill jackass who wanted to get lucky, and he was jealous that those other jackasses were not thwarted by the same inhibitions that always left him floundering forever in a frustrated loop.

He had been so preoccupied with wanting to open up Carla's pretty package—and consumed by the frustration of his failed pursuit—that he had no time for others and would condescendingly repel anyone who drew too near to his emotional hideaway. How could he whine so much about his own spurned affections when he spurned others with the same indifference, with no remorse or second thoughts? He brushed them off like pests. He didn't want to be mean. He just didn't have time to worry about anyone else's feelings. He was too busy worrying about his own. And though it went against the grain of how he liked to think of himself, he had to admit that he had a cruel streak and an arrogance that shielded him from recognizing his own insensitivity. He was hardly conscious of it except when he stopped wallowing in self-pity long enough to get his head out of its dark place and think about other people's feelings for a change.

And the thought of making that huge first move was too daunting to imagine. He didn't know how to say the things that needed to be said or how to deal with the big pricker bush of fearful and jealous thoughts that always made relationships regrettable and strangled all hope of anything promising. Part of it was that he could not fathom how anyone would want him in "that" way. How could he ever be anyone else's "the one" when there were so many other more desirable guys everywhere he looked. Smarter. Funnier. Kinder. Less self-absorbed. Not so gloomy. More mature. Guys who had something going for them, like jobs and money and cars, for a start. How could anyone settle for him, a scrawny Grasshopper League leftover pick who couldn't make the cut, when there is such a full roster of other masculine top-shelf Big League contenders to choose from? It was absurd for him to think he could be the missing piece in anyone else's puzzle. Thus, he was always suspicious of any girl who drew near, as if it were just a set up or an emotional con game or a self-serving ulterior motive where he would be the unwitting fall guy. There had been a couple of those during his post-Helen days at Henderson High. But it was also that he didn't want to waste his time on someone he wasn't abidingly interested in, someone who wasn't "the one." Or it was a distraction from his single-minded full-time-job obsession for Carla, from which he must not stray for fear of losing her, even though it had long since been obvious that she was bereft of any mutual intimate desires and that he was a total flop when it came to igniting even a faint glimmer of passion within her. Even knowing all that, he still would not take his eye off the prize, as if he knew he couldn't have her but wanted to watch her closely, like a guard dog, to guarantee that no one else could have her, either.

He figured most guys were no more refined than dogs, sniffing after whatever scent wafted near them and oblivious to all else. Maybe he would be better off as a dog. This journey had taught him that people love dogs more than they love other people. And even the homeliest of dogs gets to sniff at the prettiest of girls, who welcome their lapping tongues face-first with open arms and a warm lap. Dogs are automatically lovable and don't have to strive to prove their worthiness for the companionship they so crave. *Lucky dogs*, Matt thought, questioning whether it was pathetic or just funny that he was so hard up as to be jealous of dogs.

For whatever it was worth, he felt, well, like an asshole, for being just another asshole in Deborah's lifelong gauntlet of assholes who failed to see beyond a colorful patch of skin which, when viewed in a higher context, was actually a unique and beautiful adornment. And what gave him the right to judge others? Who the fuck did he think he was? He wished he could rewind time and accept her challenge to a night of sleeping in the desert, together, with a billion stars all around. But it was too late. He had, alas, not been the perfect stranger. He had failed that test and would always remember his failure as just more proof that he was not a good person and did not deserve the selfless hospitality that had been lavished upon him all summer long. And that he was still just a child adrift in an adult universe. Deborah had graced him with safe passage through an inhospitable desert and he had returned her grace with a harsh and shallow judgment.

Matt's imaginings were enjoying full reign, now supposing that Deborah, if she was anything like him, was busy reprimanding herself for making such a forward suggestion, only to be shot down in grand fashion. Maybe she fell for his silly act and thought of him as the world-wise travelin' man he so wanted to be, and with this rejection she was probably slipping into a depressing rut of self-invalidation, believing she should have kept her stupid mouth shut.

Then again, maybe she was nothing like him, and he was just imagining all the uncertainties and possiblies and probablies. Maybe she hadn't meant anything by her comment, and even if she did, maybe she had been toughened as a marked child and could withstand such slights with no self-invalidating aftereffects. After all, look at him. It's not like he's a big catch. Or maybe she was toying with him. Maybe he's the one who should feel foolish for making such a big deal over something that may have been an inadvertent comment spoken out of boredom, not attraction. He knew that he would never be able to make up his mind whether it was all just in his head or if she really was flirting with him. And maybe these are the exact kinds of thoughts that, for Matt, turned a simple interaction with a woman into such a complicated, ambiguous, and emotionally muddled-up ordeal.

It was always the uncertainty among possibilities, the never-ending parade of maybes, that drove Matt to distraction, turned him into "Weird Matt," got his mind running in circles, pushed him away from companionship, and fed such tantalizing ideas to the voices that taunted him at night. He grew quiet. He was afraid, now, to look at Deborah. Then, as he began to get mired in unpleasant thoughts, he felt The Watcher seep into the front seat through the air vents, and for a moment he readied himself for the inevitable assault. But he steadied his spirit and said to himself, *You get the fuck out of this car, you freak*, and, surprisingly enough, everything was fine.

Deborah stopped at a casino in Wendover on the Nevada-Utah border, which, in addition to being the line between the gambling and the non-gambling worlds, was also where Pacific Time became

Mountain Time. Deborah stayed long enough to go to the bathroom and then sacrifice several buck's worth of quarters to the clanging and clinking chaos and the multicolored madness of the slot goddess. They lost an hour when they entered Utah and began their nighttime trek across the Great Salt Lake Desert.

Deborah said, "It's too bad you're not getting to cross the salts during the daytime. It's amazing, with the mountains in the distance and the desert sands, so soft and white and, like you said before, lunar looking." Matt was flattered that she had remembered his comment from several hours earlier.

Matt now saw Deborah with different eyes. The blemishes weren't nearly as pronounced as they appeared at first sight. He had blown it all out of proportion. Or maybe he had gotten used to them or stopped caring because he recognized his reaction as evidence of a certain hypocrisy. Who knows? Maybe it's all just an illusion. What difference should it make, anyway? Her sly smile and wise-cracking attitude was refreshing, and when he surveyed her full upright stature as they strolled the casino, he saw that she had a proud self-assured womanly stride that grew more enticing with each step she took. Why couldn't he muscle up the courage to take the initiative and reopen the dialogue rather than wait for the unlikely possibility that she would do so and risk rejection a second time? He thought of opening lines, like, "You know, I think the Salt Lake Desert is safer than the Nevada Desert. Doesn't have so many snakes because of the salt." Or, "It would be nice to stop and look at the sky for a while. I bet we would see some shooting stars." Something only half-innocent and not too forward. Nothing that would risk getting himself ejected if she objected to the remark. But he dared not.

Suddenly it all seemed so simple. He could choose to make her "the one" and then nothing else would matter. Once somebody becomes "the one," she is automatically forever beautiful and all else falls in place. To hell with fate.

*The trick to finding "the one,"* he decided, with logic that made perfect sense to him at the time, *is to successfully deem her to be so before anything can destroy the illusion of romantic predestination, before your petty judgments can sour the experience, and to then allow the illusion to become your unquestionable reality. Then it's "Presto!" And then, with a magical flick of the wand to erase your own memory of having willed it to be so and be left with just the enchantment of your prefabricated love-at-first sight creation.*

*But then again,* he thought, *It's got to be mutual. You're screwed if it's not mutual.*

Matt said nothing, however, and Deborah offered no second chance, no offer of redemption for his sin of superficiality. No last minute, "It's late. Why don't you stay at my place for the night?" It was past midnight when she dropped him off on the interstate on the west side of Salt Lake City. She said, "Goodbye" and "Good luck" and left it at that, she to return home to the sanctuary of her cozy bed, he to the sentence of a cold night of remorse on the side of a lonesome far-away road.

## Circular and Synchronized

As soon as Deborah's taillights vanished, Matt launched into a severe "What a fuckin' asshole I am" session, stomping his feet and pounding his fists against his thighs. "Could've been the fantasy ride. I'm such a goddamn Waldo." The session was cut short when he got a ride from a kid who brought him halfway across town. As he exited the car, he resumed the interrupted session upon noticing that, during the ten-minute inconsequential ride, he had spilled his jug of water all over his denim coat. It was cold out, and he didn't want to spend the night freezing in a wet coat on the side of a desolate road in the mountains.

He soon got a ride with another local, Chris Johnson, who gave him a heavy down coat when he explained his dilemma. Chris said that even though it was summer, "you could still freeze your balls off in the canyon" where he was dropping Matt off, and that he would need a good coat to get through the night.

"Here. Take it," he insisted. "I keep it in the trunk for emergencies. I won't need it for a while." Matt took the down coat and wrote Chris's name and address on a piece of scrap paper and promised to send the coat back as soon as he got home. He felt blessed by such good fortune and thought that if he had somehow lost his pants he would then find a brand-new pair hanging on the next tree. Chris said, "I'm sorry I can't take you any farther. There's not a lot of traffic out here at night. You might be stuck for a while."

"That's okay. I'm used to being stuck. I'll get a ride." Then, as Chris was getting ready to leave, Matt bubbled over with a sense of thanks and said in all seriousness for the first and only time in his life, "Keep on truckin'," which was meant to sound cool but came out clumsy, so he immediately felt foolish. Chris smiled and pulled away.

Matt was somewhere outside Salt Lake City in the belly of some nameless canyon, which felt like part of a misplaced arctic econiche. Even with the down coat, he was freezing. He estimated that it was about 2 a.m. and that he'd freeze for a few more hours before thawing out in the buttery glow of the morning sun. He ran in place, did jumping jacks, and, in an attempt to conjure up the tropical essence of the state of Florida, he did the Ratso Rizzo dance from *Midnight Cowboy*, chanting "Orange juice, orange juice, orange juice." He warmed his hands in his armpits to try to loosen up his fingers enough to play the hand flute and realized upon bringing his cupped hands to his face that he was in dire need of a shower. He whistled out tunes as best he could through his cold, dry lips and hands, emitting sketchy renditions of "The Flight of the Bumble Bee," "The Rocky and Bullwinkle Theme," "The Star-Spangled Banner," and, as a grand finale, "In A Gadda Da Vida."

It was still cold and dark when he got a ride in a steamy-windowed pickup truck with a coffee-sucking fisherman who brought him to Coalville. He emerged onto the highway, his body and mind so depleted, so otherworldly, as the aura of pure daylight glows like a halo over the mountains, glowing brash and brilliant like the trumpets of dawn, and it is suddenly morning. And as the world tints to gold and the still-chilled air invigorates his face to new life, he thinks about the rosy-fingered dawn and the heroic Grecian sky, and it feels like the first ever morning. His exhaustion transports him to an exalted and nearly hallucinatory state of wonder. A voice from somewhere whispers, "Beauty is all around." There are anthems and thin hymns in the urgent flapping of geese in chevron flight above him, and the very soul of nature is chattering and chirping, saturating his alerted senses as he stands childlike and teary-eyed on the pitted shoulder of the road in one of those dazzling transformational trances that imprints itself upon him forever and sweeps him up into the poetry of life and light and flight and brisk morning breezes. He is captured within the divine splendor of a single simple moment, struck tender by the miracle of sight and the godliness of light, his wandering form rooted in the fairy tale spell of morning magic, so infused with the intangible and vibrant spirit of the wildness around him until a growl buzz-saws into his peeled senses and plucks him from his trance.

The air was playing tricks with sounds, and he could hear the echo of mechanical clugs and rumbles long before they got close enough for him to see a VW bus rounding a wide bend in the vaporous blue-green distance, looking so laughably miniscule and out of place as, in slow-motion, it climbed the swell of the mountain on this memorable morning.

### Rules of Thumb

It was only natural that the VW pulled over and a side door slid open and hailed him inward. He crossed his fingers when he saw the Wisconsin plates. The driver turned back and asked, "Where you goin'?"

"I'm goin' all the way to New York. How about you?"

"You're in luck. We're goin' all the way to Milwaukee, but we'll have to drop you off in Omaha because we've gotta make a pit stop there for a day or so and see some relatives. But we're on a mad dash to get home and are hoping you could help out with the driving."

"Fine. Great. No problem." Omaha had never before sounded so close to home. He'd be putting some miles in the bank on this one.

"Where's your stuff?" they asked. Matt laughed and told them it was a long story and they laughed back and said that they had plenty of time for long stories, so they all got to know each other through their long stories as they motored among the highlands of the spectacular Utah wilderness.

Matt's senses had been so immersed in hitching for so long that he now viewed all of life through a hitchhiker's lens. Life on the highway was the perfect metaphor for all of life's experiences, which, for him, created a coherent framework on which to hang all of his chaotic thoughts and forge them into something useful and orderly.

He had begun devising a set of principles, which he thought he might someday assemble into a book titled, *Rules of Thumb: A Journey Through the Land of Perfect Strangers*. Each rule would be derived from a specific hitchhiking experience and would provide practical insights that could be applied to everyone's everyday existence. A credo of mottos, metaphors, and morals, like a modern day "Aesop's Fables." Cautionary tales, parables, words of wisdom, hard luck stories, and songs of praise. Pithy rubber-meets-the-road kind of stuff. And it would also, he hoped, be an inspiring catechism, for his had been a sacred pursuit, blessed from the onset by his whole holy host of perfect strangers who had delivered him from evil along his pilgrim's path. Hallelujah and Amen!

He pondered his prospects and thanked his friend Vinny for teaching him the word "epiphany," for it was certainly through such experiences that his stream of realizations had sprung, fully born, in the withery nesting grounds of his thoughts. Single flashes of simple but elusive brilliance that are born of the ether and illuminated for but a mere second before they fade back into nothingness. A lost Eureka! As if a lamp in a pitch-black room had been switched on and then immediately off again, a literal blink of the eye, and you are left trying to recreate the ghostly afterimages of everything you had seen in that unexpected split second of radiance.

Hitchhiking had been Matt's liberation from the turmoil that haunted his thoughts with frightening voices, and it had also been his means of at least a modicum of salvation and self-realization in his Holy Grail quest for some semblance of inner peace. Only then, with his feet planted firmly on the pebbled shoulder of an open road and his thumb protruding like a banner from an otherwise clenched fist, did he feel like there was a place for him anywhere in this world. Only then would his burdens lift from his shoulders to be replaced with the uncomplicated sense of being fully present in the still waters of the everlasting now. A true transformation.

He now knew with certainty that if he holds his thumb out long enough, he will always eventually get a ride. And each car that passes him by brings him one car closer to the one that will stop and pick him up. And each ride, no matter how insignificant, brings him that much nearer to his destination. Little by little. Ride by ride. Through all of life's detours and dead ends, all the pitfalls and pot holes, radar traps, traffic jams, and crash sites that litter the way forward and increase your vigilance. Just soldier on and keep your thumb out, man, because your next perfect stranger is just around the bend and will be here sooner rather than later and you don't want to miss it. No. You don't want to miss any of it. You want your life to be one continuous non-stop run-on sentence with no commas and no periods. And there is something forever memorable about every perfect stranger who graces your path. And every such person has within them an inspirational story, and every life, no matter how quietly lived, is its own epic novel. No matter how sheltered and unobtrusive and unfulfilled that life may be, it is still a grand tale and through it you will find leads and clues to your own salvation and to the core and soul of all humanity. For we are each a cog in the wheel of the great everywhere and the great nowhere and in our existence as human beings we are each and all a part of the great everyone. Every one of us is every one of us and our hearts all beat as one heart and, as one, we will not face our perils alone.

Every place he had been had been stunning in its own right and had left its own indelible imprint upon him and had enriched his life beyond measure. Nature had accommodated him, had rewarded him, had punished him and tutored him with some hard-earned lessons. All for his own betterment. And he had been brave enough to face it without apprehension and fear or, at times, in spite of it. It taught him to watch the limits, watch the signs, stay between the solid lines, and, most of all, to be respectful, be reverent, and know the boundaries and always watch out for the bears, and when you're running on too little sleep and too little food, plummeting down a steep, narrow, curvy mountain road in a creaky rig with a buggy-eyed demon at the wheel and the brakes and gears are all grinding and wearing down at the same time, and every needle is in the red, just hold on tight, calculate your spin, and don't give up. And no matter how hard it rains, it's always gonna stop, and your clothes are always gonna dry, and the cold night is always gonna end, and a new sun is always gonna rise and warm the goosebumps from your flesh, and, if you're hungry, nine times out of ten, the stranger with the single sandwich is always gonna give you half, and...

Matt's brain was still brimming with a steady flow of "always gonna" maxims and more immutable truths than he could keep up with when the van swung over and reminded him of one more: a driver with a bountiful heart and room to spare is always gonna pick up more hitchhikers. And so, at Little America, Wyoming, they were joined by two Cleveland-bound guys, Bruce and Jason, who rejoiced to learn that, with this ride, Wyoming and Nebraska would soon be sinking into the western horizon.

"The mare the morrier," thought Matt.

## Ancient Teenaged Vows and Puppy-Dog Piss Squiggles

Everyone in the van was ragged, worn down, and eager for home, and the remaining miles were nothing more than an unavoidable aggravation. Their eyes were set only on the eastward horizon. Unified in purpose, they holstered their weary thumbs and obeyed the call of the same homebound desire. They took turns driving and sleeping, and they stopped only when necessary. The only time Matt saw any of the passing landscape was when he was driving. The rest of the time was spent dozing off or shooting the shit in the windowless back of the van, and he couldn't care less about the scenery.

While on his trek across Canada, he and nearly all of his fellow westward travelers were fervently pursuing adventures like pioneers in unexplored terrain. They were in the everlasting now, the timeless present, inhabited by a relentless energy. Willing to detour hundreds of extra miles for the promise of free pancakes. It was a quest for discovery. But now, heading back east, everyone was tired and living in their soon-to-be-back-home fantasies, inhibited by a travel-ravaged fatigue. Their journeys were now behind them and their futures were beckoning them home. Time was returning. The eastward trek was an impatient homeward and homesick pursuit back to their known universe, their home planet. It was not an adventure. It was an obligation.

One of the Cleveland duo, Bruce, asked of no one in particular, "What are you going to do after you get back home?"

Matt said, "Before I even get home, I'm going to stop downtown at Brown's record store and buy 'Alone Again, Naturally'. I've been hearing that song all summer. Then, when I get home, I'm going to mail this coat back to its owner in Salt Lake City and ask my mother to make some eggplant parmesan and one of her homemade cream pies with fresh strawberries and lots of whipped cream. Then I'm gonna sleep in my own bed. Then I'm gonna get a job and start saving up for a trip to Ireland."

Natalie said, "I'm going to get all my pictures of Yosemite and the rest of the trip developed and put them together in a scrapbook with all the brochures and post cards and souvenirs we've collected, and I'll write stories about each place and what we did and all the interesting people we met along the way so we don't forget. And I'm going to visit my Granny who lives up in Appleton. I haven't seen her for a long time, and for some reason I've been thinking about her this whole vacation. We used to be so close and I really miss her a lot. She's all alone now since my Gee Pa died." Matt's grandparents had all died before he was born or when he was still in diapers, and he always envied anyone who still had their grandparents.

Steve said, "I've got to make sure I've taken care of everything I need to do to start grad school. I've got a bachelor's in poly sci, and that's pretty useless. I've been accepted, and if I don't pay tuition soon, they'll drop me. Classes start in two weeks and I'm dreading it. But anyway, I've got to finish working on the house while I've still got time. Painting, wallpapering, stuff like that is the limit of my handyman talents."

Jason, the other Cleveland guy, said, "Man, that's easy. I'm not doin' nuthin' but stay home, get high and hang out with my friends, go to concerts, and try to stay out of trouble. 'Course I'll have to find a job to support myself. Or maybe I'll get back into dealing pot. That's easy money but, man, I'd be screwed if I get caught again. The first time they blowed it off 'cause I didn't have that much and it was my first offense. But they won't blow it off again."

Everyone looked at Bruce, who had posed the question. "Well, what about you?" Matt figured he would have an elaborate prepared-in-advance scheme to impress them all with.

"I don't have the slightest clue. I wish I did. I was hoping you guys would give me some ideas. But right now I can't see beyond getting back home."

The van hurtled all day on Interstate 80 through the Spin-and-Marty hills and open ranges of the Big Sky country like a rocket ship being propelled through space and preparing for re-entry back into Earth's atmosphere. For a while, the only radio station with good reception played country music and gave agricultural reports about corn and soy beans and something Matt had never heard of before: hog futures. Matt said, "The only future hogs have is called bacon." Jason said, "Yeah. They're achin' to be bacon." And then, somewhere around Rawlins, Wyoming when they passed a sign that read "Continental Divide," Jason quipped, "Hey—does that mean it's all downhill from here?"

Matt started a list of things he wanted to do when he got home: Read John Muir bio, Louis Riel, send back jacket, go to Howe Caverns with nieces and nephews, hike Adirondack trail with Tates, climb Mt. Marcy, finish writing book of poems, read Lao Tzu, learn to meditate, contemplate my future. Then, at the bottom of the list, in bold letters: "CONTACT HELEN."

Helen and Matt had once made a pact that, no matter what happened, they would always remain friends. Would she even remember that ancient teenaged vow, and if she did, would she still honor it, given the fact that he had ripped it to shreds with his dismissive behavior? He pictured her as he remembered her best, wearing a green and white polka-dotted skirt and a simple plain white blouse. She looked so beautiful that night. *If something is true once*, he theorized, *it is true forever*. He thought about that for a while, exhaled a deep sigh, and then wrote her a letter:

*Dear Helen,*

*Please don't rip this up or throw it away before you read it.*

*First of all, I want to apologize for what happened at Biagi's. I really wanted to talk with you and see you again, and I have no excuse for ignoring you like I did. I guess I was just afraid and didn't know what to say. I'm sorry.*

*I've been thinking about you ever since you called me that night, thinking about all the good times we used to have. So much has happened since then, and there's so much to talk about now. I guess we're not kids anymore, are we?*

*I've been having kind of a hard time lately. Been thinking a lot about my dad. It's difficult to explain. And the way I broke up with you. And the note I sent you. There're so many things I did that I don't understand now. I'm not trying to make excuses but I think that's why I acted like I did at Biagi's. (Maybe I am trying to make excuses.)*

*The reason I'm writing is because I really would like to see you. But not at Biagi's and not with any of my friends or your friends around. It will be easier to talk that way. But however you want will be ok with me. You can just write back and let me know and then I can give you a call.*

*How's college? You must be getting ready for your junior year. What's your major? Oh well—we can talk about all that stuff later if you want to get together.*

*I better go now before I say something stupid.*

*I miss you.*

*Matt*

*PS: Remember that weird ring you bought me when you went to the ocean on vacation? I still have it.*

It had been years since Matt had written Helen that other letter, the one that had converted him from the true-hearted soul mate into the inconsiderate and cold-hearted cad of an ex-boyfriend. He wished he had just slept on it, re-read it in the morning, regained his senses, and ripped it up. It had charted his course and sealed his fate. Thinking back, he knew that this time he had to choose each word with care. In a first draft, which he crumpled up and threw away, he had included the sentence: "I realize now that when I broke up with you I was confused and just didn't understand what I was doing." But, even though it was true, he felt uncomfortable every time he read it, so he took out that sentence and added the comment about not wanting to say anything stupid. He folded up the finished product and tucked it into his jeans pocket and prayed that he would have the courage to mail it when he got home, while still wondering: "Can I trust myself to not be despicable again?"

He cringed at the still burning sense of remorse at the memory of the last note he had sent to her those many years ago, the breakup note, delivered coldly through a go-between friend, telling her that it was over and offering a contorted explanation that was designed to make her feel like it was all her fault and that she had left him no other choice. Even as he sent it, he assumed they would patch things back together in a few weeks. He would apologize and it would be like nothing ever happened. It was as if he were trying to say something else and, somehow, this note might get her to coax it out of him. It wasn't until afterward, when he heard of her reaction, that he realized how cruel and thoughtless he had been and that he had gone way overboard. It was an unforgivable sin against Helen and everyone in her family, especially her mother, who had always been so kind to him. Something about himself changed the day he sent her that letter, as if some large boulder in his personality had dislodged and everything shifted and avalanched in upon him and left him squirming. And thus the unraveling began.

As if to rescue him from such thoughts, a stray image of Carla flashed in his mind and he noted, with a sigh of satisfaction, that he had hardly even thought about her for weeks and hoped he had finally worked his infatuation and the intoxicating procession of delusions he had spun around her image out of his system forever. *Out of sight, out of mind*, he thought, adding, *Yes. I'm most definitely out of my mind.*

"Delusion," he had once memorized, "is the elder daughter of Zeus, the accursed who deludes all; her feet are delicate and they step not on the firm earth, but she walks the air above men's heads and leads them astray." He begrudgingly conceded that his obsession with Carla had always been nothing more than a shallow longing triggered by the imagined promise of her kiss and the hypnotic hold of her ethereal eyes and her precious Madonna face. She was beautiful, it's true. But, ultimately, it was not Carla that he loved. It was the idea of her. The idea had walked above his head and had led him astray.

He coveted her form and was mesmerized by the illusion that he had created. He had been summoned by her siren's call and had repeatedly shipwrecked his hopes upon her rocky shores. But it

426

was actually him summoning himself to that self-created illusion that cast no shadow and bore no substance. He had never gotten to know the real Carla at all because he could not see behind the fantasy of who he wanted her to be. More tragically, at the root of his misfortune, was that he was so smitten and debilitated by desire that, though he pursued her and regarded her with fawning deference, he never opened himself up to her. He remained a featureless mystery who never offered her anything to love, never risking anything for fear of the rebuke that would crush his hopes. It was unfair of him to place any blame upon her for the fact that he wet himself in excited puppy-dog piss squiggles every time he saw her. A reddening crush of shame overcame him as he considered the pest he must have been, like a tick she couldn't get rid of, all bloated and burrowed in. But in that realization there was a sense of being liberated from the infatuation that had snared him and his foolhardy mind by both heart and soul for so long. He now knew that his obsession over Carla and his tired litany of regrets over Helen was just a blind alley that made a mockery of love, cheapened it, and made it look ridiculous and unhealthy, like a disease. he wondered if there were any way to salvage any honor from the mess he had made of his life.

*Love,* he thought, *should be strong, not weak; sane, not crazy; glad, not sad; proud, not ashamed; confident, not desperate; full, not empty; empowering, not depressing; an epic tale, not a parody. It should fulfill you, elevate you, and make you love life and want to live forever.*

## Flying Across A Flickering Universe

Matt took the wheel at Rawlins and drove nonstop to Cheyenne, where Natalie woke up and took over. Matt rested in the back and continued the cycle of napping, talking, and driving. He spent a long time talking with Bruce, who had said that he had no idea what he was going to do when he got home. Matt confessed that he was equally uncertain.

"I'm waiting to discover something that will keep me motivated. I was thinking that maybe I could work with people who are handicapped. You know, people with cerebral palsy and things like that."

Bruce said, "When I was a kid I had all kinds of big dreams about being an inventor or a famous writer. But something destroyed all that, and I just don't have any goals anymore. It worries me because, well, I'm a twin, and he's very motivated and already rollin' in the dough working with a cable TV company, and now I'm starting to feel like the runt of the litter. I worry that I won't amount to anything."

"I can get that," Matt said. "When I was a kid, I wanted to be so many different things. Astronaut, archaeologist, athlete, author. But I must've taken a wrong turn somewhere. But I stayed in the A's because most of the time I feel like an asshole."

"Don't say that, man. You're cool."

Matt felt silly for sounding so mopey and self-pitying, like he was fishing for insincere compliments. But he wondered nonetheless, *Am I cool?*

*Well—no. I'm definitely not cool,* he answered himself.

*But am I an asshole?*

*Well—maybe. Maybe not.*


Matt had never been to the Midwest and was awed by the rippling oceans of corn and soy beans and wheat and whatever other crop might be waving at him as they zipped past the farming machinery that looked like gigantic alien monsters, the sky-scraping silos that announced each town from miles away before there was even any idea that a town was nearby, and the sea of midsummer heat that smothered the land and set the air on fire.

They were making excellent time driving in shifts and timing bathroom breaks with all-purpose pit stops for gas and snacks. Through Ogallala and between North Platte and somewhere else, he dozed off and woke up disoriented in the pitch dark. The wide expanse of open fields was flickering with billions of lightning bugs as if all the stars in the heavens had descended into the universe of these inky farmlands and into this galaxy of crickets and bullfrogs and katydids and all the other creatures who were singing their praises in the invisible choir on this prayerful and transcendent night.

*It reminded Matt of a past summer night when he and a couple of his Hill Hood friends were driving the deserted back roads south of New Holland, getting stoned and listening to music on the radio. "Spirit in the Sky" was blasting through rattling speakers, and the whole car vibrated with the heavy fuzz-bass pulse and the steady drone of the tribal drum beat and the eerie vibrato electric guitar and the "when they lay me down to die / going up to the spirit in the sky" chant echoing in their buzzed heads. Then, just as they turned a winding bend, they came upon a wide-open pasture, all glittery and illuminated with lightning bugs. The boys gaped in stony disbelief. The driver, Harry, brought the car to a skidding halt in the middle of the country road, and they could not help but jump from their seats and run with flapping arms, laughing and prancing through the pasture as if they were flying across a flickering universe and each lightning bug was its own star. They continued running until their exhilarated state became an exhausted state, and they returned to their idling car, dripping sweat, slid back into their seats, and lit up another joint. He wanted to recapture that mystical spirit and recreate the moment out there on that Nebraska night with his new traveling friends but he knew better than to try to fabricate spontaneity.*

And on and on. They rocketed beneath a vast wash of stars through Kearney, Aurora, York and then to a gas station in Lincoln at 1:45 a.m. where everyone rejoiced when Steve and Natalie informed the bedraggled crew that they were going straight through to Milwaukee. No one would be getting dropped off in the middle of the night. As they gassed up, a girl with a backpack came over, asked for a ride, and joined the gypsy caravan as it continued through Omaha and across the wide Missouri to Council Bluffs, Iowa, where, for the first time, Matt got the joke in the Jonathan Winters commercial where he lauds his select brand of coffee as "the best coffee between Omaha and Council Bluffs." And onward, still on Interstate 80, Matt was once again at the wheel until dawn when Natalie relieved him as they refueled in Des Moines. The Cleveland duo fought like kids over who would pump the gas until one gave up and said, "Ah— stick it up your gashole."

Matt had eaten nothing since San Francisco other than breakfast in Winnemucca, a candy bar, and a few donuts. But he wasn't hungry and hardly thought of food. He slept well from Des Moines to Iowa City where he was awakened when Steve and Natalie turned off the Interstate to head north on Route 1 to Milwaukee. Everyone was remote and dull and too apathetic to exchange addresses. Matt thanked them for the ride and everybody said goodbye, shook his hand, and wished him luck. To Natalie, Matt said, "Say hi to your Grandma for me." It broke his heart, the way she smiled at him as he hopped out of the van.

### Peach Shampoo

When he lumbered out onto Interstate 80 he was in a half-zombie mental fog. He shielded his eyes from the glare of the unfiltered morning sun. He sniffed his armpits and was not pleased with the results. He didn't understand why the Cleveland guys didn't get out with him but guessed they must have changed their plans while he was asleep. A short ride took him over the Mississippi River at Davenport and into Illinois in a slick foreign car with a man who was going home to Rockford to pick up his stuff and then move out to Colorado where he had a girlfriend and a job waiting for him. Everybody was going somewhere for some reason having to do with girlfriends and jobs and futures. Except Matt. No girlfriend. No job. No discernible future. He was just heading home in a car with a stranger he had never seen before and would never see again but would always remember. For Matt, he had grown accustomed to living on the road in the everlasting present and dreaded that the luxury of timelessness was nearing its end. But he had already accepted the inevitability that he would soon become time-bound once again, that the temporarily staved-off future would resume its relentless advance, and so he stood guard to defend against the crush of its return.

*Maybe the future would come more easily if I could let go of the past*, he philosophized, thinking of two trains speeding in opposite directions and him, stuck in the middle with a foot on each caboose.

The driver turned the radio up and said, "Listen to this. I love this song."

Matt smiled when the voice on the radio sang, "I'm getting closer to my home," repeating it over and over and over like a musical mantra.

Matt was dropped off on the highway when the driver turned north on Route 2. After an enjoyable hour of walking and waiting, a car squealed to a stop as though the driver hadn't seen him until the last moment. He was a lawyer from Cincinnati who was returning home after retracing the route of a trip he had taken with his parents during the Depression when he was a teenager.

"We were gone for about three weeks. Just my mother and father and me. I was an only child. We stayed with my mother's relatives up around St. Cloud in Minnesota. One of them had a summer cottage on a lake way up north. It was a beautiful place. That was the most perfect three weeks of my entire life. My parents were getting along really good. There was no drinking, no fighting, no arguing. The weather was beautiful and we went fishing and swimming and boating and hiking every single day and sang songs and roasted marshmallows around a campfire at night. One of my cousins had a friend. Her name was Andrea, and she was beautiful. We had this very innocent one-week romance where we spent every waking moment together. It felt perfect. We had an automatic connection. On the last day just before I left, we took a long walk together in the woods. There was a secret spot we'd found during the week, and we went there together without even saying where we were going. It was like we both knew we had to go there. When we got there we started saying goodbye to each other and were making all kinds of plans and promises to stay in touch and write letters and see each other again. We were only fifteen. When it was time to leave she took my hand and then, like magic, she put her arms around me and gave me a big, long kiss. It took me completely by surprise. I had never kissed a girl before. It threw me for a loop. And then she told me that she loved me and started to cry because she didn't want me to go. I felt the same way but I didn't cry. And I didn't say anything because I was in such a state of shock. Literally at a loss for words, which is not like me, not even back then. All week long I thought she was just tolerating me and then, wham, with no warning and no preparation, I get the greatest kiss I'll ever get in my whole life. It was the happiest and saddest moment of my life. Wonderful and terrible at the same time. Well, as you might have guessed, we wrote a few times but never saw each other again. I'm not sure what happened. We were too young and too far apart. But here's what has always bothered me. When she told me she loved me, I didn't tell her that I loved her, too. I tried to and I would've meant it. But I was afraid to say it. I can't help but think that if I told her I loved her, things would've worked out differently. My whole life I've been punishing myself, regretting that I didn't tell her I loved her. And I've always thought of those three weeks, and especially that last week, as the best time of my life. It was perfect. Well, nearly. It would've been absolutely perfect if I told her I loved her. I still miss her and, lately, I can't stop thinking about her. I always thought I would eventually forget about her and that my regrets would disappear. But every few years something reminds me of her and all those memories come flooding back, this time with a vengeance. I guess I have suffered what has been called "the disastrous consequences of not listening to your heart." So for me this trip was a long-overdue reckoning. More of a journey or a pilgrimage. I had to reach way back and dig real deep. I hadn't been back there ever again until now, and I think I was trying to examine my past so I can finally learn all my earthly lessons and get over it all. I call it "the purification of experience," trying to untangle those old knots, elevate my awareness, be a better example to others and set myself free. To, as they say, "climb atop the ruins of my past and go forth unfettered, purified." Because life, after all, is filled with a thousand little splinters. And if we don't treat them, they will sting us forever." He sounded like he was reciting something he had memorized for an occasion like this or had prepared as a lecture for a curriculum instructing college freshmen on how to avoid fucking things up for the rest of their lives.

He shook his head and looked away. "I've read that the definition of suffering is to cling to that which changes. Well, son, I've done my fair share of clinging and suffering in my life. And with age comes nostalgia—and truth. I looked around but couldn't find any relatives in St. Cloud. Went to the lake but couldn't even find the cottage or that secret spot in the woods. It's changed a lot since back then. The cottage might have burned down because I think I found the lot where it was, but there was nothing there except what looked like the remains of an old foundation. I thought for sure that that place was ingrained in my memory forever. And believe it or not, I tried to find Andrea. But I didn't have any luck there, either. Who knows? It's probably for the best. I had this urge to redeem myself in some abstract way, but redemption is only as good as the confession that opens its door. I worry that maybe my purposes are selfish or that I have some kind of ulterior motive. Most people grow up and have the good sense to forget all that stuff, all that teenage stuff. I guess I'm a quart or two low on common sense. I've still got my head stuck up my past. You know, the sad fact about life is that by the time you realize what you've done wrong, it's always too late to do anything about it. But I had to repudiate my past, get it out of my system and get over my big sob story. This was a journey of atonement. Maybe now I can forget about it. After all, it's where you end up that matters. Not how you got there. But I can still see her waving goodbye. She had brown hair and a ponytail and was wearing a sleeveless sun dress with a flowery pattern and she smelled like peach shampoo."

He told Matt that he used to hitchhike home when he was on leave during World War Two. He didn't say much about the war except that he was just a kid at the time and was glad when it was finally over.

"Used to be, back then, a man in uniform wouldn't even have to wait for a ride. Cars would line up for the privilege of helping us out. But nowadays the soldiers are afraid or ashamed to wear their uniforms in public. People give them a hard time. Asking them how it feels to be a baby killer. I hate to say it, but I've seen dead babies and it's not a pretty sight. It is a sight I will take to my grave no matter how long I live. It's been almost thirty years and I still think about it every day. And I lost a lot of friends. They were just kids, but the war made them men. Braver than me. We fought through hell together, and only some of us made it back, and there was no logic as to who died and who survived. Forget survival of the fittest. It was survival of the luckiest. There is no sane reason why I am still alive and so many of my friends, who were standing in the exact spots where I had stood only seconds earlier, had to die before my very eyes in terrible ways. Those images still visit me at night."

He cleared his throat to disguise his rising emotion and sighed, "So it goes. None of it made any sense. You don't say those things to a soldier who has risked his life to serve his country. Hell, they'd be freezing in a blizzard and nobody'd pick them up now. Maybe it is a bad war, I don't know, but it's not their fault. They're just kids. It's a disgrace, the way they're treated. A national disgrace."

The man looked up at the sky, deep blue and dotted with cottony white islands of clouds, and said, "You know that expression, 'No man is an island'? He got that wrong. Every man. Every person is an island. Nobody really knows anybody else. We're all just strangers here trying to be good and do what's best and failing miserably half the time. Killing one another as though it's an honorable moral duty. It's all, excuse my French, a lot of fucking bullshit. Sometimes after I shave and shower and look in the mirror and, amazingly, there are still tiny bits of shaving cream or shampoo on my ear lobe or under my nose. It makes me question why, of all those suds smeared on my face that had washed away, how did those few little dabs survive as if nothing had happened? No logic. It makes me feel guilty." Matt didn't know how to respond. He thought it was an odd analogy, but he knew what the man meant.

Matt talked about his future plans, wanting to go to Ireland and Europe and maybe overland to India. "But as far as what I want to do with my life, I have no idea. One thing I was thinking. I knew a kid with cerebral palsy. He was a good kid. I thought I might want to learn how to work with people like him. They are a lot smarter than they're given credit for. And I guess I want to have a family someday. But I'm not ready yet."

"Well, son, when the right girl comes along you'll hear the bells and know that she's 'the one.' But you gotta hear the bells." And then, somewhat tangentially, he said, "My biggest regret in life is that I have failed as a husband and as a father to my three kids. I tried to blame it on the war, but it was all me. Too much drinking, too much working, too much yelling and, well, I drifted a bit in the wrong direction and made some big mistakes. The divorce was awful. I said and did things that I will always regret. I've tried to apologize and make things right with them, but I always blow it. My youngest won't even talk to me. I've become a stranger to my family. I always said that I would be a better father to my children than my father was to me. Little did I know."

The man had shown a fatherly concern for Matt and had called him "son" a couple of times. But even though he was old enough to be Matt's father it was hard for Matt to think of him that way because his father had been so much older and so inaccessible. In fact, in this single encounter, Matt had probably spoken more with this stranger than he had spoken with his father throughout his whole life.

As they approached Route 51, where the man would be turning south, he again assumed the fatherly role as he delivered his closing remarks:

"If I learned anything from the war worth remembering, it's this, and, once again, please excuse my French: I'm just another asshole guy who doesn't know what the fuck he's doing. It was true then, and it's still true today. But I do know this and I hope you don't take this the wrong way, but kids today are running all over creation trying to find themselves—and that's all well and good, I suppose—but if you want to find yourself, what you've got to do is stop dead in your tracks long enough to take a good, long look in the mirror. That's where you'll find yourself. You've got to be your own man. You'll never be happy if you spend your life trying to chase down dreams and be somebody else. And if you think about it and look inside rather than outside, in the mirror rather than out the window, you'll figure that one out without even leaving your house. Nobody knows you like you do. That's why everything you need to know about yourself is right there in your own reflection."

When Matt got out of the car, he told the man, "Hey, thanks a lot for the ride and the advice and everything. It's all an inside job, right? I hope your journey was successful." He reached across the front seat and shook the man's hand.

"Yeah. I hope yours is, too. But don't forget about the mirror." The man pointed to his rear view mirror ,and they both laughed, but for different reasons.

## Cubars

Matt hated his repetitive habit of dwelling on the dismal aspects of his past but felt powerless to break it. His eyes were always glued to that rear view, his brass band parade of failures, regrets, and embarrassments always marching by in full regalia. But when it came to dealing with thoughts of his father, what else was he to do but dwell on the past? It was like watching old movies over and over again searching for some overlooked clues to a convoluted plot. How else was he ever to reconcile the disparity between the deflated shadow of a father who refused to acknowledge his existence and the cabaret-partner father who took such simple delight in singing him silly songs and making silly faces and thrilling him with stories about leprechauns and shamrocks or telling corny jokes that were so bad they made Matt laugh in spite of himself? What the hell ever happened to that guy?

He could not plot out a transition between those two conflicting fatherly images, from the flesh-and-blood human being of an affectionate father to the cheap cardboard imitation, the pale replica of his father's former self. From the "Good Dad" to the "Non-Dad." He still didn't like to think about it, even after so many years and so much damning evidence. But Matt now knew more certainly than ever that it was the bourbon that had deadened the love he could only vaguely remember receiving in his early schoolboy days. It was the bourbon that had fueled that tragic transition and had stolen his father from him those many years ago. Now more than ever it was plain as day. He just didn't want to see it, but he could feel it in his gut. It was the bourbon. It was the fucking bourbon.

*Once, when Matt was 14 or 15 years old, his father had fallen ill with the flu and a stomach virus that lasted close to a month and kept him from his bourbon. After a couple weeks, Matt began to notice a change in his father's personality, a softening in his rigid face, an encouraging recognition in his eyes and voice, a slight spring in his step, as though he was awakening from a bad dream in which he had been someone else. And, for the first time he could remember, Matt felt welcomed in his company.*

*At first he thought that it might have been wishful thinking. But then one day his mother confirmed his suspicions, confiding in him in girlish tones that his father had complimented her on dinner and had even told her something funny about one of his students. That may have been the only time in his life when Matt could sense, in the optimism of his mother's voice and the light in her eyes, that beneath and beyond their travesty of years, she still truly loved that man, that waylaid traveler who was returning back home from the dark tunnels of whatever dim cave he had been lost within. She had been there all along, like John Riley's fair young maid, faithfully awaiting the return of her long-lost lover who "sails the deep salt sea." Matt felt a surge of reassurance in his mother's suppressed enthusiasm and dared to anticipate that he would once again be welcomed into the good graces of the man he had once idolized. Oddly enough, other than Mrs. Mahoney's single comment to Matt, no one else in the house mentioned anything about the quiet transformation that was taking place in their midst though it was as obvious to him as if the household climate had entered a refreshing springtime thaw after a long lonely frozen winter.*

*Then, one evening as Matt was lying on the living room floor watching television, he heard a dreaded request from his father who was sitting behind him:*

*"Matt, could you get me a cubar?"*

*The words struck like bullets. Cubar was his father's pet name for ice-cubes, inspired by President Kennedy's Bostonian pronunciation of Cuba. He swiveled and saw, to his horror, a green and gold Grecian tumbler half-filled with the familiar noxious amber elixir that Matt knew would once again steal his father away from the family and deliver him back to his self-imposed prison. Then, even more horrific, he saw himself rise like a puppet at his father's request and, in silent spineless obedience, go to the freezer and return to freshen his poison with ice cubes though inside he screamed, "No" and, condemning his own cowardice, wept an invisible and imperceptible torrent of tears.*

*That night, at about 1 a.m., unable to sleep and reeling with guilt at having been an accomplice to a detestable relapse, Matt went to the basement where the bourbon was stored. In a restrained and timid fury, fifth by fifth, he dumped a case and a half of it down the drain of the utility sink beside the washer and dryer, sobbing the entire time, enraged by his father's brutal and unrepentant indifference to his own self-destructive impulses, and hating himself for being too weak to stand up to the old man and beg him or demand of him to stop,*

*too meek and insecure to shout his angry confession, "I love you,"
or his ultimatum, "If you love me, you'll stop drinking." Before
his tempest subsided but after dumping them out, he nearly, oh so
nearly, smashed all the bottles on the cement floor and screamed,
"Fuck you, you son of a bitch" at the top of his lungs. But he didn't
quite slip off the ledge into the abyss that would have allowed him
the luxury of such insane abandon. No. He managed to hold on just
that little bit and swallow the best of his rage.*

*When the bottles had all been emptied, he left them strewn about
in a haphazard mess as evidence of his protest. He headed up the
stairs just as the door from the kitchen opened and he saw his father's
giant shadow cast down the stairway against the landing wall. His
father did not even look at him as they passed each other. But Matt
knew that it was the bourbon summoning him to the basement, so he
hurried his steps and made it to his bedroom before his father had
time to react to the shock that was in store for him. He lay in his
bed awaiting the storm, the outrage, the punishment, and fell asleep
disappointed that there had been none. Much to his dismay, there
never was any mention of the incident. The bourbon was replaced
the very next day with a brand-new case and, as always, it was as
if nothing had even happened, as if Matt and all his tantruming
emotions were of no significance and had never even existed. He
was no more than a pesky gnat against the impenetrable hide of his
father's obstinance. Though he tried with all his might to hate his
father, he knew he could never hate that broken man who had drifted
out into such a lonely and erratic Plutonic orbit. He could hate the
things his father did and those things he failed to do, but he could
not hate the man. Deep inside, in that place that never changes, he
knew he loved his father. It was the bourbon he hated and the curse
that it had cast. It was the bourbon that had kidnapped him from a
family who loved him and had exiled him to that inaccessible cave
from where no one could hear his silent screams.*

*"Fuck you, Jack. Fuck you, Jim."*

*Thinking back, Matt blamed and despised himself for giving up so easily and for not thrashing into an unbridled bottle-smashing frenzy that night in the basement, to awaken everyone in the house, the neighborhood, the whole goddamn city with a crazed display of confrontational violence, to bring this thing out into the open and cast a bright light upon it. He hated himself all the more for not dumping out the bourbon each time it was replenished so his father would know that he meant business and that his rage would not be ignored. Now he was embarrassed by his ridiculously ineffectual protest. Matt knew he had nothing to fear from the old man except a silent and passive wrath, a cold shoulder rather than the indifferent one to which he had grown so accustomed. Even when he ran away from home and totaled his father's car, the old man's only comment was an indirect "Did you learn anything?" spoken offhandedly as he walked by without looking at his son or even hesitating for an answer, a comment ingenious in either kindness or cruelty, he was not sure which. No pause in his step. No paternal comfort for the anguished son. No warmth of heart or trace of love. No cradling arm to sturdy up the agonized figure withering before him. And now as Matt, the temporarily liberated hitchhiker, struggled with the prospect of returning home to face the screamin' demons that had driven him away, he wept inside at the thought of his father as a great but misguided man entrenched in a dead-ended intellectual stoicism and who was ultimately annihilated by his own demons.*

*Matt wished that his father had lived longer and that, perhaps, in the best of all possible worlds and in that extra measure of time, they would have somehow rediscovered the love they once shared. Maybe that would have made a difference for both of them. Who knows? Even though he knew he loved his father, he just couldn't feel it. It was buried somewhere behind and beneath the debris of so many failed expectations and so many demonstrations of not-love. So much sunken hope. Matt realized for the first time that he missed his father, that drowned sailor, and that no matter how long he lived, he would never understand that man as anything other than a cold but mighty monument to the loneliness of men. In the hierarchy of tragedies that defined their relationship, highest among them was the fact that he had never even gotten to know the old man.*

*"Chip chip a little horse?"*

*"Chip chip again, sir."*

## A Beacon of Goodness

Matt flexed his thumb and for the millionth time this summer assumed the position, this time on the highway at Peru, Illinois, for only a handful of minutes when luck struck again in the form of a sporty-looking red Corvair. He ran up, opened the passenger door, and peered in to see a nun at the wheel. She welcomed him with an effusive, "Come on in. I'm Sister Veronica. What's your name and where ya goin'?"

Sister Veronica appeared to be in her late twenties and, as such, was the youngest nun Matt had ever met, except perhaps for Sister James Agnes, his study hall teacher in the tenth grade at Bishop Brannan High School. "Sister Jimmy" was kind and had a glowing smile and a face that, when seen through the miniature small-screen confines of her severe nunly head wear, was like a beautiful postage stamp in the middle of a big black and white envelope. For Matt, she had been the sole exception to an otherwise hard and fast rule.

Sister Veronica, instead of the full-metal-jacket habit, the medieval iron bonnet, and the black lasso of rosary beads and crucifix dangling from her side, was dressed in a modest short-sleeved blouse, an abbreviated shoulder length black veil, and, most surprisingly, a robin's-egg blue skirt that strained to cover her knees. The Corvair was a standard shift, and as she stretched to work the clutch and moved her feet back and forth upon the pedals, he found himself peeking peripherally at the rise and fall of her skirt upon her legs, which, she being a nun, felt just plain wrong and sacrilegious. Nonetheless, peek he did.

Matt had never seen a nun's unencumbered face or arms before, nor even the regular standard-issue human ears. He most certainly had never seen such a luxurious head of thick brown hair like that which cascaded down from beneath Sister Veronica's veil. As a child, though he had never seen them, he had correctly concluded that nuns had ears because they always detected even the slightest peep when attempting to maintain the perfect silence of classroom discipline while wielding their trusty combat-tested rulers as a warning to any transgressors. And something had to be holding up their glasses. However, he had been incorrect in concluding they were all bald. And also, until now, he had never seen a nun with such radiant hazel eyes and a smile that could fill a car with light.

"You've got to tell me all about your trip, Matt. It sounds so exciting. And here you are, after such a long journey, and you are almost home! I wish I could deliver you right to your front door!"

And so he obliged her unrestrainedly and launched into an impromptu dissertation and told her about the tragic cannibalization of his dying hometown and the indelible images of Vinny's brother, Frankie, the dead boy with the cerebral palsy kind of disease who he had barely known. And that unique little flower, Esmerelda, Queen of the Moon, and her mysterious boyfriend Roger, the King of Mars. And his last-ditch-effort pilgrimage to Canada to save himself from something irreversibly regrettable. And the dark confessionals in the drenched and capsized Wawa tent and the refugee Butterfly Princess they rescued there. About his doppelganger, Mark Olsen, and the coy waitress in the most-friendliest Over Easy Cafe in Winnipeg and the repeat doppelganger encounter with Charlie and Jerry Anne on the windswept coastline of California. The harrowing all-night truck rides with crazed long-haul road warriors speeding down the plummeting twisty-turny roads through the pitch black Canadian mountains. And the Sister of Mercy who delivered him to safety on that hallucinatory morning in Edmonton. He showed her the silver St. Christopher medal that had been gifted to him by his Indian father in Regina. He told her about the transformational double rainbow in Lake Louise and the inspirational prayer card from the Jesus freak with the Jewfro. He described the early demise of his peach-picking career during his strange sojourn in a breezy white cottage in Penticton with hyper-hippie Rob and sex-crazed Max. And he couldn't stop there. He wanted to drain himself of all his stories during this fortuitous window of time with this most-singular Sister. He shared about Jack and Donna and the Tolkienesque Avenue of the Giants and the otherworldly Redwood skyscrapers of Muir Woods. He told her about good ole Charlie and the marvelous old Mrs. Constance Hartwell and how together they all climbed Mt. Diablo and feasted on Screamin' Yellow Zonkers and Mrs. Hartwell's famous potato salad. About the sun-baked fiasco in the Nevada desert and the life-saving rescue by the Good Samaritan Indian party in the pickup truck and the kid with the swinging G. I. Joe canteen. And how he did not yet quite know what to make of it all. And that sometimes he felt blessed and other times he felt cursed.

And now, this mad dash home.

But he didn't stop there. He told her about Maureen, the Silver Girl from Michigan, and her North Star father, and Amazing Gracie in Vancouver, and her golden voice, about Deborah "not Debbie," and how guilty he felt for judging her and committing the sin of superficiality and for failing to be her perfect stranger, though he left out the whole "fantasy-ride" aspect, while also realizing in her reverent presence what a shallow pursuit it actually was, and, of course, he told her about hometown Helen of the Tolling Bells, and how his callous disregard for the sanctity of their relationship still haunted him with devastating bouts of guilt and self-hatred, and how he had let her slip through his fingers that pivotal night at Biagi's, just as the promise of redemption was so near, and how could he have been so unkind, and ultimately, how it all made him wonder what power it is that brings people together in glorious union and then tears them apart in a heartbreaking shambles and how can you ever navigate the bends and turns and the perilous pitfalls of human relations without destroying everything that you love?

When he was empty of words and sputtered to a crashing halt, certain that he'd made a fool of himself, that he should have kept his stupid mouth shut and observed his vow of muteness, Sister Veronica picked up the slack and told him, in confidential tones, "I don't usually talk about this, but when I was in high school I fell in love with a boy. We were in the marching band together." She sighed wistfully, "Picture this: I played the glockenspiel and he played the tuba. We used to joke and say that we made such beautiful music together. We had gotten pretty serious and were even making plans to attend the same college. It was all very romantic. It looked as though we were destined to get married and spend the rest of our lives together as husband and wife and raise our own family. But it ended just after we graduated high school because I felt a higher calling. It came out of nowhere, completely unexpected. It was just one of those things. Something entered my soul and changed me forever in an instant. I still have no idea what it was or how it happened, but it could not be denied. And the fortunate thing about it is that he understood and gave me his blessing. We were both heartbroken. I still love him and we are still the best of friends," she paused, "and he has never married."

Matt had spent most of his life disparaging nuns at every opportunity, and now, here he was, feeling blessed and repentant in Sister Veronica's purifying presence, a presence that defined and demonstrated nothing but love. She wore her halo well. He was bombarded by mixed emotions and by a conscience that told him he should get out of the car right now. That he was a hypocrite for accepting such kindness from someone who he would otherwise have rebuked and ridiculed outright on sight alone.

And then it happened.

His mind cleared as he felt his hatred for Sister Jeronima evaporate like steam into the deep blue distance, and forgiveness washed over his heart. And the more he forgave her, the lighter he became, and curtains opened until he found himself back in his classroom at St. Brigid's, observing invisibly from the far corner at the tidy rows of second graders, girls on one side, boys on the other, as Sister Jeronima led them through their rote morning prayers, recited in bland unison, "Are Father, who aren't in heaven. Hollow be thy name... but deliver us from eagles, Amen." He recognized his devout seven-year-old self sitting erect and still, hands pointed heavenward and folded perfectly atop his desk. Then Little Matt swiveled his head to the far corner and looked Big Matt right in the eyes and smiled. The room receded and shrank and faded away and Matt returned to the company of a saintly fair-haired woman at the wheel of a red Corvair on a highway somewhere in a mid-western state.

And then this happened.

He started to cry. Right there. Sitting beside a perfect stranger, who just happened to be a nun. He erupted into an uncontrollable fit of weeping. No matter how hard he tried, he could not stop. This was not misty-eyed sniffles. There were real tears gushing down his cheeks and he could not catch his breath.

"Are you okay, Matthew? Did I say something wrong?" He liked the way she called him by his full Christian name, just like his mother did. And when she placed her hand lightly upon his shoulder, her grace radiated throughout his trembling body and converted this sporty red Corvair, which was speeding like a rocket across the rural Illinois landscape, into a mobile confessional booth.

"No, Sister. I'm okay."

And so he told her through sobs about how he fled from St. Brigid's because he so feared Sister Jeronima Clare and that, since then, he had always hated nuns. He couldn't remember exactly what had happened that would have frightened him so much that he would refuse to return to that school and to that nun. But he was suddenly pretty sure that she must have grabbed him from behind, yelled at him, slapped him across the face, and shook him violently for some reason he would never now know, bringing him to tears in front of all the obedient students in the classroom. He now realized that ever since then, the hatred and fear he felt at that single moment so long ago had been preserved as if in amber, and he still blamed all nuns for the errant actions of just that one, and how he was condemned to become an exiled public schooler. How, as a child, he had been so terrified by the certain prospect of being sent to hell for being such a bad boy, and such a glutton, and that as a second-grader his whole life was already ruined. How Satan himself hunted him with his pitchfork to stab him and drag him down through the very Earth, down to that torture chamber of eternal flames. About his pathetic little mud hut in some soulless slum in heaven. How he had so displeased the Almighty God he had been taught to believe in, to obey and to fear, and that he had no choice but to orphan himself from such a disapproving and unforgiving father. That he was still being punished to this day and would be forever.

He thought Sister Veronica would be offended by his nun-hating confession, and he was already belittling himself for not keeping his thoughts to himself, when she said, "You were treated poorly, weren't you?"

He nodded, soothed by her gentle tone, and embarrassed that he could not yet speak without choking and gasping for air, bubbles of snot dripping from his nose, and that he had been reduced to tears by something that had happened so long ago, something he couldn't even remember, something he could only guess at.

"I don't blame you for hating her. No one should treat a child that way. She was wrong to tell you those things and to be so cruel to you." she went on to explain that Sister Jeronima was a relic of an earlier time and that her methods were now frowned upon.

"You should have mercy on her. I believe she had at one time been holy in her heart of hearts, but life in a convent could be harsh and even cruel to young nuns who took their vows with a proud commitment to their faith. She, too, must have suffered at the hands of others. It hardened her and turned her idealism and her faith into cynicism and bitterness. Do you understand what I am telling you, Matthew?" Again, the full first name.

Staring at his lap, he slipped into second-grade Catholic schoolboy mode and weakly muttered, "I think so, Sister."

"What I'm saying is that she taught you as she herself had been taught. She couldn't help it. Maybe one day you will find it in your heart to forgive her."

When he was able to compose himself and speak without tears, he said, "I understand. I'm sorry, Sister. I'm kind of a mess right now, just trying to keep it all together. I don't want to be this way. I can't help it. I'm so ashamed of so many things. I wish I could be a better person. I didn't mean to—"

"You're already a good person. If you weren't a good person, you wouldn't care about being a better person. You did nothing wrong. You were just a child. There is no need to apologize. It's my job to listen, to provide comfort. To bestow and receive grace in equal measures. To be a blessing to those who have blessed me. And, besides, tears cleanse the soul."

"Thank you, Sister."

"And Matthew. More importantly. Can you find it in your heart to forgive yourself?"

"I don't know, Sister. I just don't know. I'll try."

"Yes, Matthew. You should try. I strongly recommend that you try. And while you're at it, you must lay claim to all that is good within you."

*Could I,* he wondered, *actually forgive myself and lay claim to any goodness? Receive and retain any grace that is bestowed upon me?* The nuns had taught him to recite, "Forgive us our trespasses as we forgive those who trespass against us." But they had never taught him what those words meant or how to apply them. When he first memorized the prayer, he thought that God was telling him not to sneak into his neighbor's backyard, even if it were to retrieve the wiffle ball that would occasionally soar over their garage. Even if he did have to do such a thing, the neighbor should forgive him as long as he didn't hurt anyone or steal anything while he was trespassing just as he should forgive his neighbors if they snuck into his back yard. As for laying claim to his goodness, that subject had never been covered in any of his catechism classes, and Matt didn't even know what it meant.

After a spell of silence, Sister Veronica giggled, a pure golden giggle, and said, "You know, we're not all that bad. We're not all Sister Jeronimas. We've thrown away our rulers."

"I know," he said and managed a slight smile, but he still couldn't look her in the eye for fear of collapsing into another blubbering barrage of tears.

They ate up the fertile flatlands of Illinois through the grace of Sister Veronica's lead foot, passed beneath Chicago's sprawling shadow, and entered Indiana by late afternoon. Sister Veronica was on her way to attend a multi-denominational convocation at Valparaiso University, "The Relevance of Religion in an Evolving Society," for which she was an invited presenter. Her topic was "The Role of the Nun in the Post-Second Ecumenical Church," focusing on social and political activism and how that related to her devotional life.

"A lot of people still believe that we sisters should not become involved in social justice causes like civil rights, the war, women's rights, or anything controversial. That we should remain cloistered. That we should never express our personal opinions on current issues. They believe that the church speaks for us. But some of us disagree. We believe that we are Jesus' representatives on Earth and that we can be a force for good in the world and still remain obedient to our vows. That it is not our personal opinions that we are expressing. We are merely obeying the commands of Jesus. We are messengers. We believe that it is time to break out of the convent and speak up and have our voices heard. I guess we are changing our habits, so to speak." She smirked and said, "We see ourselves as warriors for social justice. I'm not so sure about the Pope, but I believe Jesus would approve."

The conference was taking place at the Chapel of the Resurrection on the grounds of the university. "It's a glorious chapel. The morning light through the stained glass windows is heavenly." She dropped him off on Route 90 at the intersection with 65 where she dipped south for Valparaiso. Though never in his life did Matt think he would ever regret saying goodbye to a nun, he felt suddenly empty and so alone when she disappeared from view, like how he felt when he hung up from his long distance phone calls with his mother, and all that remained was a profound existential silence.

## The In-Between Place

A no-ride slump gave Matt time to recover from the emotional aftershock of his encounter with Sister Veronica. His swollen red eyelids were still itchy, and he was still dazed and riddled by the string of epiphanies that shook him into asking himself, *Who am I really at my core?* When he did get a ride, it was in a Toyota jeep with a guy going all the way to Mt. Kisko, just north of New York City. Stan was an outdoorsy, recently graduated engineer returning home from a tour of job interviews. Matt could go all the way to Binghamton with him and then take the zig-zaggy back roads the rest of the way. He liked back road hitching even though it was slower because he got to meet the locals and see all the little towns along the way.

"Any luck finding a job?" Matt asked.

"Don't know yet. I got one of those 'Don't call us. We'll call you' handshakes when I left, o I guess we'll see."

Even though he still had hundreds of miles to go, being in a New-York-bound jeep with New York State plates gave Matt a secure feeling, as if he were no farther from home than Schenectady and this ride would bring him right to his front door. The easy green pastures and farmlands of Indiana felt so much more like upstate New York than anything he had seen in a long time. But as the idea of returning home became more of a reality with each mile, the fierce antagonism of his old hometown voice began interrupting in the pauses between the good thoughts of his new voice. Spying through the cracks of the fence separating Weird Old Matt from New Improved Matt, he knew that the vigilant Watcher still sat in silent repose, sharpening Its fangs while patiently and hungrily awaiting his arrival, Its trusty anvil and boulder tethered and at the ready. He prayed in his own way that New Matt would survive the cold shock of the hometown plunge and, armed with his new right-sized sword, would banish The Watcher once and for all.

*And so, what now?* he wondered, thinking of redemption and confessions and doors. He knew that part of him would never rest until, like a good Catholic, he confessed the sins of his thoughtlessness and made things right with Helen. He fantasized that she would pick him up hitchhiking on his final stretch and there they would be, face to face in a confined space, just like a confessional booth, from which he could not escape to dodge his shame and within which he could not hide or ignore her. He could pour out his cathartic "I'm sorry" and then maybe she would understand and remember that there had been a time when he was true and honorable and deserving of her love.

He had stored up his apologies and had rehearsed the words, the precise enunciation, the emotion, the entire delivery thousands of times so he would be well-prepared for whenever and wherever he saw her next. He would not be caught speechless. He would get it right on the first try. The happy Hollywood ending. But when he was given his golden opportunity at Biagi's, and she was right there, within sight, within reach, on a silver platter, he did nothing but freeze and watch as the promise of the evening burst into flames and was incinerated to ashes at his feet. Just another false dawn in the darkness that had become his life. If that hadn't been the opportunity of a lifetime, then what would be?

*Damn!* he thought. *If Helen was 'the one' and I've lost her forever, then I'm pretty well screwed for the rest of my life. I guess that's just the disastrous consequences of not listening to my heart!*

He could no longer afford to wait for "the one," whoever or wherever she may be, but he didn't want to end up with "the two," "the three" or "the one hundred and three." There should be a detector for such things. Besides, that whole notion was starting to sound far-fetched. On this journey alone, Matt had fallen in love about a dozen different times, his over-eager puppy-dog heart imagining each time that his newest fantasy heartthrob might be "the one," and fully convinced that she could be. Who is to say that each person could not have hundreds or thousands of potentially perfect "the one's" roaming this Earth waiting to be discovered? Sweet Frauleins and China dolls. Why should the destiny of all of his life's hopes and passions be bundled onto the shoulders of just one person? What if he was not the perfect one for "the one" who was the perfect one for him? Imagine a long chain of "the one"s and no compatible pairs, just an assortment of odd men out. At some point it turns into an idiotic academic exercise or an insoluble mathematical puzzle. And as for love at first sight? How can you experience true love with someone based solely on their apparent physical beauty without even knowing them? That left the less-attractive though nonetheless potentially perfect "the one"s at an insurmountable disadvantage. Although he had admittedly struck the jackpot with his love-at-first-sight experience with Helen, the venture was a colossal backfire with Carla, leaving him high and dry for what felt like an eternity. He realized that he knew nothing about love. At least not anymore. Would he even recognize it if it showed up again? Could he distinguish between love and infatuation? Maybe love had been there all along. Maybe it had been reawakened by the call from Helen. After all, there had always been something about her that kept drawing him, at least in his thoughts, back into her arms. She had always been able to find the happiness in him. With Helen, he had heard the bells.

In the final sift, he knew that all his turmoil was a ludicrous waste of time, that he had led a privileged life and had no right to feel so miserable, always sulking, like a spoiled kid, always polishing his urn of sorrows. But he was stuck in that uncomfortable in-between place, no longer the Holden Caulfield teen but not yet the Jack Kerouac man. He did not know what to do or how to get out of it. All he had and his only resort was his thumb, and he doubted that he would want to continue hitchhiking around the country or the world for the rest of his life, trying to avoid facing the person he had become, though such thoughts did appeal to him.

He recalled a song:

*I know all too well*
*How to turn, how to run*
*How to hide behind a bitter wall of blue*
*But you die inside if you choose to hide*
*So I guess instead I'll love you*

Stan and Matt revved on through Indiana, the last of the Triple I states, rummaging through stories and jokes like they were old high school friends. They crossed through radio zones, exhausting the reception of station after station, faint to loud and clear to annoying static. But the DJs all sounded the same as if there was really just one announcer out there saying all the same things at the same time and playing the same songs over and over again.

After a pause in the conversation, Stan broke the silence. "To be honest, I'm pretty nervous about this job hunt and the transition from being a student to being a guy with a serious job. After five years, I got good at playing the college game, going to classes, taking notes, studying for exams, trying to look as smart as possible. I've got that down pat. I just hope I'm making the right decision and that I'll end up doing something worthwhile. I wanted to change the world for a while, and I still do, but as the idea of a career becomes more real and I become more practical, part of me worries that I'm just doing this to please my parents or maybe I'm selling out because I know I can make a lot of money as an engineer."

"There's nothing wrong with making a lot of money. Might as well put your education to use and find something you enjoy. If you get tired of making all that money at least you still have the option of quitting." Matt smiled and, trying to poke fun at himself and make Stan feel more confident about his future, proffered, "I know one thing. I wouldn't want to spend the rest of my life doing any of the shitty jobs I've had so far. Except maybe as a paperboy, that was fun. Or a soda jerk. I could get free sodas and ice cream for the rest of my life. But, man. It's impressive that you worked so hard and accomplished something so important. You should be proud of yourself and try to make the most of it. The worst that could happen is that you won't like your job and will have to find something else."

Stan smirked and said, "I've got one word for you, son. Are you listening?" He paused, narrowed his eyes, and looked sternly at Matt and said, "Plastics."

They both had a good laugh, and Matt was pleased that maybe something he had said made sense to Stan.


Matt was down to a dollar and a fistful of loose change but wasn't worried about it. He was more concerned that he had been wearing the same reeky clothes and hadn't brushed his slimy teeth since California. His skin was greasy and sticky and he had black grime caked beneath his fingernails. He hoped he didn't smell too bad but wouldn't bet on it.

*This would not be the ideal time for a fantasy ride of any sort— unless she doesn't mind swapping spit with a grubby unbathed pig with bulldog breath.*

By nine or so they arrived in the Cleveland area where it was dark, dreary, and rainy. They got off of Interstate 80 amid heavy roadwork and confusing roundabout detours and attempted to follow signs for 90 East. They got lost and ended up going right through Cleveland upon congested city streets and construction sites and mingling with the stop-and-go of the local metropolitan traffic. Stan was discouraged and decided to get a room for the night. He offered to put Matt up and then bring him into New York State the next morning. Matt, however, was in too much of a hurry and knew he wouldn't be able to sleep in a motel bed when he was at such close range to his home that he could hear his own bed calling him. He hadn't talked with his mother since San Francisco and, as far as she knew, he was heading through Big Sur on his way to L.A. or to the Grand Canyon. Thus, he bid adieu to Stan and continued on alone, in darkness, with the intention of surprising his mother at breakfast time.

## Double-Barreled Earthquakes

It had stopped raining by the time Matt got out of the jeep and into the messy ménage of ramps and lights and hazard signs. In less than ten minutes, he lucked out and got a ride with a car full of maniacs on their way back home to Buffalo from South Bend, Indiana, where they had harvested a trunk-load of marijuana. They said it grew wild by the acres back a lane in some well-hidden lower forty. Every time the driver exceeded the speed limit or passed another car, the front seat co-pilot said, "Whoa! Slow down, Switch-Lane Chicane! We do *not* want to give the pigs any reason to stop us." They were all giddy over their big score, which would provide them with a plentiful private stash as well as make them thousands of dollars on the street if the shit was any good. If they got arrested on the way to Buffalo, Matt hoped the cops would understand that he was just a hitchhiker.

Matt was snugged between two passengers in the back seat. To his right was a girl named Mary from Lackawanna. They all called her "Mary Wanna." To his left, the kid blurted out, "Wanna what?" repeating an apparently tired and worn-down joke.

"That was original," said Mary, rolling her eyes and then, to Matt, said, "I don't know why I put up with these dipshits."

It was 1 a.m. when he was dropped off at a tollbooth at one of the Buffalo exits. It would be a limited-access toll road for the rest of the way home, but he was going great guns and didn't expect it to break his pace. Even with his setbacks out west, he had made incredible time, so he held his breath and crossed his fingers and toes in hopes that his luck would hold out.

He took a ride to the westernmost of the Rochester exits at LeRoy, a deserted outpost of an interchange where the skeletons of hitchhikers who had tried and failed were piled on the grass as an ominous warning to all who may dare. He risked arrest by hitching right on the thruway rather than behind the tollbooth where there was no traffic and no chance of a ride. Positioning himself in the dark and out of the way by the merging entrance lane where there was pull-off room, he waved his tiny thumb against the blinding headlights of the behemoth semis running tandem through the night. Each semi was its own double-barreled earthquake in the otherwise dead-calm darkness. He was rattled and shaken and battered by the whooshing whirlpool of wind that was attached like a lashing tail to each bellowing two-fisted whammy of urgent freight. After an hour of such abuse, a state trooper pulled over and, in stern terms, ordered him off the thruway and sentenced him to the slow death of the woebegone tollbooth where he could watch all the potential rides passing by on the highway, unaware of his existence or his epic homebound plight.

The hours crawled by. Eagerness for home dominated his mind. Although he never liked to admit defeat, if a bus headed for New Holland had appeared, he would have abandoned his strict hitchhiker's creed and pleaded for a ride. But there were no buses, no cars, and no signs of life encroaching upon his undesired solitude except for the hapless attendant in the booth.

*What a great job that must be,* Matt thought. *Man. I could get so much reading done if I had a job like that.*

With the dawn there came a beautiful pink sunrise. Sparse traffic started trickling by, and he took a ride back to Buffalo where chances for an eastbound lift would be better. After an hour and a half, he got a ride with a Toronto couple to the Waterloo exit in the Finger Lakes region between Rochester and Syracuse. He had already spent the balance of his patience overnight waiting for daylight and fighting exhaustion, and did not want to wither and die on the vine at yet another rinky-dink tollbooth while hundreds of cars passed by on the Thruway. Being close to home made him cocky and brave. After the tenth car ignored his thumb, he marched defiantly past the toll taker and straight onto the highway and at the top of his lungs shouted a mocking challenge to all the troopers of the universe, "Come and get me, you motherfuckers," with both fists extended to the heavens and a finger protruding from each. On the Thruway in broad daylight he was dead meat, but he didn't care. When a trooper did come by and waved at him without stopping, he knew it was a good omen, a sign sent by the Goddess of all hitchhikers that the remainder of his journey was to be blessed.

# PART FOUR

We shall not cease from exploration
And the end of all our exploring
Will be to arrive where we started
And know the place for the first time.
—T. S. Eliot, "Four Quartets—Little Gidding"

# CHAPTER XXXIV

## Full Rhombus

His ride home came forty-five minutes later, presto, totally out of the blue, unplanned and unpredictable but absolutely perfect, in the form of a mid-twentyish musician traveling to visit his girlfriend in Waterbury, Connecticut—yet another man with a future and a girlfriend. The man was in a happy conversational mood and was looking forward to what Matt assumed would be a romantic weekend with the woman of his dreams. Matt tried as hard as he could to be polite and alert, but his head kept collapsing forward, chin to chest, or in a sideways bang against the window, his wits dulled by exhaustion. In between a couple of the Syracuse exits, just as Matt had entered his native lands and knew he had only about 110 miles to go, the driver took pity and said, "Why don't you get some rest."

His tired eyes slammed shut and in two seconds or less he was unconscious and a mere dream second later he woke up dazed and drooling at the sight of big red letters on an old white factory wall, "Apple Orchard Foods." They were passing Mananaugua, which meant he had slept solid for an hour and a half and would be in New Holland before he knew it. He was soothed by the sight of the lush pastures and the fertile fields and the old barns and the bosomy tree-green hills of the Iroquois Valley and the sedate majesty of the silvery Iroquois River and the total mind and body embrace of being in a place called home.

Here and there, parallel to the river, he spotted remnants of the long-neglected Clinton Canal and its towpath, both now overgrown with bushes and trees, wildflowers and weeds. A red-winged blackbird swooped down and perched upon a pussy willow bobbing in a swampy culvert. There was a picture-perfect dairy farm, clusters of dappled cows huddling together contentedly in a green sea, tall white silos, the lazy patient river, and the panorama of the gently rolling valley. And above, a sky dotted by clouds that were showcased like a gallery of ephemeral sculptural masterpieces.

He laughed at the memory of Helen's father convincing him of the existence of the "Side-Hill Wampus Cows" that had evolved with two legs shorter than the others so they could stand straight and not topple over as they grazed upon the grassy hillsides. Was he really so gullible? Or did he just shrink away at the thought of disputing anything her father said? It didn't matter anymore. Either way was equally funny.

It actually took his breath away when all of New Holland came into view across the valley from the Thruway with its scenic postcard beauty. His old stomping grounds. The perfect little houses nestled between patches of trees, the hospital in the distance, the high school on the hill, the church spires, the domineering factories, and the towering smokestacks that punctuated the terraced skyline. This was his city, and he could not help but love the sight of it. No matter how far he may travel or how long he may be away, and whatever stunning places he may visit on this vast and wonderful planet, New Holland would always be his heart's home, and he would always love it above and beyond all other places. It was all so beautiful and tidy, so open-armed and welcoming. As he prepared for landing, surrendering to the gravity of its embrace, he worried and asked himself, *Have I traveled far enough? Long enough?*

Beside the exit ramp was New Holland's own unique landmark-in-progress, the underfunded and only half-finished windmill, intended to commemorate the long gone and forgotten Dutch settlers who gave name to this place. It was a large clumsy structure, and as someone had remarked, "It has all the earmarks of an eyesore." If it were ever to be finished, it might be an interesting tourist attraction,

459

but given its shoddy condition, most people passing by on the thruway thought it was a dilapidated historic ruin from New Holland's colonial days. There was something heartbreaking in the pathetic display of an unfulfilled windmill, in the very failure of its aborted structural intent and in the broken architectural promise, which was imposing itself so blatantly across this pastoral landscape, that made it the most appropriate landmark.

As he was getting out of the car, the radio played him the last song of his journey, a golden oldie:

> *If I should call you up, invest a dime*
> *And you say you belong to me, and ease my mind*
> *Imagine how the world would be, so very fine*
> *So happy together*

His weathered boots knew their way around the wide arc of the exit ramp, through the tollbooth, and across the patch of grass to dig up the pickle jar he had buried on the day he left town. He pulled out the note and was pleased that it was none the worse for wear.

"Welcome back," the note began. "My wish is that I will have done everything I wanted to do while I was gone and that I will now do everything I decided I needed to do while I was on the road. Have courage. Oh—don't forget. A souvenir for Sambo." He fumbled around in his pocket and there it was. "Yes. Redwood cone I have." Then, fingering the chain around his neck, he said, "And a St. Christopher medal."

He stumbled through the South Side in a display of triumphant defeat, down the steep hill and past the Armory, a magnificent castle-like fortress where he used to play basketball, and then past the crumbling wreckage of the old rundown factory buildings where his grandparents used to work before he was born making men's underwear, she as a cotton winder, he as a knitter. Then over the rickety wooden planks of the rusty old river bridge with a brace of nouveau confidence, thinking of parallel universes and true things and wondering, *Full circle? No. Full polygon of some sort. Rhombus? Trapezoid?* And asking his higher self, *Was this my journey of atonement?* He stood, stunned and transfixed, at the corner of Merchant and River Streets where there was no brass-band reception welcoming his return, and slipped into one last reverie, his final traveler's trance before the reality of home slapped him back into his senses.

## Needles, Shards, and Grooves

Returning home and reorienting one's self to life's mundane realities is always disconcerting and a bit disappointing. He was trying to strike a balance between the grand scheme of things and the minutiae of the here and now. He didn't know if everything mattered or nothing mattered. Was he just a tiny microscopic speck in an immense indifferent universe? Or did his existence have purpose within or beyond or independent of that grand scheme, even though he would someday be gone forever and be completely forgotten? He knew that there was no way to answer that question. But here, within the context of an existence, which at least seemed real, he thought it best to assume that everything mattered. It seemed the safest bet. He'd try it for a while. See if it worked. See if it's demon proof. To ponder the grand scheme of things and aspire to the natural state of being, all happiness and joy, but to live life in the here and now with all the minutiae, as if everything and everyone was of the utmost significance. He couldn't justify doing otherwise.

Since he had bid his uncertain farewell to his hometown, he had, by rough reckoning, hitchhiked more than 8,000 miles. He pulled his hair back into a ponytail and measured its length with his fists and estimated that it had grown about three inches since he left home. He had also grown a respectable, though shaggy, beard. He could vividly reconstruct his journey from memory, day-by-day, ride-by-ride, meal-by-meal, from day one. Every single driver and every single overnight stay stood out like its own separate chapter with its own plot, independent and complete unto itself. He remembered each meal he'd had in each of those places and could summon the aromas and flavors from each plate as though they had all been sumptuous gourmet dinners. Each face of each former stranger was presented in its own special frame of recollection. He remembered them all by name and remembered their stories and wondered how many would remember him and for how long. His whole journey had been fueled by kindness and trust and the goodness of everyone he met, all dished out in heaping portions at every bend and turn. Whether he had been deserving of such kindness had never been in question. It had nothing to do with that. It was just the way of the hitchhiker, to surrender himself to the mercy of the world's highways and to the care of perfect strangers who would never know they had opened his eyes to his better self and to the goodness of the world around him and that he would remember them forever. And, at journey's end, to be delivered back home, unscathed and braced to test his new resolve against the tectonic pressures and pitfalls of his own botched-up past.

*We are all the enemies of our own histories*, he thought.

He looked upon his tortured town with new and curious eyes and felt like he were hovering above it, not yet quite feet to ground, still straddling worlds, gauging his coolness in his uncertain strut and adjusting to the realization that he could not yet grasp the character of whoever it was that he had become since Old Matt had last laid eyes upon this place. But that is the nature of journeys. To shower you with the pure grace of a thousand perfect strangers. To cast you out to the ravages of a swiftly spinning and erratic Plutonic orbit and tempt you to struggle and clamor across grooves and shards back to the sure-footed safety of your hometown spindle. To bury you beneath the dirt of your own yearnings and then to dig you back up and mold you like a lump of clay, to poke you and prod you and squeeze you and shape you into something else, someone else, something new. Something better. And then to set you free to repudiate your past and run yet another gauntlet of one thousand potentially transformative challenges. It was all an inside job. Independent study. His earlier journeys had taught him well that not even best friends have the patience to tolerate you blustering on about your travels and the spectacular transformations that are hatching their chicks in the nest of your evolving psyche, and that attempting to force those tales upon them, hoping they will be infused by the spirit of your deep revelations, results only in frustration and embarrassment and self-invalidation.

Now the future awaited him and would swallow him whole the moment he stepped off this curb and placed a foot onto River Street. He would be swept away by its inexorable current. For a mad moment he panicked at that realization and nearly turned himself around to retreat back to the highway, back into timelessness before the time-bound world placed its noose around his neck and wrangled him back into its corral. One final yearning to unveil his thumb and disappear once more while he was still invisible and free, before anyone saw him. To return to the land of perfect strangers and continue to map the great everywhere, to sustain the spell of enchantment and become, once again, the aspiring world-wise Jack Kerouac travelin' man. Even as he considered it, he couldn't avoid acknowledging the absurdity of such an idea. He could never learn to be that man no matter how hard he tried or how far and long he hitchhiked. Yet he had, in his own way, come to know the road on his own terms and had become his own sort of travelin' man. And the road had never failed him. True to its promise, it had delivered him back to that singular place called home. It had tested his resolve and he had met its challenges and had become a different and hopefully better person, as though he had been cleansed by the waters of many rivers and many seas and oh so many tears. The challenge now before him was more arduous than his quest to become a travelin' man. The challenge now was to learn how to become himself.

He was growing tired of his own little sob story, wasting so much time on so many ugly thoughts, and he somehow now could accept that his misery was entirely of his own making and that there was a way out of the crazy maze of his emotional neediness and that it's okay if the future reveals itself day by day in inconsequential fragments. His own father had been a dropout and didn't even graduate from high school until he was twenty-four. And he became a professor. A great professor, some had said.

He thought, "You know, maybe I am a good person after all, or at least not a bad person" and "There is so much more goodness than wickedness in the world." Then the solution to his ordeal became comically apparent in a final epiphany of simple brilliance. He didn't have to get cool. That was silly. All he had to do was let go and grow up like his friends had already done. Get his needle past the shards and back into the smooth groove that would glide him away from the never-ceasing repetitive rut he'd been stuck in for so long. Snap together all those missing puzzle pieces he had collected during his journey, his pilgrimage. Become whole in his soul. Purify his experience. Avoid the stumbling blocks. Build a stepping stone. He felt like the last remaining baby bird perched on the edge of the nest, afraid to trust his wings, fearful of the big plunge. As Charlie said, "Baby birdy's gotta fledge. Can't stay in the nest forever." It was a matter of allowing it to happen and to cease resisting the inevitable free-fall leap of faith, but he felt the resistance nonetheless. It was not in a Peter Pan "I don't want to grow up" kind of way. It was more in a "it scares the shit out of me" kind of way. He wanted to put a merciful end to all his self-absorbed self-pity, admit that he has been an asshole, and just get past it and grow up. Because unless you admit you have been an asshole, you will always remain one. The cure is in identifying the disease, not admiring it.

*If only I can rake my sky clean and find the key,* he thought, *the key to that other inner self.*

The days would now begin to blend together. On Monday morning he'll have already forgotten what he did on Friday night. Any one meal will be the same as any other, and it won't even matter because the days will have lost their individual identities and the traveler's adventures will be replaced by the humdrum. He was coming to rest, and with rest comes complacency and, worse of all, disenchantment. That was it. While he was adrift in the world, his life had become enchanted, and he was already mourning its passing before it had even passed and was dreading the soldierly return of all the ugly things that had driven him away, the all-consuming depression and loneliness, and the insomnia and the irrational fears that swept over him like a tsunami.

He knew that the time for growth had come and that he was as ready now as he would ever be. He wished it would rain so as to cleanse away the residue of his Old Matt self and baptize his newborn self in one last purifying downpour before his re-entry.

*Man in motion,* Matt concluded, *is vastly superior to man at rest.*

## A Group Tube

A shrill whistle shattered his brittle stillness. A mime-like policeman positioned in the middle of the busy intersection aimed a white-gloved finger like a laser at the space between Matt's eyes, turned it upside-down, and beckoned him onward, and then extended his arms horizontally at his sides with hands bent perfectly upward and outward, so his body formed a lower-case "t," ordering all traffic to cease in its tracks so that he, Matthew A. Mahoney, could cross the street in safety and merge anonymously into the downtown pedestrian flow of his eagerly awaiting old hometown as though he had never left. He wiped his nose and made the decisive crossing.

He went to Brown's record store and bought "Alone Again, Naturally" for seventy-nine cents and then walked down River Street, where every memory-laden storefront reached out and squeezed him affectionately. The hands of the old clock on the Farmers' National Bank building were at 12:51.

The mannequins in the Holzheimer and Shaul's window display were dressed in current fashions, which were totally foreign to Matt. He could've sworn they all gave him a good-natured group tube, winked at him knowingly, slightly embarrassed by their stylish dress, welcoming him back home and saying, "Hey. We can't help it. This is just what we do. If it were up to us, we would dress cooler than this."

465

TIM KELLY

It reminded him of a *Twilight Zone* episode in which a mannequin came to life and forgot that she is not human. She lived among the townspeople for a month before she was mysteriously drawn back to the department store and confronted by the horrifying realization that she was just a mannequin and must relinquish her spark and resume her place in the display window while another got their chance to be briefly human.

Matt knew that he had been a real person throughout his entire journey, and he feared the fate that awaited him, that the spirit that had animated him during his travels would be drained from his artificial shell and that he would become a lifeless pod once again. He took a last look at the mannequins and at his own reflection staring back from the plate glass window, and thought, *Please, God. Don't let me forget who I am.*

He continued down River Street, past the Tryon Theater (Now Playing – *Now You See It, Now You Don't*) to the dingy bus station and waited for the Hen-Glen, which would take him home. While he was waiting, a friend of his walked by.

"Hey, Bones. What's goin' on?"

"Nothin' much. How about you?" He gave Matt a funny eye and a smile of recognition. Matt hadn't seen one of those in a long time. "You look kinda wasted. Your eyes are all red and puffy."

"Yeah. I am kinda wasted." He gave the thirty-second Monarch notes account of his summer adventure. Bones hadn't even known Matt had gone anywhere.

"I'll be heading back to college in a few weeks," he told Matt. "But I don't know. Part of me wants to just pack it all in and hitch to the west coast, like you did."

"Yeah, man. It's definitely the coast with the most."

## The Home Stretch

Matt counted his spare change and calculated that he'd have twenty-eight cents left after bus fare. He walked into the station past the old shoe-shine stand and the magazine racks at Ozzi's News and

466

into the stagnant waiting area and the phone booth with its stale scent of fermented urine and put the last of his cash in the coin return, hoping a lucky little kid would find it.

Five minutes later he was in the back of the bus, not a penny to his name, with the denim and down coats bundled on his lap and his lifesaving underwear tucked into one of the pockets. The big old clunker chugged and rattled and farted out black clouds of exhaust as it struggled up the steep hill, its antique gears groaning at each of its frequent street corner stops. The big round mirror inside the front of the bus gave a bird's eye view of the driver maneuvering and jamming the long skinny stick into place. All the familiar streets materialized clearly and distinctly through the big windshield, one at a time, predictably and in their proper sequence. At the ring of the bell rope, the bus stopped at the intersection of Peak and Incline, and when Matt stepped out onto the sidewalk and crossed the street and proceeded down the final stretch, the home stretch, he was no longer the freewheeling hitchhiking hippie, no longer the wayfaring stranger, no longer the Ricky Nelson travelin' man. He was the road-weary, weather-beaten, empty-pocketed, and worn-out homesick son who wanted nothing more from the world at this moment than to see his mother.

It was mid-afternoon on a hot August day. He started up the driveway and saw her in the garden, bent over on one knee, trowel in hand, planting flowers, her pant legs rolled up mid-calf. She was facing the other way and didn't see him. He stood still and watched her for a full minute and nearly wept at her loveliness. She rose to her feet with difficulty, bracing herself with one hand against the side of the house and the other hand hard-pressed against an aching hip and she was standing on the lawn and was wiping the sweat from a bandana'd brow with the back of her hand when she turned and saw him and stopped with a startled look that instantaneously transformed itself into the purest expression of recognition and happiness and love, and she dropped her trowel and walked toward him with her arms outstretched and his heart was full and glad.

# ARTIST ACKNOWLEDGEMENTS

Anyone who grew up during that renaissance of artistic creativity that took place during the sixties and seventies will tell you how important music was to their generation. Thus, there is no better way to evoke the period in which the events of this book occur than to excerpt some of the songs that formed the soundtrack for that era, whether as a Top 40 Billboard hit, an underground college FM radio favorite or an obscure cut from a favorite album. Following is a list of the songs and other writings that are referenced in "The Spider Room", listed in the order in which they appear.

"Travelin' Man" - Jerry Fuller
"American Pie"- Don McLean
"On This Day" - Ben Burroughs
"Sugar Mountain" - Neil Young
"Epistle to Dippy" - Donovan
"Hope She'll Be Happier" - Bill Withers
Baltimore Catechism #3 – Question 772
"Locomotive Breath" - Lyrics by Ian Anderson
"The New Colossus" - Emma Lazarus
"The Gift" - Lyrics by Lou Reed
"The Man Inside My Head" - Matthew A. Mahoney
"Eighteen" - Bruce, Cooper, Dunaway, Smith, Buxton
"The Loner" - Neil Young
"Alone Again, Naturally" - Gilbert O'Sullivan
"Lean on Me" -Bill Withers
"Everybody's Been Burned" - David Crosby
"Many Worlds" - Matthew A. Mahoney
Excerpt from The Legacy, The Testament, and Other Poems of Francois Villon. Translated by Peter Dale. St. Martin's Press. 1973.
"The Lessons That Nature Demonstrates" - Matthew A. Mahoney

"Sad-Eyed Lady of the Lowlands" - Bob Dylan
"One Toke Over the Line" - Mike Brewer and Tom Shipley
Excerpt of Poem by Gwyn Thomas
"Watching Betsy Dance" - Matthew A. Mahoney
"Brown-Eyed Girl" - Van Morrison
"Walk Away, Renee" - Brown, Sansone
"Can't Find My Way Home"- Steve Winwood
"Early Mornin' Rain" - Gordon Lightfoot
"Bad Moon Risin'"- John Fogarty
"I Threw It All Away" - Bob Dylan
"Carolina in My Mind" - James Taylor
"Rainy Day Women, #12 and 35" - Bob Dylan
"Looking Into You"- Jackson Browne
Incantation for Green Lantern's Light – Alfred Bester
"Sisters of Mercy" - Leonard Cohen
"Nights in White Satin" - Justin Hayward
"2000 Light Years From Home" - Keith Richards and Mick Jagger
"Ballad in Plain D" - Bob Dylan
"Love Minus Zero – No Limit" - Bob Dylan
"Big Yellow Taxi" - Joni Mitchell
Prayer by Thomas Merton
Excerpt form The Dharma Bums – "The Oriental Passion forTea"
"Who Knows Where the Time Goes" - Sandy Denny
"My Own True Love" - Grace Thurston
"When I Was Young" - Matthew A. Mahoney
"Orange Juice on Ice" - Commercial from "Midnight Cowboy"
"Comin' Back to Me" - Marty Balin
"This Land is Your Land" - Woody Guthrie
"Ripple" - Jerome J. Garcia and Robert C. Hunter
"When Men Were Men" - Matthew A. Mahoney (Possibly)
Excerpts from The Complete Works of Lao Tzu, Translation and Elucidation by Hua-Ching Ni. Numbers 47 & 67
Excerpt from The Return of the King - J.R.R. Tokien
The Story of Mosi the Cat - Johnny Rustywire

"Everything is Gonna be Fine" - Matthew A. Mahoney

"Like a Rolling Stone"- Bob Dylan

"A Horse With No Name"- Dewey Bunnell

"Everyone is a No One" - Gizmo C. (Attributed to Matthew A. Mahoney)

"Sugar, Sugar"- Andy Kim, Jeff Barry

"War" - Norman Whitfield and Barrett Strong

"Mother-in-Law" - Allen Toussaint

"Peaceful Easy Feeling" - J. Tempchin

Excerpt from The Iliad" - Homer, Book Nineteen, Lines 91-94

"Spirit in the Sky" - Norman Greenbaum

"Closer to Home" - Mark Farner

"Happy Together" - G. Bonner and A. Gordon

.

Made in the USA
Monee, IL
02 March 2021